THE JOURNEYS OF SOCRATES

DAN MILLMAN

UNCORRECTED PROOF

Title: The Journeys of Socrates

Author: Dan Millman

Classification: Fiction

Publication Date: April 2005

Price: $23.95

Approximate Length: 336 Pages

Trim Size: 6 x 9

ISBN: 0–06–075023–5

This galley does not reflect the actual size or design of the final book. Reviewers are reminded that changes may be made in this proof copy before books are printed. If any material is to be quoted or referred to in a review, the quotation or reference must be checked against the final bound book. Dates, prices, and manufacturing details are subject to change or cancellation without notice.

CONTACT THE PUBLICIST

If you would like to book an interview, are planning an article, or if you need any additional information:

Claudia Boutote 415-477-4404

CLAUDIA.BOUTOTE@HARPERCOLLINS.COM

Julie Rae Mitchell 415-477-4406

JULIERAE.MITCHELL@HARPERCOLLINS.COM

 HarperSanFrancisco

A Division of HarperCollinsPublishers

www.harpercollins.com

Other Books by Dan Millman

THE PEACEFUL WARRIOR SAGA

Way of the Peaceful Warrior

Sacred Journey of the Peaceful Warrior

GUIDEBOOKS

The Life You Were Born to Live

Everyday Enlightenment

No Ordinary Moments

Living On Purpose

The Laws of Spirit

The Inner Athlete

The

JOURNEYS

of

SOCRATES

––––––––

DAN MILLMAN

HarperSanFrancisco
A Division of HarperCollins*Publishers*

THE JOURNEYS OF SOCRATES Copyright © 2005 by Dan Millman.
All rights reserved. Printed in the United States of America.
No part of this book may be used or reproduced in any manner whatsoever without
written permission except in the case of brief quotations embodied in critical
articles and reviews. For information address HarperCollins Publishers, Inc.,
10 East 53rd Street, New York, NY 10022.

HarperCollins books may be purchased for educational, business, or sales
promotional use. For information please write: Special Markets Department,
HarperCollins Publishers, Inc., 10 East 53rd Street, New York, NY 10022.
HarperCollins Web site: http://www.harpercollins.com
HarperCollins®, [colophon]®, and HarperSanFrancisco™ are
trademarks of HarperCollins Publishers, Inc.

FIRST EDITION

Library of Congress Cataloging-in-Publication Data
TO COME

ISBN 0–06–075023–5

05 06 07 08 09 XXX 10 9 8 7 6 5 4 3 2 1

DEDICATION

Over the years, readers of *Way of the Peaceful Warrior* have asked me many questions about the service station sage I called Socrates. Where did he come from? Did he ever marry or have children? Who were his teachers? What experiences shaped his life?

Now, decades after we first met, based on notes from his journals, I can finally relate the odyssey and experiences that forged the character and tempered the spirit of the peaceful warrior who became my mentor.

I dedicate this book to Socrates—and to you, my readers, who asked me to tell his story.

Every journey has a

secret destination of which

the traveler is unaware.

—MARTIN BUBER

PROLOGUE

I'VE KILLED DMITRI ZAKOLYEV.

This thought, this stark reality, played over and over in Sergei's mind as he lay belly down, straddling the moss-covered log and paddling as quickly and as silently as he could through the dark, frigid waters of Lake Krugloye, twenty-five kilometers north of Moscow. He was fleeing the Nevskiy Military School and his past—but he could not escape the fact of Zakolyev's death.

Following a course roughly parallel to the shoreline, Sergei peered through the darkness to the shallows and the wooded hills beyond, appearing and disappearing in the mist. The lake's black surface, lit by faint slivers of moonlight cutting through the clouds, shimmered with each stroke. The sloshing water and bitter cold distracted Sergei for a few more moments before he thought again of Zakolyev's body, lying in the mud.

Sergei could no longer feel his hands or legs. He had to make land before the waterlogged timber sank beneath him. Just a little farther, he thought, another kilometer before I head for shore. This means of escape was not the fastest or safest, but the lake had one distinct advantage: Water left no tracks.

Finally he angled in toward the shore, slipped from the log, stood in the waist-high water, and waded through the sucking mud and sharp reeds at the water's edge, up the sandy shore, and into the dark forest.

He was fifteen years old, and a fugitive.

Sergei shivered not only from the cold, but from a sense of destiny, as if all the events of his life had brought him to that moment. As he threaded his way through the thicket of pine and birch, he thought about what his grandfather had told him, and how it all began . . .

THAT AUTUMN OF 1872, chill winds blew west across the moss-covered Siberian tundra, sweeping over the Ural Range and north across the taiga, vast forests of birch and pine, lichens and shrubs, bordering the city of St. Petersburg, the crown jewel of Mother Russia.

Just outside the Winter Palace, wool-capped bodyguards of Aleksandr II marched along the Neva River, one of ninety waterways that flowed beneath eight hundred bridges, then past rows of small apartment buildings and church spires topped with crosses of the Orthodox Church. Not far from the river were city parks with statues of Peter the Great and Catherine and Pushkin—tsar, tsarina, and literary master—all standing sentry, bordered by street lamps just lit in the fading light of day.

Biting breezes snatched the last yellow leaves from thinning branches, tossed the woolen skirts of schoolgirls, and tousled the hair of two young boys wrestling in the front yard of a two-story home near Nevskiy Prospekt. In the bedroom window on the second floor, a gust of wind ruffled the curtains where Natalia Ivanova, the wife of Sergei Ivanov, stood framed in the window. She pulled her shawl over her shoulders, closed the window a little, and gazed down into the small yard where her little son, Sasha, was playing with his friend Anatoly.

Anatoly ran toward Sasha, trying to tackle him. At the last instant, Sasha stepped aside and threw Anatoly over his hip, just the way his father had taught him. Proud of himself, Sasha crowed like a rooster. Such a strong boy, Natalia thought—like his father. She envied her son's energy, especially now, when she had so little of it herself—tired most of the time since her belly had swollen with their second child. Natalia's fatigue was no surprise. Yana Vaslakova, her neighbor, friend, and midwife, had warned her: "A woman of your fragile nature should not bear another child." Yet she bore this new life and prayed daily for the strength to carry this child to full term even as the fainting spells had begun and a great fatigue had penetrated her bones.

Natalia hugged herself and shivered, wondering how little boys could play outside on a chill evening like this. She called out the window, "Sasha! Anatoly! Soon it will rain. You boys come in!" Her weary voice hardly carried over the wind. Besides, six-year-old ears heard only what they wished.

With a sigh, Natalia returned to the small couch where she'd been speaking with Yana and sat with a sigh, brushing her long black hair. Sergei would be home soon. She wanted to look as pretty as she could.

Vaslakova said, "You rest, Natalia. I'll let myself out and shoo the boys inside." As her friend went downstairs, Natalia heard the patter of rain on the sill, then something else, directly overhead—the scuttle of young feet and mischievous squeals. They've climbed the trellis again, she thought. In the mixture of anger and anxiety felt by all mothers of small boys who fancy themselves invulnerable, Natalia cried up to the rooftop, "You boys climb down from the roof this instant! And be careful!"

Laughter and more scuffling as the boys wrestled on the rooftop.

"Come down now or I shall tell your father!"

"All right, Mamochka," Sasha called sweetly to curry her favor. "Just don't tell Father!" More giggles.

As Natalia turned back to lay her brush down, everything changed in one sudden, sickening lurch. Young laughter turned to descending screams. Then silence.

Natalia ran to the window. To her horror, two bodies lay below. Paralyzed, she stared down as Anatoly began to move and whimper. Sasha remained twisted and still. Vaslakova, who had just exited, ran to the boys.

The next moment, it seemed, Natalia found herself outside, kneeling in the mud. She didn't feel the rain; she didn't feel her body. As she cradled her lifeless boy in her arms, the tears and rain running down her face, she rocked to and fro in the timeless rhythm of a mother's agony.

Then a knotlike pain in her womb ripped her back from the abyss, and Natalia became vaguely aware of Vaslakova and a man standing

beside her. As Vaslakova helped Natalia to her feet, the man tried to lift
the burden from her arms. Natalia fought him off but froze when a boy's
shrill cry rang out—she looked quickly down to her Sasha, but it was the
other boy, Anatoly, whose leg was broken.

Vaslakova helped Natalia inside before the pain took her again. She
doubled over and collapsed in the doorway. Where is Sasha? she wondered. He should come in. It is cold, so cold.

When she awoke, Natalia found herself in bed, attended to by the
midwife. All at once she knew: The baby is coming . . . too soon . . . two
months early. Or have the months passed without my notice? she
thought. Where am I? Where is Sergei? He will know if this is a dream.
Sergei will smile and stroke my hair and tell me that Sasha is fine . . .
that everything is all right.

Ah! The pain! Is something wrong? Where is my Sasha? Where is
Sergei?

Sergei Ivanov arrived home to find neighbors in his front yard, standing in the rain. He saw their faces and rushed inside. Vaslakova told him
the news: Sasha was dead—a fall from the rooftop. Natalia had gone
into labor . . . the bleeding wouldn't stop . . . nothing to be done. Both
of them gone.

Their baby was alive. A son. But tiny and fragile—born so early he
probably wouldn't survive. Vaslakova had seen much new life, and much
death. Death is easy, she thought, but not on those left behind. A priest
would soon arrive to perform last rites for Natalia and Sasha, and likely
the infant as well. She placed Sergei's tiny son in his arms and told the
distraught father that the child was too weak to suckle, but a little goat's
milk, squeezed from a cloth, might sustain the boy if he lived through
the night.

Sergei looked down at the wizened, wrinkled little face and the tiny
body, swaddled tightly in a blanket Natalia had made. As grief overcame
him, Sergei sat heavily and stared at the floor, seeing nothing. He barely heard Mrs. Vaslakova's words: "Natalia's last words before she faded
away . . . she said she loved you with all her heart . . . and asked that you
give her son into the care of her parents . . . "

Even while dying, Natalia had thought about what was best for her child . . . and her husband. She knew that Sergei, a member of the streltsy, elite bodyguards to the tsar, could not care for their tiny son. Could she also have foreseen that every time he looked at his son, the child would remind him of this dark day?

The priest arrived and baptized the infant in case he should die, for the sake of his soul. When he asked the infant's name, the distracted father replied, "Sergei," thinking that the priest had asked for his own name. So it was done: The child took the name of the father.

Midwife Vaslakova offered to care for the child through the night.

Sergei nodded slowly. "If he lives until morning . . . please deliver him to his grandparents." He told her the address and their names—Heschel and Esther Rabinowitz. Jews. This did not sit well with him, but they would love the child and raise him safely. So he did as Natalia had asked. Sergei could never refuse her anything in life or in death. That day in autumn marked the beginning of Sergei Ivanov's descent into death, even as his tiny son was clinging to life.

EIGHT YEARS LATER, on a dark October night, Heschel Rabinowitz sat alone in the third railway car on a train bound for Moscow. He gazed out the window in thoughtful repose, half dozing in the manner of old men, hardly aware of the passing forests or settlement huts just visible in the first light of dawn. Heschel dozed and dreamed and stared, seeing only memories that moved through his mind like vistas flashing past the train's muddy window: his daughter Natalia in a red dress, her face bright . . . Sasha, the grandson he had never met . . . and the beautiful, aged face of his beloved Esther. Gone now, all of them.

For a moment he squeezed his eyes tightly as if to shut out the past. Then his eyes relaxed and he smiled as another vision appeared—the face of a three-year-old boy with eyes too large for his skinny body, reaching up to his grandfather.

The conductor's voice, announcing the train's arrival, jarred Heschel from his reverie. With a yawn, he stood painfully, stretching his joints, and pulled his old coat tightly around him. He scratched his snow white beard and adjusted the wire-rimmed spectacles on his large nose. Departing strangers jostled the old Jew, but he took little notice. Holding his satchel protectively in front of his chest as one might carry an infant, he descended to the platform and shuffled through a cloud of steam in the cold morning air. He looked skyward. Soon the first snow would fall.

Heschel straightened his cap and focused his wandering mind toward the north. He would have to find passage in the cart or wagon of a willing farmer, half a day's ride north, into the hills, up cold muddy roads rutted with wagon tracks, pockmarked by the hooves of horses and oxen, then on foot to the school on the shore of Lake Krugloye.

It would not be an easy journey. Heschel's back, eroded by countless hours at his workbench, was curved like the violins he fashioned from aged maple, spruce, and ebony. Heschel also made precision clocks. He had learned both trades as a boy—one from his father and the other from his grandfather. Unable to favor one craft over the other, he would first construct a violin, then a clock, alternating for variety. Even at his age, despite the aches in the joints of his fingers, he worked diligently, shaping each violin as if it were his first and each clock as if it were his last.

Soon after Heschel had learned these two crafts, his father had left him the workshop and journeyed to the East to trade in gems. Later his father's wealth and generosity enabled Heschel, a Jew, to continue living within the city of St. Petersburg, where he and his wife, Esther, had shared an apartment.

Heschel reflected on these memories as he carried his satchel out of the train station with a slow, halting gait, toward the main road out of the city.

A few hours later he sat against a sack of potatoes as a farmer's cart bumped up the narrow, rutted road leading into the hills north of Moscow. When the cart finally creaked to a stop, Heschel disembarked with a nod of thanks to the farmer and set out on foot.

As he hiked down into the valley, he thought of the many letters he had written over the past five years and the same number of refusals he'd received. Several weeks before, Heschel had sent a final letter to

Chief Instructor Vladimir Ivanov: "I have not seen Sergei since he was taken to the school. My wife has died. I have no one left. This may be my last chance to see my grandson."

Just two days earlier, Ivanov's letter had arrived, allowing the visit. Heschel had left immediately.

Now, chilled by the snow-laden wind on his neck, he lifted the collar of his wool coat. Two days, he thought—such a short time to pour my life into an eight-year-old boy. Just then the words of Rabbi Hillel came into his mind: "Children are not vessels to be filled but candles to be lit."

"I don't have much fire left," Heschel murmured aloud as he wove his way through birch and pine, down the cold and rocky grade dusted with snowflakes. His painful joints reminded him of his corporeal existence—and this one final errand. The sound of wind faded as Heschel's mind slipped back into the crevices of memory, taking him back five years to the day a young soldier came to their door with a letter from Sergei's father, instructing that his son should be taken to the Nevskiy Military School.

An hour later he approached the main gate of the Nevskiy Military School. Heschel surveyed the enclosure, bordered like a castle with walls about four meters high. Just ahead he could see a spartan complex of blockhouses. No hedges or adornment softened the stone battlements, where, he surmised, efficiency and function molded the young soldiers' lives.

A cadet showed Heschel across the large courtyard into the main building and down a long hallway to a door and sign that read, V. I. Ivanov, Chief Instructor.

He removed his cap, brushed back his thinning hair, and entered.

Part One

THE BITTER
AND
THE SWEET

I have a sad story to tell, and a happy one.
In the end, you may find that they are one and the same,
for the bitter and the sweet each has its season,
alternating like day and night, even now,
as I pass through the twilight hours . . .

FROM SOCRATES' JOURNAL

. 1 .

SERGEI WAS WORRIED, that October day, when he was summoned to his uncle's office.

He was supposed to think of Vladimir Ivanov not as his uncle but as Chief Instructor Ivanov. He also was not supposed to ask personal questions, though he had many—about his parents and about his past. The chief instructor had said little about either one, except on that day four years ago when he'd announced that Sergei's father had died.

Being summoned—a rare event for any young cadet—usually meant bad news or punishment. So, in no hurry to stand before the chief instructor's stern face and downturned brows, Sergei wandered across the school compound at a distinctly unmilitary pace.

Each spot Sergei passed in the inner courtyard held memories of earlier years and experiences: the first time he'd ridden a horse, bouncing wildly, clinging to the reins in a death grip and trying to look brave . . . one of many fistfights he'd gotten into due to a quick temper.

He passed the infirmary and the small apartment of Galina, the elderly school nurse, who had watched over him when he'd first arrived. She had wiped his nose when he was sick and brought him to meals until he found his own way around. Too young to live in a barrack, he had slept on a cot just off the infirmary wing until he was five. It was a lonely time, with no place of his own and nowhere he fit in. The cadets treated him like a mascot or pet dog—petted one day, beaten the next.

Most of the other boys had mothers or fathers at home; Sergei had only his uncle, so he worked hard to please the chief instructor. His efforts, however, only earned the wrath of the older cadets, who called him "Uncle's Vlad's boy." They would trip, push, or punch him at every opportunity—a moment's inattention might mean bruises or worse. Older cadets routinely bullied the younger ones, and physical beatings were commonplace. The instructors knew about it but looked the other way unless someone was seriously injured. They tolerated the fights because it spurred the younger boys to toughen up and stay alert. It was, after all, a military school.

The first time Sergei was accosted by an older cadet, over in the corner of the compound, he started swinging wildly, sensing that if he backed down there would be no end to it. The older boy gave him a good beating, but Sergei managed to get in one or two good punches, and the boy never bothered him after that. Another time he had come upon two cadets beating a new boy. Sergei had attacked them with more rage than skill. They had backed off, treating the whole thing like a joke. But it was no joke to the new boy, whose name was Andrei and who had been Sergei's only real friend ever since.

Just after his fifth birthday, Sergei was moved into a barrack with the seven- to ten-year-olds. Older boys lived upstairs, and anyone over sixteen lived in another building. The older boys ruled the barracks. Every cadet dreaded a move to the next floor, where he again would be the youngest and therefore the prey. Meanwhile, Sergei and Andrei watched each other's backs.

Of the years prior to his arrival, Sergei had only hazy impressions—as if he had been cocooned in another world, not yet awakened into this one. But sometimes, when he searched his memory, he glimpsed fleeting images of large woman with arms as soft as bread dough and a man with a halo of white hair. Sergei wondered who they were; he wondered about a great many things.

He had gazed at maps of Mother Russia and other countries on the classroom walls, and his finger had circled the globe on his teacher's desk, tracing lines across sky blue seas and lands colored orange, yellow, purple, and green. But he no more expected to visit such places than he thought to visit the moon or stars.

His world—until that day in October of 1880—was defined largely by the stone walls, the blockhouses, barracks, classrooms, and training grounds of the Nevskiy Military School. Sergei had not chosen this place, but he accepted it, as children must, and passed his early years in orderly routines of class work, physical training, and discipline—military history and strategy and geography, riding and running and swimming and calisthenics.

Whenever the cadets weren't in their classrooms or on work assignments, they practiced fighting skills. In the summer Sergei had to swim under the cold waters of Lake Krugloye while breathing through a hollow reed, and practice elementary skills with the saber, and shoot arrows with bows he could barely bend. When he was older he would shoot pistols and carbines.

It was not a bad life or a good life, but the only one he knew.

As Sergei drew closer to the main building, he tucked his dark blue shirt into his dark blue pants and gazed down at his boots to see if they were clean. For a moment he wondered whether he should have fetched his more formal dark coats or gloves but then decided against it. Most of the taller boys looked trim in their uniforms; on him everything still looked baggy. When he finally grew out of one size uniform, they gave him another hand-me-down.

Still daydreaming, Sergei shuffled down the long stone hallway toward his uncle's office. He thought about the last summons, four years ago. He could still recall his uncle's lean face and severe countenance as the chief instructor told him to sit. Sergei had climbed into a chair with his legs dangling—he could barely see over the top of the desk—and his uncle had spoken the few words now imprinted in Sergei's memory: "Your father has died. His name was Sergei Borisovich Ivanov. He was once an elite bodyguard to Tsar Aleksandr. He was good man, and a Cossack. You must study and train hard to become like him."

Sergei did not know what to feel or how to respond, so he only nodded.

"Do you have any questions?" the chief instructor had asked.

"How . . . how did he die?"

Silence. Then a sigh. "Your father drank himself to death. A great waste." Then Sergei was dismissed. He remember how white his uncle's face had looked that day.

He had left the office awash with so many feelings it was hard to sort them out. He was sad to hear that his father had died. It also meant that his father had been alive but had never come to see him. Yet he felt proud to know that he had a Cossack's blood coursing through him and that he might someday grow strong like the father he never knew.

Sergei reached the door of his uncle's office. About to knock, he paused as he heard muffled voices inside. "This visit you propose," said his uncle. "I will allow it. But several others disagree . . . They have no love for Jews, the killers of Christ."

"And I have no use for soldiers, the killers of Jews," said an older voice Sergei didn't recognize.

"Not all soldiers hate Jews," said his uncle.

"And you?" said the other voice.

"I hate only weakness."

"As I hate ignorance."

"I'm not so ignorant as to be tricked by your Jewish intellect," said the chief instructor.

"And I'm not so weak to be intimidated by your Cossack bravado," said the other man; then, in a more friendly tone, he added, "You know, with your bravado and my intellect, we could have done great things . . ."

In the silence that followed, Sergei found the courage to tap three times on the door.

It opened to reveal his uncle and an old man. Sergei's uncle spoke curtly: "Cadet Ivanov. This is your grandfather."

The elderly man rose from his chair and faced him. He had white hair and seemed happy to see Sergei. Then he spoke softly, almost in a whisper—it sounded like a name: Sokrat . . . Socrates.

. 2 .

Heschel reached out to embrace his grandson; then, realizing that the boy did not recognize him, he lowered his arms and, more formally, reached out to shake the boy's hand. "Hello . . . Sergei . . . it's good to see you. I would have come long ago, but . . . well, I am here now."

Chief Instructor Ivanov broke in: "Get your things ready, Cadet Ivanov—I will allow you two nights' leave." And to Heschel: "See that the boy returns by midday Sunday. I expect him to be ready to train. He has much to learn."

"That he does," said Heschel, taking Sergei's hand.

When the chief instructor dismissed them both with a wave of his hand, Sergei hurried to the barrack to gather a few belongings; then he and his grandfather took their leave, passing through the dark hallways, out the iron gate, across the fields, and up a snow-covered path toward the forested hills.

Heschel, somewhere in his eighties—he had stopped counting when Esther died—walked with faltering steps. Sergei, intoxicated by a sense of liberation, skipped ahead, then rejoined his old grandfather. The boy had no words to explain or express this elation, this new sense of himself. It was as if he were no longer just another cadet but a real boy with a grandfather, a family.

They angled through the trees until they came to a stone outcropping and a large boulder. Heschel took out a map and showed it to the boy. "You see the lake and the school? Here is the boulder, shown on the map, and there is our destination," he said, pointing first to an x on the map, then upward into the hills. It seemed a good map, showing the landmarks. Sergei had learned only the rudiments of map reading, but he knew enough to understand and to remember.

Putting away the map, Heschel peered up the narrow path, hardly discernible in the snow. Then he checked his pocket watch and frowned. "We have to reach our destination before dark," he said.

Sergei was accustomed to doing what he was told and not asking questions. Now his mind overflowed with curiosity. He sensed that it was safe to ask and that his grandfather might answer. "Are we going to your house?" Sergei asked.

"My house is too far away," Heschel answered. "We'll spend the next two days and nights with Benyomin and Sara Abramovich. I have known Benyomin for many years, but that is a story for another time, perhaps."

"Do they have any children?"

Heschel smiled, having anticipated the question. "Yes—two of them. Avrom is twelve years old, and little Leya is five."

"Their names sound . . . strange."

"They are Jewish names, and tonight we celebrate Shabbat—"

"What's a Shabbat?" asked the boy.

"Shabbat is a sacred day set aside for rest and remembrance."

"Like Sunday Sabbath?"

"Yes. But Shabbat begins Friday night when the first three stars appear. So we will have to be getting on," Heschel said.

As they trekked upward, the old man concentrated on each careful footstep while the nimble eight-year-old hopped up from rock to rock like a mountain goat. Sergei heard his grandfather's breathless voice behind him. "The stones are slippery—be careful, Socrates."

There was that name again—the one he'd heard in his uncle's office. More boldly, Sergei asked, "Why do you call me Socrates?"

"Your grandmother and I called you little Socrates ever since you were a baby. It was our special name for you."

"Why?"

A faraway look came to Heschel's eyes as his mind drifted again to the past. "When your mother, Natalia, was just a girl, I would read to her from the Jewish Talmud and the Torah . . . and from other books of wisdom, including the commentaries of the great philosophers. Her favorite was a Greek named Socrates. He lived a long time ago . . . and he was among the wisest and best of men." Heschel looked away, into the hills or the sky, and said, "We called you our little Socrates because it made us feel close to your mother . . . to our daughter."

"Did my mother like Socrates for his wisdom?"

"Yes, but even more for his virtue and strength of character."

"What did he do?"

"Socrates taught the young men of Athens about higher values, virtue, and peace. He claimed to be the most ignorant of men, but he asked clever questions that revealed both falsehoods and truth. He was not only a thinker, he was also a man of action. As a youth, Socrates wrestled, and he was a brave soldier until he finally put war behind him. So I suppose you could say that he was a . . . peaceful warrior."

Satisfied, Sergei turned to gaze back down at the snowy landscape. The afternoon sun sparkled off the white hillside, illuminating the trees and moss and lichen. Invigorated by the crisp, cool air and by this adventure, Sergei bounded ahead, then forced himself to slow down and stop so his grandfather could catch up. As he waited, he thought about the word Jew. He had heard it uttered at the school, most recently in his uncle's office.

"Grandfather," Sergei called down the trail, "are you a Jew?"

"Yes," panted Heschel, approaching slowly. "So are you . . . your mother was Jewish, and your father . . . well, he was not . . . but you have Jewish blood."

Sergei looked down at his hands, reddened by the cold air. Cossack blood and Jewish blood. "Grandfather—"

"You may call me Grandpa if you like," he said, sitting down on a snow-covered rock to rest a moment.

"Grandpa . . . would you tell me something about my mother . . . and my father?"

Hearing this, Heschel stopped, brushed the snow from another large stone, and beckoned Sergei to sit beside him to rest a bit and talk. After

Heschel had contemplated his response, he told Sergei the story of his birth—all that Heschel had learned from Vaslakova, the midwife, who was with Natalia on that fateful day.

When Heschel had finished the story, they stood and continued their upward hike in silence. It was a good thing, Heschel thought, to let the boy walk and absorb what he had learned. Finally, as if the story needed a postscript, Heschel said, "You were that little child, Socrates—a single ray of light on a dark day. And you had a mother and father who loved you . . ."

Sergei glanced just behind him and saw his grandfather wiping tears from his cheeks. "Grandpa? Are you sad?"

"Just give me a moment, my little Socrates—I'll be all right. I was just thinking about your mother—about Natalia . . ."

"What was she like?" Sergei asked.

Heschel's gaze grew vacant again before he continued in a wistful voice, "Every daughter is lovely in her father's eyes, but not all were so wise or gentle as your mother. She would have been a prize for any Jewish man worthy of her—if he didn't mind a little debate," he said with a smile. But then it faded as he continued, "I don't know exactly how she met your father—perhaps in the market—but when he came to our apartment we learned that he was not Jewish. Even worse, he was a Cossack and body-guard to Tsar Aleksandr, who is no friend to our people."

"But he married my mother, and he was good to her. You said—"

"Yes. But you see . . . your mother could not marry your father unless she renounced her Jewish faith and converted to the . . . Christian Church." Heschel stopped to let Sergei absorb the enormity of this terrible thing.

"Did she stop speaking to you?"

"No." Heschel's face contorted again.

"Grandpa . . . are you all right?"

He held up his hand. "It was me who stopped speaking to her. I treated my daughter as if she were dead." He started to cry again, this time openly, as his words poured out. "I don't expect you to understand how I could do such a thing, little Socrates—I don't understand myself.

But cruel words poured from my mouth. I turned my back on her as I believed she had turned her back on her people. I could find no other way. Your grandmother Esther had no choice but to do the same, although it broke her heart."

Heschel forced himself to go on. "Your grandmother Esther wanted desperately to speak with her daughter—to embrace her one more time. Did she think I wanted anything less?" Heschel said to himself, his mind again drifting to the past.

When he spoke again, he sounded weary. "When we learned that our first grandchild was born—your brother, Sasha—Esther and I had a terrible argument. She begged me to let her go to her daughter, ask her forgiveness, and see her grandson. But I would not let her . . . I would not even allow my beloved Esther to answer my daughter's letters.

"We never did get to see little Sasha," he said. "We learned about his childhood only from your mother's letters—letters we cherished but never answered. I could not bear to read them myself, but your Grandma Esther would tell me of their contents. We never spoke with your mother or saw her again. Not while she lived."

Heschel blew his nose and wiped his cold wet cheeks on the sleeve of his coat. This made Sergei want to cry too.

A light snow had begun to fall again as they continued upward. Heschel grasped Sergei's hand and said softly, "There is one more thing you should know, Socrates. The midwife who brought you made a point of telling us that your mother was able to hold you close to her for a little while before she died."

"Why did she die, Grandpa?"

"Why does anyone die? It is not for us to know." He stopped for a moment, reached down slowly, and plucked a blood red winter blossom from the snow. "Your mother was fragile, yet strong, like this flower that grows in the winter. It is an innocent flower, yet I've just plucked it from the snow. God picked ·Natalia; it was her time. I only wish . . . " Once again Heschel withdrew from this world, and his face took on a more peaceful visage. "Yes, Esther," he said to a ghost Sergei could not see. "I know . . . it will be all right."

Heschel put his hand on the boy's shoulders, and they walked in silence, side by side. Sergei thought about what his grandfather had told him—how his mother had held him close before she died. And for a little while, he didn't feel so cold anymore.

Now he knew the story of his birth, and of the deaths surrounding it. He sensed too, as much as any eight-year-old can, that his grandfather would carry his own sorrows, like a weight in his knapsack, to his own death, when all weights would be lifted. But for now the boy saw that his grandfather's brow had relaxed, and he was glad for it.

After a time Heschel emerged from his thoughts and spoke again: "So that is how things are, little Socrates—I lost my daughter and my wife; you lost your mother and father. Each of us is alone now, but we have one another. The truth may hurt, but it sets us free."

Sergei hoped he might someday make his mark upon the world so that when he was as old as his grandfather, the world might be a better place because he had lived.

. 3 .

A COLD SUN, barely visible through the blanket of clouds, disappeared behind the trees. Somewhere in the darkening woods ahead a wolf howled, marking the coming dusk.

A few minutes later a clearing came into view, and a cabin. From its windows poured a soft light, offering the promise of comfort and warmth. The falling snowflakes appeared gray in the twilight—all except those drifting past the lighted windows, which sparkled white in a final moment of glory before settling to the earth.

The cabin appeared well built and larger than Sergei had imagined, with a plank-and-shingle roof and smoke rising from a stone chimney. Heschel stepped first onto the porch, removed his cap, and shook the snow from his boots. Sergei did the same. Then Heschel knocked firmly on the large oak door.

A few moments later the door opened. After a warm welcome and much-needed washing, Sergei and Heschel sat at the table with the first real family in Sergei's memory. The mother, Sara, a small-boned woman with brown hair almost covered by a white babushka tied beneath her chin, brought food to the table. Visitors were rare here, and friendly faces all the more so. Both children glanced at Sergei, and he glanced back. Avrom, a tall, slender boy of twelve, appeared formal but friendly; Leya, a pretty little five-year-old with a mop of copper-colored hair, glanced shyly at him.

Sergei's eyes drank in all he could of their orderly home. He felt a little shabby in his plain clothing next to Avrom in his coat and smooth trousers and Leya in her dark dress and white babushka like her mother's.

The father, Benyomin Abramovich, explained for Sergei's benefit, "During our Sabbath we set aside all of our weekday concerns and devote ourselves to literature, poetry, and music. This day reminds us that we are not slaves to work. On Shabbat we are free of the world."

Sara lit two candles and said a blessing. After Benyomin recited a prayer over wine, he invited Heschel to say a prayer over two loaves of a bread braided like a rope, which they called "challah." Sergei gazed at the array of food set out before them as Sara pointed out each dish: a thick barley soup, chopped eggs, a spicy beet salad, crackers, chopped vegetables from the garden, potato knishes, rice with apples, and a honey cake with stuffed apples for dessert.

As everyone ate their fill, Sara apologized with a shrug of her shoulders. "In this weather I would have included chicken broth, but the chicken declined."

So this is what a mother is like, Sergei thought, gazing at her. He envied these children for getting to see her every day.

It was the best meal in his memory. There was laughter, and easy conversation. The evening glowed with a special light, provided by a fire on the hearth and candles everywhere, and he was embraced as a member of their family. It was a night he would never forget.

THE NEXT DAY passed quickly. Avrom taught Sergei to play checkers. As they played, Sergei noticed a scar on Avrom's forehead over his right eye. Avrom saw him staring at it and said, "I was climbing a tree and fell—I think a branch did this," he said, pointing to the red line. "Mother said I almost put my eye out. Now she won't let me climb so high anymore."

That afternoon, when the sky cleared, the family went for a walk in the woods, and Benyomin pointed out the trees whose wood he prepared for Heschel's violins and clocks.

When they returned, Heschel took a spontaneous nap that began midsentence. Later, he woke up grumpy, not quite sure where he was. Sara brought him a steaming tea, then left him alone to come around on his own.

That evening, when the first three stars appeared, the Sabbath ended with more blessings recited over wine and candles. As Benyomin lit a new fire on the hearth, Heschel reached into his sack and took out gifts—spices and candles for the adults and sweets for the children. Then Benyomin handed Heschel a violin that Heschel himself had crafted, and he began to play.

Sergei stared openmouthed. It was as his grandfather had come alive in a new way. No longer a mere mortal, he was now a Maker of Music who brought the instrument to life. It sang of private sorrows one moment and lifted their spirits the next. Leya danced and twirled as Avrom and Sergei clapped for her.

When his grandfather finished, the cottage was full of music and light. Then, with a yawn, Heschel excused himself to retire early.

Sergei lay down in front of the hearth with the children. That night he slept in the fold of a family and dreamed of music.

O N S U N D A Y, soon after dawn, they said their farewells. Sergei took in every impression he could, to store away so he might draw upon these memories back at the school. He memorized Sara's face and voice . . . Benyomin's laughter . . . Avrom, his face buried in a book . . . Leya sitting by the fire helping her mother arrange a bouquet of tiny winter blossoms . . .

He wondered if he might someday be such a husband as Benyomin Abramovich, with a wife like Sara and with children of his own.

Before they parted, Sara Abramovich knelt and embraced Sergei; little Leya gave him a hug too. Avrom and his father shook his hand. "You are welcome here anytime," said the father.

"I hope to see you again," said the son.

Grandpa pulled on his winter coat and lifted his sack over his shoulder. Sergei did the same. He looked at Heschel and realized that his grandfather, after all his meals alone in an empty apartment, had also found comfort in this home. With a last wave, they turned and headed down the path into the forest.

The body can forget physical sensations. After feeling cold for hours or days, one can sit for a few minutes by a fire, and it's as if the cold never existed. How different are the emotions, which leave traces in memory that come alive with each recollection. In the difficult days and years of his life that followed, Sergei's memories of that family—of a fire on the hearth, the smell of fresh-baked bread in the stone oven, and Avrom and Leya, not young soldiers but regular children his age—would help sustain him.

Sergei had attended many masses in the school chapel when Father Georgiy spoke of a heavenly realm. But Sergei had never understood heaven until those two days with his grandfather in that cabin in the woods.

Except for the crack and shush of a snow-laden branch breaking, the whispered gusts through the pines, and the rhythmic crunch of their feet in the snow, Sergei and Heschel descended in silence. Words would only intrude in the thoughts and feelings that each savored. Besides, they had to concentrate on each step; the path was more hazardous on the downward journey. Sergei slipped once and reached out to grasp his grandfather's hand.

Then Heschel said, "You're a good boy, Socrates."

"And you're a good grandpa," Sergei responded, glad he had spoken when he saw the old man smile.

Too soon, it seemed, the school came into sight. Sergei looked up at his grandfather. His face looked drawn and weary, older than before. Sergei knew that a long journey awaited his grandfather and that at the end he would find an empty apartment, inhabited only by memories. He felt a sudden impulse to go with Grandpa Heschel to St. Petersburg, but he couldn't find the courage to speak. It had been his father's will that he be raised at the military school. Besides, as much as he might wish otherwise, he would not be permitted to leave.

They reached the edge of the school grounds, then drew near to the main gate.

They stood for a long time as the autumn sun passed overhead. Finally, Heschel spoke: "My little Socrates, no matter what the coming years may bring, even in the most difficult times, remember that you are not alone. The spirits of your parents—and your grandma Esther, and your grandpa Heschel—will always be by your side . . . "

Staring down at his feet, Sergei felt his shoulders sink with the full weight of their parting. Sergei shivered as the possibility snaked into his awareness: He might never again see his grandfather. Heschel bent down and straightened his grandson's shirt and coat. Then he pulled him close.

Sergei feared his grandfather was about to leave him then, but instead Heschel smiled and said, "I have something for you—a gift from your mother and father." He reached inside his coat and held out a silver chain, from which dangled an oval locket. The boy blinked as its silvered surface caught a ray of light.

"The midwife gave it to me on the same day she gave you into our care," Heschel told him. "This locket belonged to your mother. It was a gift to her from your father. The midwife told me that your mother wanted you to have it when you were old enough. You are old enough now."

Heschel placed the locket and chain in Sergei's open palm. It had touched his mother's skin . . . and now it was his to keep.

"Open it."

Sergei looked at his grandfather, uncomprehending.

"Here, I'll show you—" Heschel opened the clasp, and inside Sergei saw a small photograph—the face of a woman with dark curly hair and skin like milk, and a man with high cheekbones, an intense gaze, and a dark beard.

"My . . . parents?"

His grandfather nodded. "I think it was her most precious possession, and now it is yours. I know you will keep it safe."

"I will, Grandpa," Sergei murmured, still in awe, unable to take his eyes from his parents' faces.

"Quickly now, Socrates, listen carefully! There is something else—I couldn't bring it with me—another gift, hidden in a meadow near St. Petersburg." He reached again into his coat and pulled out a folded piece of paper and spread it out on his chest so that the boy could see it: a map that marked a spot by a tree in a meadow, bordered on three sides by forest, near the banks of a river. The map also had other markings.

"You know the story I told you on the way to the cabin—the one about my favorite spot in the forest, on the banks of the Neva River where I learned to swim? Here it is, just north of St. Petersburg," he said, tracing a line with his finger. "And here's the city . . . and boat docks . . . and the Winter Palace. If you follow the river ten kilometers north of the palace, out of the city and into the forest, you will come to a clearing . . . "

He turned over the paper to reveal a more detailed drawing of the shoreline, a tree, and a small x. "This is where the box is buried, on the side of a tree opposite the river . . . the only large cedar tree standing alone near the center of the meadow. The tree was planted by my own grandfather when he was a boy. In the box, buried between the two roots, you will find it."

Grandpa folded the map and placed it in his hands. "Maps can be lost, or stolen, Socrates. "I want you to study it carefully, in private. Commit every line and every marking to memory. Then destroy the map. Will you do that?"

"I will, Grandpa."

They walked to the gate. "Remember this gift. It will be waiting for you. When you find it, remember how much we love you."

"I'll remember," he said.

Heschel looked up into the sky and took a slow, deep breath—the kind he took when he had completed a new violin or clock and was pleased by what he saw. "That is good," he said. "That is good." He then lowered his gaze. "I want you to know, Socrates . . . to share this Shabbat with you—it has been one of the great joys of my life."

With that, Heschel Rabinowitz turned and set out toward the hills, murmuring to himself, "Yes, Esther . . . yes, it will be all right now . . . " Sergei watched him grow smaller, until he faded from sight, out of Sergei's life and into his memory.

. 4 .

WITH THE MAP TUCKED SAFELY AWAY, Sergei entered the gate. The cadet on guard duty said, "You're late for chapel."

He ran through empty halls to his barrack and dropped his knapsack into his footlocker. As he turned to leave, Sergei noticed a traveling bag on the bunk next to him, vacated several weeks before. This bag might indicate a new arrival.

He quickly slipped the locket and map into a hole in his mattress—the safest hiding place he could find. Then he hurried down the hall toward the chapel. His half run slowed to a walk as he imagined his grandfather, stooped over, hiking slowly up toward the main road.

As he reached the door and made the sign of the cross, Sergei asked God to keep his grandfather safe and give him strength for his journey. It was the first time he remembered praying with all his heart, the way Father Georgiy had instructed. He'd never had a reason to do so before.

Sergei hoped his prayer might be answered, even if Grandpa Heschel was a Jew.

AS SERGEI WALKED QUICKLY down the aisle of the chapel, several boys stole glances at him, smiling either in friendly greeting or gloating that he would be punished for his lateness. He looked up at Father Georgiy, standing in his black robe before the raised altar and icons of Christ, Mary with child, and St. Michael, St. Gabriel, and St. George, the guardian of their school and patron saint of Russia. The sun cast rainbows of light through the stained-glass window.

A hymn had begun; Sergei found his place and joined in, but his mind drifted. Both Father Georgiy and his grandfather Heschel had spoken of a God he couldn't see. To Sergei, God was a cabin in the forest, and heaven was a mother's embrace . . .

"Grandpa," he had asked on their return to the school, "what do the Jews say is the path to heaven?"

Heschel had smiled upon hearing this and said, "I do not speak for all Jews, nor am I wise enough to know this, little Socrates. But I believe that one day you will blaze your own path . . . You will find your own way."

As THE SERVICE ENDED, Sergei snapped out of his reverie and joined the orderly lines out of the chapel. That's when he first encountered the new cadet—tall and unsmiling, three or four years his senior. They happened to walk side by side up the narrow aisle as they filed out of mass. There was room for only one person at a time to pass through the door, and Sergei was about to step aside and let the new boy go first when the taller cadet shouldered him aside so roughly that Sergei nearly fell into the pews.

This first act of dominance would define their relationship.

It turned out that the bag on the bunk between Sergei's and Andrei's did belong to the newcomer. His name was Dmitri Zakolyev. From that day on, Sergei would think of him only as Zakolyev, a name he came to fear and despise.

Rumor had it that a man had brought Zakolyev to the entrance, handed an envelope to the cadet at the gate, and said, "Here is payment," and without another word or even a glance back, the man had turned and left.

Being twelve years old, Zakolyev should have been assigned to a sleeping room on the next floor among the eleven- to fourteen-year-olds. But they had a temporary shortage of beds upstairs—something about airing the mattresses because of lice. So for his first week the new cadet had to sleep in the "little boys' barrack," as he called it. He took his embarrassment out on everyone around him—especially on Sergei and Andrei, since their bunks were the closest.

In the following weeks Zakolyev elbowed his way to a certain status in the student hierarchy and earned a grudging respect from his peers— the kind one might give to a passing snake or bear.

Everything about Zakolyev seemed larger than life. He had huge hands, with knuckles scarred and calloused from punching trees or stones, and big ears, mostly covered by straw-colored hair that he left as long as he could get away with. Zakolyev hated the mandatory haircuts; he hated anything mandatory. His other features were fair enough, but they didn't quite fit together, as if they belonged to different faces. And he had a pasty complexion, as if the skin on his face never got enough blood.

What stood out most were Zakolyev's eyes—flint gray and cold, deep-set above a prominent nose, eyes that made you shiver. His eyes never changed when this strange boy smiled—a frightening, mirthless grin that appeared when others might frown or cry, revealing Zakolyev's crooked teeth. Anyone who stared at those teeth might lose some of his own. Nor did anyone stare at his birthmark—a red-white blotch on his neck, just beneath his left ear, another reason he hated the haircuts.

In a school where power meant respect, Zakolyev quickly estab- lished dominance over the younger cadets as well as most of his peers. He possessed a self-assurance that drew the admiration of some cadets, and they competed for Zakolyev's approval, which he doled out in small portions so that it seemed rare and valuable. Disgusted by this fawning display of servility, Sergei did his best to stay out of Zakolyev's way—a fact that did not escape the bully's notice.

Zakolyev came to be feared not only for his brutality but also for his unpredictable nature. Quiet one moment, cruel the next, he might lash out for the least cause or for no reason at all. Once he befriended a smaller boy, defending him against several bullies; the next day he gave the boy a worse beating than the hapless cadet would have suffered at the hands of his previous assailants.

Zakolyev seemed to view everyone at the school—cadets and instructors alike—as either potential followers or obstacles, and each was treated accordingly. An acute observer of human nature, he was wary of all those in authority who were older, stronger, or more powerful. Those people he would deceive or manipulate; the rest he could coerce.

Sergei was never certain how he got on Zakolyev's bad side. Maybe it was because he saw through Zakolyev's ruses, and he refused to be intimidated. Sergei was not stupid, however—he avoided confrontation, knowing the extent of the bully's wrath if provoked. There were other bullies in the school—probably a third of the upperclassmen. But Zakolyev seemed as threatening as anyone Sergei had ever met. He once overheard Zakolyev say to an older cadet, "There are men . . . and there are sheep." That summed up his philosophy—and it was clear to Sergei in which camp he and Andrei fell.

In fact, they became Zakolyev's whipping dogs—"runts of the litter," he called them. Sergei received no serious beatings at first, only bruising and humiliation. Andrei studied the bully's expressions the way a dog watches its master to learn whether it will be fed or beaten. And when Zakolyev turned his ire on Sergei, the smaller boy did his best to fend off the bully's angry blows. He did not strike back; it would have driven Zakolyev into a frenzy.

Zakolyev made his own rules but followed none—unless he was under the direct gaze of an instructor. Then he would make a pretense of obedience but do as he pleased once the instructor was out of sight. In one eerie incident, Zakolyev was mercilessly kicking a fallen cadet when two instructors rounded the corner. Instantly, Zakolyev knelt down like a ministering angel, and all the instructors saw was him calmly and gently touching the contorted, moaning face of the cadet. "I think he's had some kind of seizure," Zakolyev said in a concerned voice. The injured boy dared not contradict him. Not then, and not later. After that story got around, Zakolyev more or less took charge.

He could even manipulate some of the senior cadets. Sergei saw how it worked: At first he might ask only small favors, until they got used to saying yes, but gradually his requests increased until they became demands. Occasionally, when a senior cadet had had enough and refused to be intimidated, there would be a fight. Zakolyev won for two reasons: First, he showed no sense of fair play; second, he didn't seem to care what happened to him. That made him a formidable foe—one who fought with the instincts of a cornered wolf.

Among the cadets, especially the younger ones, an atmosphere of fear now pervaded the hallways and training grounds. Zakolyev required immediate obedience to any "request," and his punishments for insults real or imagined were absolute and inescapable. He never forgot or forgave, and eventually all transgressors suffered. It became easier to obey than to resist.

O<small>N THE LAST NIGHT</small> before Zakolyev was moved upstairs, Andrei stepped around a corner and collided with Zakolyev, causing the older cadet to stumble. He turned and put all his weight into a punch to Andrei's belly that doubled him over. Andrei fell to the floor groaning, gasping for air as Zakolyev stepped over him, walked to his bunk as if nothing had happened, and lay back with his hands behind his head.

Sergei rushed to Andrei's side, his fists clenching with rage as he helped Andrei, just starting to breathe again, back to his bunk. Sergei looked up at Zakolyev, who stared down at Sergei with that cold smile. Sergei stared right back in a small gesture of defiance.

Later that night, as Sergei drifted to sleep, he thought once again, as he had many times before, of that cabin in the forest—of Sara Abramovich and Benyomin and Avrom and Leya. Wishing he were with them, he drifted off to sleep and dreamed that he had awakened by their hearth on a Sabbath morning, with Avrom and Leya nearby, and that he was part of their family and the school had been only a dream after all.

Morning came as a great disappointment.

I<small>N THE DAYS AND WEEKS</small> following Zakolyev's move upstairs, that late winter of 1881, school returned to its usual rhythms of class work and combat training, meals, chapel, and sleep. But early one morning a senior cadet woke Sergei and his bunkmates at dawn and led the twelve sleepy boys—wearing only shorts and hugging towels and bundles of clothing to their chests—down the long passageway beneath the school.

It was cold and dank in the dim light. Dripping water echoed along the walls as twelve pairs of bare feet slapped the wet stone floor. Shivering, the boys came to a massive iron door. It creaked as the cadet pushed it open. Sergei stepped outside and found himself on the shore of the lake, now glowing in the first light of day. Chunks of thin ice and slush, remnants of winter, still floated in the shallows. The eastern hills stood in dark silhouette, and all was quiet. Not for long, however.

"Take off your shorts!" ordered the cadet as he removed his own clothing and waded out into the frigid water, up to his shoulders, up to his neck, then he submerged for a few seconds. He surfaced, his cheeks red, and returned to the shore, with tiny bumps showing on his now rosy skin. The senior cadet took his towel and rubbed himself briskly, then issued the command: "All of you, do the same!" But Sergei noticed that the cadet was fighting back a grin in anticipation of their agonies.

Like the other boys, Sergei edged into the water, gasping and screeching, followed by spasms of shivered laughter. The cold cut into his skin as he ducked under the water, then clambered quickly out and rubbed himself dry. The boys pointed to one another's blotchy red faces and chests and arms. Sergei still remembered feeling flushed with warmth and giddy after this exhilarating experience—but not one he wanted to repeat anytime soon.

As he and the other boys slipped into their clothing, the cadet announced, "You will do this immersion every morning from now on! You will never like it, and you will never get used to it—but it will make your body and spirit strong. Such disciplines will shape you into soldiers who can defend the Tsar and Mother Russia from foreign invaders. And from the best of you, we will choose the elite bodyguard."

Sergei thought about the elite bodyguard and wondered whether he would follow in his father's footsteps.

. 5 .

A FEW WEEKS LATER Sergei's group was about to start riding practice when Lieutenant Danilov called out, "Sergei Ivanov, come with me!" Sergei guessed that they were going to the chief instructor's office. At the first summons, years before, he'd learned of his father's death; the second time he'd found his grandfather waiting for him. So he didn't know whether to feel excitement or dread.

He found out soon enough. The moment he arrived, his uncle announced, "I just received word that your grandfather has died." The chief instructor waited a few moments for Sergei to absorb this information, then added, "He must have made arrangements—so you would know when the time came. You may go to the chapel if you wish to pray for his soul. That is all," he said.

Sergei did not go to the chapel. He returned to his empty barrack, checked to make sure he was alone, and retrieved his mother's locket. He gazed at the photographs of his parents. Now his grandpa Heschel had joined his parents and his grandma Esther. This locket would remind him of them all.

He placed the silver chain around his neck. He decided to wear it whenever he could safely do so and to hide it again when the others were asleep.

Then Sergei took out the map and committed every line, every marking to memory, until he could close his eyes and trace it in the air with his finger. When he was sure, he tore it into small pieces, scattering them in several different receptacles.

ONE MONDAY AFTERNOON in March of 1881, the school was shaken by news that dwarfed Sergei's personal concerns and reminded him that he was part of a larger world—a world of conflict and turmoil. On this windy day, he and about fifteen other cadets were outside in the compound, training with wooden sabers, when a bearded Cossack rode in through the main gate. They all stopped to watch this proud rider pass.

When all the cadets were convened in the chapel, the Cossack was introduced. His name was Alexei Orlov. He had once served with Sergei's Uncle Ivanov in a Cossack regiment. Then the chief instructor announced that the Little Father, Tsar Aleksandr II, had been assassinated.

That evening they returned to the chapel for a special mass so the instructors and cadets could pray for the tsar's soul. Like the other boys, Sergei dressed in his best uniform—dark blue with shiny buttons down the jacket and the academy logo, a two-headed eagle with a rose and saber in its claws.

Alexei Orlov stood straight and tall, his handsome face filled with grief. He said, "Cossacks are a free people, loyal to the Tsar and to the Mother Church." He offered a respectful nod to Father Georgiy before he continued: "I was among those serving as the tsar's royal guard. But despite our best efforts to protect the Little Father, he was killed by an assassin's bomb. The Tsar Liberator, who had emancipated millions of serfs, reformed the legal systems, and allowed greater freedom than ever before, was nevertheless hated by revolutionaries dissatisfied with their lot. Aware of the threat to his life, the Little Father had varied his travel routes under our direction. I was not yet on duty at that time, but one of my men told me what transpired.

"Despite precautions," Orlov continued, "as the tsar's carriage reached the upper section of one of the city's canals, a young man suddenly loomed up and threw what looked like a snowball between the horses. The bomb exploded but wounded the tsar only slightly. His Imperial Highness insisted on getting out to express his concern for a Cossack and a delivery boy who had been severely wounded.

"As Tsar Aleksandr turned toward the carriage, another man made a sudden movement toward him. There was an explosion. Within the hour, both the assassin and the Little Father died of their wounds. The man who threw the first bomb informed on his comrades. We know that at least one of the conspirators was a young woman named Gelfman— a revolutionary and a Jew."

When Sergei left the chapel, he found himself walking alongside his uncle. The chief instructor looked down and said under his breath, "If your father were alive, it would not have happened . . . not on his watch."

Soon Sergei heard news of the coronation of Tsar Aleksandr III— and fragments of conversations about a wave of violent pogroms sweeping through Russia and Ukraine as word spread that a "cadre of Jews" had murdered the Little Father. That rumor turned out to be false: The sixteen-year-old, pregnant Gelfman woman, who later died in prison, was the only Jew, a naive but idealistic girlfriend of another revolutionary. Still, the pogroms continued.

Mutterings about revolutionaries and Jews continued at the school, especially among those closest to Zakolyev. This talk made Sergei conscious of his own Jewish blood. He grew more concerned, as the weeks passed, for the Abramovich family. In this dangerous time, their isolation in the sanctuary of the wooded hills might work in their favor—but it could just as easily work against them. What might happen if a roving band of brigands, or even Cossacks, came upon a family of Jews in the forest?

Sergei had to warn them.

THAT NIGHT Sergei slipped past several cadets on guard duty and passed down the long tunnel under the school to the back door by the lake. He had traversed that hallway so many times he could do it blind-folded. His eyes might just as well have been covered, since no lamps were lit there at night.

Sergei pushed open the heavy iron door with a creaking sound that made him grit his teeth. He wedged a small branch between the jamb and door to keep it open, then moved quickly around the school's perimeter. Skirting the field, he found the stone outcropping that marked the beginning of the path. Now he had to rely solely on memory and instinct. Fortunately, the night was clear, and a waxing moon provided enough light for him to make his way.

Despite the darkness, he had to hike at a much faster pace than the last time. He only hoped he could find his way. Having slipped out without being caught, he now had to contend with other dangers: hungry wolves—or getting lost. If he lost his way, he could find the school in the morning, but by then his absence would have been discovered. Such absence without leave was a serious infraction; he would be punished severely.

Several older cadets, caught after they sneaked out during the night, had to walk with their heads lowered between two long rows of cadets, who whipped them with heavy reeds. At the end of the line they were whipped by the instructors. After that, the bruised and bleeding cadets were put in isolation cells without food or water for three days. Chief Instructor Ivanov announced to the cadets, "If they had committed this offense while in real military service, the punishment would have been far worse."

No one had repeated that offense, as far as Sergei knew—until now.

Once he found the cabin, he would tell Benyomin about the assassination, the pogroms, and his grandfather's death. After he savored a cup of tea, which Sara would insist on giving him, along with another embrace, he would return before dawn. He planned it all during his march up the moonlit trail.

Sergei was breathing hard but keeping his pace. His light frame and improved endurance served him well. Awash in the adventurous optimism of youth, he suddenly realized that he could be leaving the school for good. The idea had not occurred to him until that moment. What, after all, was keeping him there? He would miss Andrei, and maybe even Uncle Vladimir. He might feel a certain nostalgia for the school grounds. But he would not miss the day-to-day life—and he would gladly put Dmitri Zakolyev behind him forever.

Sergei was wearing the locket; he had no other possessions worth keeping. If only he could find the courage to ask! Could he claim Avrom and Leya as his brother and sister, and Sara and Benyomin as his parents? Would it be possible? Yes, he decided. He would be a good child, and be helpful, and make them proud. Excited by this possibility, Sergei pushed onward. The moon was nearly overhead. It couldn't be much farther—

In the next moment, thick clouds covered the moon and the path disappeared. Sergei could scarcely see his hands in front of his face. He looked up to see stars spread across the sky to his left and right. Only the moon was obscured. He shuffled forward, his arms reaching out in front of his face, feeling his way. Sergei was nearly there.

Then he froze as some primitive part of his mind recognized that it wasn't clouds obscuring the moon. It was smoke.

Sergei found himself careening headlong toward the cabin, racing around the boulders, lurching into the small meadow, to stop dead still, his mouth agape. Then moonlight revealed it all, and his dread turned to horror. Where the cabin had stood he now saw only charred ruins. Flickering illumination from some still-burning timbers lit the nightmarish scene.

He felt the smoldering heat. Stumbling through the burning embers like a drunken man, he found no living thing. He prayed that the Abramovich family might emerge from the forest to greet him. Together they might rebuild—

No, he told himself—the truth: Their lives, and his hopes and dreams, were burned to cinders. Coughing and wiping his smoke-blackened face, he searched the piles of smoldering rubble and found the damning evidence he most feared: the blackened bones of a forearm and hand reaching up through the timbers.

Squinting from the heat and fetid air, Sergei threw off the smoking logs to reveal a man's skeleton with glistening flesh still clinging to the bones. The stench and sight of it burned a place in his memory. The body was almost certainly that of Benyomin Abramovich. Forcing himself to dig farther, Sergei found what remained of a little girl's shoe and wooden doll. He had to face what he wanted to deny: The rest of the family lay buried somewhere beneath the smoking nightmare that was once a home.

He turned and retched onto the earth and ashes. He somehow dragged Benyomin's remains away from the ruins and into a shallow indentation he had found. The earth was loose, and he managed to scoop it out deep enough with his bare hands, now bleeding, and to cover Benyomin's remains and say some words. There was no way he could dig alone through the rubble to find what was left of Sara or the children. Sergei had done what he could.

With his eyes burning from the acrid air, Sergei stumbled and ran back down through the wooded hills. Before dawn threw himself, fully clothed, into an icy stream to clean the smell of death from his hair and clothing. But he couldn't clear it from his mind, where questions raged: Why didn't I come sooner? he asked himself. I might have saved them! Only one day sooner . . .

His head throbbed, and his breath came in gasps.

An hour before dawn, with nowhere else to go, a Sergei finally reached the school. The iron door was still ajar. He entered like a ghost, hardly caring if he was seen. Maybe I'm dead too, he thought, only a wraith, invisible to living beings. He climbed into bed and fell exhausted into a barren, gray dreamscape.

When his eyes opened to the wan light of the day, Sergei thought, for a moment, that it was only a nightmare. But then he saw the soot and dried blood on his hands. He could tell no one, not even Andrei, what he had seen.

Part Two

SURVIVAL
OF THE
FITTEST

*What is to give light
must endure burning.*

VIKTOR FRANKL

. 6 .

During his tenth, eleventh, and twelfth years, Sergei fell into a trancelike routine at school, going through the motions—growing in strength, in centimeters, in skill. He faced each task as it came but without any real sense of meaning, connection, or purpose. He still thought about his grandfather at times and clung to his memories of the Abramovich family—but each time they came to mind, the specter of smoldering ruins rose up before him.

Then news circulated among the cadets that Zakolyev, now sixteen years old and living in the senior barracks, had almost killed an older cadet in a fight. Sergei heard two of the senior cadets whispering that Zakolyev had acted "like a crazy man" and beaten their friend with a chair. The cadet's injuries were reported as an accident.

A few days after the beating, six of the injured cadet's friends overpowered Zakolyev and gave him a beating of his own. They sent a clear message that he might overcome one man but not many. Zakolyev seemed quieter, less domineering, after that. Yet over the following months, every one of those six boys suffered a painful "accident." One boy tripped on a loose stone and broke his ankle; another was struck by a falling object that almost crushed his skull; a third rounded a corner where his head collided with an unspecified object; a fourth fell down the stairs.

Zakolyev had learned from the experience: divide and conquer. The others got the clear message. None of them would talk about their accidents; they feared for their lives.

On a hot summer's day in 1885, a few months before Sergei's thirteenth birthday, Alexei Orlov returned. Chief Instructor Ivanov announced, with some satisfaction, that after negotiation with higher authorities, he had succeeded in getting Instructor Orlov assigned to the school.

"As you will soon learn," his uncle continued, "Alexei Igorovich Orlov is as skilled as any man alive at tracking, outdoor survival, riding, and combat. I have seen him stand atop a galloping steed and leap over a tree branch, landing lightly again on the horse's back. Even our Instructor Brodinov might find Alexei Orlov a challenging foe in hand-to-hand combat." Sergei glanced at Instructor Brodinov, who scratched his balding head and grinned.

This high praise from his uncle turned out to be fully justified. In the coming weeks Alexei the Cossack, as the cadets referred to him, had occasion to demonstrate his skills. Sergei found himself observing the Cossack the way he had once watched his uncle. He admired the confident yet relaxed way the Cossack walked, and his friendly manner—as if he didn't need to bluster or posture or threaten because he knew he was deadly.

Sergei felt as if he was awakening from a long sleep. Suddenly he wanted to learn from Alexei Orlov; he wanted to *become* him. Now it seemed manly and romantic to be a warrior—like his father, like a Cossack.

Sergei had heard older cadets talking about women—making jokes about what men and women did together to make babies. This subject, which he had previously ignored, now fascinated him. And it was generally agreed that to win a woman a man needed to be able to defend her from other, lesser specimens; he must fight off brigands and protect the weak. In short, he must be like Alexei, the sturdy Cossack with wavy brown hair and a neatly trimmed beard, whose face lit up when he smiled.

The Cossack's one physical flaw—a saber scar on his neck—only added to his dashing persona. He told the boys that the scar served as a reminder about the value of practice, which he had pursued intensely since that mishap. He was never cut again.

Unlike the other instructors, Alexei the Cossack treated Sergei and the others with courtesy and respect. He expected even the slowest students to surpass him someday, allowing the young men to believe that anything was possible. "When we're in the woods," he told the cadets, "you may call me by my first name—as if we are colleagues and friends. But you must work hard to earn this friendship."

Sergei would have done anything for him.

Alexei, he learned, had grown up in a village of Don Cossacks. When Alexei's father was killed in battle, he had redoubled his training. He was driven by a sudden awareness of the reality of death but also from the desire to make his father proud. He was later taken into the tsar's elite guard.

"You will become Russia's finest soldiers," he told them, "and leave your mark upon the world." And the cadets believed every word.

"True warriors," the Cossack added, "bring death only when necessary and protect life, including their own, whenever possible. What good to conquer an enemy in battle, only to be vanquished by hunger or cold? Napoleon and his men were defeated not only by Russian soldiers but also by the Russian winter. So my aim is to show you not merely how to kill, but how to live—how to survive on the bare essentials of life, relying on no one but yourself. There is a difference, however, between knowing how to do something and actually doing it. You will discover that soon enough."

SINCE HIS HIKE in the forest with his grandfather years before, a love of the wilderness had slumbered in Sergei—and it awakened now as a wanderlust. He found himself gazing at the mountains in the distance. He continued applying himself in the classroom and in wrestling, riding, swimming, saber, and shooting, but survival training became his passion.

The cadets made camouflaged shelters out of pine branches and learned the skills of hunting and trapping and fishing. Alexei showed

them how to find edible plants—nature's medicines he called them—
and how to avoid poisonous plants and other hazards of the wild: bears,
snakes, and insects. They learned how to adapt to different terrain and
any kind of weather. "Outdoorsmen do not seek hardship or adversity,"
Alexei explained. "We do not delight in sleeping on the cold earth or suffering unnecessary discomfort. Use your wits and skills to soften
nature's sharp edges."

Alexei the Cossack did not waste time, motions, or words. "Every
action or statement," he said, "must have a purpose." His words
informed them, but his actions inspired them. Through Alexei the
Cossack, Sergei came to take pride in his father's lineage.

One morning before training, Alexei paced back and forth in front of
the attentive cadets, gesturing with his arms as he spoke: "We Cossacks
are a peaceful and devout people, but fearsome when provoked. When
the gospel is read, we draw our sabers halfway out to show our readiness
to defend church and country.

"Legends abound of the Cossacks' nearly magical skills in horsemanship and combat. Our people can make sounds to imitate the gait
and voice of different animals; we can howl like a wolf, cry like an owl
or a hawk to signal our compatriots. But it is not magic; it comes from
training."

The younger boys begged him to demonstrate, which he did so well
that he could hardly continue after that because the young cadets were
all howling and making animal sounds too. "Stop!" cried Alexei in mock
consternation. "You sound like a barnyard of animals in mating season."
This predictably sent the boys into peals of hysterical laughter, which no
other instructor would have allowed—and that was why they loved him.
Even the younger boys quieted down at the prospect of learning more.

"The Cossacks bow to no one but the tsar. We fight his enemies, but
beyond this we make our own laws. We kill any marauding bands, and
thus we form a kind of Great Wall like that of China, but a wall that can
move faster than any enemy, protecting Mother Russia on the frontiers
and borders of this vast land. But we will not allow soldiers to arrest runaway serfs whom we have accepted into our communities."

"But won't soldiers make you give back the serfs?" asked one of the younger boys.

"Soldiers do not 'make' Cossacks do anything," Alexei answered. "We have developed effective fighting methods on any terrain and in all kinds of weather—on frozen rivers, in snowy forests, and on tropical plains—against many different invaders, fighting styles, and weapons. I will teach the best of you some of these skills."

Sergei smiled, seeing some of the younger boys sit up straighter, trying to look taller and stand out as more disciplined than their peers. Alexei then led them into the woods once again. When a few of the younger boys treated this time as play, throwing berries at each other instead of paying attention, Alexei appeared to ignore their antics, until he stopped abruptly and said, "Those who listen, live." The cadets froze as he added, "If any of you gets lost or injured—or if you die during survival training, which can happen—it will be your failure. But it will also be my failure . . . so you must take care."

There were no slackers after that.

Alexei the Cossack's strengths even earned the grudging admiration of Dmitri Zakolyev. For all Zakolyev's flaws, he trained harder than most for reasons of his own. When the Cossack gave Zakolyev an occasional nod of approval, a jealous Sergei strove even harder to earn Alexei's respect.

As the weeks and months passed, Sergei began to win more wrestling matches than he lost, even with some of the older boys. He also learned to shoot a rifle and pistol while riding across the nearby fields, imagining himself a great Cossack like Alexei, like his father. During this period Sergei outgrew his clothing almost as fast as he was issued larger sizes. His uniforms no longer looked baggy; he felt new muscles on his arms and legs and chest.

IN MARCH when he was fourteen, Sergei overheard Lieutenant Danilov talking with one of the senior cadets. At the word Jew, he listened more closely, and caught a few more words: ". . . Constantine

Pobedonostov, the tsar's procurator . . . one-third of the Jews forced to convert, one-third expelled . . . the rest killed . . . pogrom . . . Cossacks." Times were growing darker for the Jewish people—as his grandfather had predicted.

On a Friday afternoon, after a survival training session, Sergei managed to catch Instructor Orlov in a rare moment alone and asked if he could walk with him back to the main gate. Alexei's smile and nod gave Sergei the courage to ask, "Are Cossacks killing Jews?"

Alexei seemed surprised by the question. He kept walking without offering an answer. For a moment Sergei feared that his instructor might ask, "Why are you so concerned about Jews?" Instead, he said, "Your uncle told me a little of your history, Sergei. I understand your concern. But your secret is safe with me," he added. "After all, your mother converted, and you have Cossack blood as well. But . . . to answer your question about whether some Cossacks have killed Jews . . . I would have to say yes.

"Cossacks feel a deep connection to the Tsar and the Mother Church. The ways of Jews seem strange to us. But we are a free and tolerant people. Those who plague, pillage, plunder, and hunt Jews like animals are not Cossacks but nationalists who resent any outsiders. True Cossacks have honor, Sergei. We engage in battle with the enemies of Russia; we do not slaughter a devout people even if they are different."

He paused before adding, "Yet among even the Cossacks there are lesser men who have raped women after battle and who have behaved badly. There is no doubt that violence against Jews has increased, at the hands of angry peasants, the Okhrana—the secret police—and even soldiers on orders of the tsar. I'm afraid that a small number of Cossacks have also raided Jewish settlements. Sometimes there are deaths. It is a shame."

NOT LONG AFTER his conversation with Alexei, between classes, Sergei was washing his face in the latrine area when Zakolyev entered, brushed past him, and said, "Well, if it isn't Sergei the Good."

Sergei was caught off guard. Is that what Zakolyev thought of him? And how should he react? If he ignored the comment—pretend it hadn't happened—he would suffer for it. So he shrugged and muttered, "Not always so good." Then he exited the latrine as soon as he could.

Sergei had no wish to fight Zakolyev, four years his senior and equally dedicated to his training. But Sergei suspected that a confrontation might be inevitable. And he thought: Alexei the Cossack would not let a bully dominate him, so neither will I.

After that he began to observe Zakolyev during hand-to-hand combat matches, seeking to discover the older cadet's weak points. It never occurred to Sergei that Zakolyev was also watching him.

A few days later Instructor Orlov called the cadets together and told them that the next morning at sunrise they would all set out on a seven-day survival test. They were to work in pairs, each comprised of a senior and junior cadet. He then instructed the older cadets to choose a younger partner.

Zakolyev chose Sergei. The phrase "survival test" took on a new meaning.

. 7 .

THE NEXT DAY at dawn Instructor Orlov explained, "Now that you understand the strategies of survival, you and your partner will hike to isolated parts of the forest, away from the others, to the spot marked on your map. Each team of two will work together to survive. Now remove your clothes."

The cadets were not sure they had heard correctly; it was late April of 1887, and although the snow had begun to melt, patches still lay on the ground and a chill remained, especially at dawn. "You may keep your shorts," Alexei said, "but you must walk barefoot to learn the importance of footwear. Each of you may take one of these," he said, issuing a knife and sheath to each cadet and a small military shovel to each pair. "I expect you to return here by midday seven days from now—well rested, well fed, in good health, and wearing footwear and clothing you made yourself. Any questions?"

As Sergei squatted down to pick up his clothing, he stole a glance at Andrei, who gave him a worried look.

Sergei had to run to catch up with Zakolyev, who had already taken the map and set out toward the forested hills.

Four hours later, after following a small stream up into the thickly wooded hillside, they arrived at the location marked on the map. Or Sergei guessed it was the right location, since Zakolyev had made no move to show him the map. It looked like a good spot—a small clearing about fifty meters from the stream. The stream meant fish, and equally important, it meant animal trails leading to the water. An overhanging rock wall formed a shallow cave that would serve as a partial shelter; the rest they could build.

Sergei examined his feet, reddened with cold—numb, already blistered—and was about to find material to make various traps when Zakolyev issued his first order: "Make us a fire!" So he found dry moss and small twigs for a starter fire. He then tried striking his knife against several different stones to create sparks but made little progress, so he shaped a fire stick and began rubbing for friction and heat and blowing gently. It took nearly an hour—precious time, longer than he had thought—but soon he had heat, then smoke, then glowing embers. Despite the blisters on his hands matching those on his feet, Sergei felt a primal excitement when the twigs burst into flame. He had made fire in training sessions, but this was for real. This meant survival.

Meanwhile, Sergei noted, Zakolyev had gathered branches, stones, and the tuberous fibers they could weave into string for their snares. So, after placing some larger branches on the fire and then larger logs he had cut from a fallen tree with the shovel, Sergei approached Zakolyev to help construct their traps.

"Go get your own materials!" said Zakolyev. "This is for my traps."

So that's how it was. Sergei knew better than to refer to the crackling flames as "my fire."

He moved quickly into the forest to find the materials he would need for his traps. After some difficulty, and with an eye to the sun's lengthening afternoon shadows, he managed to build and set seven traps at likely spots upriver and upwind of their site along animal trails. He made two fish traps and set snares and deadfalls—and where a supple sapling grew, he made two spring traps near the stream. He was careful to camouflage them well.

By the time he returned to camp, dusk had brought cold gusts of wind from the north. Shivering, he slapped himself and danced around to keep warm. He found Zakolyev completing a primitive shelter from birch branches and leaves, propped against the hillside next to the fire. It had room for only one.

The fire, now little more than embers, needed more logs. Sergei gathered a few and set one on the fire Zakolyev had claimed. Then he gathered more twigs and logs and built a fire of his own.

By the light of his fire, Sergei managed to throw together a makeshift overhang of interwoven pine branches near another granite overhang. He finished just as a light drizzle began. The cloud cover served as an insulating blanket, keeping the night from turning frigid.

Shivering, wet, and naked except for his shorts, Sergei sandwiched himself between layers of pine boughs he had gathered, shifting until he found a warmer position.

Zakolyev's huddled form, faintly visible in the glow of his fire, revealed that he had made similar preparations. Sergei lay awake for a few moments, too cold to sleep, and listened to the rain. Despite the cold and hunger that churned in his belly, a wave of satisfaction washed over him. He had set snares, made fire, found shelter. For the present, he was alive and well. In the morning he would check his traps, and they would see what the day would bring. These thoughts gave way to a deep fatigue that pulled Sergei over the edge of sleep and into the dream world.

W HEN SERGEI next opened his eyes, his breath misted in the chill morning air. He scrambled out of his bed of pine branches, hoping for a patch of sunlight, but found none this early. Leaving Zakolyev asleep, he walked gingerly on sore feet to the stream, where he drank, then splashed the icy water over his face and chest and shoulders. He brushed the water from his body, slapping himself all over, and did knee bends and jumps until his body warmed.

Sergei then returned to camp, grabbed his knife, and headed upstream. Despite marking trees at eye level near the traps, he couldn't find the first snare. Alexei had reminded them, "The wilderness teaches hard lessons and has little tolerance for mistakes." Why didn't I pay better attention? Sergei thought, chastising himself for his carelessness. Backtracking, he found the second trap he had set. Empty.

But nearby, in a spring trap he had placed along the trail, he found an exhausted weasel, dangling in midair. He approached the animal cautiously. It struggled weakly. Sergei realized that he was going to have to kill this creature. As he reached up to grasp the weasel, it made a low growl and sliced his hand with a sudden swipe of its claw. Then it tried to bite him.

With a primitive rush of energy, Sergei grabbed the back of its head and slashed the weasel's throat so forcefully he nearly took off its head—and narrowly missed cutting his own wrist in the process. The creature kicked a few times, blood pulsing from its neck. Then it was still, and dead.

Panting and trembling, his heart pounding, Sergei found the presence of mind to open the snare rather than cut it; he would need it again. He hoped the killing would be easier in the future. But then he thought, Should killing get easier? Did he have the right to kill? No—he had only the power. He did what had to be done under the circumstances. He felt no animosity toward this animal, which had only tried to defend itself. And Sergei had only killed to survive. In an instinctive gesture, he thanked the weasel for its life, which would sustain his own. He would not waste it.

In killing that weasel, he had put his childhood behind him. He realized that his life too could be snuffed out in a moment. It had nothing to do with fairness, only chance. By paying attention—through knowledge and skill—he might better his odds. This was his first real lesson in the wilderness. As he padded quietly toward the next trap, Sergei wondered what kind of snares might be waiting on his own path into the future.

The third trap was empty and undisturbed; so were the fourth and fifth. The next had snared a squirrel, which he killed as quickly and mercifully as he could with one blow of a large stone. The remaining traps were empty, except for the last, in which he found a large rabbit. This meant food for several more days, and new shoes as well.

The cut on his hand from the weasel's claw was beginning to throb.

So he swung his arm rapidly around to make the cut bleed to cleanse the wound. Then he washed and scrubbed and scoured the shallow gash with sand from the stream. Finally, he peed on it, remembering Alexei's dictum that fresh urine could help guard against infection.

After Sergei tied the creatures together with several vines, he reset the last snare and turned back toward the camp. He didn't expect any more catches until the next morning, but he would check again in the late afternoon. Just in case.

The hunt had awakened his instincts and sharpened every sense. He listened to rainwater dripping from budded branches overhead and birdsong in the distance. His eyes drank in every hue and texture of the forest as he headed back to camp. He found a morose Zakolyev skinning his catch—a single squirrel, one small meal and one shoe.

Sergei knew it would not go well for him when Zakolyev saw his three animals, but he could hardly hide them. So he casually walked up and dumped the other squirrel next to Zakolyev's, followed by the weasel and rabbit, saying diplomatically, "These are from our other traps."

Zakolyev stared at them. All he said was, "Sergei the Good does it again," before turning back to his skinning. Sergei butchered the carcasses as well as he could. It was messy work, made worse by his inexperience. In training, he had only helped butcher one rabbit and a deer.

By early afternoon they had hung strips of meat from vines tied between nearby trees. They stretched the skins on frames made from flexible saplings. The weasel skin wasn't large enough to cover Sergei's shoulders, but it was a start. When he handed Zakolyev the squirrel skin and said, "For your other shoe," the senior took it without comment.

They cooked strips of rabbit flesh, their first meal in nearly two days. With a full stomach, Sergei brought back more saplings and pine boughs to reinforce his makeshift shelter.

That night, as Sergei and Zakolyev squatted by their respective fires, neither having spoken more than a few words, Sergei watched the stars appear, sparkling like ice crystals scattered across a velvet sky. White smoke and glowing embers rose up, then disappeared into the night. After a glance toward Zakolyev, staring into the flames of his fire, deep in thought, Sergei slipped into the cover of pine branches. As he drifted into sleep, he wondered: Why had Zakolyev chosen him?

THE NEXT MORNING Sergei found a squirrel crushed by one of his deadfalls; another trap had snared a raccoon near the stream—the same trap that had caught the weasel. Rather than trying to grab the hissing, growling animal, he fashioned a club from a heavy log and knocked the creature unconscious before taking its life.

Sergei also found two fish in the fish trap before returning to camp.

Zakolyev's traps had caught only one squirrel and a sickly looking skunk—good for its hide but not for meat. When he saw Sergei's bounty, Zakolyev just stared at him, saying nothing.

Awkwardly, Sergei set down the two fish, the squirrel, and the raccoon on a flat rock. "I got lucky," he said. "We can eat well." Then he said no more, wondering what Zakolyev was thinking.

After the meal, his stomach satisfied, Sergei went out exploring—anything to distance himself from the sullen Zakolyev. He spent about two hours making a wide circle around the camp, checking the streams for fish and familiarizing himself with the surroundings. He was returning to camp when he heard the distant tapping sound of a deer's hooves. He froze, waited, and listened. Silence . . . a few more hoof sounds . . . then silence. Sergei was downwind of the sounds, which would make it less likely for the animal to detect his scent. Sergei crouched low and moved in slowly and quietly.

A few minutes later he spotted it—a huge buck, barely visible, about twenty meters away, nibbling on fresh shoots of grass. Every few moments its large ears would turn, and it would look up. Sergei stayed absolutely still. The deer moved a few more feet in his direction. That's when Sergei realized that he was standing on a deer path, between the deer and the stream.

A crazy idea occurred to him: He'd hunt the buck. There was no time to go back and get Zakolyev. It had to be now, or he'd lose the chance. This one creature would provide them with enough food and

clothing to meet their needs. So, driven by desperate need, Sergei slowly shimmied up a tree right next to the deer trail.

Once he reached a thick branch directly over the trail, Sergei found
a stable position and waited. He could no longer see the deer, but he
would wait as long as it took, on the chance it would pass under him.

About fifteen minutes later, there it was—walking and grazing below
him. Now or never, he thought. Hardly breathing, his knife in hand,
Sergei dropped from the branch and landed on the buck with a thud,
one arm wrapped tightly around its neck. As the creature kicked wildly,
he reached around and cut its throat—once, then another cut. The panicked buck, bleeding profusely, kicked wildly. Sergei realized that if he
fell off, the buck would likely kill him with those antlers before it bled
out. So, before he was thrown, in a hunter's act of mercy, he aimed just
above the front foreleg and stabbed deeply into the buck's side, through
its ribs and into its heart.

He had been trained well. The creature fell over and lay still.

Panting hard, his own heart pounding, Sergei was awash with elation
as well as sorrow for this brutal, violent act he had committed.

On the way back to camp, he remembered something Alexei had
told them: "When in the wild, you must become wild."

Entering the clearing, still bloody and breathing hard, Sergei told
Zakolyev about the deer. He didn't think Zakolyev believed him, but the
senior cadet went back with him to find the proud creature lying dead.

Sergei watched Zakolyev closely as his strange companion took in
this sight. He saw Zakolyev's face change from surprise to . . . a contained fury. The senior said nothing, however. He just pulled out his
knife, cut the vines, and began to gut the deer. "Come on!" he ordered
Sergei. "Don't just stand there—make yourself useful!"

They left most of the internal organs for the scavengers, then made
litters and dragged the carcass back to camp. It took them the rest of
the day to butcher the animal, stretch the hide, and prepare the strips
of meat. It was such a large buck that they now had enough food to last
the rest of their stay in the forest. More important, with the other animals, mostly trapped by Sergei, they had enough for fur-lined shoes

from the rabbit and deerskin shirts and leggings. Sergei also had a raccoon cap.

That night, just before dusk, Sergei washed the blood off his bare chest and legs. Then he padded through the forest and dismantled his traps. There was no sense killing more animals.

I⊤ TOOK a good part of their final two days for each of them to fashion a pair of stiff buckskin pants and shirt. They had to let the hide soak for hours in the stream before scraping off the hair and flesh and washing the hide several times more to remove any grease. They couldn't tan them properly, lacking salt or lime. But they rubbed the hides with the brains of the deer, then with ashes from the fire, as they had been taught.

Finally, after cutting leather thongs—narrow strips to tie together the leather shirt and pants—they were clothed like real woodsmen. That final day passed quickly. Still, Zakolyev only spoke to Sergei when necessary, every remark curt or insulting.

Then, an hour before dusk, Sergei was alone in camp, thinking about their hike out on the following day, when he thought he heard a distant cry. Thinking it must have been an animal, he went back to tending the fire. Then he heard it again. It was Zakolyev. Going quickly to investigate, he heard him cry out again: "Ivanov!"

Sergei found Zakolyev at the bottom a steep and slippery embankment over the stream. It was so slick with moss that Sergei almost lost his footing as well. In the fading light he could just see Zakolyev struggling to free his ankle, wedged between two rocks.

Furious—as if Sergei himself were somehow responsible—Zakolyev snarled, "Don't just stand there, idiot. Get a branch! Hurry!"

Sergei had his knife, but it hadn't occurred to him to bring the military shovel, which also served as a hatchet. "I'll be right back," he yelled, and ran as fast as he could in the deepening dusk to retrieve the tool. On his way back from camp he spied a straight and sturdy branch that might be used as a lever. Sergei hacked at the limb until it came free.

By the time Sergei got back to him, Zakolyev was so enraged he could hardly speak. This was the ultimate embarrassment, and Sergei knew it. Not only had he out-trapped Zakolyev, and caught and killed the great buck, but now Sergei the Good was rescuing him—maybe saving his life.

Sergei knew that if he was able to free Zakolyev, there was no way to predict what might happen next, but it wasn't likely to be a humble thanks or a handshake. He felt an impulse to leave Zakolyev there. But it passed.

Once Sergei got the heavy branch under one of the stones, it didn't take long to move it enough for Zakolyev to pull his ankle free. The ankle was sore but not broken. Sergei knew better than to offer any further help. He silently handed him the sturdy branch for a walking stick and left him alone.

A dread came over Sergei as he walked back to camp. He knew that in saving Dmitri Zakolyev, he had made an enemy for life.

W HEN ZAKOLYEV finally returned to camp, Sergei busied himself by adding branches to his lean-to, fearing that a single word, or even a look, might set off Zakolyev. Sergei needed more branches overhead because the heavy clouds threatened rain, and he hoped to sleep well this final night in the forest.

As it turned out, he hardly slept at all, alert to any sound that stood out against the patter of rain.

Sometime in the night, after drifting off, Sergei was startled awake by flashes of lightning in the distance—then the explosive crackle of thunder. His eyes snapped open, but he saw only the thick overhang of pine boughs.

Still, he lay wide awake, feeling a foreboding. Something was wrong. The lightning flashed again, and he saw—or thought he saw—legs and a torso just outside the shelter. He turned his head imperceptibly, nearly frozen with fear. The lightning flashed again to reveal a momentary glimpse of Zakolyev, squatting nearby, staring at him. There was a knife in Zakolyev's hand. Sergei thought he was about to die.

The light vanished in an instant. Unable to breathe or make even a sound, Sergei stared into the darkness. Then another flash of light revealed that the figure was gone.

Could he have dreamed it? Imagined it? He couldn't be sure. Sergei lay back, gulping shallow breaths as the downpour continued and the thunderclaps receded in the distance.

The next thing he knew, his eyes jerked open to the light of dawn. He sat up quickly to see Zakolyev, lying asleep under his lean-to.

As Sergei broke apart his lean-to and scattered his fire, Zakolyev rose, took his knife and the shovel, and without a word walked out of the camp.

Again, Sergei was completely mystified as to why Zakolyev would have chosen him as a partner. It didn't matter now.

Later, making his way back through the rocky, forested terrain, Sergei thought about how he had survived not only the wilderness, but also his strange companion. He now knew that he could survive in the wild—like Alexei and others before him.

Sergei made it back to the meeting place by midday, as Alexei Orlov had instructed. Soon most of the original thirty-two cadets had returned. Some distance away, Sergei saw Zakolyev standing in the middle of an admiring group of half-naked younger boys. Zakolyev also saw him—he pointed toward Sergei and said something to the boys. They laughed.

Ignoring them, Sergei looked around for Andrei, wondering how he had fared, but he wasn't back yet. When he turned back, Zakolyev and those with him now stood nearby. Some of the young boys snickered. One of the bolder cadets, probably trying to please his idol, said in a sarcastic tone, "Found your way back, did you?"

Sergei stared at the young cadet; he could only imagine what Zakolyev must have told them all.

As the group of boys walked away, one of them called back, "It was lucky Dmitri gave you part of the hide, or you'd be as naked as some of the others!" Then he scurried off to follow Zakolyev.

Sergei spotted a tired but happy-looking Andrei approaching with his older companion. They had pieced together rough-looking long shirts but no pants, and pieces of leather were strapped to the soles of their feet with thick cords. He saw them smile at each other, half-naked boys barely covered in motley skins made of rabbit, raccoon, shrew, skunk, fox, and squirrel.

It had been one of the most intense experiences of Sergei's youth. He only hoped it was the last time he would ever have to spend time alone with Dmitri Zakolyev.

. 8 .

AFTER SURVIVAL WEEK, Sergei returned to the daily routines at the school, yet something had changed in his inner world, and in his body as well. He looked at himself in the mirror and now saw a muscular youth, with hair growing under his arms and elsewhere. He thought about women more often—about their bodies and their mysteries, all in a confused state of longing.

He also began to notice flaws and small hypocrisies in the adults around him, such as Brodinov preaching about the importance of training hard and staying fit while he grew heavier with each passing month, or Kalishnikov, who would lean over his desk in the classroom and pontificate about telling him the truth while he lied about the Jews.

Sergei's life seemed even more complicated and confused than before. He thought about what it might be like to leave this place, to find a home where others were more like him.

Sergei felt the urge to be free in a world where few freedoms existed—except in the wild. And even nature had its own strict rules and consequences. Questions raged inside him about his future. He had never thought much about the future; now it preoccupied him.

When the chief instructor allowed it, Sergei made more frequent visits to his uncle's library. Vladimir Ivanov owned an impressive selection of books, and Sergei read works ranging from religious philosophy and military science to ancient Greek philosophers like Plato, who described the lives and teachings of Socrates and the other sages and statesmen.

Sergei discovered that certain phrases seemed to unlock within him a vast storehouse of insights about subjects he had never before contemplated, questions he had never asked: What is the purpose of living? What constitutes the good life? Are people innately virtuous or selfish? Sometimes he had to shut a book, close his eyes, and hold his head in his hands as his heart raced with excitement—not merely because of the words he read, but because of what they revealed. It was like discovering foreign lands in his mind.

Then came Sergei's fifteenth birthday, near the end of summer in 1887. He thought of his mother on that day, as he thought of her on every birthday and other times as well. He slipped the chain of the locket around his neck and under his shirt. He wore it almost daily, taking this risk for the simple pleasure it provided him in a place with few pleasures, simple or otherwise. After dark, or before training or the cold-water immersions, he would hide it again within his mattress.

IN DECEMBER of that year, Chief Instructor Ivanov made a rare appearance during morning exercises in the school compound. In recent months he had seen little of his uncle, a distant and private man who remained behind the scenes. So the chief instructor's presence spoke of the importance of this announcement. Without preface or explanation, he said, "Step forward if you hear your name called." He began reading from a list. Sergei heard the names of several senior cadets; then his name was called, and that of a few of the more hardworking boys his age, including Andrei. Sergei stepped forward with the others. Why are we being singled out? he wondered. When his uncle called out the last name on his list —"Cadet Dmitri Zakolyev"—no matter what the purpose, Sergei knew he wanted no part of it.

His uncle announced, "You twelve have been selected for special training and duty as elite soldiers and possible future bodyguards to the tsar. You are to be congratulated." These were the closest thing to encouraging words any of them had heard from the chief instructor.

Out of the corner of his eyes, Sergei could see proud smiles forming on some of his companions' faces. He was glad to see Andrei smile as well. But Sergei had nothing to grin about; it only meant that his life had changed once again at the whim of others. And more likely than not, he would see more of Zakolyev.

Chief Instructor Ivanov dismissed all but the chosen twelve. When the others had left, the chief instructor began to pace slowly and speak in measured tones, as if he were imparting secrets for their ears only. "Thus far," his uncle said, "you have learned what all young soldiers must learn—the fundamentals of wrestling and boxing, horsemanship, water skills, basic weapons, military strategy, and survival in the wild. The other boys will continue to refine these skills. But elite bodyguards need elite training."

He paced in silence before continuing. "Long before the birth of Christ our savior, Greek merchants traded with tribes on the shores of the Black Sea. As centuries passed, Sarmations were overrun by Germanic Goths, who fell to Asiatic Huns, later defeated by Turkic Avars. Then, twelve hundred years ago, heirs of the Vikings gave way to eastern Slavic peoples who settled in a land now called Ukraine, home of the Kievan Rus. These various peoples, who spoke a hundred and forty different languages and dialects, who had risen up through a history of sacrament and sacrifice, of struggle and blood and toil, formed the largest country in the world, known by its peoples as *Rodina* . . . Mother Russia."

Sergei remembered this speech vividly—not only because his uncle spoke so rarely, but also because he saw the chief instructor pause and wipe away the tears that came to his eyes at the mention of *Rodina*, this land he so loved. He quickly recovered, however, and said, "Throughout her history, Russia's people—not only Cossacks and soldiers, but farmers, merchants, and others called to duty—have been forced to repel invaders from the north, south, east, and west. We have fought on sandy plains, frozen rivers, muddy bogs, and thick forests. Our varied enemies forced us to develop a versatile system of combat. As elite soldiers, you will be shown an approach to fighting more natural and deadly than what you have studied up to this point.

"Alexei!" he called, and the great Cossack teacher stepped forward as Chief Instructor Ivanov turned back to the twelve boys. "We need a volunteer," he said. Immediately, Anatoly Kamarov, one of the senior cadets and the wrestling champion, stepped forward. Gesturing in a good-natured way, his uncle said, "Please attack Instructor Orlov." Cadet Kamarov crouched and circled Alexei, who only smiled and stood relaxed, not even bothering to face the cadet squarely. When the cadet thought he saw an opening, he lunged in and threw a front kick.

Alexei hardly moved, but the cadet was suddenly off balance and falling awkwardly to the ground with a thump. It was as if the cadets were watching a magician rather than a fighter. This performance was repeated several times before his uncle thanked Kamarov for his courage and Alexei for his illuminating demonstration. "The tsar has many loyal soldiers," he continued, "but those who protect him and serve on special missions must be the best fighters anywhere, able to overcome even the best soldiers. So at this point your training will intensify to the breaking point, and sometimes beyond. Anyone who wishes to step down may do so with honor. To remain in the regular barracks, step forward. You will have our permission to contribute to the regular ranks of brave men."

The chief instructor waited. No one stepped forward. "There is no shame in the regular ranks," he repeated. "It takes courage to know your limits." Sergei stood frozen like the others.

"So be it," said his uncle. He nodded in approval, then announced, "The regular cadets will continue to train with Instructor Brodinov. The elite group will train under the supervision of Alexei Orlov."

THE NEXT DAY their elite training began. As soon as the cadets had assembled in two straight rows, Alexei told them the Cossack code: "The life of your friend is more important than your own. You may die yourself, but always save another. It is your duty to risk your life to save a comrade, a friend, or a loved one."

He paused as they absorbed this—Sergei felt lifted to a place above his usual world—and then the atmosphere changed abruptly with

Instructor Orlov's next words: "Each of you must now pass an initiation. It may seem cruel, but it serves many useful purposes. You are about to suffer pain and injury. Each of you must choose whether to receive a deep knife cut or have your arm struck by a hammer with a force that may break it.

"You will be the first, Cadet Ivanov," he announced. "The others will follow." Hoping this was another kind of test—that he might escape this situation—Sergei asked, "Instructor Orlov, you've taught us to look for creative solutions to any problem. Are those my only two choices, or might I negotiate another option?"

Alexei the Cossack smiled gently. "A good question," he said. "I might have asked the same thing myself years ago. But in this case, you only have these two choices; both involve pain and injury. Which shall it be?"

Sergei thought about it for a moment and chose the blade. Immediately, but without pleasure or rancor, Alexei sliced open his arm. For an instant Sergei felt no pain—only the shock of watching the skin of his arm part and open to the thin white layer of fat. Then the wound filled with blood, as the deep, throbbing pain began, and the blood ran down his arm and dripped to the earth.

"You two," said Alexei, pointing to two of the older cadets. "I want you to stitch up Cadet Ivanov's wound and apply a field bandage. And do a clean job—you will soon have your turn." He gestured toward a table with various bandages and splints and supplies. Galina, the old nurse, stood by to supervise. She told Sergei to drink two small glasses of vodka to help dull the pain. He did so—and wanted a third but could not bring himself to ask.

After the nurse sprinkled a powder into the gaping wound, she held his arm and watched an older cadet clumsily stitch his skin with a curved needle. Sergei turned away, clenched his teeth, and tried not to gasp or cry out each time the needle pierced his skin.

The throbbing pain had increased and the needle punctures made him wince, but he held on as Cadet Yegevny pulled the thin twine taut, drawing the edges of the wound tightly together. After what seemed an interminable few minutes, Sergei's wound was covered with a bandage, and the pain faded to a deep ache.

"You're a brave boy," she said. He hardly heard her, distracted as he was by the continuing tests a few meters away. At least the worst was over for him.

Now every cadet stared in morbid fascination as the next boy, after seeing Sergei bleed, chose the hammer. He yelped then whimpered but did not faint when Alexei hit him with the hammer. They all heard a crack but couldn't tell whether the bone had broken. The cadet came over, breathing rapidly, in great pain. Two other cadets applied a splint while the rest of the cadets observed.

They continued in this manner, with some choosing the knife and others the hammer. Andrei hated blood and chose the hammer. He cried out but then gathered himself together once it was over. Zakolyev chose the knife and didn't even flinch. In fact, he smiled throughout.

One of the cadets had declined to take the test. Alexei told him, with formal courtesy, to return to Brodinov's group. Soon a line of eleven, pain-racked cadets remained, standing at the medical station. Most drank the vodka and, like Sergei, wanted more—anything to help dull the pain.

At the end Alexei called them all together and said with great formality and respect, as if each had leaped across a chasm that separated them from the other cadets: "Sometimes words alone cannot teach. Each of you has received an injury, as you might in battle. The wounds will heal. Meanwhile, pay attention to the wounds. Learn from your body. Will yourself to heal quickly. Continue to function as well as you can despite your injuries, as you would have to do in battle.

"This was not a lighthearted exercise," he continued, "and I do not enjoy inflicting damage. But it was necessary. Now you've experienced a small degree of the pain that you, as soldiers, will inflict on the enemy when necessary. This is the ugly reality of battle. Never forget that it is better to wound ten men than kill one. The wounded require more care and slow the enemy, and I tell you this for higher reasons as well.

"Wounds may heal, and a soldier can return to his family, but death is permanent, and an adversary's soul rests heavily upon your con-science. So kill an enemy only when there is no other way. Now return to your rooms until your next class and think about what I've told you." After that the cadets were issued pants with a red stripe down the sides, just like the officers.

As the eleven cadets walked back toward their respective barracks, Sergei noticed a certain camaraderie among them, forged by the com-mon bond of having endured this painful lesson together.

One of the older cadets had taken a bottle of vodka from one of the instructors—a daring act. Now, as a show of trust and bravado, he shared it with the others. They passed around the bottle, and Sergei got drunk, and funny, and sick, like some of the others. Later he found him-self craving more, but there was no more to be had. Then Sergei remem-bered that his father had drunk himself to death, and he wondered if there was something in his blood too.

His wound healed within a few weeks, but he would have a scar for the rest of his life that would remind him of this day he became one of the elite.

Soon after, those in the elite group had to go without food for seven days, with no water either for the last two days. The purpose of this, according to Instructor Orlov, was multifaceted. "First," he said, "you will overcome the instinctive fear of not eating, so that if you are cut off during a battle, it will be of little consequence to you whether or not you have food. Second, occasional fasting—going without food, and for shorter periods without water—purifies the body and strengthens the constitution."

"Third," whispered one of the cadets, "not feeding us saves the school money." Several of the other cadets stifled laughs. But no one was laughing by the end of the first day. They all felt ravenous, and not in the best of spirits the second day either. That day another cadet dropped out, so ten cadets remained. Meanwhile, they were assigned extra work and training during this period, so their lack of food was no excuse to rest or slack off.

During those seven days Sergei and the others experienced periods of lassitude alternating with a sense of lightness and higher energy. The last two days without water were the hardest. They ended the fast with purifying rituals involving a kind of second baptism. "You become elite soldiers through elite training," Alexei reminded them. "And one day you'll make the shift from soldiers to warriors, like the three hundred Spartan Skiritai of ancient times who held the pass at Thermopylae for three days against three hundred thousand invading Persian soldiers."

"What happened to them?" asked one of the other boys.

"They all died," he said.

. 9 .

SERGEI FELT EVERYTHING quickening—his thoughts, desires, his mind and body. He was moved into the men's quarters. Zakolyev was now nineteen, and a senior cadet. He all but ignored the younger students, which was fine with Sergei. Meanwhile, the training continued in firearms, camouflage, field medicine, and winter survival training.

Hand-to-hand combat training with Alexei continued as always. A few weeks later the elite instructor announced, "Today we will practice choke holds and escapes. When your partner tries to strangle you, do what you can to escape without inflicting serious damage to your fellow cadet. Explore possibilities. Find out what works, and what doesn't. When you are choking your practice partner, he will not be able to speak, so he will slap his hand on his leg to signal you to release the choke immediately. Otherwise, he will pass out . . . but if you hold it too long, you might just kill him. So do not hold a choke after your partner has slapped!"

Near the end of the day, Zakolyev chose Sergei as his partner. The moment Zakolyev's arms wrapped around his neck, Sergei couldn't breathe, couldn't speak. As the choke tightened, Sergei's head felt like it was exploding. Spots floated before his eyes. He slapped his thigh once, then again, as he was sucked down into a maelstrom of panic, an encroaching darkness.

Finally Zakolyev released the hold. Sergei collapsed to a sitting position, semiconscious. He looked up to see Zakolyev staring at him. "What's that around your neck?" asked the senior cadet.

"N-nothing," Sergei answered, furious at himself for having forgotten to remove the locket before combat training. A moment's carelessness, and there would be hell to pay.

"Let me see it," Zakolyev said casually.

Sergei almost found his hand reaching for the clasp. Zakolyev had a way of asking for things that made it seem unreasonable, even silly, to deny him. But Sergei came to his senses. "No," he said. "It's personal." Zakolyev shrugged and walked away to work with another cadet.

With a few final comments, Alexei ended the class and departed. All of the cadets, except for a few still practicing, filed out of the practice room. Anxious to find a few moments alone, Sergei was turning to follow his departing classmates when he heard Zakolyev's chilling voice close behind him. "Now you can show me your little treasure."

Sergei knew instantly that Zakolyev didn't merely want to just see it; he wanted to possess it. "It's private," he said. "I want to keep it that way."

As Sergei turned to leave, Zakolyev's right arm again wrapped around his neck; the other locked behind his head. Sergei willed himself to fight the panic, to breathe—but there was no breath, only an agony of pressure bursting in his head. Through the gathering darkness he caught a final glimpse of a few of the straggling cadets, who glanced in their direction then turned and walked away, thinking that they were still practicing. But this was no practice. Zakolyev could kill him.

As the light faded from his mind, Sergei experienced a flickering premonition—an image of his lifeless body sprawled on the floor. Then blackness.

W HEN HE CAME TO, Zakolyev was gone. So was the locket.

From that moment on, Sergei knew what it meant to be obsessed. He had but one goal: to reclaim what Zakolyev had taken from him. Zakolyev could not be allowed to steal Sergei's parents, his lineage.

Sergei searched for him everywhere—in the senior barracks, on the grounds, and behind the classrooms where Zakolyev would smoke and drink—but could not find him.

The two were not scheduled to practice together for a few days. Meanwhile, Sergei's concentration suffered. Everyday life faded into a fog except for this one thing: to take back what was his.

Three days later he caught up with Zakolyev and confronted him. Despite the senior's greater size, strength, and capacity for brutality, anger burned in Sergei's belly. "Give it back!"

A few other cadets who had arrived early to practice circled around, drawn in by the unfolding drama.

"Give back what?" Zakolyev said calmly, apparently amused.

"You know what."

Zakolyev smiled that hateful smile. "Oh, you mean that little girl's trinket you had around your neck?"

"Give it to me . . . now!" he said, his voice a growl.

"I told you . . . I don't have it."

"You're a liar!"

Zakolyev studied him as he might observe a bug, intrigued that Sergei the Good, nearly four years his junior, was crazy enough to make such demands. Still, the boy would have to be punished—

Sergei's kick caught Zakolyev unaware, snapping his knee to the side. It might have hurt Zakolyev badly, but, anticipating the attack, Zakolyev had let his knee give way and twisted his body to trap Sergei's leg, forcing him to the ground. Now the muscular senior sat on Sergei's chest and methodically pounded on his face.

Sergei's hands came up protectively as the blows rained down, and he managed to strike back once. Using his fingers as a spear, Sergei thrust them into Zakolyev's eye, infuriating him.

Just then Brodinov showed up and broke them apart. But not before Zakolyev had broken Sergei's nose, loosened some teeth, and cracked his cheekbone, sending him to the infirmary.

The next day Sergei peered through eyes swollen almost shut to see Andrei kneeling by his bedside. In an excited whisper, Andrei said, "No one dared say anything about Zakolyev's black eye or his limp after the fight. It was a brave but foolish thing to do, Sergei. I heard Zakolyev tell some older cadets that if you ever troubled him again, you might have a serious accident.

"And that's not all: There's a rumor that one of the other cadets saw Zakolyev choke you after class and take the locket. Somehow the instructors heard about it," Andrei said, smiling. "Brodinov demanded that Zakolyev return the locket, but Zakolyev insisted he didn't have it. They know he's probably lying, but no one can prove anything, and no cadet would step forward to accuse him. Zakolyev has to sit in detention all his spare time as long as you're in the infirmary. He's been punished like any other cadet; now it's out in the open. And some say that he's going to be expelled."

Then Andrei's elation vanished. "I think you've made a bad enemy, Sergei. But I'll watch your back."

"And I'll watch yours," Sergei managed to reply. He felt no elation at Zakolyev's punishment or satisfaction in Zakolyev's shame. It would only make things worse. Sergei sighed. Zakolyev would never return the locket now.

SERGEI SLEPT and daydreamed through the rest of the day. But that night he awakened from a deep sleep to see Alexei the Cossack standing nearby in the shadows. For a moment Sergei thought he was seeing an apparition. His elite instructor was dressed, not in the school uniform, but rather in his Cossack garb—the way he had first appeared years before, when he rode into the compound to bring news of the death of Tsar Aleksandr II.

Sergei blinked, still unsure whether he was asleep or awake. Alexei's appearance so surprised him that he was too disoriented to ask about the clothing. Then Alexei spoke, and Sergei knew he was awake. "Practice holding your breath, so you will not be concerned about lack of air. And if you are ever choked again," he whispered, "relax completely—it will give you twenty or thirty seconds. It's the pressure of the depleted blood that causes blackout. Life can be hard, Sergei, so you must be harder. But sometimes softness overcomes rigidity, the way a river can cut through stone. It only takes time. All you need is little more time."

Then he added, "You did a brave thing, confronting Dmitri Zakolyev. Your father was also a brave man . . . a good man, as you will become. Yet I don't think you will become a soldier."

Hearing his last words, Sergei felt a pang of deep disappointment, but it vanished as he saw Alexei smile at him as one might smile at a friend. And before Sergei could say anything, or thank him for his guidance, Alexei Orlov stepped back into the shadows and was gone.

THE NEXT MORNING Andrei returned to Sergei's bedside with the news: "Alexei the Cossack is gone! He had to report back immediately to the palace, and he left before dawn. Instructor Brodinov will continue our training. Chief Instructor Ivanov conveyed to us Instructor Orlov's farewell and regards. Then he said—let me see if I can remember—he said, 'This is a soldier's life. People appear and disappear. Comrades may fall in battle right next to us, but we must continue without missing a step.' After that he dismissed us until the afternoon—that's how I could come to see you." Andrei paused. "You know, Sergei, I think the chief instructor will miss Instructor Orlov."

Not as much as I will, thought Sergei.

. 10 .

It was bitter cold that January day in 1888 when Sergei was released from the infirmary and Zakolyev's detention ended. Still intent on recovering his locket, Sergei had considered his options. He realized the futility of another confrontation; if he again challenged Zakolyev, he would either get beaten or he might get lucky and hurt the older cadet. In either case, Zakolyev would never tell him where he had hidden the locket.

The wisest thing he could do was to wait. But he would not forget. Sergei knew he had made a formidable enemy. But then, so had Zakolyev.

Another change had occurred since that night Alexei had visited. A part of Sergei's spirit had departed with him. He felt a growing sense of detachment, as if he were an observer rather than a participant in the life around him.

In the coming months Sergei spent more time alone, withdrawing to the quiet of his uncle's library in every spare moment. He would turn the globe on his desk, gazing in a reverie, letting his fingers drift across Russia to the north, south, east, and west.

Soon after the spring thaw Sergei was sitting in the library reading the dialogues of Socrates when the strangest thing happened: The face of a man appeared in his mind—a rough-hewn face with a nose that looked as if it had been broken, chin and cheeks covered with a beard, and coarse, curly hair. Yet the face had an air of strength and integrity. The man's eyes somehow reminded Sergei of thunder and lightning.

Then Sergei heard the words, "I am a citizen not of Athens or of

Greece but of the world . . ." It suddenly dawned on Sergei that this vision was Socrates himself. The apparition spoke only a few more words before it vanished: "A new world . . . to the west . . . "

Then all was quiet. Sergei was back in his uncle's library at the Nevskiy Military School. He had no idea what had happened or why. He did not believe that the spirit of the Greek philosopher had actually visited or spoken to him. After all, the words were not in Greek but in his own language. Yet he remembered those words, and he wondered: What new world? Where to the west? Then Sergei recalled something that Andrei had told him soon after they had met: "Sergei, I wasn't born in Russia, but in a land to the west, across the sea . . . in a place called America."

He looked once more in the book, hoping for another vision—but all he held in his hands was an ordinary book. Or perhaps not so ordinary, for it was about his namesake. He replaced it on the shelf and was turning to go when something caught his eye—some sort of official letter lying askew on his uncle's desk. Curious, Sergei stole a glance:

NOTICE:

To Vladimir Borisovich Ivanov,
Chief Instructor, Nevskiy Military School:

In one week's time, a garrison of soldiers will pass your school on the way south to the Pale of Settlement for Jewish duty. All seniors and elite cadets will join this garrison for three months. This will provide field experience, so prepare your cadets. Remind them they will act in the name of the Tsar, the Holy Church, and Mother Russia.

Vasiliy Aleksandrovich Artemov
Field Commander

Jewish duty. The word chilled Sergei. As one of the elite group, he would be expected to harass innocent people like his grandfather—like the Abramovich family. An unwelcome image appeared of the charred remains of their cabin.

He would not do it. He could not. Not for his uncle or for the tsar himself.

Sergei had come to a crossroads, and his mind cleared. The time had come for him to disappear in the night like Alexei the Cossack. He would go to St. Petersburg to find the treasure his grandfather had left for him. Then he would go to America, where they did not send soldiers to kill people because they were Jews.

As this decision penetrated him, he reflected on the consequences: They would conduct a search. He would have to travel fast and far. And he could never return. Then he reflected upon his father's decision to send him here and his uncle's willingness to take him in and provide a home and a way of life. He would be turning his back on them. It was a life he could no longer abide. He was not only his father's son, after all; he was also his mother's. It was her blood calling to him now.

Sergei felt as if he were about to leap from that tree onto that wild buck once again. He couldn't know what the future might hold, but it would be a future he would choose.

He must depart. Soon—that very night. But not without leaving a letter for his uncle. He owed him that. He snatched up a blank piece of paper from his uncle's desk and a fountain pen and wrote:

Dear Chief Instructor Ivanov,

I offer my apologies for leaving in this way to find another life. I have taken a map, a compass, and some supplies I will need for my journeys.

I can only guess what hardships I would have faced if you had not accepted me as a student. Under your care I became stronger, and I learned much. Someday I hope to make you proud, and to honor my father's memory. I wish that I could have known you better. Even though you are stern, I have always seen in you a good and kind heart.

I will remember you always and hold a place for you in my prayers.

Sergei signed the letter, folded it, and put it in his pocket. Before he left the office, he searched hurriedly and found what he was looking for—a map that might prove useful—and from a file drawer that held the cadets' legal records, Sergei quickly grabbed the few documents in his folder.

THAT NIGHT Sergei slipped into bed with his clothes still on. His knapsack was packed with whatever essentials he could gather, including the documents, which he had wrapped in oilcloth for protection. He packed dried food he had pilfered from the kitchen, along with a survival knife and the small and versatile military shovel, as well as fishing line, map, and compass.

During the evening meal Sergei gazed at Andrei and his fellow cadets and said a silent farewell. Before bed he walked to the barrack window and gazed out across the central compound, where he saw his boyhood self, clinging fiercely to the mane of that horse on his first ride.

After curfew he feigned sleep until he heard the familiar sounds of slumber all around him. Then Sergei slipped the letter to his uncle under his pillow. Someone would find it soon enough, and his uncle would send the best cadet trackers, maybe even one of the instructors. But they would not find him; they had trained him far too well.

Once again he reviewed his escape plans. First he had to slip past the sentries—he knew their routines well enough. And during their last cold-water immersion, he had seen a log floating in the shallows.

SERGEI AWOKE with a start. What time is it? he thought. Have I overslept? He slipped out of bed and peered through the narrow window to see the moon still rising, nearly overhead. The time had come. He lifted his pack and padded soundlessly out of the room, barefoot, carrying his boots, moving like a shadow along the wall to avoid any creaking sounds on the stairwell, then down a long corridor, where he thought he saw a crack of light under the door of his uncle's office. He passed through the old oak doorway and down the stone steps. In the tunnel he put on his boots, laced them, and hurried down its length—several hundred meters, slanting downward under the main building and grounds as it followed the curve of the gentle slope.

His heart pounding with excitement, Sergei finally stepped out into the moonlight on the shores of the lake. So far, so good. The lapping sounds at the water's edge seemed unnaturally loud with all else quiet, except for a distant loon singing across the water. As he stood there, a young man alone in the night, the bird's melancholy song pulled at his chest.

Taking a deep breath, Sergei walked toward the place where he had spied the floating log. It wasn't there. He couldn't find it anywhere nearby. The wind was blowing north, toward his left, so he moved quietly in that direction, peering through reeds and waist-high grasses and the gathering mist, searching for the log. His boots made slushy sounds where the sand gave way to mud.

Thankful for the dim light of a waning moon, he knelt down among the reeds and grasses in case the log had washed to ground and lay hidden. Finally he spotted the old timber; he hoped it wasn't too waterlogged to float.

Just then Sergei heard the sound of someone walking nearby. Still squatting, hidden among the grasses, he froze and listened. Instantly, the mystical night turned dank and dour as a familiar figure appeared. A bitter bile rose in his throat. Had he followed him ? Or was this just some bizarre coincidence?

ZAKOLYEV ALSO CARRIED A PACK. Could he be running away on the same night that Sergei had chosen? Zakolyev stared straight ahead, peering through the mist, as if searching for something. Or someone. Sergei had only a moment to decide whether to remain hidden and let him pass by or to stand and confront him. The first choice seemed far wiser; if he let him pass, he could avoid any confrontation. But then he would never learn Zakolyev's purpose. As Sergei weighed caution against curiosity, Zakolyev drew close. A few more meters and he would pass by . . .

Then Sergei saw the faint glint of moonlight upon a chain around Zakolyev's neck, and his decision was made. He stood and whispered, "Dmitri Zakolyev!" just loud enough for the older youth to hear.

Zakolyev jerked his head around but didn't seem entirely surprised to see Sergei. "So," he said. "Out enjoying the evening air?"

Sergei said nothing but only stared into those ghostly eyes as he closed the space between them, focused on only one thing. "Give me the locket, then go where you wish—to hell for all I care." He had spoken louder than he had intended, but his voice would not carry through the mist.

Zakolyev smiled again and shook his head, as if disappointed. "Good Sergei . . . wasn't one beating enough for you?"

A fight might attract the sentries' attention, and they both knew this. So they had reached a stalemate. Several thoughts flashed through Sergei's mind: What would the others think about two cadets disappearing on the same night? Would his uncle assume they had gone together? Not likely. They might conjecture any number of things . . .

Then he remembered the letter to his uncle. Yes—he at least would know—

As if reading his thoughts, Zakolyev pulled a sheet of folded paper from his shirt. "Such a nice farewell letter to your uncle Ivanov," he said smugly, flashing that hateful smile again. The blood pulsed in Sergei's temples as Zakolyev tore the letter to bits and threw it into the water lapping at their boots.

Zakolyev grew cocky, feeding on Sergei's expression of dismay. "You should know I have spies everywhere, Ivanov. How could you be so stupid?"

The locket, he told himself. Concentrate on that—the rest can't be helped. "Give me the locket, and I won't yell out an alarm," Sergei said.

"Go ahead," Zakolyev replied.

Sergei's gaze pierced the older youth. "Are you so sure I won't?"

Zakolyev hesitated only slightly. "Sure enough."

Sergei's mind searched for a solution. "Keep the locket, then. I only want the photograph of my parents, Dmitri. Give me back this one thing, and we will not part enemies."

In the silence that followed, Sergei knew his answer.

What happened next surprised even him. Without warning—as if his body acted on its own accord—Sergei lashed out with a front kick to Zakolyev's midsection. The kick caught the older boy square in the solar plexus; Sergei heard the air whooshing out of him as he doubled over. Sergei followed up with a snapping side kick toward his head, but Zakolyev managed to redirect the kick with one hand, and Sergei found himself spinning off balance. Then Zakolyev had his arms around Sergei's neck, and his every instinct told him that Zakolyev intended to kill him this time.

A moment of panic washed over him, but this time it was followed by a cold clarity. His first impulse was to lock Zakolyev's arm with his chin, bend quickly forward at the waist, and throw his adversary—but the placement of Zakolyev's weight told Sergei that his opponent was prepared for that. So he did the unexpected, turning his head toward the crook of Zakolyev's elbow. It was a mistake, and Zakolyev knew it and took full advantage. But he didn't know that having his air cut off did not concern Sergei, who could now hold his breath for more than two minutes. As long as he relaxed, he might buy some time . . .

Sergei felt the familiar pressure building and saw the first of the black spots. He feigned a frantic struggle for a few moments, waiting as long as he could, then he went completely limp, as if unconscious. Now Zakolyev either had to release him or hold his dead weight up off the ground. He did the latter, squeezing even harder—he fully intended to take Sergei's life. So Sergei played dead, buying himself a few more precious seconds. More black spots appeared. If Zakolyev did not release him soon—

All at once Zakolyev let go. Sergei felt his back thud to the muddy ground. Lying still, his eyes closed, he sensed his opponent standing directly over him, one boot on either side of his head. He stayed dead for one second . . . two . . . three. And with explosive speed, Sergei simultaneously grabbed the backs of his ankles, locking Zakolyev's feet to the sides of his head. At the same time, Sergei lifted both his knees to his chest, then thrust one leg up and back, directly into Zakolyev's groin. It was a solid shot. Zakolyev made a noise between a grunt and a deep groan and went down, his whole body contracted, unable to move.

As Zakolyev vomited onto the muddy ground, Sergei rolled to his feet. Grasping a short, clublike log heavy with moisture, he swung with a burst of strength and hit Zakolyev on the back of his head, knocking him unconscious. He lifted the log again, high over his head, ready to smash the bastard's skull, when something stopped him.

At war with his own impulses, Sergei willed himself to drop the log. And in a fit of unspent rage, he grabbed Zakolyev's knapsack and flung it as far as he could into the lake. The muffled splash made no more sound than a duck landing on the quiet waters.

Zakolyev might awaken soon, Sergei thought. So he knelt down quickly and removed the locket from his neck. He blew on it instinctively, as if to clear any lingering traces of Zakolyev from it. Sergei fastened the clasp around his neck and picked up his knapsack. About to set out, he glanced back one last time at Zakolyev, lying askew and still. Sergei couldn't see any rise or fall of his chest. That's when the thought occurred: I might have killed him.

In the heat of the moment, Sergei had hit him hard—maybe too hard. Even in the pale, fog-shrouded moonlight, he could make out the dark wetness on Zakolyev's scalp, and his eyes, half open and staring, sightless. His face looked gray. Sergei put his hand to the older cadet's throat. No pulse.

With a shudder, Sergei backed away from the body. Away, away, away, said his mind, no longer thinking clearly. Sergei slipped back down among the reeds. And with a strength born of desperation, he managed to pull the large timber out into the water. It floated. With his pack fastened tightly to his back, he lay on his belly, his legs straddling the log, and pushed away. The numbing chill on his arms and legs cleansed his mind of thought for the moment. Balancing precariously, he heard only a gentle slosh of water as he began to paddle away from the shore. A moment's distraction would roll him, rucksack and all, into the lake.

He paddled out into a thick cover of fog. No sentry could spot him now; neither would he be able to see the shore. If he paddled too far out, he could lose himself forever in the expanse of icy water, never to return. As it was, Sergei couldn't stay out too long or he would freeze. Even this brief exposure left him shivering uncontrollably—from the cold, and from the shock of what he had done.

I've killed Zakolyev. I'm no longer a runaway but a fugitive, he thought. Never mind that it was an accident. It will not look that way. Everyone knew I held a grudge against Zakolyev over my locket.

He thought of going back, of explaining—explaining what? That he had been running away and so had Zakolyev? The letter was gone. There was no evidence, no excuse that would satisfy his uncle. What was done was done. Zakolyev was dead, and Sergei would have to live with it for the rest of his life.

. 11 .

A NEAR SPILL into the icy water pulled Sergei back to his senses. The past is behind me, he thought. Focus on this moment, then the next. He paddled away from the Nevskiy Military School, pulling through the water with all his strength to fight off the chill now creeping into his bones. His chest heaved with the effort, as the full import of his circumstances bore down on him.

Another few minutes, then to the shore . . .

Sergei's destination was the mouth of a stream that emptied into Lake Krugloye about six hundred meters east of the school. Estimating that he had traveled nearly that distance, he paddled into the shallow water, abandoned the log, and walked through waist-deep water, mud, and reeds up onto the shore.

Still shivering, his teeth chattering, he took careful, measured strides over the gravel-covered ground. After he had hiked briskly for another hundred meters east along the shore, his blood began to warm. But he worried that he had passed the stream. He stopped and listened intently—ah, there it was, a rushing sound ahead. Dropping on all fours, he crawled through the thick foliage until he found it.

Sloshing up the shallow streambed, he headed south another hundred meters; then, after reaching a rocky area where his tracks disappeared, Sergei walked backward in the same tracks he had left and returned to the stream. Leaving this false trail behind him, just in case, he continued upstream before finally turning east. Given Sergei's means of escape, his pursuers could only guess at his direction.

If he were only a runaway, they would soon give up the search. But now everything had changed: Zakolyev's death meant he could no longer go north to St. Petersburg; they would notify authorities there. His search for his grandfather's treasure would have to wait; so would the voyage to America. One year, maybe two, or longer . . .

Now he must flee to the mountains, far to the south, and put the ghost of Dmitri Zakolyev behind him.

Sergei circled back within a thousand meters of the school before he turned east again, then south through the forest, into the wooded hills. He heard a distant wolf howl as he pushed onward, racing the dawn, breaking into a run where moonlight and terrain allowed.

He had once heard of men from Mongolia or Tibet who could run hundreds of kilometers, over rough terrain in the dark of night, while gazing straight up into the sky. Sergei wasn't ready to attempt such a feat. He ran, then walked, then ran again, his eyes not fixed upon the sky but peering ahead through the misty darkness.

He hoped that the dawn would bring a new light to his soul because he had lost any sense of his path into the future. How had all this happened? he asked himself. Seven hours before, all was well; life was routine. He was an elite cadet, respected well enough by his instructors and peers. He had a friend in Andrei, a comfortable bed . . .

Had he made the right decision or the worst mistake of his life?

No, he had done what he had to do. The alternative—"Jewish duty"—was unthinkable. Sergei did not regret his decision to leave, but he had not intended to leave a corpse behind.

The manhunt would begin in a matter of hours. His only safety lay in the faraway mountains of Georgia, twelve hundred kilometers to the south. There he would find sanctuary.

Thus Sergei's journey began. It took him down the Kiyazma River toward the great Volga, that spring of 1888.

In those first days of flight he glanced back repeatedly, haunted by the sense he was being pursued by soldiers or by ghosts. Each night he fought with shadows in his dreams; each morning he immersed himself in the river, washing away the last traces of the night. He made camp in the late afternoons, finding or building shelter, then hunting, fishing, or foraging as need arose.

Several weeks later, when Sergei reached the great Volga, he found an abandoned skiff in some bushes on the shore. Its flat bottom had several small leaks, which he was able to fill with tree sap. Soon he was rowing his way downriver. As time passed, he measured his days by the rhythms of the circling oars. His life merged with the river and with a sense of the eternal.

On warmer days Sergei dove into the clear, deep water to bathe, with one end of a length of twine tied to his ankle and the other end to the skiff. After the river had washed the sweat from his body and soothed the heat from his blistered palms, Sergei climbed back in and lay in the sun as the rowboat drifted down the widening waterway past ever-changing landscapes.

The days lengthened, and his shoulders turned to copper. Some days he ate little or nothing; on others he feasted. From bamboo cane growing along the river he made a primitive spear, then a bow, fashioned from the flexible limbs of a yew tree, and arrows made of thick reeds flocked with quail feathers, their tips weighted with stones sharp enough to pierce tough hides, and he bow-hunted hares too far off to spear.

In this manner, through the summer and early autumn, Sergei rowed a thousand kilometers downriver until he reached the Caspian Sea, continuing south along the coastline toward the thriving port of Baku. But well before he reached Baku—about a hundred kilometers south of Makhachkala—he reluctantly abandoned his little skiff and set out on foot, east toward the Caucasus Mountains of Georgia.

Now, as he hiked south and west toward the Caucasus range, Sergei occasionally glimpsed a *stanitsa,* a fort where Cossacks were stationed. He doubted that news of Zakolyev's death had traveled this far, but he could not forget that he was still a fugitive, and he resolved to avoid contact with military men. He would bide his time in the high country for one or two full cycles of the seasons, maybe longer, until he could safely return to St. Petersburg, where he might find the treasure his grand-father had buried, then sail across the sea.

Sergei broke his resolve only once, in the first chill days of autumn, as he made his way into the foothills. Out of curiosity, and a loneliness that came with the season, he risked passing through a farming village of free Cossacks. He gazed wistfully at wisps of smoke rising from warm hearths, then his eyes drifted to a young woman returning to her cabin. She glanced toward him and nodded and smiled, stirring in him a long-ing to belong, to become part of a community, a home. He had never been with a woman, and he yearned for this too. He wondered again whether he might ever have a family of his own.

Sometimes he fell into reveries of the past or thought about his grandfather's treasure and what the future might hold. But all that seemed pointless to dwell upon, so he returned to the present.

SERGEI'S ASCENT into the mountains took several weeks as he searched for a more permanent camp that offered protection from the elements. It would be a cold winter in the high country, but the moun-tains would offer the safety and solitude he needed. In late autumn he found a cave not far from a waterfall, with salmon and trout, and a beaver dam not far away. He built a sturdy lean-to against the face of the cave, with an opening above his fire pit, packing it with a thick clay that would dry solid enough to keep out the coming winds and snow. And before the streams froze and game grew scarce, he hunted and then dried as much food as possible. That, with some ice fishing and his remaining supplies, would have to last him until the spring thaw.

On the cold, clear days of winter he explored the local surroundings, hunting or trapping what he could, but mostly he hibernated like the bear, and he slept, and he dreamed. Huddled in his burrow when the winds howled outside, he stitched together a fur coat and gloves lined with tufts of fur to keep his hands from freezing. He lined his worn boots as well.

Some mornings he would rub snow on his naked body and then exercise to maintain some vigor before slipping back into warm clothing and burrowing back into his cave. It was a long winter of solitude.

The spring of 1889 was worth the wait. He caught sight of a bear and her cubs in a meadow far below. Later, near dusk, he spotted a shy leopard passing above him like a shadow along a snow-covered ridge. He now felt a part of it all, no longer a visitor here. He rarely spoke aloud, and then only to reassure himself that he still had a voice. But sometimes he practiced birdcalls and howled with the wolves at night.

In this manner, the seasons passed into a second year of his mountain hermitage. And one morning it struck Sergei how everything had changed—how he no longer belonged to a school, a society, a religion, a group, or even a culture. He was a wolf and a woodsman. When he stopped to drink in a highland pond and glimpsed a rippled reflection of his bearded, sun-burnished face, he hardly recognized himself. Even his eyes had changed, somehow deeper. Autumn had come again. He was eighteen years old, but the face he saw was that of a man—a mountain wanderer. Once a visitor to the wilderness, he had become a part of it.

In THE SPRING OF 1891—nearly three years after he first took flight—Sergei was squinting directly into the rising sun as he threaded his way through a narrow canyon whose vertical walls stood about four meters apart, forming an alleyway. He stepped carefully, avoiding stones left slippery from a recent rain, his senses sharpened by necessity—but not sharp enough.

As he stepped around a huge boulder in his path, Sergei nearly found himself facing the largest bear he had ever seen. Its back was turned to him, but only for a moment. As the bear turned, he backed away as quickly as he could while the creature snuffed the air and decided what to do about him. Fresh from her winter lair, well rested and full of terrible hunger, the bear was far more pleased than Sergei by this chance encounter. It saw him not as a man, but as a meal.

Sergei did not in fact know whether he was about to be killed by a she-bear or a he-bear. But as the bear rose on two legs and towered above him, blocking the sun, both their instincts took over, and several things happened at once: The bear dropped to all fours and thundered toward Sergei. He pulled off his rucksack, threw it between him and the furry giant, and scrambled up the nearest rock face like a frenzied spider. He had never known that he could climb so fast—that *anyone* could climb so fast.

Throwing that rucksack gave him precious seconds, and his rapid climb had saved his life, at least for the moment. Just out of the bear's reach, he hugged the sheer wall. Bears were good at climbing trees but not rock walls, he hoped.

The bear stood and reached as far as it could, swiping razor claws within centimeters of his quaking boots while his legs shook so badly he could barely retain his footing.

The frustrated bear paced and growled, then tore open his pack. Sniffing for food, finding none, it lumbered off, disappearing down one end of the narrow passage. Sergei climbed down a few steps, listened as the seconds passed, then leaped, landing hard and rolling to his feet. With a quick glance behind, he grabbed up his torn pack, knife, shovel, and other essentials and sprinted in the opposite direction.

If the bear returned, it would have no problem running him down. That thought provided a burst of speed that took him down the rugged course of that mountain.

By late afternoon Sergei sat beneath a rocky overhang, sorting through the remains of his torn rucksack and ripped blanket. He built a small fire on either side of him in an attempt to keep warm. And he reflected on his near-death encounter. He realized how close he had come to violent death, and the incident affirmed—in a way no words could have done—the value of his life and the opportunity it represented. And he thought, How will I spend my remaining time on this earth?

That night he fell into a troubled and restless sleep. Over and over he replayed his narrow escape from the bear, then two bears, and three, which shifted into human predators roaming the steppe, and villages burning . . .

He sat up with dark images still flashing through his mind: the charred Abramovich cabin, the cries of innocent people as mounted men rode them down with whips and sabers . . . And as a faint light illuminated the snowcapped peak of Mount Elbrus, Sergei went to the stream to clear his mind.

That very morning he reversed his course and began his long trek north, out of the mountains and up through Ukraine. It was time to return to St. Petersburg to seek a buried treasure that might take him to a new land across the sea.

Part Three

―――――

GAIN AND LOSS

From the beginning,
love has been my undoing . . .
and my redemption.

FROM SOCRATES' JOURNAL

. 12 .

AT THE SAME TIME that Sergei Ivanov set out on his long trek north, a different sort of man—riding a stolen horse and carrying a Cossack saber purchased with money he had not earned—pursued another course. With a certainty possessed only by sages or zealots, Gregor Stakkos aimed to become a leader of men. "Leaders make their own laws," he said aloud, savoring his words, rehearsing speeches waiting to be spoken. "And the weak live by rules imposed by others."

Stakkos, riding through southern Russia in the region of the Don Cossacks, viewed himself as a volcano ready to erupt, a man who would achieve his goal by any means necessary. His plan was simple: he would join, and eventually lead, a Cossack band. As a boy, he had heard of the Zaporozhian Cossacks—and the Kuban, Terek, and Don Cossacks as well—and of their clever tactics and fighting skills. He also knew that they often welcomed strangers who showed bravery in battle. He would find his place among these warriors, then rise above them.

They would call him Ataman—leader—as Cossacks called those in power. Beyond this single-minded ambition, he had no other aims but one: to rid the land of Jews. He despised them for reasons not entirely clear, even to himself.

Gregor Stakkos was not troubled by uncertainty. He feared nothing, except the screams that plagued him nearly every night. He hated falling asleep. In the waking world Gregor had no equal; against the netherworld he had no defense. Unable to turn away, he could not shut out the staccato shrieks and jagged, bloody images that appeared. His limbs were strong, but he had no power to banish that grisly scene from his ninth year of life, when he had lost both parents in a single night—murdered by a monster.

Gregor's father was a former officer in the tsar's army and a drunk for many years. He had stayed sober for nearly a year, until an accident left him lame. He had smelled of vodka ever since. The colonel, as Gregor called him, lived in the back of a small outpost store near the city of Kishinev with his wife and young Gregor. On a cold night in December, as on many other nights, Colonel Stakkos sat fuming in a drunken sulk. He sought a reason for his anger but found none, until Gregor ran inside to escape the great gusts of snow and the wind-driven door slammed shut.

Young Gregor went straight to the warmth and safety of the hearth, as always, where he would sit quietly and whittle, trying to shape another hollow reed into a flute. It was all he did at night—whittle quietly and stay out of his father's way.

The colonel, startled by the slamming door, found an object for his smoldering rage. Which meant that Gregor would either have to flee outside into the cold until the colonel passed out or take another beating.

These beatings were neither rare nor brief. While the colonel's heavy belt raised welts on Gregor's back, his mother would look away in dismay, busying herself with the cleaning, never raising a hand or saying a word in her son's defense.

The senior Stakkos stood and tottered toward Gregor, blocking the exit. "Little bast'rd," he muttered. "Come take y'r med'cine, you son of a dog . . ."

"But I'm *your* son, Father," said the boy.

"Thass wha' you think," the colonel slurred. "'Bout time you knew. Took y'in when y'r father gave y' away . . . some Jew kid . . . the mother'd run off'r died, dunno which . . . " The colonel fumbled with his belt buckle and pulled the heavy leather strap free. "Now come 'n' get yer beatin'! Didn't want no damn kid . . . wife said you'd help with the chores . . . dirty Jew . . . should've known . . . good f'r nothin' . . . useless . . . you owe us your—"

The colonel never finished his sentence. Because on hearing these words and learning that he was a Jew, Gregor swiveled around and with surprising ease caught the belt and jerked it from his old father's hand.

"Get away from me!" Gregor screamed and struck out with all his might, hitting the older man until he felt a wetness. Then Gregor opened his eyes and saw the whittling knife in his hand, glistening red, and his father, stumbling back, eyes wide. The colonel fell, grabbing blindly at the table, knocking over the chair, striking his head with a sickening thud on the cast-iron stove. Then he lay still, staring into nothing.

Gregor turned to face his mother, who was gazing wide-eyed. She let out a deep sigh, maybe of relief, then cried, "Oh, my God, my God!" Gregor had finally gotten her attention; she had stopped cleaning. And as she turned to the small boy standing there, his hand shiny and red, she began to scream. "Monster! Monster! You've killed him!"

That's when the monster came, and Gregor saw the blade sink deeply into the woman's belly, and she screamed, and the sound cut through him, and he saw the knife flash again, and the monster stabbed her until he was spent and the cries faded to a whimpering and she lay quiet.

Gregor dreamed of a fire, the flames leaping high into the air and the smoke mingling with the falling snow. Neighbors came and found the ruins and the boy who had dreamed it all, sitting in the snow, and they took him in.

. 13 .

By MIDSUMMER, Sergei had journeyed up out of Ukraine along the eastern edges the Pale of Settlement, that region of Russia from the Baltic to the Black Seas, where most Jews were required to live. In a few weeks he would pass to the west of Moscow on his way north. Now nearly nineteen, with long hair and beard, he was no longer recognizable as the young, clean-cut youth who had fled the Nevskiy School, so he risked the open road, at times even riding in the wagon of a farmer or merchant.

As he trekked through the summer heat, Sergei reviewed all that his grandfather had told him, including his reminders about his map to the buried treasure. He sensed that along with the map, Grandpa Heschel had somehow attached his love and his blessings, which might somehow guide him along the way.

He had committed the map to memory ten years before. The gift was buried north of St. Petersburg . . . in a meadow . . . on the shore of the Neva River . . . ten kilometers north of . . . the Winter Palace.

By late September of 1891, on a muggy summer's afternoon, St. Petersburg finally came into sight. Sergei entered the city, walking along cobblestone streets. Some passersby, more accustomed to seeing city folk than a wandering woodsman dressed in buckskin and worn boots, gave him wide berth. Their stares made him self-conscious for the first time in a long while, and he decided to get cleaned up to blend better into his new surroundings.

Only now—seeing city people in their carriages, and the lamplighters at their work outside shops and businesses—did Sergei realize how long he had lived without any need to pay for food, clothing, or lodging. If he found the treasure, he would have the resources to afford a room, a hot bath, and a barber.

He made his way to the Neva River, not far from the Winter Palace, and headed north with a growing excitement. He now saw the map clearly in his mind's eye: a drawing of the Neva River and, near its bank, bordered by forest on three sides, an x marking the spot beneath a large cedar tree planted by his grandfather's grandfather when Heschel was a boy. He walked through the deepening darkness and finally slept in a forested area just north of the city, his bed a pile of leaves on this humid night.

Early the next morning Sergei found his way to the large meadow ten kilometers north of the palace. For all the years since he and Grandpa Heschel had parted, Sergei had remembered that some kind of buried treasure awaited him.

As he searched for the lone cedar tree, a great doubt filled him. This had to be the place, yet he saw no great tree marking the spot.

Just then, a sudden breeze at his back—or maybe an instinct developed in the wild—caused him to turn. He spied four riders in the distance—two hundred meters away and closing fast. It might be nothing, but when riders are racing toward a lone man, it is rarely a good sign. He took a deep breath. He had nowhere to run in this open field, so he just stood and did his best to relax. But he couldn't help wonder: Are they still hunting for me? What has happened to my instincts? Have I grown complacent?

From this distance they looked like Cossacks, with black fur hats and black capes flapping in the wind. As they loomed closer, he could see their red vests, loose black pants, and black boots, then the sabers hanging at their sides and rifles strapped across their shoulders.

For a moment he thought they might ride him down, but at the last moment they reined in their horses, spread out, and surrounding him, as if they were hunting and he was the prey. Their action affected Sergei at a primal level: the hairs stood up on the back of his neck. He took slow, deep breaths, willing himself to stay calm despite his pounding heart. His combat skills were strong, but against four trained men with sabers . . .

"Greetings," he said, forcing a confident demeanor.

"Your name?" demanded their leader.

"Sergei . . . Voronin," he said, at least having the presence of mind not to use his last name. Two of the men turn to look at each other. One of them rode over to the leader and whispered something, but he shook his head and it ended there.

"Do you live nearby?" he asked him.

"No—as you see," Sergei answered, "I'm just a traveler, come to visit St. Petersburg." Then, speaking more boldly, like a man who has nothing to fear, he said, "Do you question every visitor to the city?"

The leader answered curtly, "We're looking for unauthorized Jews who might be wandering about." He gave him a hard look, searching for any signs of fear. "You haven't seen any, have you?"

"No, I have not," he said, with all the bravado he could manage. If they knew about Zakolyev's death . . .

He waited in silence. Then he heard wagons approach on a nearby road. The leader looked over at the passing farmers and decided that Sergei might be more trouble than he was worth. "Let's go!" he shouted, and they were off. Cossacks or not—and it was difficult to tell—they rode well. And could fight too, he ventured. The way they were armed, if they had tried to stop or search or rob him, things would not have gone well.

THAT INCIDENT left Sergei troubled—something about how those two men had looked at each other.

Still, the incident had resolved itself—and he had more pressing business. Finding no cedar tree in the meadow, he hiked farther along the banks of the Neva; then he backtracked in case he had passed the site. But he found no other meadows that better fit his grandfather's description. He was certain he had reconstructed the map in his mind.

This had to be the meadow—but without the tree, how could he ever find it?

The September afternoon had turned hot. Hoping to clear his mind, Sergei set aside his knapsack and clothing and immersed himself in the cold, clear waters of the Neva. After a few minutes he waded up onto shore and squatted for a few moments in the shallows, feeling the cold gravel between his toes as tiny waves lapped at his feet. He imagined his grandfather as a boy in summer, floundering in these same shallows, learning to swim . . .

Sergei washed his clothing and hung it to dry, resting in the sun as it dried his skin. All the while, he pondered the possibilities. It's exactly as my grandfather described, he thought—except for the missing tree where he had marked the x. He could still recall his grandfather's voice: "A small x by a lone cedar tree . . . a box is buried, on the side of the tree opposite the lake, between two large roots . . . "

After putting on his still-damp clothes, Sergei let them dry as he crisscrossed the meadow, searching for the base of a tree that might have fallen years before. He also explored the edges of the meadow, since new trees might have grown and the land changed over time. It made no sense; he must have forgotten some essential clue—or the cedar was here but had vanished. Maybe a local farmer had taken it for lumber.

He walked to the edge of the meadow and turned to face the center. He could just make out what appeared to be a slight mounding in the soil near the center of the meadow. He returned to that mound and found the trace of a tree root—a good-sized root, now dead and rotted, just below the uneven surface. His pulse quickened.

He fetched his shovel from his knapsack and dug, searching for any remaining roots. Soon he had cleared a three-meter circle and found a pattern of disintegrating roots that seemed to radiate outward, indicating where the tree must have stood.

The map had shown the x between two roots and away from the lake. He looked toward the lake and stood on the opposite side of mound where the tree had grown. Then he marked off a square and began digging—shallow at first, then deeper, until the shovel hit something solid. He fell to his knees and cleared away the soil with his hands.

Panting with exertion and excitement, Sergei found a box and pulled it free of the soil's tight embrace. "I found it, Grandpa!" he cried aloud, as if Heschel stood nearby. The box was bigger than he had imagined, and heavier as well. Kneeling on the rich earth, Sergei pried it open to find a large canvas bag inside. For a moment he wondered if it contained an heirloom, a treasure that might pay for his voyage across the sea—maybe enough to purchase land or even a house.

He opened the drawstring and reached inside, trying to guess by feel alone. It felt like wood. Another box? he wondered. Then he could wait no longer and pulled the object out to reveal . . . a clock.

Sergei stared at the treasure numbly, unable to sort out the mixed emotions of disappointment . . . guilt over the disappointment . . . and gratitude. The truth was, he had hoped for something more. But it made sense—Grandpa Heschel did, after all, make both violins and clocks. And it was a fine clock, to be sure, a fine gift. It was just that he had hoped for something more valuable.

Then he noticed something else—a small bag, tied to the back of the clock. He touched it and heard a clinking sound. It sounded like pieces of metal or . . .

He quickly opened the small sack and found five gold coins and a folded piece of paper. Eagerly he opened the paper and read, in Grandfather Heschel's fine script, "To my dearest grandson, Socrates. Always remember that the real treasure is within." It was signed, "Your loving grandfather, Heschel."

His eyes stung and spilled over as he read his grandfather's words. Tears born of fatigue from the long journey—or perhaps it was the gratitude that welled up inside, and a longing to see his grandfather once more. Sergei imagined how Heschel must have smiled as he placed the five shining coins into the pouch—a small fortune for a young man who had never before had a coin in his pocket.

Sergei had little sense of the cost of anything, including passage to America—but these coins might be enough. All told, they might be worth a hundred rubles or more. Still, he would have to earn more before leaving, so he would arrive with money in his pockets—and his grandfather's clock.

He slipped Heschel's note and the coins into his coat. Gently setting the clock down beside him, Sergei reburied the box and covered it, and out of long-bred habit, he erased all signs of his presence. Then Sergei admired the clock once again, with its fine glass cover over the face and the carefully carved and polished wood. He turned it around to view the short pendulum and weights—and that's when he noticed something scratched into the wood. Blowing off a fine coating of dust, he saw letters and numbers—a street address, quite likely his grandfather's old shop . . . or even his apartment!

Sergei felt a sudden impulse to visit his childhood home. But then he thought, My wild appearance may frighten whoever lives there. I'll need a bath . . . a haircut . . . new clothing for my voyage to America . . .

The sun was already dropping to the west; his search had taken the better part of the day. Placing the clock back into its original sack, he decided to stay another night in the woods.

. 14 .

THE DAY was already warm on that September morning when Sergei exchanged one of his coins for rubles and purchased shoes, dark pants, and a shirt and coat. He carried this bundle of new clothing to the barber, then the bathhouse. Afterward, he paused to glance at his clean-shaven, well-groomed self in the mirror.

Later that morning he would inquire about the cost of passage to America via Bremen or Hamburg or Liverpool. Then he would find a room. But first he would find his grandfather's apartment.

Carrying his knapsack and few belongings, including his grandfather's clock, Sergei looked again at the piece of paper on which he'd written the address. When he looked up, he saw a vision that made him forget where he was going: She stood less than ten meters away, across the street, apparently bargaining with a street vendor. Her gestures were so animated, her expressions so full and graceful, that she seemed to appear in color while the rest of the world faded into a background of gray.

Sergei couldn't quite make out her words, only the sound of her voice, which wafted across the cobbled street like the aromas of fresh bread and flowers. Clearly, she was getting the best of this vendor, who alternately frowned and smiled. Finally, she threw her head back and laughed, and Sergei thought that no music could ever be as sweet as that sound.

He could just make out hair of auburn, the rich color of autumn leaves, beneath her headscarf—a slim young woman about his age, maybe younger—a full mouth and large eyes.

He couldn't take his eyes from her, and without even realizing it, he followed her as she completed her business and moved off through the street market.

Sergei, who had survived in the mountains, was nearly struck by a carriage as, desperate for a closer look, he fixed his tunnel vision on her retreating form. He hardly dared speak to her, but for a closer look at least, he would give—

"Young fool!" Another warning shout from an irate carriage driver as Sergei dodged deftly out of the way without taking his eyes from her graceful form. Clearly, she was at home, in her element, while he was lost in every sense of the word.

He saw her stop and greet and touch the shoulder of a ragged old man, and drop a coin into his hand. A few more words and she moved on, crossing the street—

Just then, looking both ways, she turned to catch him staring at her, and Sergei realized in a sudden fit of self-conscious awareness that his mouth was hanging open.

Had he detected a faint smile on her face before she looked away? Yes! And she glanced back! Only once, briefly. Maybe he could find the courage after all to—

The shrill cry of a child, like the shriek of a wild bird, snapped Sergei's head to his left to see a mother trying to comfort a little boy who had fallen and bumped his head. The mother held his head and murmured to him . . .

He quickly turned back to the young woman. She was gone.

Sergei raced forward, searching right and left, scanning the tangled lines of vendors calling out the best prices. He who could track a hare or deer through the brush had just lost this most beautiful quarry of all.

That's when he realized that this was no mere game. He felt wretched, consoled only by the hope that she might return the next day.

After lingering there for half an hour longer on the chance she might appear, Sergei again recalled and resumed the purpose that had brought him into the city of St. Petersburg.

Thirty minutes later Sergei ascended the stairs of a vaguely familiar address, knocked, and just had time to straighten his coat and brush back his neatly trimmed hair before the door opened and he saw the dead come back to life.

He stood frozen, his mouth agape, and stared. More than ten years had passed, but she had hardly changed. As she gazed back with a growing recognition, her expression shifted from puzzlement to amazement to delight. It was the face of Sara Abramovich.

"Sergei?" she said. "I can't believe it's you!" Sara clasped his hands and drew him inside. He followed her obediently, in a kind of trance. In his mind she was still incinerated with her husband and children ten years before.

"Mrs. Abramovich . . . how did you—?"

"I still can't believe it!" she said. "As soon as we moved here, I had sent word to the school, but they said you had gone—"

"The children are all right?"

She smiled. "Quite all right—but as you will see, they are no longer children. Sit for a moment, Sergei. I'll make us tea and tell you everything." She led Sergei into a sitting room brightly lit by the morning sun, then she went into the kitchen, leaving him on a chair by the windows, overlooking the cobblestone street below.

He touched the chair; it was somehow familiar. And the polished wood floor as well. He had played there. Sergei heard her call out from the kitchen in her high, soft voice, "Oh, Sergei, . . . your grandfather would be so happy to know you are here!"

"And where are Avrom and Leya?" he asked loudly enough for Sara to hear as water boiled over the *primoos,* the kerosene burner.

"They no longer go by their old names . . . nor do I," she said, emerging from the kitchen with tea and small cakes. "Now eat! I made these myself, last night. You must tell me how you found—"

"Mrs. Abramovich—Sara—*please,*" he said, interrupting her. "How . . . are you here . . . alive?"

"How handsome you've grown," she said, ignoring his question. Then she turned to the old windup clock on the wall. "Oh, will you look—the clock has stopped again. I never know the right time anymore—I must get it fixed. But I expect the children home soon; I can't imagine what might be keeping them . . . oh! I haven't told you—Avrom is now named Andreas, and Leya is now Anya, and I . . . I am Valeria Panova. Our new names were arranged by your grandfather, just in case anything should ever . . ." Her words faded into silence, and her eyes took on a faraway look.

"What did happen?" Sergei asked again.

"Yes," said Valeria. "I suppose you should know." She gripped his hand more tightly, perhaps for courage. Not knowing where to begin, she started with a question. "You asked about the children, Sergei. But you didn't ask about Benyomin," she said with a tremor in her voice, afraid to hear his answer.

"In March of 1881," he began, "almost a year after my grandfather and I visited you—after the tsar's assassination—there was talk around the school about Jews. I was worried about your family. So I sneaked out of the school at night and found the path into the mountains."

"In the night? But . . . you were so young!"

"I had to warn you . . . and I found my way to the cabin . . . right after it happened . . ."

"Then you know."

He nodded. "If only I had arrived sooner. I wished it so many times—to warn you . . . nothing was left . . . only a pile of smoking rubble. But I . . . found a body that I believe—that I'm certain—was your husband. I managed to take his remains to a place where I had scooped out the earth . . . I buried him safe from the elements . . . "

Valeria's face slowly collapsed, and she cried.

AFTER A TIME Sergei asked how she and the children had escaped.

She spoke slowly, not sure where to begin. "You know that Benyomin loved to work with wood. He admired beavers for their ability to build lodges with secret tunnels. So when Benyomin built our cabin, he dug his own tunnel from the root cellar extending forty meters to a concealed trapdoor in the forest. I remember chiding him about this odd project . . . It took him longer to dig that tunnel than to build the walls of our cabin . . . "

Valeria sighed and looked out the window for a few moments before adding, "It might have saved Benyomin's life as well, had he not run back. I thought about it later. Many times. I should have known that he would meet them at the door, to keep them from finding the tunnel. Oh, Sergei, they came so quickly—then the cabin was on fire . . .

"They must have expected all of us to run outside so they could . . ." Her words trailed off for a time before she said in a rush, to get it all out, "After he hurried us all into the cellar and closed the door, Benyomin quickly handed me and Avrom—Andreas—a knapsack, with food and the papers your grandfather had arranged, with new names, just in case . . .

"We walked quickly, crouching, into the tunnel. It was pitch-dark, but he was right behind me. Then he was no longer there. I only heard his voice, muffled by the earth, far behind. 'Run!' he said. 'When it's safe, go to St. Petersburg!' Those were his last words.

"We waited in the tunnel for an hour or more. Once, I felt the pounding of horses' hooves above us, and a dusting of earth fell through the stifling air. Finally there was only silence. We waited like moles in the earth. We smelled the smoke. I knew that Benyomin would not return to us." A pained look crossed her face, and she spoke more quickly. "I wanted to run back, to beg him to come with us . . . only the children held me back. Only the children . . . " Her eyes brimmed with tears and she sighed.

"Just before dawn we slipped out and made our way through the forest. We slept under cover in the day and traveled by night until we reached St. Petersburg."

Sergei imagined Sara and Avrom and Leya, without any training or skills, making their way those many kilometers on foot, as Valeria continued, "My husband saved our lives by his cleverness and courage. Your grandfather gave us a new life," she said. "We were a shambles when we arrived. We didn't know where else to go but this apartment—"

"But by that time my grandfather had died . . . "

"Yes, but he had made arrangements—you see, Sergei, we had all become like a part of his family by the time Heschel brought his little grandson to visit." She touched Sergei's hair, and for a moment Sergei felt like that boy again.

"Most Jews," Valeria continued, "are required to live in the Pale of Settlement, far to the south, where conditions are hard, and where the pogroms continue. My husband refused to be told where to live and decided to build our cottage in the forest; Heschel was able to make a different choice. His regular income allowed him to live in St. Petersburg . . . in his own apartment, which he left to us."

"But why did you have to change your names?"

Realizing that Sergei knew little of Jewish traditions, Valeria explained, "In the Talmud it is written: 'Four things can change the fate of man and they are: charity, humble prayer, change of name, and change of action.' After we were attacked in the mountains, we left our old names, our old identities, behind us. Now we blend in. We attend services of the Russian Orthodox Church. Heschel even arranged for our baptismal papers, to complete our masquerade.

"Andreas and Anya both cling to their Jewish faith, but only in private. But they understand the risk that Heschel took, and the expense . . . and that it was their father's wish to keep us safe. In our hearts we are still Sara, wife of Benyomin . . . and Avrom and Leya. But you must call us by our new names, Sergei . . . for all our protection."

Sergei nodded, resolving to remember, though it would seem strange at first.

Valeria's thoughts returned to her children. "Heschel's apprentice, Mikhail, has trained Andreas; he is now a violin maker. He is more serious than his father, but so like him in other ways. And Anya has also grown into a young woman of good character and—"

Just then the door opened. Sergei turned to see Anya framed in the entry, her cheeks flushed from exertion, her arms filled with packages.

Aₙya's eyes were green as emeralds, illumined by an inner light. Her curly auburn hair, highlighted gold by the sunlight, crowned a radiant face. In that moment, as Anya's lips parted in a smile—as she set her parcels on the hallway table, and her hand reached up to brush back a stray curl—Sergei fell in love for the first time.

It was as if he had lived in one world and was suddenly catapulted into another one more refined and elevated.

The rest of the evening passed in a dream.

When Valeria reminded Anya that Sergei had visited when she was a little girl, a look of recognition came into her eyes, and something else as well, mysterious and intangible, that gave him hope.

Anya and her mother went into the kitchen, and the light seemed to fade in her absence. Sergei felt a pang of disappointment when Valeria returned alone, even when she said, "I hope you'll stay with us for a few days, Sergei. Your grandfather would want this, and so do I. You'll find the spare room quite comfortable—"

"Is it all right with . . . Anya if I stay?"

Valeria put her hands on her hips. "The last time I checked, Anya was not in charge of this household, but I'm sure she has no objections. None at all."

When Anya returned, she looked even more radiant, in a deep blue dress that highlighted her figure. Sergei knew it was rude to stare, but he couldn't seem to pull his eyes away. At least he had enough presence of mind to close his mouth. And when their eyes met, the world vanished.

The spell was broken by Valeria's voice: "Sergei, would you put a few more logs on the fire while Anya and I prepare the evening meal? Andreas should be home any minute, and you two can get reacquainted."

They retreated to the kitchen, and Sergei was feeding the fire when the door opened and Andreas entered. Still tall and slim, he had not changed greatly from his boyhood self. Valeria emerged from the kitchen and made the introductions. Andreas greeted Sergei in a formal but not unfriendly way—as he had years before.

Then came dinner and small talk, but Sergei could hardly concentrate; he kept glancing at Anya, hungry for another look at her soul, shining through her eyes. When he told of his plans to emigrate to America,

Sergei thought he detected a trace of disappointment on her face. Did she feel something for him, or was she just being polite?

Then Sergei remembered the clock. Excusing himself, he retrieved his knapsack, returned to the dining room, and took out the timepiece, briefly explaining how his grandfather had given him a map years before, and how he had only just found it, buried in a meadow just outside St. Petersburg. "It was my grandfather's last gift to me," Sergei said, handing it to Valeria. "As you can see, it had this address . . . on the back. I believe it belongs here, on your mantel . . . "

Valeria smiled. She passed it to Andreas, who set the hands and arranged the weights and pendulum so that it began its rhythmic swing. Even after all these years beneath the earth, it worked perfectly, ticking like the beat of Sergei's heart as he turned again to Anya . . .

"A beautiful timepiece," said Valeria. "We can leave it on the mantel for now. When you take it with you to America, it will remind you of the time we had together."

In the guest bed that night, Sergei finally drifted to sleep, acutely aware that Anya slept only just down the hallway. He hoped that she might also be thinking of him . . .

And she was.

In THE FIRST FEW DAYS of his visit, Sergei helped fix things around the apartment, making himself useful. Still, it felt strange to see Andreas off to work each day while Sergei tinkered around the house. He also offered to help pay for groceries, an offer that Valeria graciously refused.

Sergei knew that the sooner he found employment, the sooner he would have enough saved beyond his four remaining gold coins to finally voyage west, across the sea. His deepest wish was that he might buy two tickets—not in steerage but in the far more expensive second class.

He went out each day after that, and ten days later he found a job at a foundry, in the industrial section at the outskirts of the city. He would assist the blacksmiths who shaped and repaired horseshoes and carriage wheels as well as decorative metal fences and gates for homes of the wealthy. It was hard work, but after his active life in the wild, Sergei welcomed it. The fatigue of honest labor felt good to him.

He returned home each evening covered with sweat and grime. Valeria heated water and insisted that Sergei take a hot bath before supper. He did so but continued his long-standing practice of pouring a bucket of cold water over himself afterward.

Sergei needed these cold-water dousings more than ever, given his growing ardor for Anya. He thought about her many times each day, certain that he could not leave without her.

One night at dinner, in the most important and difficult minutes of his life, he announced that he had fallen in love and that it was his deepest wish that Anya would consider him as a suitor for her hand in marriage. He had planned, out of respect, to direct his words to Valeria, with Anya a spectator to his declarations. But when the moment came, Sergei knew he had to speak to Anya directly, with her mother and brother as witnesses. "As surely as I have ever known anything, I want to dedicate my life to your happiness, if only you will consent to our engagement."

Sergei did not know where such eloquence came from, or such courage—for in the next moments he might be both rejected and made a fool. He watched Anya acutely for any sign. She did not smile or frown, but her green eyes were wide open, not quite believing what she had heard.

Valeria broke the silence: "Anya, I expect you have some things to do in the kitchen—no, I think in your room. It seems that Sergei and Andreas and I have things to discuss."

Anya responded softly, but with firm resolve: "Mother, I'm quite sure I have nothing more pressing in the kitchen or my room than what happens here, so I shall stay."

Then she turned to Sergei, and he looked at her face and knew even before she spoke to him, and she said, "Yes."

Andreas, however, was less than entranced. "Sergei," he began, "you say you want to share your life with Anya. What life would that be? What are your prospects for providing for her safety and security?"

It was the best and the worst question Andreas could have asked. And for the first time in Sergei's life he wished he were a wealthy man. What could he offer besides devotion?

He answered as well as he could. "I understand your concern, Andreas. I have only a modest salary, right now, but I have discipline. I've survived alone in the wild. My hands are skillful, my mind quick to learn, and I don't mind hard work."

"That is all well and good," Andreas responded as the man of the house and Anya's brother. "But you've known my sister only a few weeks; you should take more time to get to know each other."

Sergei spoke to Andreas but looked directly at Anya. "There is nothing in this world I look forward to more." Then, turning to Valeria, he said, "I love your daughter with everything I am or ever will be. And I will do anything for her. I'm trained in combat, and I'll protect her with my life if need be. This I promise."

Then, speaking to them all, his hoped-for family, Sergei concluded, "I will go to school, work long hours, and improve himself in any way possible to bring Anya a good life."

"Still, Sergei—"

"Andreas, enough!" interrupted Valeria. "Let the poor boy eat."

"Sergei is not a boy, Mother," said Anya.

And Sergei knew that all would be well.

He could not know that a few days later all his hopes might be destroyed.

. 15 .

I T B E G A N with lighthearted conversation over dinner, when Valeria asked Sergei about his plans for the future.

"Well," he said, "I'll do whatever I can to better myself. There are many opportunities in America . . . "

All movement stopped around the table.

Andreas spoke first: "Did you say *America?* But I had assumed—"

"We *all* assumed," said Valeria, her voice flat.

Sergei stared at Andreas, then Valeria. Indeed, they had all made assumptions. In a flash he understood. After all, he had a job; he was getting settled. They all believed that his plans had changed—that he would continue to live there, with Anya, until they had found a suitable place nearby.

Sergei, for his part, had informed them more than once of his intention to emigrate and had presumed that they understood: he and Anya would make a new life together across the sea.

The silence that followed was so profound that they could hear one another's breathing. Valeria, broke the silence, saying, "I will not allow it. You will not take my daughter across the sea. I would never see her again."

"Mother," said Sergei. "Please. I know how much you love Anya, and would want better circumstances—"

"What 'better circumstances' do you refer to in this America-across-the-sea?" she demanded.

He took a moment to gather himself. "You know the times have never been easy for Jews—with the Cossacks roaming, and the pogroms—"

"You don't have to tell *us* about Cossacks or pogroms!" Andreas interrupted, his voice strident. "We have had ample evidence of animosity toward the Jews. We are reminded by our father's empty seat at the table—and why we play this sham of fitting in, why you see before you 'Valeria,' and 'Anya,' and 'Andreas.' Do not tell us of difficult times!"

"You're right, Andreas—and I apologize for my thoughtless words. But these difficulties are all the more reason for you and Valeria to come with us to America! Take back your names and your heritage. Build a new life! In America you can celebrate Shabbat openly, and families can worship however they choose."

Sergei turned to Valeria. "Mother, I don't want to take Anya away from you. I only want to take her to a better life. Come with us!"

Valeria stood. "I . . . am going to my room now, to think. Anya, the dishes—will you . . ." She turned and hurried out, but not before they all saw the pain on her face.

Anya started to rise but stopped, knowing that her mother would call when she needed her. So she remained at the table with Sergei and her brother as they sat in silence. Sergei wanted to speak, to bridge this chasm that had opened, to heal this fresh wound, but he had said all that he could.

He wondered: Is it selfish of me to pull Anya from the only family and home she has known, to take her so far across the sea? He gazed at Anya as she stared down at her hands, then raised her chin, met his eyes, and said in a whisper, "Sergei . . . whatever happens, wherever you go, I will stand by your side."

Sergei wanted so much to embrace Anya, but until Valeria returned, they could only sit and wait. But he knew this: they would be married; he would be her husband, and they could go where he deemed best. But how could Anya do so without her mother's blessings?

Sergei sighed, realizing how love and family could pose more challenges than a winter in the mountains. In the wilderness, the rules were simple—but there are no maps to the human heart.

"Mother won't go," Andreas said, "you know that, Anya. She is deathly afraid of the sea. She will never cross an ocean." After that, they waited in silence.

Some long minutes later, Valeria appeared in the doorway. "Anya, come here, please." Anya rose and disappeared into her mother's room. Now it was the men alone, waiting.

Finally Valeria returned, and her voice halted any further discussion: "I will not go to America," she said. "I was born and will die on Russian soil. It is where my husband . . ." Her voice trailed off, and then she looked at Anya, squeezed her hand, and said, "Although I give my blessings for this marriage, I will never give my blessings for Anya to go across the sea . . . but I do give my permission. She must go where her husband goes.

"But I beg one thing of you both, if you bear any love for me: Do not leave right away. Give me a little time with my married daughter, so I can get to know my new son-in-law better."

Sergei could not refuse Valeria; he agreed to stay for a few months longer. Only then did a smile come to Valeria's face. It was a brave smile, willed there by a mother's desire for her daughter's happiness above her own.

Only then did Andreas say, "So be it." And he embraced Sergei as a brother.

Busying herself with arrangements, Valeria told Sergei, "You and Anya will have to be married by Father Alexey in the church, or it will not be legal. They will require your baptismal certificate, Sergei. I presume you were baptized at that military school, and that they have such records. So you should contact them soon . . ."

On hearing this, Sergei nodded and smiled. But behind the smile, a flood of dark thoughts emerged that he had tried so hard to forget.

Years past, he had taken all his records, including the required certificate, from the school. So this practical matter posed no problem. But Valeria's request was a painful reminder that Sergei could never contact the school; that he had killed a fellow cadet and fled as a fugitive; that he was still a fugitive—another reason he could not wait long before taking Anya to America.

Valeria knew none of this, and he would not tell her or Andreas or even Anya—especially not Anya.

T HEY WERE MARRIED on a Friday morning, November 6, 1891, in a small chapel—six weeks after Sergei's arrival in St. Petersburg. It snowed on that fall day, and the world was cold and beautiful and good.

As a boy, Sergei had dreamed about becoming a part of this family. Now it had happened, so it felt as if he was still dreaming.

Later that afternoon, at home, before her mother and brother and a few close Jewish friends, they once again declared their vows and their love in the Jewish tradition. It could not be a formal ceremony with a rabbi because Valeria could not risk bringing the required minyan, the minimum of ten witnesses, according to Talmudic law.

Sergei and Anya received a wedding gift from his new family: a baker's cart Andreas had painted like new, pulled by an old but reliable horse—a splendid gift for rides in the country.

When the guests left, Valeria sent them outside. "For your first walk together as husband and wife," she said.

"Is this a tradition I hadn't heard about?" Sergei asked.

"Yes. A new tradition we are just starting. Now go out and get some fresh air," Valeria ordered, falling into her role of mother-in-law as easily as snow fell from the clouds.

So Sergei and Anya bundled up and strolled through the frosting of falling snow. The flakes caught the light of a nearby gas lamp as they passed under it. The night air—the glowing street lamps, the scent of snow mixed with smoke from many hearths—took on a new clarity, as if Sergei were seeing St. Petersburg for the first time through Anya's eyes, and she through his.

"Mother was right, you know, as always," Anya said. "She pushed us out to get some fresh air—and do you notice how especially *fresh* the air is tonight?" They both laughed. Then she removed a mitten and asked him to do the same. "I want to feel your hand, Sergei. I don't want gloves between us. I don't want anything between us . . . "

He looked at her. "Let's go back home," he said. "I think it's time for bed."

Anya smiled, and the flush that rose to her cheeks was not just from the cold.

On returning, they discovered that while they were out, Valeria and Andreas had moved their belongings into Valeria's larger bedroom and Anya's own things into her old room.

"It is only right," she said, as she wished them good-night.

Earlier that day, Andreas had reminded him that according to Jewish law, on Friday nights husbands are directed to give pleasure to their wives.

Sergei intended to follow the law to the letter. And maybe surpass it.

O N   T H E I R   W E D D I N G   N I G H T, Sergei gave Anya his mother's locket. He told his bride about its history. Then he cut five strands of her auburn curls, wound them into a small coil, and slipped this lock of hair behind the photograph of his parents. He told her, "This locket was once my only treasure. Now you are my treasure, so I pass it on to you." After that he held Anya in his arms under the warm covers of their marriage bed and whispered, "We were married the moment our eyes first met."

"When you were eight and I was five?" she teased.

"Even then. Even before this life."

After her initial anxiety melted away, Anya gave herself to him completely. Overwhelmed by desire, Sergei and Anya learned the ways of love as they lay together each night that followed, as they rose and fell in each other's arms and become one.

One night in bed, as Anya giggled softly at his touch and tenderly touched the white scar on Sergei's arm, she whispered to him, "This is the happiest I have seen my mother in years."

Puzzled, he asked, "She's happy because we traded bedrooms?"

"No, silly—men can be so dense—she's happy thinking about her first grandchild."

"Ah . . . then we will have to do everything we can to increase her joy," he said, kissing Anya in the hollow of her throat.

Anya pressed herself against him and whispered, her voice breathy in his ear. "My husband, we must begin working on the project right now." And as they had done nearly every night, they renewed their vows with each kiss and every caress.

After their first Friday night, each day that followed, Anya's enthusiasm for their embraces grew, and they shared a private joke as lovers do: Sergei might be fixing a lamp or reading in the sitting room or shaving, and Anya would slip up behind him and whisper in his ear, "What day is it today, my husband?"

Every day his answer would be the same: "Why, I believe that today is Friday."

And she would answer, "My favorite day . . . and my favorite night . . . "

In the days and nights that followed, whether in the bedroom or kitchen or strolling through the streets and canals of St. Petersburg, Sergei told Anya of his young life. He also memorized every detail of her past joys and sorrows, as he committed to memory every part of her. They shared everything with each other. Almost everything.

In THE FOLLOWING WEEKS a vague foreboding, no more substantial than smoke or shadows, intruded upon Sergei's happiness. It was the sense one gets before an approaching storm. The source of his unease centered on his promise to remain for a time in St. Petersburg. If it had been up to him alone, Sergei would have booked passage on the next train to Hamburg and from there the first ship to America. He had resolved to honor Valeria's plea, but he would not delay much longer.

In mid-January he had a private conversation with Valeria, reminding her of his intention to leave for America as soon as it was feasible. "I will have enough money saved in another month, Mother—two at the most. So prepare yourself for our departure."

"Of course, I understand," she said. "But everything is going so well, and we are all so happy. You don't need to rush across the sea." She kept finding things that needed repairing and asked if he might help a little with the expenses, so his savings grew more slowly. Sergei could not refuse Valeria's requests; after all, he was living under her roof, and it was only right that he assist with expenses.

He knew that Valeria still had a difficult time accepting the idea of Anya leaving, and this created tension between them as the weeks passed.

Their anxiety only grew as news of pogroms in the south and rumors of other isolated incidents reached their ears. But despite the urgency gnawing at Sergei's insides, their day-to-day life in St. Petersburg was peaceful and good. Sergei convinced himself that his fears were natural but groundless.

. 16 .

GREGOR STAKKOS set out each day with clear purpose, untroubled by the petty concerns or morality of lesser men. Disinclined to meaningless labor, he stole food and funds and a better horse, leaving the injured or dead behind. Certain that he was a giver of life or death with powers and rights beyond ordinary mortals, he already thought of himself as Ataman—Cossack leader. Soon enough, others would do likewise.

Men such as Gregor Stakkos have become leaders of nations—but to lead, they need followers with the loyalty and skills to become the leader's eyes and ears and limbs. Gregor learned much by observing and asking questions, but where he traveled he left no friends or goodwill behind.

Lean and sinewy, Gregor arrived at a Cossack settlement near the Don River, an outpost maintaining the southern border from marauders. After a few days' stay, he faced an accusation from a young man about his own age, who claimed that Gregor had stolen a knife. For this slander, Gregor beat the boy badly, nearly putting out an eye. The knife was never found.

A few days later a young girl whispered in shame that Gregor had taken her by force. She could offer no proof, but she was the daughter of the village ataman, and Gregor had to leave, before the ataman returned, and go seek a more suitable settlement.

These events taught him that he would have to show more restraint in the future, until he got what he wanted. He considered this as he sharpened his newly acquired knife.

After his stay in this particular settlement, as Gregor rode away, he was followed by a tall, one-armed horseman about his age, a man the villagers called Korolev. Gregor had already noticed and asked about this Korolev, and he'd learned that while everyone knew of him, few knew anything about him. Korolev stood a full head taller than Gregor himself, with chiseled features, deep green eyes, and long black hair tied in the back. A powerfully built and handsome brute, save for a large scar on one cheek, eyes too small and close together, and the missing left arm.

"He keeps to himself," said an elderly Cossack villager. "Arrived half a year past but never fit in." Now, apparently, Korolev was following Gregor.

Deciding there was only one way to discover this man's intentions, Gregor stopped and confronted him. "What do you want?" he asked.

"I have seen you handle yourself. I want to find out if you are a worthy companion."

"I am no one's companion, but I can be a generous leader to those who ride with me."

"Then you will have to best me in battle," Korolev said with a smile. His voice had an odd sibilant quality, like the hiss of a snake.

Stakkos nodded. "Let us find out." Although his adversary looked formidable, Stakkos's hidden power was his willingness to accept pain or death rather than defeat. This impressed Korolev, who had never been bested and who usually intimidated most men into cowering before the fight even began. So they circled one another and then fought, each testing the other's ferocity and commitment.

Korolev fought well—amazingly so for a man with one arm. In fact, he would have won, as he always did, except that he made a slight error. Like most men, he had underestimated Stakkos. Stakkos took full advantage of it and threw Korolev down, at the same time drawing his knife. With his knee on Korolev's massive chest and his knife on the giant's cheek, Gregor said, "I see that you have some artwork to complement your pretty face; would you like a matching scar on the other side? Or perhaps I should take off your other arm to improve your balance?"

"As you wish," answered the one-armed man, "but I will ride with you, in any case, and follow you while it pleases me."

"Well said. I will leave you as you are."

Gregor reached down to help Korolev to his feet, but Korolev sprang up on his own and mounted his horse. As they rode they spoke, not as trusted friends—they would never be that—but as allies.

When Stakkos asked direct questions, Korolev answered them without embellishment: the scar was self-inflicted as a boy to make his face "less pretty." The loss of his arm had come three years earlier, when he had attacked an ax-wielding man with nothing more than a knife. Before Korolev killed the man, the bastard had cut into Korolev's left arm so deeply that it would be useless and might become infected. So after the he tore open his opponent's throat, he took the man's ax and finished the job, then jammed his stump into a nearby brazier to seal it. He lay sick for a time after that but survived.

Gregor also learned that, like him, Korolev had left home early. Beyond that, he would say no more except, "There was trouble at home. They were afraid of me after that."

"They threw you out?"

Korolev shook his head. "One morning I woke and they were gone . . ." He turned his blue-eyed gaze on Stakkos. "What I have told you is for you alone. We must have an understanding: if you repeat it, I'll kill you—or die in the attempt. But more likely, I will succeed."

Nodding, Gregor placed Korolev under the same conditions, adding, "I'm good to those who are loyal and not so gentle with those who betray me. You understand as well?"

They looked into one another's eyes, and for the first time in his memory, Korolev felt something akin to fear. He shook it off and added one more condition: "I have a strong appetite for women. So when we take prisoners—"

"We will take no prisoners—"

"Before they die, I will have the women first. Do you agree?"

Gregor Stakkos agreed readily. He lusted far less for sex than for authority. Korolev could have his women.

In this way they formed an alliance. Over time these two men would form the core of a new breed of Cossacks, with Stakkos as Ataman. And like-minded men would be drawn to this Ataman and his right-hand man as flies find their way to fresh dung.

. 17 .

In MID-FEBRUARY, on a rainy morning just before they got out of bed, Anya whispered, "I have something special to tell you, Sergei."

He whispered back, "Everything you tell me is special, my sweet."

She nudged him in the ribs. "This is more special. Are you listening? Really listening?"

He turned toward her, vaguely aware that after work he needed to fix the basin in the kitchen. "When do I not—?"

She touched her finger to his lips. "Don't talk. Listen. A new life has begun inside me. I can feel the baby . . . "

Sergei was not sure he had heard correctly. It was as if Anya had just announced that she could float from the ground and fly. It felt like a miracle. "A baby?" he said. "Our baby?"

Anya laughed. "I don't recall making a baby with anyone else, but let me think . . . "

"But when did you know?"

"I suspected something in January but wanted to be certain. It must have happened soon after we married. Maybe even on the first night," she said.

He reached out to touch her belly. "Can I feel it moving?"

Anya rolled her eyes as she did when amused or exasperated. "Sergei Sergeievich, you wise and silly man, he is probably still no bigger than your fist. It will be months before you can feel him kick like his father."

"He? His?"

Anya hesitated. "Yes, I think the baby is a boy, but—"

"Then a boy he shall be!" he pronounced, thrilled by the prospect of making his own family. "We shall have a house full of children, and . . ." Then he thought of Valeria. "Does Mother know?"

"Of course not! Do you think I would tell anyone before I told you?"

"We must tell her and Andreas! Our son shall be born in America!"

Anya leaned against him. "Yes . . . in America . . . "

"I'll teach him all I know—how to survive in the wilderness . . . "

Anya laughed. "Aren't we getting ahead of ourselves? We mustn't plan his future just yet. After all, he could be a she."

His eyes widened at the possibility. "A daughter? As graceful as her mother? Then she shall be a ballerina!"

Anya paused then, glowing with happiness. "Is it not a wondrous life, Sergei? Four months ago you didn't know I was alive. And now you're planning our daughter's life as a prima ballerina in the Marinsky Theater—"

"Anya," he said, more seriously, "not in the Marinsky Theater—you do understand that our child will grow up in America . . . "

"Of course, Sergei—it was only a slip. Do they have ballet in America?"

"I expect so—and hot water in the kitchen, and indoor commodes . . . "

"No more trips to the *kolonka* at the corner to draw water? Or running downstairs to the toilet? Or heating bathwater on the *primoos?*" Anya asked. "That alone is enough to draw me across the sea! Oh, Sergei, if this is a dream, I never want to wake up."

Sergei embraced her gently. "I won't break, you know," she said, giving him a quick squeeze before she slipped out of bed.

Before he left the apartment that day, they agreed in whispers not to tell Valeria until dinner, when they would all be together. "It's never easy," she said, "to keep anything secret from Mother."

At the dinner table, Anya and Valeria brought in the food as usual. Sergei just sat grinning until Andreas said, "Well? What is it?"

Valeria turned toward Anya. "You have something to tell us." It wasn't a question. From the expression on Anya's face, Valeria had already guessed the truth but was waiting for confirmation.

Upon hearing the news, Valeria got up and rushed into the kitchen. Anya and Sergei looked at each other, bewildered—then Anya quickly followed her mother. A few minutes later Anya emerged, smiling as she wiped a tear from her eye, and explained, "It's okay. Mother just didn't want us to see her cry again. She is making a honey cake to celebrate."

With the coming of spring, Anya and Sergei took walks in the fresh evening air as her constitution allowed. In the early months she had some bad days, but now, in her fifth month, she felt in the best of health. On Sundays they took long walks and spoke of their future together.

But on the first Sunday in June, in the sixth month of Anya's term, Sergei took her on her first ride to the meadow where he had found his grandfather's clock, now sitting on the mantelpiece.

As they walked the perimeter of the meadow, in the shade of the trees, Sergei glanced often at his wife, checking to make sure she was all right. He needn't have worried—Anya glowed in the outdoors, pointing out birds, delighted by her brief sighting of a doe and her fawn.

Ankle-high grasses waved in a soft summer breeze, with red, yellow, and purple flowers scattered everywhere. "It's beautiful," she said. "Let's spread our picnic blanket over there." They ate their fill and spent a rare day alone. If Sergei had suddenly died and found himself in heaven, it would not have been different from that day in the meadow.

The afternoon was marred only slightly by a cloud of dust to the east, reminding Sergei of the riders who had confronted him nearly a year before. He could just make out a small band of passing horsemen. It didn't look like they were heading their way, so he lay back down. A few minutes later he looked again and they were gone.

He was left with that restless feeling again, glad that very soon they would leave so their child could be born in America.

That night at dinner Sergei announced that he had saved enough for their tickets and initial expenses, and in a few more weeks they would depart. He said nothing about his sense of urgency. There was no point in burdening others with his concerns.

When Anya took the dishes into the kitchen, Valeria sat next to Sergei, took his hands, and said spoke almost in a whisper, "Sergei, have I not loved you and been good to you?"

"Yes, Mother . . ."

Having gained this concession, she continued, "You know that I may never see my daughter again, the world being what it is. May I at least see my grandchild?"

Sergei had seen this coming. Next, he thought, she will be asking us to stay until the child's confirmation or bar mitzvah. He would not be swayed so easily. "Andreas will marry," he responded. "Then you'll have many—"

"Who can predict?" she said, outflanking him. "Andreas has not yet thought of marriage, much less children. Sergei . . . I'm not asking you to stay forever—I would if I thought there was a chance—but can you at least find it in your heart to grant this one delay? Let me assist my only daughter as she gives birth to her first child!"

Sergei turned from Valeria's anguished, imploring face to see Anya in the doorway, listening and waiting in silence for his response.

Despite his misgivings, Sergei heard himself say, "All right, Mother. You will see the birth of your first grandchild—but as soon as we are able to travel, we will go without delay."

An ecstatic Valeria embraced him. "You are such a good man, Sergei—"

"And a good husband," said Anya.

. 18 .

WHEN GREGOR STAKKOS and the one-armed giant Korolev arrived at a village of Cossacks in the region near the Caucasus Mountains of Georgia, both spoke and acted with discretion. As mounted warriors, they were provisionally welcomed into the everyday activities of the settlement. They worked for food and lodging and bided their time, waiting for an opportunity to prove themselves. They did not have to wait long. A few weeks after their arrival, Cossack warriors returning to the settlement after a scouting mission told of Abreks, Chechen bandits, who had crossed the river to raid the Russian side. This time they had killed two Russians. The Cossacks expected more raids and doubled their sentries, with each watching out for the other so no sentry could be taken without alerting the others.

Gregor saw his chance to earn a hero's welcome. He had already drawn the admiration of several younger men with stories of his conquests. Some of the stories were true, and the rest were drawn from his imagination. The fact that the one-armed warrior rode with him only added to his reputation.

Gregor told his young admirers, "I do not think we should wait for the Abreks to cross the Terek. Korolev and I will cross this very night, find the Chechen encampment, and kill them all. We will bring back their weapons, horses, and boots. And some souvenirs—maybe an ear or two," he added, holding up a leather pouch. Two of the youths, impatient for glory and adventure, volunteered to join them; three more, not wanting to appear cowardly, followed.

So it was that Gregor Stakkos and his small band silently approached the camp in the predawn darkness. He warned them to save the single shot from each pistol until absolutely necessary—to favor the knife and saber for their silent efficiency.

These Abreks were hardened fighting men. But they had never expected such a daring preemptive raid in their own camp by seven young warriors who would have slaughtered the bandits in their sleep had not one of the enemy gotten up to relieve himself and seen a movement in the bushes. He just had time to shout a warning before his cry was cut short.

Suddenly alert, the Abreks leaped up to grab for their knives, pistols, and rifles. Seeing his surprise unravel, Gregor led a determined charge, nearly decapitating one warrior with a stolen saber as he drew his pistol with the other hand and fired. The young men, inspired by their leader's bravado and Korolev's apparent invincibility, fought like demons.

Eight men and two women had lived in the enemy camp. Gregor killed the first woman as she leveled a carbine at one of his men, but Korolev captured the second woman alive—and then raped her with his young followers until she begged to die. In this manner, the Ataman and his first lieutenant, Korolev, initiated the first of many new traditions for these youths whom he now called "his men." And so they were.

Their band of seven returned to camp leading enemy horses, their tunics covered with blood—mostly that of their enemies. Only two boys had received wounds minor enough to be worn proudly, like medals. Gregor Stakkos had proven his abilities at strategy and leadership as well as his bravery in battle.

They were welcomed as heroes—until the younger men bragged about Korolev's as well as their own treatment of the woman. When the elders heard this talk, and heard these young men call Gregor Stakkos Ataman and saw Stakkos's bag of "souvenirs," they spat on the ground, lending a bitter taste to this day of bravery and infamy. After earning the adulation of the youth and the enmity of the elders, Stakkos left with five young Cossacks, the beginning of his band.

In the coming months, under the Ataman's authority, the band began scouting for small Jewish shtetls, or cabins or farms. At random, every month or two, they would ride in like a storm, leaving fire and death in their wake. Other times they rode on normal patrols, as did other Cossacks bands, hunting other enemies of Russia.

This pattern of roaming patrols, changing camps, and the occasional slaughter of Jews continued until a scouting party Stakkos had sent out returned to camp. Soon after, the Ataman announced to his men, "Break camp. We ride far north!" They moved like a force of nature, wreaking havoc along the way, then disappearing without a trace.

. 19 .

As JUNE SLIPPED into early July and the full heat of a St. Petersburg summer, Sergei decided that his uneasy feelings were normal for a husband and father-to-be. Yet he worried all the more because he had never before known such happiness, and he wanted nothing to change. He recalled his grandfather telling him, "There will be times, little Socrates, when you'll want things to change, and other times when you will want everything to remain the same. But life is God's book, not ours, to write."

He thought of these words as he read *Bibliograficheskie zapiski,* which reported both facts and rumors about raids in the Jewish settlements to the south. He had that sinking feeling again in the pit of his stomach—but in a few short months his family would be on their way to America. And someday Valeria and Andreas might follow.

As each day brought them closer to their departure, family gatherings took on an air of the sacred. Valeria became possessive of Anya and wanted to sit and speak with her daughter alone. Sergei was glad to accommodate a mother's wishes. He and Anya would have a lifetime together, but Valeria's time with her daughter was drawing to a close.

When Valeria came in and sat near him, he put down the news publication.

"I hope you enjoyed your dinner, Sergei."

"I did, thank you."

"Anya has gone to your room to read. I thought we might talk."

"Of course."

With some difficulty, she said, "Motherhood is sweet, Sergei, but sometimes bitter. Because, those we most love, we miss all the more when they are gone. Now, when I speak with Anya, my words fall far short of what I want to tell her. I want her to know how much I love her . . . how much she means to me . . . but she cannot know, she will not understand—not until her own child grows up. Then she will know . . . and she will miss me too, Sergei. She will miss me terribly."

Valeria began to cry softly. Sergei did not know what to do, so he just sat with her. He did not speak, for what words could console a mother when the hour came to part? After a time she released his hand, which she had been squeezing without knowing it, thanked him for listening, and started toward her room.

The next words he heard were not meant for him but were whispered thoughts only—as if she were talking in her sleep. She said, "A grandmother should be near her grandchild . . ." Then, with a sigh, Valeria disappeared through the doorway.

Her turmoil was clear: she wanted to come with them—but she could not, would not, allow herself to do so. Her roots lay in Russia, but her heart would soon reach out across the sea.

Even though her grandchild wasn't expected for many weeks more, Valeria grew more anxious by the day—not so much about the birth itself, but because it signaled her daughter's impending departure.

Valeria and Sergei maintained a sort of détente. She cared for him; he knew that. But he was also the man who would take away her daughter and grandchild to a faraway land.

As they waited those final weeks, Sergei gave his notice at work and planned their passage, obtained luggage, and helped Anya pack their few belongings. Meanwhile, Valeria kept busy, cleaning and preparing for the arrival of her grandchild. Arrivals and departures.

On the third Sunday in July, Anya asked Sergei to take her to their "happy spot" in the meadow for a picnic, where she might cool her tired feet in the shallows of the Neva.

He had misgivings and thought she should remain close to home, just in case. "Aren't you far along for a bumpy ride?" he asked.

"I feel farther along than any woman who has ever lived," she said. "Still, I'd welcome a carriage ride out in the fresh air and another day alone with my husband."

Sergei helped Anya up to her seat. A worried-looking Valeria handed Sergei the picnic basket. "We'll be home long before dark," he assured her, flicking the reins.

As they rode along the canal passing beneath Nevskiy Prospekt and turned north, Sergei said, "Anya, my sweet, do you believe in fate?"

"I believe in you."

"I know you do," he said, leaning over to kiss her hair. "But do you believe in destiny?"

Anya laughed. "How could he *not* believe when such strange and wondrous events brought you to me?" She rubbed her abdomen. "And now we have another miracle." Drawing one of his hands from the reins, she held his palm to her round belly. "Do you feel him?"

Nothing at first—then a thump, and another. "He is already practicing his kicks and punches," said a smiling Sergei, glad for this day, glad for this life.

Making their way out of the city limits and up a country road, they passed a farm. Anya, in love with the world, smiled and waved to the farmer, who nodded back in greeting.

Soon after, they arrived at the meadow. Sergei had planned on setting their blanket in the center of the clearing, atop the rise where he had found his grandfather's final gift. But the oppressive heat sent them closer to the edge of the forest, where they rested in the shade. They set out the food and gazed out across the meadow.

. 20 .

DURING THE REIGN of Tsar Aleksandr III and the period of counter-reform, violence increased against the Jews and gypsies. The *Chernosotentzi*, extreme nationalists, were one source of the scourge. Another source was Gregor Stakkos and his men.

Unlike the nationalists, Stakkos had no ideology; his hatred of Jews was personal, his motives unquestioned. And unlike the Cossacks, who might kill enemies of the tsar but would not steal like common thieves, Stakkos had a passion for acquiring anything of interest or value before they burned all evidence of their crimes. He left no witnesses to provide clues to their whereabouts. Stakkos was obsessive about security and would never ride off directly toward camp but would circle back over rocky terrain and streambeds. So he and his men seemed to disappear like ghosts, and their raids produced rumors both terrifying and confusing.

Over the past few years, the Ataman had attracted restless youths and hardened veterans as they passed through towns and villages. Several women had joined too, for reasons of their own. A few were married or attached to new recruits. Some were willing to service the other men, so rules were made and order maintained.

During this time, Stakkos began a new custom: every year or two, he would spare a Jewish infant and give the child over to the women to raise. This way, even as he murdered and burned, he adopted the mantle of "savior of children," to be raised as good Christians. Eventually, this nomadic tribe came to resemble the makings of a Cossack village.

Each small atrocity opened the way for a greater one, until no act

was unacceptable. By their standards cruelty was necessary, even virtuous. Armed not only with swords and firearms, but with the certainty of
any zealot, they indulged every kind of impulse.

In their temporary camps they appeared to be like men, with huts
and hearths and women and children. But they were men without
humanity. Intoxicated by a growing sense of invincibility, setting themselves above both law and decency, they rode across Russia and wrought
the horrors of hellfire on their victims.

Thus it was that Gregor Stakkos and his men rode into a peaceful
meadow on a Sunday afternoon in July.

. 2 1 .

They had just finished their picnic meal, and Anya rested her head against Sergei on this languid afternoon. They listened to the birdcalls and the summer wind blowing through the trees and across the Neva.

As he was about to lie down in Anya's arms, Sergei saw a dust cloud rising in the distance. He sat up and saw riders coming their way—most likely soldiers out on patrol.

Maybe if he had taken immediate action at first sighting—maybe if he had trusted that sinking feeling in the pit of his stomach—they might have gotten away. In sudden alarm, leaving their belongings in disarray, he might have gotten Anya up onto the cart, then whipped the old horse into a gallop. But such actions would have seemed alarmist, cowardly— a needless and confusing panic. After all, it was just some men riding in their direction.

Riding fast. And now it was too late. Mounted men have an immeasurable advantage over those on foot. As the men approached, Sergei thought he recognized one of the same men, then another, who had surrounded him on the previous September. Then his dread grew when he saw among the fourteen riders a giant, one-armed man who looked like a Mongol warrior.

The rest of the men drew near, and their leader pulled his horse up a few meters away. The man had a scar angled across his forehead and was older now, but there was no mistaking him. Towering above him,

astride his warhorse, and gazing down with a smile he would never forget, was the face of Dmitri Zakolyev.

Sergei stood immobile, reeling from revelations and contradictory
emotions: relief that he had not killed Zakolyev, then regret that he was
alive, followed by a sense of impending doom.

He quickly turned to Anya, who was still sitting, not yet frightened,
only puzzled, looking up at Sergei for a sign of reassurance. "It's okay,"
he said. "I know him—we're old schoolmates." But his mouth was suddenly dry, and his voice rang hollow. He looked back at Zakolyev.

"It's good to find you, Sergei—I believe you've already met a few of
my men," he said, gesturing toward the four riders who had surrounded
him months before. "When my scout told me of a man he had encountered who fit your description—a Sergei Voronin, I believe he said—I
was quite cross that he had not brought you back to the camp for a
reunion. I was going to properly chastise him, but he assured me that he
could find you again. And so he has. An opportune time for us to catch
up, don't you agree?"

Not waiting for Sergei's response, Zakolyev continued, "I inquired
about you for a considerable time, but no one had heard of Sergei the
Good. And after the way we parted on such unfortunate terms, I truly
wanted a chance to make things right. And now here we are, together
again, and you with a pretty wife, no less. And with child. "

Zakolyev's voice was so gentle, his manner so courteous, that for a
fleeting moment Sergei believed that his old schoolmate might have
changed. Until some of his men laughed, and the muscles on Sergei's
arms twitched as he snapped back to cold reality: Zakolyev was going to
humiliate him; then he was going to kill them both.

"Well, Sergei," he continued, "where are your manners? Will you not
introduce us?"

Sergei's mind raced, searching for a way out. He took stock of the
situation: if Zakolyev was dangerous, his men were even more so—they
were followers, anxious to please their leader, to rise in rank and status.
No doubt they were well-trained fighters. He might be a match for a
few, make an heroic effort—

If he fought, Zakolyev would kill them both; if he pleaded and humbled himself, they might spit on him, beat him . . . then make him watch while they—

He would not allow his mind to go further.

Sergei searched desperately for the right words or action that might at least save the life of his wife and child. All this passed through his mind in the time it took for Anya to climb to her feet—Sergei reached quickly down to help her. She came to his side and took his hand. It was cold, and it was trembling. In that moment he felt a raging, primal power. Contain it, he thought. Use it. But not yet . . . not yet.

"I asked whether you were going to introduce me to your woman," Zakolyev repeated, an edge in his voice.

"Dmitri," Sergei heard himself say, calling on better times. "Do you remember when I was under your guidance during our survival training? How we helped each other—?"

"I remember everything," said Zakolyev, cutting him off.

Sergei knew, upon seeing Zakolyev alive, that he must have been waiting for this day, that he must have rehearsed and anticipated everything Sergei might say or do, every desperate attempt to escape. But Zakolyev had not foreseen the sweet surprise of Anya.

"I appeal to you as a Cossack and a man of honor," Sergei said. "Let my wife go home. I give you my word—"

A bored-looking Zakolyev raised his hand to silence Sergei. Then he asked, politely, as if he were merely curious—as if reminiscing about old times—"Do you still have that old locket?"

"I . . . I gave it away," he answered. "As a gift."

Anya's hand automatically reached up to her neck.

"Indeed you did," said Zakolyev. Then he barked, "Korolev!" and gestured with his head in Anya's direction. The huge one-armed man with the black braid dismounted and walked slowly toward Anya. The stench of him hit Sergei's nostrils—not just the scent of sweat, but the rank odor of a man possessed.

"Back off!" said Sergei, stepping between his wife and the muscular giant. "Call off your attack dog, Zakolyev!"

Korolev paused. The chieftain nodded toward his men, and six of them dismounted immediately and surrounded Sergei, with Anya outside the circle.

"What is this?" said Sergei.

"I need a man to search you," said Zakolyev.

"And the others?"

"In case you try something stupid."

Sergei decided to cooperate. So far, no one had been injured or even threatened. There was still a chance. But he stood balanced on a powder keg.

Then the keg exploded as all six men restrained Sergei and the giant grabbed Anya's wrist, pulled her to her feet, and dragged her away from Sergei.

In the next five seconds, with a burst of energy, Sergei disabled two of the men, one with a blow to the windpipe and the other with a kick to his knee. Both fell back, one gagging, the other unable to stand. But the other four managed to grasp his arms, his legs, his neck—a crushing weight of bodies as more men dismounted to hold him—and they took him down, smashing his face to the ground, immobilized.

Instantly, Sergei relaxed as if he had given up. He would wait for a few moment more, until they least expected it . . . but there were too many. He managed to lift his head and spit out dirt and blood, and watch in helpless fury as the scene unfolded.

ZAKOLYEV NODDED ONCE AGAIN. Korolev released his one-arm grip on Anya's wrist, and rapidly, like a snake striking, ripped the locket from her neck and, in the same motion, backhanded it up to Zakolyev. Anya gasped and held her neck as a red line appeared on the soft throat Sergei had kissed only minutes before. She was frightened now—terrified for her husband, herself, but most of all for her child.

She would not take her eyes from Sergei—as if she could imagine that no one else was there but the two of them and that by sheer will she could make them all go away. Her eyes searched his for a glint of hope.

His eyes said, "I love you," but nothing more.

Zakolyev spoke. "Thank you for keeping this for me all these years, Sergei. And on such a lovely neck." He sniffed the locket. "Ahhh, it has her scent. I rather enjoy the aroma . . ."

Some of the men laughed, and a blood red sea flooded Sergei's vision. "You have the locket," he growled from his belly-down position. "It's yours . . . and I'm at your disposal."

"Yes, you are," Zakolyev with a lifeless smile.

"Then let my wife go—she's not part of our business. Let's face each other if that's what you want . . . but for God's sake, Dmitri, we were fellow cadets—"

"I find you tiring," Zakolyev replied, as if bored. "I have always found you tiring, Good Sergei."

He turned to Anya. "Is our Sergei also good to you in bed?" he asked. "Does he say 'please' and 'thank you' before and after?"

Zakolyev's men barked like dogs thrown a scrap from their master. He was a cat playing with its prey.

Korolev tightened his grip on Anya's wrist, and she winced, beyond Sergei's powers to help. He could feel her dread; he knew her mind and heart. She had narrowly escaped from Cossacks as a child, and it tore at Sergei's guts to watch her brave face, even as her eyes repeated the same silent prayer: "Protect the life inside me."

But Sergei lay impotent, a pawn in Zakolyev's game.

As one man searched his pockets, the others let up a little. In a rapid movement, Sergei whipped his elbow up and broke the searcher's jaw. He managed to turn and kick another man in the groin when the others fell on him with again with crushing force so that he could hardly breathe. They forced him belly down again, pinning him.

Zakolyev spoke: "So you see, Sergei, how I have become a leader of men?"

"I see what you've become."

"And you have remained what you always were—a weakling anxious to please the parents you never met." Zakolyev opened the locket. "Ah, yes, here I see your sainted mommy and daddy. I always liked this family photograph. I found it touching," he said to no one in particular as he stared at the tiny faces. Then his gaze shifted back to Sergei. "Then you stole it from me."

Sergei tasted bile rising in his throat. In that moment he knew that their luck had run out, that their prayers would not be answered. His last act would be one of desperation.

Zakolyev turned to Anya and looked her up and down. Sergei tried again to throw the men off. "This bauble means nothing to me now," he said. "Maybe I'll even give it back to the pretty wife in exchange for a little kiss."

Anya's eyes, frantic now, like the eyes of a young doe, looked to her husband. Even now she had faith that he had a plan or power to save them. Even then, with her husband pinned by all those men, a thread of hope still remained—until the leader of those men added, "On second thought, with all the trouble I've gone to over my locket, I believe it's worth more than a kiss."

Wallowing in his power, knowing that Anya was Sergei's weakness, Zakolyev said to her, while looking straight at Sergei, "Little wife, it's such a warm day, why don't you remove a little clothing so the men can enjoy a look—" He nodded again to Korolev, who released his viselike grip on Anya's wrist and ripped open her blouse. She stood, terrified, trying to cover herself and protect the child in her womb.

Sergei exploded with a superhuman ferocity, breaking free of the five who now held him down. "Run Anya! Run!" he cried out as he broke the ribs of another man before four more—all the remaining henchmen save Zakolyev and giant—fell on him like an avalanche, burying him under their weight, breaking his nose and cheek as they smashed his face down again into the dirt.

Sergei felt no pain—only an overwhelming need to protect his Anya and his absolute inability to do so. He drew upon every skill, every ounce of strength or cunning he had, to no avail.

Two words spat from Zakolyev's mouth: "Hold him!"

A hand grabbed Sergei's hair and pulled his head up to watch Korolev release Anya's wrist and roughly squeeze her full breast. Anya spat in his face, in a maternal fury now, fighting, kicking, clawing at Korolev's eyes—

Enraged, his face bleeding, Korolev reached around Anya's head, grabbed her jaw, and twisted.

With a sickening sound, Anya's neck snapped. She died three meters from Sergei's grasp.

Everything happened in slow motion after that. Sergei no longer felt as if he were in his body but rather floating above as Korolev threw Anya like a rag doll to the earth and she lay still, staring sightlessly up into the pale blue sky. His benumbed mind refused to believe what his eye beheld. It couldn't be true; it was only a nightmare; he was asleep.

But the nightmare wasn't over. Zakolyev dismounted, his brow furrowed, and walked toward Korolev. Drawing his sword, he approached the man who had just murdered Sergei's wife.

"Korolev," he said, his voice sharp, "you really must learn to control that temper of yours. You've spoiled a moment I had hoped to prolong."

The giant wisely remained silent, backed away, and remounted his horse, waiting for the Ataman's next words: "Well, not all is lost."

As Sergei stared, horrified, Zakolyev knelt by Anya's body and, almost tenderly, drew his saber across her swollen belly, opening her lower abdomen. Then he reached inside her and pulled out an infant, hanging the tiny newborn upside down, its cord still connected to its mother.

Zakolyev shook his head grimly as he saw, along with Sergei and the others, that his saber had cut too deeply—the infant was dead.

Disgusted by this ruined triumph, Zakolyev turned to face Sergei. "It was a boy," he said, dropping the dead child next to Anya's body.

Sergei screamed, trying to drown out the pain he couldn't bear. Out of the corner of his swollen eye, Sergei glimpsed a pistol swinging toward his head. Then he saw no more.

A FTER TAKING A SOUVENIR, as was his custom, Zakolyev remounted. Korolev dismounted again, drew his knife from the sheath at his side, and approached the unconscious Sergei Ivanov.

"Leave him," said Zakolyev. "I want him to live. I want him to remember."

"You have made an enemy for life—now my enemy as well," Korolev responded. "A man with nothing left to lose may be dangerous; it would be wise to kill him before he returns the favor."

"He's a weakling and a fool, and no threat to anyone," Zakolyev said sharply, aware that his men bore witness to this conversation. "Now in case you didn't hear me the first time, I said, leave him! You have done enough damage for one day." It was not a request—and the Ataman did not like to repeat himself. Ever.

Korolev hesitated, but not for long. With a shrug, he returned to his horse and remounted. To break the tension, he asked, "Ataman, why did he call you Dmitri Zakolyev?"

"It was a name I took in my youth," he said. Then louder, he called out to all his men, including those limping or being carried back to their horses, "From this day on, Gregor Stakkos is dead! I never want to hear that name again. To commemorate this day, my name to you and all concerned is now Dmitri Zakolyev—but you will call me only Ataman! To signal your assent, raise your sabers!"

They drew their sabers and pointed them skyward. After a moment's pause, Korolev did the same. Zakolyev and his men wheeled their stallions and rode out of the clearing. With a last look back at Sergei Ivanov, who lay facedown and still, Korolev turned and followed the others.

. 22 .

Sergei Ivanov came back to life with a gasp, to another life, a hellish life, called back by the shrill cries of carrion birds. Leaping to his feet, flailing and screaming like a madman, he vented his rage on the winged harpies tearing apart the remains of his wife and child. His bloody head throbbing, he forced himself to look down, but his mind could make no sense of the shards of skin hanging from the bones of a tiny hand, stretched out toward the breast of a waxen figure whose abdomen lay open to the sun.

Wrapping his family's remains in the blanket, he tried to dig a grave, scraping at the earth with his hands until his fingernails were torn and bloody, but the hard soil of summer would not yield. He could not save them, and he could not bury them. So he pounded his fist against a flat stone, watching from faraway as his knuckles cracked open.

Sergei would gladly have lain down with them upon the quiet earth but for his last duties—to find and kill Zakolyev and the man Korolev and then to tell Anya's mother and brother what happened. Only then could he face Anya's mother. If he still lived.

A hollow man, he had no fear left in him; they could not kill a man from the netherworld. Seeing nothing beyond a dark tunnel, he stumbled and groped his way toward the river, where he vomited. When the ripples cleared he saw the face of a stranger who meant nothing to him—a weakling, a coward, a fool.

Anya, the love of his life, had thawed the ice of his past until it flowed into the warmer seasons of love. Now he was chilled to the bone, shivering as he staggered aimlessly into a shadow world. Another sharp pain pierced his skull, and a sickly light flashed behind his eyes. Sergei fell to his knees and prayed for an end to memory, for an end to suffering, but neither prayer was granted. He knew who he was, where he was, and what had occurred on that day: Dmitri Zakolyev was alive; his wife and child were dead. She was the purity and goodness in this world, and it had died with her. There was no God left for him, no justice, no light remaining.

Then his head exploded again, the earth tilted, and he fell.

H E   A W O K E in darkness, as the throbbing pain flooded his head, hands, everywhere. He found himself lying on a soft bed. As he threw off the covers and started to rise, his legs gave way and he fell, knocking over a table. An older woman appeared and helped him back into bed.

"You rest," she said. "Later we'll talk if you want."

"My wife, my child . . . in a blanket—"

"Hush now. My husband saw men riding off . . . saw them taking your horse and cart. He found you and buried them proper where they lay. Now sleep."

When he awoke again, it was still dark. He heard snoring not far off as he rose on shaky feet, then sat back heavily as the haunting came and a demon whispered, "But for you, she would be alive." He could not deny this truth, or bear the pain, or end it. His penance meant living with it every moment. He would die many deaths before he could join them. Soon enough, but not yet. He had men to hunt and a mother to face.

Sergei stood again, trembling, and found his clothes, now cleaned and folded next to the bed. He turned his head and winced. Reaching up, he felt a bandage; his hands had been washed and covered with a poultice. Dressing quietly, with his shoes in a shaking hand, he wove his way toward the door. In the bare outlines of predawn, Sergei found a pen and paper on an entry table and scribbled a few words: "Thank you. I will not forget your kindness. I must go."

Back in the meadow, in the first light Sergei knelt at the mound that marked his family's grave. He spoke words of love and sorrow—but when he offered an apology, his words died in his throat. Despising himself, Sergei swore on his family's grave that he would avenge their deaths.

The tracks were not difficult to follow, at first. He traveled as quickly as he could manage on foot, limping through the day and part of the first night. His smashed nose, loose teeth, and swollen face left him in constant pain. That was good—it would keep him awake. But he had to maintain his strength, so he found a stick and sharpened it on a stone to spear fish from a stream. He ate it raw as he walked, eyes on the ground, following the hoof marks. The next day he found bird's eggs, and he picked fruit. No fires, little rest. He had no appetite but forced himself to eat, to keep moving.

Time passed in a daze of light and darkness, a sunlit, moonlit dreamscape of changing shadow. As he pushed on, reading the signs, following a map of trampled earth, Sergei thought about his father, and he finally understood how a man could drink himself to death.

Like his father, he had lost a wife and son in a single day. But Sergei's family was not taken by God; they were taken by the will of twisted men. And in taking their lives, Zakolyev and his men had ended a lineage, for Sergei would not marry again—he knew this as surely as he knew these men would die by his hand. No mere punishment would suffice, no redemption was possible. He didn't want their contrition; he wanted their heads. And from that day on, he would live for their deaths.

On THE MORNING of the third day it rained—a sudden downpour—and the tracks disappeared. He found a few broken branches, then nothing. He had lost them. With this realization, he slumped to the ground, too weak to go forward or back.

Then he thought of Valeria. She would be crazed with worry. He had to return without delay to complete the dreaded task.

On his return to St. Petersburg, Sergei's preoccupation was so deep that he did not notice the passing scene except to take bearings. When he stopped to drink from a pond, he saw reflected back to him a swollen, grime-stained face. He also noticed that his hair had turned completely white.

Then he saw the spires of the city, and he returned to the world of men. He would bring news of another world to this woman whom he had come to love as a mother, to whom he had made a promise.

GAZING UP at the apartment window, Sergei recalled the moment he had first asked for Anya's hand. And now . . . a moaning sound escaped his lip. If a man could feel worse agony, he did not know how. He walked slowly up the stairs and knocked upon the door. He heard the rush of footsteps, then as the door opened, Valeria's voice, frantic yet filled with the relief. "My God, where have you . . . " When she Sergei standing alone, her words fell away.

Her face was ashen, her graying hair disheveled, with dark circles under reddened eyes. Sergei was less recognizable than she. With his broken cheekbone, swollen nose and lips, hollow eyes, and stark white hair, he looked like a grotesque mask of his old self, a reflection of what he felt like inside.

But Valeria knew who it was, and with a horrified glance she looked past him, searching down the stairs. "Where is Anya?"

Sergei stood mutely, unable to speak.

"Where is Anya?" she repeated, her voice a whisper and a shriek. Then she looked at Sergei, and her heart knew the truth before her mind would grasp it: Anya had not come back. She would never be coming back.

Sergei caught her as she fell and set her gently onto the couch.

When her eyes opened, Valeria sat up abruptly. "Tell me what happened."

In a clipped monotone, Sergei said only, "A band of evil men came to the meadow. I was overpowered and knocked unconscious. Anya was killed. I followed them to avenge her death, but I lost their trail . . . "

Valeria refused to accept this—far better to believe he was cruel or deranged to tell her such terrible lies. Sergei sat with her in silence until the truth penetrated her heart. She finally spoke in a voice so weary it was almost a whisper. "Six days . . . and six nights of not knowing. At first I feared that you had both run away . . . later I prayed that you had . . . I tried to convince myself. But I knew that Anya would not . . . "

Then Sergei read her unspoken thoughts: Valeria had begged them to remain in St. Petersburg so she could see her grandchild. For this self-ish act of love, she would blame herself for the rest of her life.

Words would change nothing, and nothing he could say would make a difference. Sergei imagined Anya's brother, even now hard at work, losing himself in his craft while praying for his sister's safe return.

Valeria took a deep, gasping breath and with great effort asked, "Did you at least bury my daughter?"

He nodded slowly. "She's . . . in the meadow . . . "

He reached out to take her hand, but she pulled away. She finally spoke the words he most dreaded and knew were coming, the question he had asked himself a hundred times: "How is that Anya is dead and you are alive?" Sergei had no answer, so she asked another: "Here, in this room, did you not promise to protect her—to give your life for hers? Did you not make this promise?" They both knew the answer.

His eyes looked into hers, searching. "Mother, I—"

Valeria stood stiffly and said, "You let them kill her. You are a coward. You are no son of mine. Now leave this house."

He nodded and stood slowly, then entered their bedroom for the last time to fetch his few belongings. Sergei gazed at her pillow and touched the nightdress folded neatly for her return. He held it to his face and inhaled her scent. Images appeared—moments they had shared. The pain was so intense his legs gave way.

Sergei pulled himself to his feet, gathered his rucksack, knife, shovel, and a few items of clothing, and left as he had come, a lone wanderer without a family.

V ALERIA LEANED against the door. Her dry eyes stared at nothing. She hardly breathed until she realized that Andreas would soon be home, and she would have to tell him. Then a gasp escaped her, a spasm of breath. "Oh! Oh!" she sobbed and couldn't stop.

Later, like a sleepwalker, she rose and walked across the living room, hugging herself, suddenly cold. The apartment, like her body, felt empty, barren. She turned toward the hearth. Then another shrill cry of grief burst forth, a final acknowledgment that she would never see her daughter again.

Valeria pounded her fists upon the mantelpiece—once, and again—and her blows dislodged the clock resting there. She watched it tip and fall, somersaulting . . . this clock made by Heschel, from wood prepared by Benyomin's hand, tumbling down . . .

Its corner struck the floor, and with an off-key clunk it broke apart, scattering pieces that sparkled like jewels across the floor. But Valeria saw only ashes and dust before she collapsed, broken like the clock, on the living room floor.

H IS FINAL TASKS BEHIND HIM , Sergei returned to the meadow where his wife and child now lay buried and prepared himself to die. He had thought it through: he would not let his life's blood stain the earth where Anya lay; he would only lie near her grave and let hunger and thirst do their work.

One day passed. Then two . . . then three . . . then he stopped counting. Hunger had long passed. His parched lips served as small penance, his death a mere pittance on a debt he would never clear.

He did not plan to rise again.

A stream of thoughts, sounds, and emotions rose into his awareness as he lay in dreamlike reverie, random images of bygone days mixed with what might have been: his father, drinking alone in a darkened room . . . his grandfather disappearing in the distance . . . Anya, nursing their child . . . their children playing in a park in America . . .

Then mysterious impressions arose from the dark, mythic realms of his mind. He saw Charon, ferryman of the dead, a sulky old man waiting for him on the shore of Acheron, the river of woe, waiting to carry him across to the underworld, across the river Styx. But he had no coin to give the ferryman and was doomed to wander through the mists, along the rivers of the dead.

Sergei saw the river before him as he stood naked on the shore of no return, gazing down into the black water, seeing only moon and stars reflected upon the rippling surface. Then it came to him that he was not imagining this, that his body had somehow risen from the dead, and he stood on a small outcropping on the shore of the Neva. He leaned out, tipped forward, and fell down toward moon and the stars.

The shock of hitting the surface roused Sergei's heart, and it beat strongly. He gasped, then drank deeply, and the waters had a strange sort of curative power. In a moment of grace, the demon of self-hatred was cast out from him, and he turned away from the path of death.

Sergei struggled out of the river like the first creature to emerge eons past from the sea. Dripping wet, reborn on this warm summer night, he heard the voice of Alexei the Cossack in his mind: "A man is measured twice—first by his life, and then by his death." Sergei's life had come to nothing, but his death could still count for something. He decided then that he would not throw away his life, that his death would not be cheaply bought. Anya had fought bravely; he could do no less.

"Why are you alive?" Valeria had asked. He'd had no answer then, but now he knew that he had survived for a purpose. As he stood naked under the starry sky, his purpose crystallized, and it had carried him back from the underworld to the world of men.

The face of his grandfather appeared, then his mother and father, bringing a moment of sanity, a memory of love. But the moment passed. Memories alone would not sustain him; only one man had that power— and his name was Dmitri Zakolyev.

Sergei thought back on his deluded attempt to hunt down those men. How could he have imagined himself succeeding? Was he hoping for divine intervention—for a burst of superhuman strength? His training as a youth had prepared him to fight one, maybe even two or three untrained men, not an entire band of seasoned fighters. Dying was easy. It was time to live, to accomplish this task: he would train as no man had done before; he would suffer any hardship and grow stronger so that the next time he faced them he would be ready.

Even a dark purpose can keep a man alive.

On this night, as a warrior spirit possessed him, Sergei Sergeievich Ivanov became his father's son. With new clarity, patience, and resolve, he trusted that the necessary power would come in time. He would seek out those who might help prepare him. And when he was ready, he would find Zakolyev and Korolev—and he would send them to hell.

Part Four

———————

THE
WARRIOR'S
WAY

*I had not always believed
that strength could come from brokenness,
or that the thread of a divine purpose
could be seen in tragedy.
But I do now.*

MAX CLELAND

. 23 .

In THE SUMMER OF 1892, nearing his twentieth birthday, Sergei Ivanov set out on his quest to become an invincible warrior.

As he walked south, Sergei could still picture Alexei the Cossack pacing before his enthralled audience of cadets, reminding them, "One does not cut down a tree with a dull ax or rush into battle unprepared. To defeat an enemy, you must know the enemy. To know the enemy, you must first know yourself. Face your own demons now before you confront them on the battlefield."

His inner demons. Of late Sergei had made their intimate acquaintance: He still had trouble focusing on a task for more than a few moments before the recent horrors rose up to haunt him. And his emaciated body needed to heal before he could even begin to train seriously.

He had returned to the forested hills again, where he found a quiet stream and made camp. There he set traps and fished and hunted. He drank the pure water of rushing steams and returned to his cold-water dousings each morning. In the evenings he sat in quiet contemplation, gazing into the flames of his campfire.

At first his ribs stuck out, but as the weeks passed, the late summer brought ripe fruits and berries to supplement his simple, nourishing diet. He began to stretch in a relaxed yet rigorous way, and he added strength-building exercises for his abdomen, back, arms, and legs. At first he recalled what he had learned as a youth, but as time passed he relied more on his instincts.

The hills and woods offered many opportunities to increase his vigor.

He walked, then ran uphill and upstream. He would go on long, slow runs for ten kilometers over hills and rough terrain, with intermittent bursts of speed as spirit moved him.

Each day he imagined that he was facing the giant Korolev, then Zakolyev, then two, then three, then four. He fought phantoms, boxed shadows, ducked and evaded and rolled, refining movements he had learned in the past. He fought until he was drenched in sweat—ten minutes, twenty minutes, thirty minutes, or more—imagining enemies leaping out from behind the trees and boulders, from every possible line of attack, with every weapon. He formulated how he would respond— and he defeated them all.

It was easy enough to do in his imagination. But when the time came, he would have to end each confrontation in seconds, not minutes. To destroy these renegade Cossacks, he would seek out the best Cossack fighters and train with them. By mid-October, Sergei was ready to travel farther south.

H E   J O U R N E Y E D   O N   F O O T —walking, running, and fighting shad- ows, developing his stamina, looking for any opportunity to better him- self as he traveled south along the River Don.

As the December winds blew and the snowfall deepened, it came to Sergei that he needed a horse. If he were to find the training he sought from Cossacks, he needed to arrive on a mount. Besides, a horse would allow him to cover more ground in less time, and time was precious.

The three remaining gold coins, and nearly two hundred rubles he had earned, remained in the pouch in his knapsack with his other pos- sessions. The coins would enable Sergei to purchase a suitable horse; the rest would serve for future needs that might arise. When a man has learned to live without money, a few rubles can go a long way. That was good, because he had a long way to go. Had Sergei thought about it, he would have left money for Valeria, but she would not have accepted it, and at the time he had not been able to think about anything.

He inquired at each farm he passed whether they had a horse for sale. Some days later, in exchange for the three remaining gold coins and a hundred of Sergei's remaining rubles, a farmer was willing to part with a strong-looking stallion. He also gave Sergei a blanket, saddle, bridle, and bit.

"He's a bit skittish, doesn't take to the plow or wagon," the farmer said as they closed the deal.

As it turned out, the horse didn't much take to a rider either. But Sergei had learned enough about horses in his youth to reach an understanding with the animal. After some bucking and bargaining, the horse calmed down. He named the horse Dikar, "wild and crazy."

After another week in the saddle, a bond grew between Sergei and Dikar. He reminded himself that the horse was a creature, not a possession like his knapsack or the saber or clothing he had purchased in a nearby town. The horse carried him, and he would care for its needs.

THE WINTER went easier atop his horse, with Sergei wearing the long Cossack waistcoat and the burka, a long felt cape, to keep out the winds that sometimes threatened to tear him from his mount. But Dikar was stolid enough, and if he could weather the storms, so could his rider.

Several months after heading south, in early spring just before the thaw, Sergei came to a settlement near the shores of the Don. This small community had the appearance of a simple village, but only the most ignorant of bandits would venture among these men and women, among the most formidable fighters the world had seen.

Chimney smoke mixed with a late powder of snow as Sergei entered the settlement, passing between the first cabins of birch logs scattered under a sparse covering of shade trees. The clearing was about two hundred meters from the river. He could see that its placement was strategic. The encampment rested on ground high enough to escape flooding should the Don overflow its banks. A forest of birch and pine stood near enough to form a windbreak in rough weather but not so close as to provide cover for unfriendly observers. He saw a few boys scurry about; an elderly man, wrapped in a woolen coat, sat in a chair and smoked a pipe.

Hearing hoofbeats behind him, Sergei turned to see a rider pull up alongside until their horses walked shoulder to shoulder. With a glance, he took in the man's traditional Cossack dress—the soft leather *cheviaki,* or boots, and a *cherkesska,* the belted, long-sleeved black coat, and a row of cartridge pouches on his chest. His burka, which served as a blanket, tent, or head cover from winter winds or the burning summer sun, was folded neatly over the man's saddle. He also carried a saber at his side and carbine slung over his shoulder.

A few sturdy-looking women came out to greet the riders who followed close behind. Several younger women carried infants on their backs, leaving their hands free to fight if need be, according to custom.

The Cossack riding alongside Sergei—about ten years his senior, with a powerful frame and a shaggy mane of light hair—nodded in welcome. Taking his measure, Sergei sensed that this man could be a good friend or dangerous adversary. The Cossack asked in a clipped local accent, "Do you pass through, stranger, or look for shelter?"

Sergei answered in kind: "I come to learn."

"To learn what?" he asked.

"To fight," he said.

The Cossack laughed and turned to smile back at a few other riders near enough to hear. "Well, you've come to the right place," he said.

"And the right man," said one of his companions.

He introduced himself as Leonid Anatolevich Chykalenko. As the men were in need of some light amusement, that afternoon a match was arranged in the barn—a relatively private affair, with friendly bets among the spectators. Sergei lost the first match and won the second, surprising Leonid and the spectators and earning their respect. The third was called a draw. Sergei found Leonid swift and skilled and clever in his tactics. But his own intense physical preparation and training had paid off. This match—the first with a real adversary since his overwhelming defeat against Zakolyev's men—boosted his confidence. He had expected to fare worse.

Sergei offered his compliments, telling the Cossack quite honestly that he was one of the most formidable men he had fought and that he had learned much of value from him during their match. He left with friendly farewells and a personal reminder that there were good people in the world—and for a fleeting moment, he felt a pull to stay for a time, here in this quiet village, and become one of them. But the moment quickly passed, for his path led elsewhere and allowed no such delays.

Sergei met with a similar experience in the next Cossack settlement, and the one after. Each victory revealed the strength, speed, and skill he had acquired over those months, fighting with shadows. But to defeat Zakolyev and his Cossacks, Sergei would have to go beyond Cossacks. Fighting friendly matches with a single opponent was one thing; battles to the death with multiple opponents were quite another. Sergei needed another mentor like Alexei, who rose not only above other men but above other Cossacks as well.

He recalled a conversation with Leonid Chykalenko and a few other men after their evening meal. When Sergei had expressed his wish to find a master of combat, no one responded. But few minutes later, as the men gazed into the crackling fire on the hearth, Leonid said, "I've heard rumors about a swordsman who lives alone in the forest, southeast of the Don—somewhere near a kut, a few Cossack huts, in the hills around Kotelnikovo. I was told that he traveled widely as a young man . . . trained with the samurai of Japan . . . and gained audience with their last great ataman, the Shogun, where he disarmed one of their samurai before the warrior could even draw his blade."

"His name?" Sergei asked.

"No one knows for certain, though I've heard he calls himself Razin."

. 24 .

On a windy March day in 1893, Korolev returned from hunting with a deer carcass slung over his back. As he entered the temporary camp, he saw one of the new men, Stachev, a heavy drinker, stumble unevenly toward his hut, then fall facedown.

Oddly, the way Stachev fell reminded Korolev of the day, some months before, when the Ataman had found that man Ivanov and his woman and thrown him facedown, then let him live—a foolish thing to do. No matter now. They had traveled south again to the warmer plains between Kharkov and the river Dniepr. Besides, Ivanov was no more than a pissant to Korolev, certainly not worth remembering.

Yet the one-armed giant did remember because of the change in Stakkos since that day. Not only had the Ataman taken a new name—Dmitri Zakolyev—but having settled a score, his mood had improved. Except for an incident that had occurred a few days later, Korolev recalled.

After every raid, as a cautionary measure, Zakolyev sent Tomorov the scout back along their trail to check for any signs of pursuit. After the incident with Zakolyev's old foe, Tomorov returned and reported, "I saw only a family traveling by wagon, and a white-haired old man resembling the one we left behind, stumbling along on foot—"

When Tomorov saw Zakolyev's expression, the scout quickly added, "He couldn't have been the same man, Ataman—his hair . . ."

Zakolyev sent Tomorov to find the man, kill him, and bring back the body.

When Tomorov returned empty-handed, Zakolyev announced that the band would move on once again.

A month later they found a camp far to the south and west, not far from Romania's Carpathian Mountains. From that camp, they patrolled the border like regular Cossacks. They also resumed their methodical raids, once every few months. Everything returned to normal, including Zakolyev's nightmares.

Korolev knew of the Ataman's troubled sleep; he made it his business to know everything. The few men who courted his favor, and the women who were terrified of him, were quick to report anything of interest they had learned. But they could not inform him of the contents of Zakolyev's mind. Korolev would have cut off his braid to know what disturbed the Ataman's sleep. Yes, that would be worth something. He studied the Ataman as one might study an animal in its natural habitat. But Zakolyev remained an enigma, and Korolev did not like puzzles; he either solved them or smashed them to bits.

At first it seemed that Zakolyev had no weaknesses. He lived like a Spartan; he no longer seemed interested in the women. He drank rarely. The Ataman was a model of virtue, except for his penchant for killing the Jews. It was just his nature, Korolev surmised: Scorpions sting; Zakolyev kills Jews.

Korolev found only one possible flaw in Zakolyev's armor, and that was the Ataman's strange attachment to children. Zakolyev actually *liked* the little beasts, especially the young suckling whelps who didn't know any better, who would smile and coo at the devil himself. Only when the children grew past infancy, and the Ataman saw the fear in their eyes, did he lose interest in them except as servants or new blood to carry on his dynasty.

Among those born or adopted into the tribe, the Ataman seemed especially taken with two of the new children—a boy, Konstantin, and a girl he had named Paulina. Just after her arrival—when her cry was heard in the night—Zakolyev had claimed the child as his own. He proclaimed that the woman Elena was the child's mother but that Shura would care for his daughter; the older woman was better suited for such maternal duties.

Once, after the child had grasped the Ataman's finger, he remarked with paternal pride, "A strong baby, is she not?" Shura agreed, as she always did. Whatever the Ataman said became truth.

In her forties, Shura was the oldest woman and first female to join the band. Disfigured by scars on her cheek, neck, and one breast as a result of childhood burns, she was befriended by Great Yergovich, the only other elder in the tribe. He did not approve of the younger men inflicting their lusts on the poor woman, but things were as they were. Fortunately, she was one of the few women that Korolev ignored.

Shura had a foul mouth and would complain loudly to anyone who would listen. Mostly she talked to herself. Careful not to complain in front of the Ataman, she grumbled about little things: the weather; the knots in the girls' hair as she pulled out their tangles. The girls would run the other way when they saw Shura with her wooden comb.

Widowed years before when her man was killed in a drunken brawl, Shura had followed her son, Tomorov, when he had taken up with Zakolyev. The Ataman permitted her no motherly indulgence. "If your children become a problem," he told her, "they will be left behind." She understood what this meant. She also understood that when the girls were old enough to attract any of the men, they would be used as the men pleased.

All but the child Paulina.

The Ataman's other favored child, Konstantin, knew his place and played the admiring pup. It was a natural role for this curious boy with large dark eyes and a tousle of hair to match. When Zakolyev looked upon the boy, sometimes he almost smiled, and other times one might even think he was sad—about what, Korolev could not guess.

For his part, Korolev could barely tolerate the Ataman's displays of sentiment—patting his favorites on the head and insisting that they call him "Father Dmitri." It was disgusting. Still, Korolev was glad he had found this one flaw, because once you know what a man cares about, you know where to stick the knife.

Korolev also found distasteful Zakolyev's passion for stealing the belongings of the dead Jews. Killing was one thing, but acting like a common thief was another. And the way the Ataman pored over these mementos back in camp made no sense. Taking money, gold, and jewelry one might understand—but coveting soiled goods, journals, and photographs of those they had killed? Trinkets and memorabilia? Korolev was not a superstitious fool, but any man could see that one should not bring such things back to camp.

Although the Ataman had grown more eccentric as time passed, he maintained his authority—and the raids remained the same: The scouts continued to ride at least two days' distance—north, south, east, or west, never the same direction twice. They would note the locations of isolated huts, cabins, or small farms, observing from a distance until they could determine who lived there and whether they were Jews. Sometimes one scout would leave his horse with the others and walk to the door asking directions. If they saw women, all the better.

Eventually two other women, Oxana and Tatyana, had joined the band—bored girls plucked not unwillingly from their native villages. Now four of the nine children in the tribe had been born to Elena, Oxana, or Tatyana, but no one kept track anymore.

Despite their normal appearances, the men and women of Zakolyev's camp were outsiders and outlaws. Friendly enough to their own kind, they had lost any veneer of civilization when seeking prey. Murdering on orders of the Ataman—some with reluctance, others with pleasure—they had given their souls to Dmitri Zakolyev and become extensions of his mind, servants of his will.

.25.

SERGEI RODE SOUTH along the river, then east, where he found several more Cossack camps. He considered seeking more contests but thought better of it; to defeat Cossacks he had to go beyond them. That meant finding the swordsman Razin. He was committed to this. Leonid Chykalenko's mention of this man seemed more than chance. His search concentrated into a single-minded passion.

Looking for a few small huts hidden in the shade of a forest was no simple task. Sergei asked many locals, but their directions were vague and conflicting. After three months he began to doubt the man's existence. He had heard other legends about warriors, but most were folktales. Still, he pushed on.

A few weeks later Sergei's pulse quickened when he came upon a likely group of huts in the forest. He saw an old woman peering out of a makeshift door, and he asked her if she had heard of a skilled swordsman. She stared at him for a time, as if trying to discern his intentions. Then she pointed toward a thatched roof on a rise barely visible among the trees. Her door closed before he could thank her.

Sergei rode to the hut, dismounted, and knocked lightly on the door. No answer. He tapped again. Suddenly he felt a saber point between his shoulder blades.

Sergei considered spinning and taking the saber as he had been trained but thought better of it. If this swordsman had wanted to kill him, he already would have done so. A husky voice behind him said, "Your business?"

"I wish to learn from the sword master Razin," he said. The point of the saber pierced the first layer of his skin.

"Who sent you?"

"A . . . a Cossack . . . he had heard of your skills . . . "

"I no longer teach. Go away!" Lowering his blade, he glided past Sergei into his hut and closed the door.

Sergei knocked again.

"I said go away!" His voice was soft but guttural, like a growl. There was no mistaking it—this was a dangerous man.

"If I could explain—I believe that I am meant to learn from you—"

"Do not disturb me again!" said the gruff voice. Sergei caught only another glimpse of the lean, almost emaciated face—the sharp cheekbones, dark eyes, sun-darkened skin, and shaved head—before the door slammed again.

Sergei had found the sword master—he had no doubt—the teacher who might make the difference between success and failure. He had searched too many months to turn around and go. Sergei's horse was weary, and so was he. The sense of destiny infused him once again.

He remembered something Alexei had said—or was it his uncle Vladimir? "The soldier must commit fully to any action."

There was nothing else to be done but to sit in place until Razin accepted him as a student.

Dikar had not volunteered for hardship duty, so Sergei led the stallion twenty meters off into the forest near a stream and hobbled him under the cover of pine trees. Although it was cold, the air was not biting, and short of a late blizzard, Dikar's winter coat would keep him warm enough. He had eaten a generous helping of hay at a farm the day before and could graze at the river's edge.

Sergei returned and sat cross-legged, his back against a tree, in front of this reclusive master's hut. An hour passed . . . two hours . . . four hours. His body grew cold and stiff, then numb. He could no longer feel his hands or arms or legs. A fit of shivering came and went, and then he grew drowsy. Sometime in the night he fell over and painfully forced himself back to a sitting position. The motion brought back a little circulation, biting painfully at every nerve.

He grew hungry, but the hunger passed. The new day, clear and cold, brought a stream of memories—some welcome, others not: Anya and he walking, laughing, through the streets of St. Petersburg, in the sunlight—then the horror came, and he saw Zakolyev's dead smile, and Korolev, tearing her clothes—

Sergei sat up straight, his resolve turned to iron.

As the sun crept overhead, providing scant warmth, it occurred to him that Razin didn't even know he was here. He might have gone away. Even as these concerns arose, he heard the door open, then barely audible footsteps recede into the forest and, later, return. No, Razin could not fail to notice Sergei's vigil but was apparently ignoring him.

By nightfall of the second day, Sergei wasn't sure he could move if he'd wanted to. His tongue snaked out from between cracked lips in search of water, even if from the random snowflake. Then dawn came, and time ceased to have meaning. Another night, then a third day. During moments of clarity, between random dream images, Sergei wondered whether he had lost his mind. Where did determination end and obsession begin?

The day passed by, and then it was dark, and he drifted in and out of awareness. Then he thought he saw a trace of light, and he remembered nothing more.

A VOICE called him back into the world. "All right," it said, from a faraway place. Suddenly louder: "I don't want your corpse stinking up my place. Get up!"

Sergei tried to move but couldn't. He felt strong arms lift him, but he couldn't stand. So Razin left him sitting and returned with a pail of water. He poured most of it over Sergei's head—like heaven raining down—and it woke his arms and legs. Sergei couldn't tell if the water was hot or cold. Then Razin gave him a sip of water. "Not too much!" he said curtly.

After a time Sergei could move a little more. He rubbed his feet with increasing vigor. Finally, he rolled over and struggled to stand, dizzy and weak. Razin brought him into the hut and gave him a dried apricot. "Chew it slowly!" he said, handing Sergei warm tea and a cube of sugar through which to sip the liquid in the Russian manner.

"Sit there!" he said, directing Sergei to the large fireplace. Over the fire hung a large iron cooking pot. Inside was a steaming soup of barley and pieces of winter vegetables, with a little meat. "Stir the soup well, then fill both our bowls!" he instructed, and left Sergei alone for a time.

He did as Razin had asked.

When Razin returned, he told Sergei that he was to eat by the fire; Razin would eat at his small table. Then he gave Sergei more water to drink.

When Sergei had finished, Razin told him to wash both their bowls, adding, "I may consent to teach you. We will see . . . "

Razin pointed to the cooking pot over the hearth. "Most important— for my soup every night." He showed Sergei his stores of barley, oats, and kasha—buckwheat groats—and a small garden of winter vegetables he was to tend. He pointed to the pit toilet outside. "Keep it clean!" So Sergei was to cook Razin's food, sweep the floors, wash his clothes, and clean his latrine, burying the waste in a hole he would dig in the woods.

He pointed to extra oats and barley. "For the horse," he said, then pointed back toward the old woman's hut and the small barn nearby. "Keep your horse there. Go now and take care of it. Then return and begin your chores."

Sergei rose and left the hut. He attended to Dikar, feeding him a good portion of oats and barley, then took him to the small barn, where he removed the saddle and blanket. Then he returned to the hut and prepared to clean.

OVER THE NEXT FEW DAYS Sergei did his best to please this sinewy old warrior, without success. Razin always seemed irritated, barking one order after another. Without comment or complaint, Sergei made soup, stirring the vegetables and groats with a large wooden spoon, covering it to simmer with the heavy iron lid. Razin only grunted when he tasted it. After he ate, he indicated with another grunt that Sergei could also take some.

Between chores, Sergei also went foraging in the forest, gathering eggs and catching a few rabbits. He also managed to walk Dikar, explore his immediate surroundings, and do some limbering exercises.

As the week turned to two, then three, Sergei went beyond what Razin demanded and made simple improvements and repairs—fixing the door and a loose window that rattled in the wind. Finally he grew impatient. Surely I must have earned at least some goodwill, he thought—at least a relaxing of his sour demeanor. But Razin showed no sign of changing. With all of Sergei's sweeping, cleaning, washing, folding, and cooking, Razin said nothing about teaching him.

Four weeks had passed; it was the middle of May. He could wait no longer. That evening, as he served his food, he said, "Master Razin, I hope—"

"Not Master Razin," the sword master interrupted. "Just Razin."

He nodded, then continued: "I've done my best with my duties . . . I hope you have found them satisfactory."

Razin answered with a grunt.

"So I need to know whether I have earned the right to train with you." Razin glared at him in a way that made the hairs stand up on his neck. He started to turn away, with the question unresolved, so he added, "I am on a mission that I can't delay much longer. It is a matter of life and death."

Razin turned back slowly to face Sergei. "It is always a matter of life and death with you young people."

Sergei decided he had to tell him; there seemed to be no other way to gain his cooperation. "Some men posing as Cossacks murdered my family. They will kill many more innocent people. I have to stop them. You had promised to teach—"

"I promised nothing!" Razin said, then stormed out of the room.

Sergei was at a loss. Was this old man a charlatan? A liar? Was Sergei being used—taken as a fool? Had he spent this time for nothing?

That evening, as Sergei sat near the fire stirring the stew, he was suddenly struck in the head with such force that the blow nearly knocked him unconscious. Stunned, thinking a log had fallen from the ceiling, he rolled over.

Razin was standing over him, holding a wooden staff.

The man's face was blank—no scowl of anger, nothing. He turned calmly, walked over to his chair, leaned the staff against the wall, and sat. Then he took out a book and began to read. Sergei's hand went to his bleeding scalp, where he felt a large lump rising.

So Razin *was* crazy. And mean-spirited. Sergei was about to head for the door, but something held him in place. It was already night, after all; he would think more clearly in the morning.

As it turned out, he didn't get much sleep that night. As soon as he drifted off, whack—he awoke in a panic, sitting up, waving his arms at nothing. He glimpsed Razin's back as the old man returned to his cot.

Rubbing the welt on his shin, Sergei finally fell back to an uneasy sleep, but not for long. Sometime before dawn he was awakened in a similar fashion, to a new bruise. Yawning, he went outside for his morning immersion in the stream. The icy water numbed his aching body.

That day, and every day for the next week, each time Sergei was distracted or preoccupied, Razin would strike, quick and silent as the wind. Sergei would have defended himself, but Razin continually caught him unaware. Pain became such a constant that Sergei forgot what it felt like to be free of it.

Each time he was nearly ready to end the abuse, he realized that he was not a prisoner—that any moment he could walk out, mount Dikar, and ride away. That thought kept him in place. One more day, one more hour, one more minute. This might be an initiation for all potential students—a test of sincerity. If he passed this, Sergei felt certain that Razin would teach him something of value.

Day and night the blows rained down—ten, twenty, thirty—until he lost count. Meanwhile, Sergei continued with his duties and slept with eyes half open.

Two nights later, Sergei jerked awake without knowing why. He did not sense Razin near, so he was about to go back to sleep. But just then the idea came to him that he would turn the tables . . .

It took him nearly twenty minutes to move the five or six meters from his sleeping pad to Razin's cot, feeling his way through pitch darkness until he reached the cot. Anticipating the surprise he was about to deliver, Sergei lifted the straw pillow he had carried and swung it down—

It struck an empty cot.

The hairs stood up on the back of his neck as Sergei realized that Razin might even now be stalking him in the darkness—not with a stick, but with a sword. He whirled around—

No one was there. Disappointed, Sergei walked back to his mattress, where he found Razin, asleep in his bed.

Sergei didn't sleep the rest of the night. And in daylight he felt a constant state of nervous alertness and anxiety, expecting a blow any moment, feeling his way around corners, ready to raise a protective hand.

Then it happened, when he least expected it: One evening, just as he was lifting the lid off the pot to stir the stew, his arm abruptly moved the lid above his head, just as Razin's blow came whipping down. The stick clanged against the iron lid. Surprised, he spun around to see Razin gazing at him.

A smile spread across Razin's face—the first Sergei had seen.

Emboldened, he said, "Razin, does this mean my training can begin?"

"No," the old man answered. "Your training is complete. You may leave."

In that moment Sergei understood Razin's gift. All those attacks . . . an initiation . . . Razin had been teaching to move instinctively.

Sergei was finally ready for Zakolyev.

IT WAS TIME TO GO. Sergei had saddled Dikar and prepared to mount when he sensed someone behind him and spun around to see Razin standing nearby.

Razin nodded. "Good. You haven't wasted my time."

"Then you think I'm ready to face these men?"

"Of course not! But you may be ready to learn . . . "

Razin was a man of few words, so Sergei thought he had finished. But as he mounted Dikar, Razin added, "There is a master—far better than I. "

"With the sword?"

"With everything. Anything. Nothing. I saw him fight a hundred opponents, one after the other; he was never defeated. He could throw a man without touching him."

Razin paused again. "I heard he lived on the island of Valaam . . . in Lake Ladoga. He may be useful . . . "

Razin stopped himself, deciding he had said enough. With a nod, he turned and disappeared into the woods.

. 2 6 .

SERGEI THOUGHT about Lake Ladoga as Dikar carried him west toward the river Don. He thought about the two long journeys he had made to the south of Russia—after fleeing from the school and now, to prepare himself to kill Zakolyev and the others. They were likely raiding in this southern region, in the Jewish Pale of Settlement to the west. He had no intention of riding a thousand kilometers north once again, simply because Razin mentioned a mysterious warrior from years past on some island, who might not even be there and might not teach him anyway.

But the mention of Lake Ladoga, less than a hundred kilometers from the meadow, brought a sharp stab of anguish. Sergei shivered, thinking about his wife and child in the cold ground. No, he would not delay his hunt any longer. He turned his horse west.

That May of 1893, Sergei crossed the Don and headed toward Ukraine, the Dniepr River basin, and the Jewish territories.

Two days later, the enormity of his task sank in. Looking at his map, Sergei traced his finger across a few centimeters of area. How easily his fingernail traversed hills or seas, flying over prairie, forest, and farmland. But when he gazed at the terrain before him—rivers to ford, rocky grades, and vast stretches of land across Ukraine—he realized what little chance he had to find his quarry. He had nothing to go on but rumors. It was like trying to catch a fly that someone had seen buzzing through a room three days before.

A<small>FTER MONTHS</small> riding zigzag patterns—passing Kharkov, Poltava, Kiev, across the region—Sergei had made almost no progress. One Jewish shopkeeper had heard talk of Cossack brigands to the west; other locals were certain such men were last seen in the east . . . or north . . . or south. One farmer reported hearing from a friend who had heard from another friend about phantoms who rode in the night to kill and burn, then dissolved into mist before the morning light.

Another year had passed, an eternity of days in which hope dwindled with the passing hours and died with each sunset, then was born anew with the dawn. By August of 1894, under a baking sun, as he wiped his brow and sweat stung his eyes, Sergei thought fondly of winter snows. Dikar was thirsty and ornery, pulling at the reins and dropping his head at any sign of water. Summer passed as had the previous spring.

That autumn Sergei turned twenty-two on the open plains, riding on from one settlement to the next. He found the ruins of several farms but nothing more. No tracks or traces remained by the time he arrived. Maybe that farmer was right; he might as well have been following ghosts.

In the summer he had slept under the starry sky; now that the autumn winds had come, he and Dikar occasionally took shelter in the barn of a farmer.

By December, after marking his map with the few, isolated, burned-out farms, and putting dots where people had heard rumors of attacks, he looked for patterns or meaningful lines, but it all seemed entirely random. Discouraged, he rode on. There was nothing else to do.

As flakes of scattered snow drifted down near Vinnitsa, on the shores of the Southern Bug River southwest of Kiev, Sergei learned that Tsar Aleksandr III had died and the reign of Nicholas II had begun.

Such news seemed faraway as his hunt for Zakolyev continued.

By THE END of a long winter, growing doubts pulled Sergei into a deepening depression. He had trained. He had fought skillful Cossacks. Razin had honed his instincts. But Sergei was nowhere closer to finding Zakolyev than the day he had lost their tracks three years before. Had he wasted those years? Would he spend three or six or ten more years like them?

Even Dikar walked listlessly, like a riderless horse. The pale sun had no power to thaw the rivers or his bones. But Sergei rode on despite fading hopes, under gray skies, through falling snow. In moments, Sergei believed he had already died and now rode through a purgatory of lost souls. He put his head in his hands and wept.

But spring did come, and the season brought warmth if not hope. One month followed the next. Summer came and passed. Then, on an afternoon in October, when sky was threatening a cold rain and the wind began to gust, Sergei approached a village. He set up camp in the woods outside of town, hobbled Dikar to graze, and set out to stretch his legs by walking into the town where he might find a clue or scrap of information. Or maybe just a friendly face.

Just outside the town walls, he encountered four men, roughly dressed—sauntering as if they had been drinking. Sergei kept his gaze forward, but one of the men blocked his way and accosted him. "Why do you come to our village, stranger? Do you need food or women?"

"You will find the food better than the women!" said one of the others, elbowing the first, apparently their leader. All four of them laughed.

Sergei smiled. But when he tried to walk around them, their mood changed abruptly. A second man stepped into his path. Then the leader explained, "You must pay the toll to enter the town on this road."

To avoid trouble, Sergei shrugged and turned to leave, only to find the others blocking his path. "This way is even more expensive," said one of them, the largest.

"I don't wish to trouble you," Sergei said. "I'm only looking for a band of—"

Their leader interrupted him, mistaking Sergei's courtesy for weakness or fear. "Maybe you didn't hear. You must pay us now."

Clearly, these ruffians were set on robbing Sergei and giving him a beating in the bargain. He observed them calmly as they took his measure, a lone, white-haired man.

"I don't want any trouble," said Sergei. "Just let me pass and I'll wish you a good day."

"Not without your toll," said the one, pulling a knife from his belt. He moved closer; the others followed. Just as the thug with the knife stepped forward, Sergei kicked the inside of his knee, throwing him off balance; he then grabbed the man's hair and twisted the knife from his hand. Having disarmed him, Sergei threw him to the ground. The others, surprised, were caught off balance, giving Sergei time to deal with the two closest men. He stunned one with a trinity of blows and held the other off with a kick. Then the fourth ruffian got in a lucky shot from behind—he clipped Sergei on the side of his head—and for a moment everything went dark. On the ground, Sergei felt a kick to his side, then another.

Lying there, covering his head, Sergei saw flashing images from a time past, when he suffered other such blows, outnumbered by Zakolyev's men. Suddenly enraged, which may have saved his life, Sergei rolled abruptly away from the men and came up facing them. He took down the first man who came in, then disabled the next man with a stomping heel kick to the thigh. The third man threw a sloppy, glancing kick. Sergei grabbed his leg and twisted—he heard a snap and a cry of pain. Then his arm went up instinctively and deflected a punch he didn't even know was coming. Kicking his heel back and up, he connected with the groin of another man behind him. At that point the last man still standing lost heart—and they all withdrew, limping off, sulking.

Panting, Sergei took stock: His head hurt, and his ears were ringing—he would be sore the next day—but he had no disabling injuries. Shaking it off, he continued into town to make the usual inquiries. Learning no more than he already knew, he was soon heading back into the forest to spend another quiet night with Dikar for company, as he had done many nights before.

That evening, from under his lean-to, Sergei gazed into the flames of his crackling fire. He thought of the four swaggering drunks who had nearly beaten him. "Never underestimate an adversary," he muttered to himself, recalling Alexei's advice of years before. Then an old proverb came to mind: I hear and I forget; I see and I remember; I do and I understand.

Now Sergei understood: Drunk or not, those men likely had been soldiers in their youth and were hardened by past battles. He had underestimated them, a nearly fatal mistake and a lesson he would not forget.

His own combat experience was limited to boyhood wrestling matches, a few fights, and his struggle with Zakolyev outside the school long ago—then his utter devastation by Zakolyev's men . . .

As Sergei's eyes grew heavy, scenes flashed before him of his training these past months—fighting shadows, and Leonid, and Razin. That's when the sword master's words came back to him, about the master of combat on an island in Lake Ladoga . . .

He fell into a restless slumber and dreamed he was fighting phantoms . . . five Zakolyevs, ten Korolevs, then more and more and more . . .

Then they vanished and he found himself lying on his straw bed in Razin's hut, unable to move, staring up at the swordsman standing over him, about to strike—not with a stick but with a saber. Sergei could only stare, wide-eyed, as Razin cut downward—

Jarred awake by a crack that sounded like a gunshot, still half dreaming, Sergei threw his body to the side to avoid Razin's anticipated blow just as a large tree branch crashed down, with a crackle and a thud, smashing the lean-to where he had been sleeping moments before. The ground shook with the impact. Sergei leaped to his feet, confused, half expecting to see Razin there, until dreams and reality sorted themselves out.

He took a deep breath, a new resolve taking shape in his mind. Then he turned toward Dikar, to find that dreams and reality had merged. Sergei's breath caught in his throat as he saw his horse lying crushed and broken beneath the trunk of the fallen tree. He rushed to the stallion but found no signs of life.

Using his shovel, Sergei dug for half the day in a deep sorrow. When the large area was hollowed out, he rolled over his brave and loyal horse into the shallow grave. He covered him and said a few words. "You carried me far, valiant friend, and never complained." A sense of loss overwhelmed him. He had lost too much in his life—parents, grandfather, wife, and child—and now this innocent animal, a good and loyal a companion.

The sharp pangs of loss reminded Sergei once again of the reason for his journey. Not that he needed any more reminders. After stripping off his sweat-stained clothing, he immersed himself in the icy stream, ate the last of his stored food, and set out on foot, leaving behind the saddle to mark his horse's grave. He followed the river Don, north once again.

Razin was right, thought Sergei; I'm not ready to confront Zakolyev or the others. Not until I've found the master on Valaam. If he exists at all.

Then as he set out, once again on foot, over rolling hills and across broad plains, another understanding grew in Sergei's mind: To bring down Zakolyev and his minions, it would not be enough to train with a master. He would have to become one.

It took six more months to reach St. Petersburg on foot. Once again Sergei drew upon his survival skills and his will, each step of the thousand-kilometer trek. Leaning into frigid winter winds, he was bone tired as he drew near the city of St. Petersburg. Once again Sergei had arrived as unkempt as before, with his beard and long white hair.

Seeing Valeria and Andreas was out of the question; he would not open old wounds. Far better to leave them to whatever peace they had made with their loss. Neither would he rent a room for the night. He would need his few remaining rubles for passage by boat across Lake Ladoga to the monastery island of Valaam.

Near dusk, near the banks of the Neva, he reached the meadow and his family's grave. The site was overgrown, but the small marker remained. Before he slept, Sergei sat by the weathered mound of earth and spoke to Anya. He renewed their marriage vows in spirit and promised again that her death would serve some higher purpose. He also renewed his pledge to save innocent lives by ridding the world of Dmitri Zakolyev and his henchmen. Then he bid Anya good-night as he had while she lived: "You are my heart," he told her, reaching down and touching the earth where she rested.

His dreams that night were peaceful and sad, filled with love and longing. He felt Anya with him, as if her hand were stroking his hair, her kisses cooling his brow, as the night winds blew.

So it was that in the spring of 1896 Sergei walked to the docks and boarded the next boat heading up the Neva, north across Ladoga, to the monastery island.

Part Five

THE

MONASTERY

ISLAND

Softness triumphs over hardness, gentleness over strength.
The flexible is superior over the immovable.
This is the principle of controlling things
by going along with them,
of mastery through adaptation.

LAO-TZU

. 27 .

During the twelve hours it took for the two-masted ship to sail across windblown waters, Sergei spoke with several pilgrims on their way to the monastery. He learned that Valaam was the largest of many islands in Lake Ladoga but measured only seven kilometers side to side, with a few smaller islands just offshore. Dense forest and steep cliffs guarded the island's coast, but as the schooner rounded an outcropping, a small bay came into view, followed by the topmost tower of the main monastery—a huge, gleaming white fortress, eight centuries old, with spires of brilliant blue topped with gold. It was as if he were sailing into a bay of dreams.

Several pilgrims had spoken of tranquil inner lakes hidden in the primeval forest, bluffs, and glades. In addition to the main monastery, the center of community life, they told him, smaller, secluded hermitages called *sketes* were scattered about the island. These were inhabited by monks seeking deeper seclusion. Even more isolated were the tiny hermitage huts and caves, and even some holes in the ground where hermit monks worked and prayed in complete solitude. As one pilgrim put it, "No one lives there but the monk and God, until only God remains."

One brother returning to the monastery told him that it had been destroyed many times in the past since the pacifist monks refused to fight when Swedes annexed the island before Peter the Great reclaimed it. Strange, thought Sergei, looking for a warrior in a community of nonviolent monks. Sergei expected that this kind of man might stand out in such a place. In any case, if he were here, Sergei would find him.

If he wanted to be found.

SERGEI MADE a temporary camp in an isolated section of the forest covered with lichen, ferns, and growing blossoms as the late spring took hold. In the days that followed, he crisscrossed the island, walking past the small farm that supplied the island with milk and vegetables, past the isolated sketes and the tiny hermitage huts scattered about the woods. As the weeks passed, Sergei carefully watched the black-garbed monks. He also tried to catch a glimpse of the hermits, in case one of them was the one he sought.

Razin had referred to a master he'd seen many years past, so this master would most likely be middle-aged, in his forties or fifties . . . or maybe older. Whether monk or recluse, if this warrior still lived among them, he might reveal himself by the way he moved.

Sergei started recognizing familiar faces among the various brothers, as well as several of the elder fathers, as they went about their duties. One such elder stood out in his memory: Sergei was in the main monastery building when he noticed one of the black-robed elders, a man with a snowy beard and long white hair, ministering to a bedridden monk in the infirmary, giving the monk his last rites. A few minutes later, on his way back down the hallway, Sergei saw the same elder, his eyes closed in concentration as he laid his hands upon the chest and fore-head of another patient. Then the elder looked up and gazed directly at Sergei, who stood transfixed . . .

The spell was broken as a monk brushed by to enter the room. He glanced back to see Sergei's expression and smiled. "The father's name is Serafim. He is a *starets*."

Only later did Sergei learn that the term *starets* referred to elder fathers of extraordinary character and wisdom. He made a note to speak with this Father Serafim, who might be old and wise enough to recall the warrior he sought.

Meanwhile, he continued to question other monks. He could not openly state that he was seeking a master of combat on an island of pacifists, so he phrased his question this way: "I once heard about a man who lived here. He was a skilled warrior before he found peace. Have you heard of any such man?" His inquiries attracted puzzled looks. No one seemed to know anything, and he found no signs of any such warrior.

As summer slipped into autumn, and frigid breezes began gusting off the lake, serious doubts arose as to whether such a master existed—at least on Valaam.

Even as Sergei watched the monks, they had been observing him, the young pilgrim with white hair, who wandered the island asking questions. Soon after, a monk who introduced himself as Brother Yvgeny brought the following message: "The elders know of your presence here but not your spiritual purpose. Since you seem to follow some inner calling, you may stay for a time if you are willing to serve. Are you so willing?"

"Yes, I am."

Satisfied, Brother Yvgeny nodded and continued, "Since you cannot live outdoors through the winter, you are to live and work at the skete St. Avraam Rostov. This hermitage is located five kilometers to the south. It is separated from the main island by a narrow channel—"

"I am familiar with the location," said Sergei.

"Good," the monk replied. Then he added one last thing: "You will be allowed to stay there for only seven days. When the elder returns, you may ask his permission to remain and serve the brothers in hermitage. Otherwise, you will need to leave the island soon. In another few weeks, high winds and blocks of ice make the lake impassable until the spring."

Sergei had only one question: "The father whose permission I need . . . what is his name?"

"Father Serafim," he replied and, with a nod, departed.

Sergei gathered his belongings, removed all traces of his camp, and found his way to the rocky shore, where he descended stone steps and was taken by cutter across the channel. He arrived in the late afternoon, when all the monks had retired to their cells for several hours of prayer. During this time Sergei walked quietly through the skete—the small kitchen, dark hallways, and common room now empty. A good place and time, he thought, to practice.

On the fifth morning after his arrival at St. Avraam Rostov skete, as Sergei swept and cleaned, he asked one of the brothers when he could speak with Father Serafim.

"He should return in a few more days," the monk replied before departing for other duties. Sergei continued with his tasks until the brothers retired and it was time for training.

In the waning afternoon light, as Sergei headed toward the common room, he passed Father Serafim's empty cell. Curious, he stopped and peered through the open doorway into the darkened room. He found no furniture except for a small table and a chair. And in the corner, where a bed would normally be, stood an open coffin.

With a shiver, he continued down the hallway as rolling thunder marked an approaching storm.

The silence was so profound at Rostov skete that Sergei's breathing seemed unnaturally loud, and the dim lighting lent a dreamlike quality to the winter days.

As Sergei moved through a warm-up routine, practicing kicks and strikes in the air, a lone figure appeared in the dimly lit doorway holding a candle. This sudden apparition startled him, until Sergei recognized the face of Father Serafim. Sergei was about to speak but found that he had no voice.

The old monk's stillness, and the way he stood watching, reminded Sergei of a snow leopard before it springs on its prey. A flash of lightning filled the room with stark, garish light, for an instant turning the monk's face into a death's head—a skull with a scraggly mane of white hair, whose empty sockets stared at nothing.

In the grip of a primal fear, Sergei stared at the death's head in the darkness—until Father Serafim raised the candle higher and Sergei saw only an elderly monk, his serene face illuminated by the flickering flame.

The next instant the doorway was empty. It wasn't that the father had turned and walked away or even backed into the shadows. He was standing there, then he wasn't. Sergei heard no footsteps receding down the hallway.

I must have closed my eyes, looked away for a moment, he told himself. Only he couldn't remember doing so.

Two hours later, in the candlelit room, as Sergei served a meal to the six brothers in residence, he expected to see Father Serafim, but his place remained empty.

As soon as the meal ended, Sergei said to Brother Yvgeny, in whispered tones, "I saw Father Serafim this afternoon. Why was he not—"

"You say you saw him?" said the brother.

"Yes, he was in the doorway."

Shaking his head, Brother Yvgeny said, "You must have seen someone else. Father Serafim is not due back until tomorrow."

W HEN THE ELDER RETURNED on the following day, as expected, he summoned Sergei to his tiny cell and beckoned him to sit on the only chair. A soft glow seemed to surround the old monk. His mane of long white hair and full beard made him appear somehow larger, more imposing. Sergei, overcome with a sense of awe and reverence, had never before met a man of such spiritual presence.

"I am Father Serafim," the elder said softly, then smiled. "But then, I believe we've already met."

Sergei cleared his throat and, with difficulty, found his voice. "I'm pleased to meet you, Father. I . . . I would like to ask your permission to stay in this hermitage through the winter."

"And then?" asked the old monk.

"Then? I . . . don't know," Sergei answered.

The father closed his eyes, took a slow, deep breath, and remained that way for nearly a minute. He finally opened his eyes and said, "It is unusual for a layman to stay in a skete, but . . . I've looked into it. You may remain through the winter—possibly longer . . . "

Seeing Sergei's eyes steal a glance toward the coffin, the father smiled and said, "The box serves as my bed, but also a reminder to make use of the time God has given me. And one morning, when I do not rise, it will save the others some trouble."

It just didn't seem like the right time for Sergei to ask Father Serafim if he had met any great fighters.

. 2 8 .

Thus began Sergei Ivanov's official residence at the Avraam Rostov skete, living with celibate, ascetic monks in hermitage, eating their plant-based diet, observing silence during meals, and searching for the man who wasn't there. There never seemed to be an opportunity to speak again with Father Serafim, so often away or doing his healing work at the monastery . . . tending to the needs of the brothers in residence as well as praying in solitude. With silence at meals, and Sergei's duties before and after, he rarely crossed paths with the father at an opportune time.

Meanwhile, on occasional errands to the main cloister, Sergei continued his search for the elusive, or nonexistent, warrior.

About six weeks after their first brief meeting, he encountered the father gazing out the window at a snow-covered landscape. Sergei approached quietly, so as not to disturb him, and for a moment also looked upon the winter scene, as if seeing it through the old monk's eyes—the snow, highlighted by emerald green pines and shrubs with tiny red bulbs . . .

By the time Sergei came to his senses, the monk was walking away. "Father! Father Serafim!" he called, startled by the volume of his own voice.

The elder monk turned. "Yes, Sergei?"

"I've been meaning to ask you—but now I'm not sure how . . . You've been here a long time, I take it?"

He nodded. "Yes, a long time."

"Well, during that time, some years ago . . . did you happen to know, or see . . . someone—a monk or pilgrim—who was a skilled fighter? Some kind of master?"

Sergei suddenly felt dull and silly as this starets looked at him, a blank expression on his face.

"A fighter, you say? A soldier?" said the father. "I . . . have nothing to do with such people." Excusing himself, he departed.

Sergei could think of no one else to ask and nothing more to do.

Nonetheless, he worked diligently, serving wherever he could, and he joined the brothers in their customary two meals a day—porridge, bread, mash and vegetables, sometimes with fish, and herbs. They drank kvass, a beverage made from bread, and tea on holy days. It was a simple, ascetic life of work and contemplation and training.

During one of these times of reflection, Sergei realized with shock and regret that he had never taken time to write to his uncle Vladimir— an oversight all the more serious as he recalled how Zakolyev had destroyed his farewell letter. To this day, his uncle might still believe that Sergei was dead.

So he composed his thoughts and set quill to paper:

Dear Chief Instructor Ivanov,

I write this long-overdue letter to express my apologies for leaving the school without your consent—and my regret for not having written to you sooner. I did what I had to do, and I offer no excuses. I thank you for the kindness and care you showed me during my early years. It is not forgotten. You are not forgotten.

I have enclosed a map I took from your library. I return it to you now, somewhat the worse for wear. It has served me well, and I thank you for this "loan." As to the knife, shovel, compass, and other supplies, I will one day return them or pay for them.

During the course of my long journeys through Russia, the skills I learned at the Nevskiy Military School enabled me to survive arduous conditions in the wild. I am now twenty-three years old. Despite the manner of my departure, I want you to know that both your care and your training may yet serve some higher good.

I respected you and your position as chief instructor, but I have always thought of you first as my uncle and family. You were the closest man I had to a father. You will forever remain in my memory and in my prayers.

Your nephew,

Sergei

As he sealed the letter with candle wax, he saw his uncle's stern face in his mind. Sergei felt no longer the fear and awe of his youth but rather a deep affection for this good man, Vladimir Borisovich Ivanov.

That letter completed a small part of his past. A far greater portion of his past remained unfinished. Until he concluded that task, Sergei had no future.

THROUGH THE SHORT BITTER DAYS, Sergei followed the same routine: work, reflect, train, eat, and sleep. It was like being back at the Nevskiy Military School—as if he had gone nowhere, done nothing. Each day his frustration grew.

More than three months had passed since Sergei had begun his residence. He thought back to his time at the school, among soldiers, when he had wished for a sense of peace. Now, in this place of peace, he sought a warrior. Meanwhile, he continued training on his own. No progress, no change; winter outside, winter inside. Sergei faced the reality that he might soon be leaving, having wasted another year of his life.

Then all at once Sergei's fortunes changed—not because of anything he had done or deserved, only a matter or timing or luck. Or perhaps a master's change of heart.

On the last day of March 1897, Sergei had just completed the movements of his routine, ending in a stance with his arms in a guarded, ready position, when out of the corner of his eye he noticed Father Serafim watching him.

The old monk's arms were crossed over his broad chest. He was shaking his head as if to say that all of Sergei's skills added up to nothing. "Whatever are you doing?" asked the puzzled father.

"I'm training . . . preparing myself," Sergei answered.

"In a real battle," said Father Serafim, "there are no warm-ups, no rehearsed techniques, no rules." He shook his head again. "I don't believe that such movements will prepare you to face the men you hunt."

Upon hearing those words, Sergei's mind raced, then slowed, and finally came to rest on one thought: Could this man be . . . ?

"Yes," said Father Serafim, answering his unspoken question. "I am the one you seek, and I know why you are here. But you do not."

"What?"

"You still believe that you were sent by Razin, but you were sent by God. And when you leave, you will not be the same man who arrived."

He spoke with an authority that seemed to stretch back into eternity. And those words marked the beginning of a different way of training and living than any Sergei had ever encountered.

W ITHOUT ANY FURTHER WORDS, Serafim took up the role of teacher as if it were both natural and inevitable. He began appearing in the common room each afternoon to observe practice. One day soon after, Sergei stopped to ask him a question: "Father Serafim—"

The elder man held up his hand to silence Sergei. "Do not call me 'Father' again, except in the presence of other monks. 'Serafim' is enough."

Before Sergei could ask why, Serafim explained, "Training you to vanquish other men has nothing to do with my calling as a monk. I've taken vows of nonviolence, and I will die before killing another human being. I have seen . . . and done . . . enough killing." He would say no more about it. But he set his gaze upon Sergei, who suddenly felt naked, then transparent. And Serafim said, "I see that you also have another name. So when we are alone I will call you Socrates."

When Sergei finally managed to speak, he stammered, "H-how . . . ?"

"I . . . looked into it," said Serafim.

"If you . . . look into such things—and if you knew I was here—then why did you make me wait before revealing yourself?"

Serafim paused. "I needed to observe, assess your heart, and your character, so I waited . . . until the time was right."

Sergei looked at the old monk. It was like gazing down at the rippled waves of Lake Ladoga: He could not see beneath the surface, but he sensed great depths.

In TRUTH, it was difficult for Sergei to imagine Serafim as a great fighter. In the past, perhaps, when he was young and strong. But now, thought Sergei, despite the force of his words, Serafim looked more like someone's elderly grandfather than a master of combat.

Serafim must have sensed Sergei's doubts because he said, "Attack me any way you wish. But make your attack sincere. Do your best to strike me." Serafim's tone carried the clear message that he would not tolerate a halfhearted effort. So Sergei gave it his best.

Sergei couldn't even get near the old monk. Sergei didn't understand what the man was doing; he only knew that he couldn't seem to connect with, or even *find,* the elderly father.

Whenever Sergei tried to kick or punch or sweep or trap or grab or throw, he found himself on the ground, again and again, without any clue as to how he got there. And Serafim held him down with one hand, one knuckle, one finger. Sergei was physically unable to rise. Once, he found himself falling, only to realize that Serafim had not even touched him.

Razin had been right. Sergei had found the master—and it was one of the most frustrating encounters of his life. When the old monk challenged Sergei to push him off balance, he tried many times without success. He recalled the time he'd tried to push over Alexei the Cossack— it was like trying to push over a mountain. But with Serafim, it was like trying to push over a feather—and not being able to do it.

The old man would evade Sergei, trip him, twist him, turn him, and throw him to the ground with his hands, with his feet, and only with his mind, it seemed. Serafim never actually struck him until near the end of their session, when the old monk administered a light blow that left Sergei stunned and unable to move for several minutes. Had Serafim intended to injure him, Sergei wondered what damage he might have done.

The next day Serafim asked Sergei to join him for a walk through the snow to a small orchard above the farm. As they walked, Serafim began, "There is a reason the Bible says, 'Vengeance is mine, sayeth the Lord.' What gives you the right to play the avenging angel?"

"I have no right at all. Nor can I know if my wife's soul will rest easier for it. I only know that mine will . . ."

"So you believe . . ."

"So I believe."

"You can't undo what these men have done—"

"But I might stop them from destroying more lives." What Sergei left unsaid was that in fulfilling his vow, and perhaps dying in the process, he might find salvation for his soul and join his wife and child in a better place, if such a place existed.

"Is there no way I can dissuade you from this course of action?" Serafim asked.

"It's something I have to do," Sergei replied.

The old monk sighed. "All right, then, I'll take you into the shadows. I'll show you the road to hell . . . so that one day you may want . . . what I want to give you."

"What *do* you want to give me?" Sergei asked.

"Peace."

"There's only one way I'm going to find peace."

"Through death."

"Theirs or mine. Or maybe both," Sergei replied. "And I can't wait much longer. I need to find them soon—three months, six months, a year at the most."

Serafim's eyes again fixed on Sergei. "The time things take is not for us to say."

"You believe it may take longer?"

He nodded.

"How much longer?"

Serafim paused. Then he said, "In an instant a life may turn around; a heart may open in a moment of grace. But preparing for that moment can take a lifetime . . . " Serafim began to pace as he continued, "Learning may happen quickly. Unlearning takes longer. Old habits die hard . . . and tense warriors die young. If you're willing to start fresh . . . well, it may be less than ten years—"

"I don't have years!"

Serafim's eyes blazed. "You must be an important man to make such demands on God. And supremely wise to know how long it should take . . . "

As they left the orchard and turned back toward the skete, a chastened Sergei changed the subject: "How many other students have you taught?"

Serafim sighed. "None have learned from me what you seek."

"Why are you willing to teach me? Isn't there some sort of initiation?"

"You've already been initiated—by Razin and . . . by your life."

"What do you know of my life?"

"I've seen enough."

Sergei shook his head in wonder, still mystified by what the old monk could have seen. "So you're going to teach me, just like that, for nothing in return?"

"It would be a mistake to view my instruction as a personal favor, Socrates. I'm not doing it for you; I only serve God's will. And I do this because . . . helping you may yet serve a higher good that neither of us has foreseen."

. 29 .

Most of Zakolyev's men, and all of the women they had collected along the way, desired a permanent camp—a settlement like those from which some of them had come. But their leader's response remained the same: "It's harder to hit a moving target."

So it was a surprise to all when the Ataman called his men around the fire in their temporary campsite near the Romanian border and announced, "Prepare yourselves! Tomorrow we ride north to build a permanent camp. Long ago I found a site deep in the forest north of Kiev. No huts this time but real cabins. And, listen well!—I make this prophecy: We will soon have more women and children to form the beginnings of a new Cossack dynasty. A new beginning in a new camp. Our time has come! From this hidden place we'll ride forth and strike at the Jews, then vanish. We will leave behind only rumors but no living witness, except for one child each year, too young to remember, whom we will make one of our own. Thus our legend will grow. We ride for Church and Tsar!"

This last exclamation, which drew cheers and raised swords, was said for the benefit of any remaining believers. His men needed to feel that they served a higher cause. Zakolyev served his own will, and his will alone.

And so it was that he led his growing community of would-be Cossacks to their camp in the north, hidden within a forest. With tools acquired in various ways, the men set about cutting trees and erecting real cabins. The work was good for morale, the women seemed glad enough, the children played, and for a time they did not murder or pillage. It was a time of settling, and even a restless Korolev contented himself with simple labor.

Soon after the men finished building the cabins, the Ataman announced that Paulina's mother, the woman Elena, should move her belongings to his cabin and live with him in order to watch after the child. Elena did as she was instructed.

Zakolyev's sudden domestic decision seemed out of character. But for the first time in his life, he felt something like love. Not toward Elena, but toward the child. Elena's place in his household was utilitarian at best; she did not share his bed but slept on straw matting in Paulina's room. It would always be called Paulina's room, and the child would remain, along with the boy Konstantin, the primary object of Zakolyev's affection.

It is good that fathers tell stories to their children. So one night Father Dmitri told young Paulina, "One day, not so very long ago, there lived a man and his wife, and they were happy and good, so a beautiful little girl was born to them. And I was that man, and you were that little girl."

"And my mother was Elena," she said.

He shook his head sadly. "Elena is not your true mother, but you must never reveal this secret."

This revelation was not really a surprise to Paulina; Elena had never felt like a mother to her. "Is Shura my true mother?"

"You are lucky to have old Shura, but no, she is not your mother."

"Then who—"

Father Dmitri cut her off. "Do not interrupt your father!" Then, in a softer voice, "You must be silent until I finish, Paulina. Your true mother—my beloved wife—was murdered by a monster . . . "

Paulina's eyes opened wide with horror. On the Ataman's strictest orders, she had remained insulated from any mention of violence or death or even the purpose of the raiding parties. She knew only that her father and his men went out on patrol to serve someone called the Tsar.

"What . . . what did the monster look like?" she asked, afraid and fascinated by this dark revelation.

"He looks like any other man—about my age, yet his hair has turned white. He is also a wizard who has the power to enchant with his voice, telling sweet lies that confuse before he kills. The only way to destroy this monster is quickly, before he can speak and weave his spell."

Father Dmitri was utterly convincing in his tale, which he told in a trembling voice, as if he actually believed it himself.

Every child has nightmares—and for the remainder of her brief childhood, Paulina's took the form of a monster who looked like a man with white hair.

The men were puzzled by the Ataman's new paternal role, and the women were quietly bemused to see any endearing quality in a man they feared. Some of the women asked Elena whether the Ataman had become a husband as well.

She would not speak of it.

THE NIGHT that Ataman Zakolyev adopted his new domestic role, a period of relative normalcy entered the camp as the men concentrated on building rather than hunting Jews. Oddly enough, it was the dogs that completed this settled atmosphere.

Prior to finding a permanent settlement, Zakolyev had killed the growling canines along with their owners. But now he allowed those dogs whose loyalty could be bought with a few scraps of food. On occasion, Zakolyev was seen scratching an animal behind the ears. They would lick the Ataman's hand, and they showed absolute obedience.

The smarter children did the same. Zakolyev let the youngest do as they pleased—running wild like the dogs and amusing themselves. But as soon as were old enough, they were given menial duties such as cleaning the outhouses, washing clothes in the river—whatever the adults found distasteful or dull.

Like the children, the dogs earned their keep: No stranger could approach without warning. The dogs also cornered stray horses and herded sheep acquired from recently deceased Jews. So the animals became a part of the camp, hunting with the men and watching with rapt attention as the women prepared the food, hoping a hand might drop a slice into their waiting jaws.

So the dogs barked and chased sticks thrown by youngsters, men built hearths in sturdy cabins, and women prepared food and cared for the children, as in any other Cossack camp. But fires were allowed only at night, when the smoke would dissipate in the darkness, or during rain or snow, which would suppress any sign of smoke. Few could ignore the Ataman's growing preoccupation with security—but no one detected the seeds of a growing obsession, as Zakolyev started seeing Sergei Ivanov lurking in the shadow of a tree, peering out from behind the barn, or staring at Zakolyev from the foot of his bed late at night.

Soon enough, Zakolyev's nightmares grew worse, and he showed the effects while awake: the twitch of an eye, the jerking turn of a head, a muttered phrase directed at no one. At times he appeared distracted— he would stop whatever he was saying or doing and stare into a black hole only he could see. Circles appeared under his eyes, and he grew more remote from his men. During this time the Ataman came to view himself as a mythic figure, strengthened by his suffering, rising above other men. Fraternizing with a shrinking inner circle of men, he now gave orders through Korolev, who made sure they were carried out with brutal efficiency.

Meanwhile, life went on in the camp. The men returned from hunting—sometimes animals, sometimes Jews—to sit by the campfires and tell stories of their youth and drink toasts. They had learned to choose their words carefully when their leader was nearby—or even when he wasn't. Zakolyev declared a death penalty for anyone who undermined his authority or compromised their location.

There was little danger of detection. Their cabins lay hidden deep within an expanse of forest in a small clearing a hundred meters from a flowing stream. And a short distance through the trees, the stream turned to a waterfall, pouring over the cliff and thundering down nearly twenty meters to the rocks and shallows far below. Below the base of the falls, the stream became a torrent of white water, with steep drops and rapids. Because it was not a navigable stream, no small boats would pass, and the camp lay far off any beaten path. They would remain undisturbed.

T HE NINE CAMP CHILDREN—four girls and five boys—glad for this permanent camp near a real waterfall, played happily in the shallows until one of the boys waded into the stream too close to the edge, slipped, and was washed over to die on the rocks below.

After that, the Ataman forbade Paulina or Konstantin to play near the top of the falls. The boy who died, he remarked, had neither intelligence nor luck. He would not be missed, except perhaps by Shura.

Like the other boys his age, Konstantin enjoyed exploring the woods, carrying on make-believe adventures, and riding when he was allowed. Spending time with a young girl was not high on his list, even if little Paulina looked up to him. But from the time he had first seen the infant girl years before, he had developed a fondness for her that brought him both delight and mortification.

He still recalled how, when Shura had first asked him to hold the infant while she tended to another, her tiny hand reached out as quick as a trained fighter to clutch the sleeve of his woolen shirt. She squeezed the cloth and cooed so sweetly and looked up at his face. In that moment, as he gazed into her large eyes, he saw the world as she saw it—a place of mystery where all people were good and all things were possible.

That luminous moment ended abruptly when one of the older boys walked past and called him "wet nurse." As soon as he could, Konstantin disengaged himself and rushed away to help the men.

Later, when Paulina had learned to walk and talk a little, she would follow Konstantin, running on her little legs, trying to keep up with him, crying out, "Kontin! Kontin!" because she couldn't say his full name. From that day on he would become her Kontin. As time passed, he would watch over her protectively.

The Ataman had given Elena strict orders that Paulina was not to play with any of the other girls, only the boys. His daughter was to dress as a boy and would be trained in hand-to-hand combat by Great Yergovich and all his best fighters. In the meantime, if anything happened to her, the responsibility would rest heavily on the shoulders of Elena and Konstantin. Which meant that if she came to harm, nothing would be resting upon their shoulders at all.

Although Father Dmitri clearly favored Paulina, he sometimes seemed to care about Konstantin too—but there were times that the Ataman looked at Konstantin so strangely that the boy felt afraid and didn't know what to think.

Konstantin was glad for Paulina, that she lived in a cabin with people who cared about her, or at least took care of her. Sometimes he wondered where he came from and who his parents were, but such thoughts led nowhere, so he let them be. Still, he made it his business to listen closely to the men in case a stray conversation might provide a clue to his past.

At night he would sit sometimes and draw pictures or whittle in the corner of the barn where some of the men drank and talked. A boy with sensitive ears could overhear many things because Konstantin was as invisible as the dogs who curled up beside him.

When he was younger, he had wanted to go out on patrol with the grown men. But when he heard them speak in hushed tones about all the killing, he wasn't so sure. One day the time would come when he'd have to choose whether to become one of them or . . . or . . .

His young mind could find no other option. This life was all he knew; the rest was only dreams.

. 30 .

Some weeks later, as Sergei prepared to begin the next session, Serafim threw a punch toward his face. The movement took Sergei by surprise, but he evaded, as he had learned in the past. Serafim swung again; Sergei parried.

"Move naturally," said the monk, taking his shoulders and shaking them, pushing this way and that. "Less like a soldier, more like a child. You're far too tense. Even as you move, relax . . . always relax."

"I am relaxed."

"There's relaxed," Serafim said, "and then there's *relaxed.*"

"Even in mortal combat?"

"Especially then," he said, continuing his attacks. "More men die from fatigue than from lack of skills. Only when you learn to relax under pressure, to relax in motion, can you fight longer and live longer. So practice relaxing in all that you do—in the kitchen, in the laundry. Let movement happen instead of making it happen."

For the next week Sergei repeated the word relax under his breath a hundred times a day, taking a deep breath and releasing any unnecessary tension—especially while doing physical labor or training. "Your training is not just about punching or kicking," Serafim reminded him. "It's about everything you do. Remember: Here and now . . . breathe and relax . . . in battle and in life."

Exasperated and feeling more tense than ever, Sergei begged, "Please, Serafim, I don't need you to constantly remind me to relax and breathe. I understand your point!"

"*Doing* is understanding," Serafim chided. "So show me."

As they walked the island paths, Serafim had Sergei inhale and exhale in time to his footfalls, until he could inhale for twenty counts and exhale in the same manner. Serafim could add ten counts more—he had lungs like huge bellows.

As another frozen winter passed into the new year, practice became only more frustrating. "You still cling to the familiar, Socrates, to rote techniques you've practiced a thousand times. But you can't preplan for every situation. Reality will surprise you every time."

During this phase of training, Serafim began to attack him at random, as Razin had done. The elder monk would strike Sergei day and night, at odd times: when Sergei was running errands on rough or slippery ground, by a lake or in the forest, and sometimes even in the hallways of the hermitage. No place was safe—the old monk once even attacked Sergei while he was relieving himself.

Finally, Serafim made his point: "Each situation is unique. Your opponent will be unpredictable; so must be your defense. Confrontations get messy, sloppy, slippery, off balance, unorthodox, and unpredictable. Anything can and does happen: Your opponent may have a concealed weapon or companions waiting nearby. He may seem drunk, then suddenly alert. He may turn out to be stronger or faster than you. Don't assume; don't predict; don't guess what your opponent will or will not do next. Just stay aware and respond naturally to whatever arises in the moment."

"Are you saying I should move without thinking at all?"

"In combat, there's no time to think. Beforehand, you may plan and strategize, but all plans are tentative and must change on the spur of the moment. Whatever happens, there's only one certainty: It will not go exactly as you expect. So expect nothing, but be prepared for anything. Relax and trust your body's wisdom. It will respond on its own."

"I think I experienced that . . . with Razin."

Serafim nodded. "You've experienced it, but now you need to master it—even when injured, overwhelmed, on your worst day. That means throwing away any preconceived notions about your adversary's personality or emotions. None of that matters. Whether it's a fist or a stone or saber or charging horse, a force comes in—you move, you breathe—and in any given moment, your body will find its own solutions."

"Easier said than done," said Sergei.

Serafim smiled. "I think you're starting to understand."

I T B E G A N when Serafim picked up a fist-sized stone and, standing three meters away, said, "Hold up your hand and catch this rock!" He threw it with such force that it nearly broke Sergei's hand. "Remember the pain," he said. "It's called *resistance*. In life, stress happens when you resist what arises." He added, "The same is true in combat. No matter what comes your way, if you take a rigid position, you experience pain. Never oppose force with force. Instead, absorb it and use it. Now you can learn how yielding can overcome even a superior force."

Serafim started swinging underhand, gently tossing fist-sized stones toward Sergei's chest. He was to step out of the way and catch them smoothly, matching the speed of the stone with his hand so there was no sound at all.

Then the monk brought out a heavy oak staff and swung at Sergei from the side. First he instructed Sergei to take a rigid stance, like a solid vertical wall, and experience the pain of impact. After that, Serafim instructed Sergei to swing the staff at him, and he demonstrated how, by moving and leaning away from the staff at the last moment—the way Sergei absorbed the stones with his hand—Serafim could absorb the blow, reducing its force by more than half.

"That's fine if someone swings a staff," said Sergei. "But suppose it's a saber? I can't just absorb the cut of a blade."

Serafim scratched his beard, as if pondering the question. "In that case, I suggest you get out of the way."

The next week, and the week after that, Serafim threw more stones, faster and faster. Sergei was to move off the line of force and silently catch the stone, absorbing its force. As time passed, he graduated from stones to knives—thrown slowly at first, then faster. Later he learned to evade and absorb pushes, punches, and kicks in addition to blows of the staff.

Finally, Sergei wanted to move on. "These games are well and good," said Sergei in a sudden fit of impatience. "But when will I be ready to learn advanced skills—and work with weapons and learn to fight like animals, like the Chinese monks do?"

"First of all," said Serafim, "there are no advanced skills; there is only skillful movement. Imitating tigers or monkeys or dragons has a certain artistic appeal, but I suggest you become the most dangerous animal of all—the human animal, who uses both instinct and reason. And your most formidable weapon is between your ears. Those who focus only on strength can be defeated by cleverness, unpredictability, flexibility, and deception."

In early autumn, as the cold winds again bit at the flesh, Serafim led Sergei to the edge of a sheer granite cliff that plummeted down to waves breaking twenty meters below. "Stand with your back to the water and your heels just at the edge," he instructed. "There are times you may find yourself having to fight at the edge of a precipice— on a bridge or a cliff like this. At the moment fear arises, you tense up; that's precisely when you need to soften, breathe, absorb, and evade. If you tighten, you fall."

Sergei glanced behind and almost lost his balance. "If I fall—"

"You will not likely die," said Serafim, "but it will be . . . unpleasant."

As Serafim gently pushed, Sergei swiveled, giving way. Serafim continued, pushing the right shoulder, then the left; the hips, the torso. Sergei evaded, gave way, maintaining his balance as the pushes grew more forceful. He did the same as Serafim poked at him with the tip of a knife.

Then Serafim said, "Turn around," and Sergei faced the crashing waves far below. Now he couldn't see the pushes; he would have to sense them and instantly give way. A moment of tension, and he would fall over the edge—

Serafim began slowly, gently, all the while softly reminding Sergei, "Fear is a wonderful servant . . . but a terrible master . . . Fear may produce tension, so breathe and relax . . . You don't have to rid yourself of fear . . . just train yourself to respond differently."

Sergei called forth the memories that reminded him why he had dedicated his life to his training as Serafim's pushes came with more force, then turned to slow punches. Then came the knife—the sting of the blade, poking, pushing, piercing his skin as he moved like water—

Then the knife was gone, and Serafim punched Sergei's shoulder blade. It took him by surprise. He was plummeting down. For a moment he felt a sickening loss of orientation—everything seemed to spin—but his instincts took over, and he managed to stay upright by flailing his arms and legs. He closed his legs before he hit the water with a ka-fump.

The impact punched up through his legs, hips, spine, and neck. Then silence under the icy water. He could move everything, but his stomach had cramped and he felt like someone had kicked him in the groin. Struggling back up toward air and light, Sergei mentally scanned his body for injury.

He broke the surface with a gasp and heard the crash of waves and the caw of gulls. Looking up, Sergei saw the small figure of Serafim high above, pointing to Sergei's right. He swam that way and found a small beach—none too soon, for he could no longer feel his arms or legs. Shaking to bring feeling back to his frozen extremities, he hiked and climbed to the top.

Serafim said nothing; no words were necessary. Shivering, Sergei realized how much more he still had to learn.

A WEEK LATER Sergei was limbering up when Serafim suddenly lunged at him with a knife. It came out of nowhere. One moment Serafim was smiling, relaxed, standing with empty hands. The next moment a blade was whipping toward Sergei's throat. Instantly, Sergei's hands came up and he leaned away from the knife. Not a very sophisticated defense, but at least he had moved without thinking.

"Everyone responds differently," said Serafim. "Some fighters flinch and turn; others lean forward or back. We begin with your own instinctive response. Here, I'll show you what I mean." He handed Sergei the knife. "Thrust the blade toward my throat." Sergei did so halfheartedly. Serafim slapped the knife away with such speed that it stuck into a wooden beam three meters away. Then he slapped Sergei's face. "A sincere attack!"

The next time Sergei attacked—sincerely—Serafim leaned back and to the side, bringing his hands up to his throat. "This was my own instinctive reaction the first time I was tested," he said. "Notice how I build upon it."

When Sergei attacked again, Serafim moved the same way but followed up with a slight turn of one elbow, and Sergei found his knife hand trapped. Then Serafim swiveled smoothly back, and the knife was torn from his grasp and pointed back in his direction as Serafim held his wrist in a painful lock. "You see? We begin with a natural response, then let each body take the path of least resistance to solve the problem. There are no wrong movements. The only mistake is not moving at all."

Nearly every afternoon, unless he was called away, Serafim joined Sergei to observe and instruct—correcting, demonstrating, giving new exercises, and sparring with Sergei, testing his slow and steady progress.

As Serafim revealed clever and deceptive ways to move in at angles to disarm and defeat an assailant armed with a pistol or a saber, he corrected Sergei's mistakes not with words, but with pushes, touches, and taps. Working silently in this way, Serafim taught Sergei directly, physically, without the intrusion of abstract concepts.

When Serafim finally did speak, at the conclusion of one session, it was to remind Sergei, "In lethal combat, it won't matter what brilliant concepts your mind understands. The outcome depends on your physical preparation—not what your mind knows, but what your body knows. That's why we will talk less and practice more."

After that, Serafim would make a single point and have Sergei then practice it ten times, fifty times, one hundred times. And over time Sergei passed through many stages of practice. He trained when he was feeling vigorous and also when he was fasting or ill or tired. As Serafim explained, "By training through fatigue, on occasion, you discover that you can handle yourself even in the worst of times. And when physical strength and speed are lacking, you develop relaxation, balance, timing, and leverage."

Nearly a year had passed since his training had begun. Not an easy one. When even Sergei was about to quit from exhaustion or frustration, Serafim would say something like, "When running up a hill, it's all right to give up, as long as your feet keep moving." The only thing that kept his feet moving was his memory of Anya and his vow to avenge her death.

Patience failed him each time he thought about Zakolyev and his men. Every month's delay would mean innocent lives lost—but if he attacked before he was ready, he would lose any real chance of success.

As precious time passed, this dilemma continued to plague him.

. 31 .

W HEN PAULINA was about eight years old—no one kept track of exact ages in Zakolyev's camp—she remained, more than ever, Konstantin's friend and admirer. But much had changed since her training with Old Yergovich had begun. Now she had her own pursuits, and Paulina no longer had much time to spend with Konstantin except when she could slip away during a rest period. Since they had less time together, they valued it all the more.

Konstantin had changed too. His bright mind was hungry for challenges, and his curiosity grew. He could understand things the others did not. And what he didn't yet grasp, he could figure out. He actively sought to learn whatever he could from his elders. One of the few men who could read, flattered by the boy's admiration, showed him the Cyrillic alphabet. After that, Konstantin taught himself to read. He had found several books thrown in a pile of discarded belongings, taken from people the men called Jews.

One of these books, written by a man named Abram Chudominsky, told of a voyage on a great ship, across an ocean, to a land called America. Word by word, Konstantin made his own journey through the book; then he read it again, and then again. He thought that someday he would like to voyage in a great ship across the sea to such a place. Konstantin wished he could have met the great man who wrote this wondrous story.

To read and to dream undisturbed, Konstantin built a special hiding place—a little cave he had hollowed out of the foliage, just across the stream near the top of the waterfall. Later, he revealed his secret place to Paulina, and they met there whenever their duties allowed. Tucked away from the world, they would make fun of things and laugh, and he read to her from his favorite book and showed her the alphabet and taught her how to sound out the words and to write the letters.

THEN, on the eve of 1900, a restlessness and malaise gripped Zakolyev's camp. Some of the men, whose childhood religious devotion had degraded to childish superstition, were worried about Judgment Day and feared for their souls. While they believed their continuing raids were righteous, the blood and screams spoke otherwise. Only Korolev slept well, as if he were too powerful to be touched by judgment or just didn't care.

The Ataman continued to rule with quiet courtesy and random terror. If you pleased him, he could be generous. If you betrayed him, it would not go well for you. For all his moodiness, Zakolyev was not lazy. He held the respect of his men by training harder than most. Yet he maintained his real power not by speed or strength, but by keeping Korolev and the others off balance. Korolev could be more ruthless, but no one was less predictable than Ataman Dmitri Zakolyev. None of the men, women, or children ever knew what he would do next.

On one occasion some months back, a drunken Brukovsky had muttered complaints about the Ataman's strange behaviors these past few years and suggested that he could lead as well as the Ataman, maybe better—perhaps hoping someone would affirm this. But no one spoke a word. Konstantin, along with the few silent men, overheard this. All looked down at their hands, pretending they had heard nothing so it would not taint them. But the Ataman, who had a way of learning every secret, got word of the incident. Some said he could read men's thoughts, which left most of his men in a state of constant anxiety.

Soon after, Konstantin was allowed to join the men on a routine patrol as serving boy—another privilege given to him by Father Dmitri. So he was present when the Ataman and twelve of his men sat around a large table. They were eating and drinking their fill when Zakolyev, in a good humor, observed, "We sit like Christ and his disciplines at the last supper, only I'm not going to be crucified anytime soon." Then he looked around, searching each man's eyes.

As they raised their glasses quickly, toasting the Ataman's long life, he walked casually around the table, his approving hand on some men's shoulders. But as he reached Brukovsky, who had just taken a long drink of vodka, Zakolyev reached around his head, pulled Brukovsky's jaw to the side, and cut the man's throat so deeply that vodka spilled out with his life's blood. Brukovsky, who had served the Ataman for nearly twelve years, died facedown on the table. The Ataman glanced at the blanched faces of his men, each attempting a stoic expression, most failing miserably, as he casually threw the body to the floor, sat at his place, and finished Brukovsky's meal. "We must not waste food," he advised, always the thoughtful leader.

Despite a growing concern in camp over the Ataman's behavior and state of mind, there was no more talk of rebellion. For a long while after that incident, any talk at all was careful, and rarely above a whisper.

Not even Korolev was safe from the Ataman's ire. One cold evening in February, Zakolyev found Korolev in the barn, having just returned from hunting. The Ataman looked around the loft and in the stalls to make sure they were alone, then Zakolyev asked his lieutenant, "Do you remember the man Sergei Ivanov, whom we left facedown in the dirt some years ago? You snapped his woman's neck, if that helps refresh your memory."

There had been so many incidents, so many faces that meant nothing to the one-armed giant. But he did remember that incident and the woman and the man Ivanov, whom the Ataman had sought and finally found—then foolishly ordered Korolev to leave alive . . .

Korolev was wrenched back from his recollection by the sharp edge in Zakolyev's voice. "I ask you again, Korolev, do you believe that he was still alive when we left him?"

"You asked me to leave him," Korolev answered. "I did so. Yes, I believe he was still alive, but his head was bloody—"

"I didn't ask for speculations; I asked what you remember!"

Zakolyev had grown more anxious. His visions of Sergei Ivanov, both dreaming and awake, had increased of late. Now he deeply regretted his impulsive decision to let Ivanov live. It was eating at him; his head ached and stomach churned just thinking about it. Korolev had been right: Ivanov's sorrow would turn to anger, and sooner or later he would come for vengeance. Even now the monster Ivanov searched for Zakolyev in his dreams.

. 3 2 .

At the turn of the new century, a sense of peace and celebration reigned at St. Avraam Rostov skete, and the brothers prayed for humanity at this auspicious time. Then the new year dawned like any other day, with a cold sunrise and prayer and service—and for Sergei, more training.

Then spring came with the usual signs of migratory birds, the trickle and rush of streams, and a colorful array of blossoms as the island was born anew. The work that Sergei did in the fields, the laundry, and the kitchen gave him a sense of connection to the community at large. This practical service, he noticed, gave a healthful balance to his combat practice.

In this manner, and with these routines, four years had passed on the timeless island of Valaam, where change was measured in centuries. Word reached the monastery of a Boxer Rebellion in China; warriors had banished Japanese and Westerners from their land, and Mother Russia had sent soldiers to occupy Manchuria. When this news trickled down to skete Avraam Rostov, it was met with brief nods then forgotten.

Meanwhile, Sergei's training progressed: Serafim taught him to move his arms, legs, hips, shoulders independently. "Allow your mind to be concentrated on a single point yet everywhere at once," said Serafim. "So relax the body, release the mind. By remaining fluid and open, you can strike one opponent in front of you while your leg is kicking another behind you, even as your body is moving or turning. Your opponents will think they are battling an octopus."

And he reminded Sergei that no matter how many men surrounded him, he would never have to fight more than one man in a given moment. "Even if ten or twenty men attack, most of them get in each other's way. Of the three or four who threaten, you move toward the closer man—don't wait for him to reach you."

That very day Serafim taught him to juggle two stones, then three. "Fighting multiple opponents is very much like the juggler's art," he said. "You toss objects into the air one at a time, but in rapid succession. If your attention fails in juggling, you drop a stone; if concentration fails in battle, you lose a life. So stay relaxed, focused, and always moving as you face one man . . . and the next . . . and the next . . . with an expansive mind and flowing body . . . with a peaceful heart and warrior spirit."

ALTHOUGH SERGEI had first come to Valaam for combat training, he and Serafim also had other obligations that were a necessary part of the skete's existence. Serafim was constantly busy, engaged in his spiritual guidance to the monks and his healing work with the sick and injured. But each afternoon, for the most part, was dedicated to training.

As frustrating as these sessions could be, Sergei looked forward to each one because he never knew what was coming next. One day, and for weeks after, Serafim showed him how to throw knives with his right or left hand—overhand, underhand, from standing, lying down—and while running or rolling.

Then Sergei learned to apply the right force to devastating pressure points that could paralyze an arm or leg—and how to strike two or even three men at once in a spinning, whipping motion, and redirect an opponent's kick or punch to hit one of his fellow assailants.

During this phase of training, Serafim caught Sergei staring intently at an intimidating ax he had raised. "Relax your gaze!" he instructed. "Stay aware of everything around you. Don't fixate on your opponent's arms or legs or eyes. Such a narrowed focus hinders your ability to move properly. An open gaze not only expands your awareness but also conveys a powerful message to your adversary's mind that he is only a temporary problem you will soon put out of the way. Keep your gaze open, above and beyond the opponent, as if you are hardly concerned with the attack, yet you remain completely aware."

"Is that possible?" Sergei asked.

"You'll find out soon enough," Serafim assured him.

As the months passed, Sergei came to realize that his hermitage duties—his hours of service and contemplation—were not merely a distraction but an integral part of his training, so that movement practice and the rest of life began to blend into a unified existence. Almost without his noticing, the practice of combat shifted to the practice of living.

"How could it be any other way?" Serafim said. "I would not have wasted my time merely teaching you how to vanquish your enemies. Our time together has far more to do with living than with fighting. And I still hope you will find a way to let go of your vendetta."

Sergei said nothing because there was nothing he could say.

B Y THE MIDDLE of Sergei's fifth year on Valaam, the results of his training began to manifest with increasing depth. Because Serafim always pushed him to the edge of his abilities, he noticed this gradual transformation not in his combat, but in his everyday life—the way he moved more easily and gracefully when sweeping the floor, opening a door, or washing the bowls and utensils. His body felt . . . different, somehow. Without doubt, Sergei's skills improved, but there was something else as well: He had become as much a part of the skete as young trees were part of the island. The outside world, engaged in its own pressing affairs, knew nothing of a young man named Sergei Ivanov, who had finally learned to move like a child.

Some weeks before, Serafim had reminded him, "A young child responds freshly to each moment, without plans or expectations. This is a good way to fight . . . a good way to live." Now Sergei had made another kind of journey, back to innocence. He could no longer recall what his mind or body were like when he had first arrived on Valaam seeking a mysterious master. He could not yet match his teacher's prowess, but Sergei had gained the ability to see what old Serafim was doing—and it intrigued him as never before.

He recalled a story Serafim had told about a man who was always tired and who prayed each day for more energy. His prayers were never answered, until one day, in a fit of despair, he cried, "Please, oh, Lord, fill me with energy!" And God answered, "I'm always filling you, but you keep leaking!"

Sergei was no longer leaking—not as much, anyway—and his energy seemed to build with each passing day. He would need it, because Serafim never let up. What kept Sergei going was the memory of Anya, as he prepared for the task ahead.

In the coming weeks Serafim pressed, prodded, poked, twisted, and struck sensitive pressure points to cause increasing discomfort. "Notice," he said, "when I push here, you feel fear; when I press here, you feel anger. No two people are exactly alike in this. But whatever emotions arise, let them pass through you as you focus on your goal."

The old monk also began to slap Sergei in the face to momentarily stun him, until the time came that he could concentrate and move right through the pain. Afterward, one of the monks noted the "healthy glow" in Sergei's cheeks as they worked in the kitchen. "Your practice must be invigorating," the brother said.

Sergei smiled, thinking, If you only knew . . .

One evening soon after, Father Serafim called in four of the brothers to assist with an exercise. As ethical pacifists, the island monks did not approve of such fighting practice, but the good brothers trusted Serafim's wisdom in this unusual form of service. So they agreed to hold tightly to Sergei's legs, arms, and head as he lay on his back on the floor. As instructed by Father Serafim, each pulled and twisted rigorously in a different direction, inflicting some pain. Sergei's task was to stay relaxed. He found this exercise surprisingly difficult; it brought back sensations of having been pinned down on that day of horror years before. But by not resisting, and instead using creative movements, he was able to escape each time.

Afterward, when the brothers had departed, Serafim remarked, "So you see, Socrates, as long as you stay relaxed and mobile, you'll never again become weighed down by many hands."

Sergei recalled the day, many months before, when he had finally told this island father the details about what had happened that drove him on this quest. Once again Sergei had the eerie sense that his words had only confirmed what his old teacher had already seen.

By the time that momentary reverie ended and his attention returned to his teacher, Sergei heard, "Rather than immediately trying to break free, maintain physical contact; it enables you to know the location of an opponent. If he grasps you, you actually have him. Then move your body in such a way as to throw him."

The instructions, and practice, went on and on and on. And that winter Sergei grew agonizingly aware of his every weakness, imbalance, and point of tension. When he told Serafim that he seemed to be getting worse, the monk smiled. "You're making the same mistakes you have always made, Socrates, but to a lesser degree. Life is not about perfection but about refinement. And yes, you still have refining to do."

The next afternoon Serafim was administering more pain training with a short leather whip that stung fiercely when one of the brothers walked past, shook his head, and muttered under his breath, "They would have lined up for this in the Middle Ages."

As the brother departed, they both laughed. Then, more seriously, Serafim said, "No healthy person seeks pain, Socrates—nor do I enjoy administering it. But such training, judiciously delivered, conditions you so that pain in battle has less power to shock or discourage or slow you down."

Each time Sergei felt the sharp blow, he thought of Zakolyev.

In the spring of 1903 Serafim blindfolded Sergei for a part of each session to enhance his sensitivity and awareness. He led Sergei through the forest, saying, "In case you're temporarily blinded, you need to fight on using whatever senses you have remaining."

After some falls and bruises, Sergei began to sense his way around obstacles, developing greater acuity in hearing. Sometimes he felt the energy of objects around him. All the while, Serafim provided sudden pushes from the back, front, or side, and Sergei had to soften instantly and move or roll. If at any time he lost track of his teacher's where-abouts, Serafim would hit him over the head with a stick. On their return to the skete, Serafim led Sergei into a room where he had to guess how many other monks, if any, were present.

And at random, Serafim would instruct Sergei to close his eyes and describe his surroundings in as much detail as he could. This encour-aged him to pay acute attention to his surroundings rather than getting lost in thought. "You are learning," Serafim said, "how to think with your body—how to leave your mind and come to your senses."

Serafim tied thin ropes to Sergei's ankle and elbow and pulled him off balance as he fought imaginary opponents. He also tied one then both of Sergei's arms behind his back, forcing him to fight with his shoulders, chin, hips, head, feet, knees, or torso. "If you can't use any-thing else," Serafim urged, "use your wits. You may surprise yourself with your abilities, even against great odds."

Sergei also learned new ways to escape from holds and twists—head locks, arm locks, and different chokes—by striking in clever ways to a variety of targets. He then studied ways to defeat one or more opponents while standing or lying on his back or side or stomach and while rising to his feet, so he could fight when disabled or on difficult terrain or from awkward postures.

As Sergei's mind turned to his mission and those he would fight, he told Serafim, "Some of my adversaries are larger and stronger than I. One of them is a giant—"

"It doesn't matter," the monk answered. "Big men can fight well at a distance—they have reach—but softness or fluidity or speed can overcome size and strength. A shorter man can work on the inside, at close range. Every body type has its strengths and weaknesses, so work to minimize your weaknesses and focus on your strengths. You can even overcome superior speed by responding instantly to an attack rather than waiting until it is launched."

That summer, when Serafim decided that Sergei was "finally ready to learn," they met in the forest clearing, and Serafim showed him several extremely clever movements for evading and disarming a swordsman. Holding a razor-sharp saber, gliding across the earth, and cutting through the air, Serafim said, "Learning to use a blade helps you defend against it."

After Sergei had practiced for weeks with various attacks and strikes in the manner of the samurai of Japan, Serafim asked him to draw a saber from a scabbard as quickly as he could and strike him.

As Serafim stood relaxed and alert, three meters away, Sergei was about to draw the sword and advance quickly and strike as Serafim had instructed. But as soon as he started to draw the sword, Serafim was standing next to him, locking Sergei's sword arm so he could no longer draw—and he demonstrated how he could then disable Sergei in several ways.

"Never fear the weapon, Socrates, only the man wielding it. Focus on your opponent even as he focuses on his knife or saber or pistol. As he invests his power in the weapon, he forgets the rest of his body. And in an instant—the very moment you might want to back away—go in without hesitation! Close the distance and disable him before he can draw it out. Stop the attack before it begins."

It took many more weeks of patient practice until Sergei could close the distance between himself and an adversary in a fraction of a second.

THEN ALL AT ONCE, it seemed, Sergei's training took a different turn. As they walked back to the skete in the brisk air of late September, Serafim spoke about patience, and the ethics of combat. "You have done well these past years, Socrates, but skill training is only the beginning.

The movements of the highest warriors are relaxed and expansive because they fight for a cause larger than themselves. Only by surrendering to God's will does one find victory in battle and serenity in life."

Serafim started pacing again, as he did whenever he was about to emphasize a point. "The true warrior, Socrates, retains his humanity even in battle. In winning a brutal victory, you may still lose your soul. Those who fight the dragon may become the dragon."

These words, and the spirit behind them, penetrated not only Sergei's mind but his heart as well as he gazed at this loving old warrior-monk. Over the past seven years, Serafim had assumed the role of mentor. But he was more than that, and it seemed ironic that Sergei was never to call him "Father," because that is what he had become, filling a role that Sergei had missed since childhood.

That night, after Sergei had said a prayer of love and remembrance for Anya and his son and had thanked Razin and God, who had sent him to Valaam, he offered a prayer of thanks for Serafim's generosity of spirit and his simple humanity.

Sergei had known from the beginning that the old monk had no wish for him to follow this course, yet each day without fail—unless church duties took him elsewhere—this island father gave Sergei a part of his life and experience. He received nothing in return except Sergei's gratitude. For Serafim, it seemed reward enough to serve the mysterious will of God.

This truth made Sergei love him all the more.

. 3 3 .

AFTER HER MORNING SESSION with Yergovich, Paulina laughed with delight, barely escaping Konstantin's grasp as they raced through the woods toward the river. Konstantin might have caught her, but he chose to let her get the better of him. The way she was training, he would not be able to catch her for long.

No longer a boy but a tall youth, Konstantin remained her protector and friend. Not that Paulina needed protection anymore; she was learning to handle herself amazingly well for an eleven-year-old. How he'd had to protect her in years past! Not from the older boys—none would be so foolish as to bully Zakolyev's favorite—but from herself. When she was younger, Paulina had tried every kind of risky stunt with wild abandon: climbing trees to the high branches, walking a slippery log over a deep culvert. Now she was growing up as wiry and swift as any of the boys.

And with Great Yergovich training her, Paulina would soon be able to outrun and outfight even the older boys. He was training her in the traditional Cossack style of fighting, which depended more on flowing movement, balance, and agility than brute strength or size. All in the camp agreed that she was agile and had a talent for it—although no one knew why the Ataman was so obsessed with her training. Once she had learned all the basic elements, Zakolyev insisted that every man teach her everything he knew. All but Korolev, who privately declined to involve himself in "children's games."

The Ataman doted on Paulina more than ever these days, alternating between maudlin sentiment and fatherly severity when it came to her combat training. He demanded nothing less than her best effort each day—at morning, afternoon, and evening practice sessions. For her part, Paulina had both the willingness and energy. Now she took pride in her newfound expertise and applied herself with a focus that impressed all who watched her progress.

KONSTANTIN KEPT TO HIMSELF much of the time, dreaming and reading and drawing images in the dirt or sketching on parchment with charcoal from the fire. He thought about Paulina more than ever. He missed her gentleness and innocence, qualities that he had lost somewhere along the way. Having her with him felt like stepping out of a dirty, crowded hut into a fragrant forest. Sometimes he watched from the shadows as Great Yergovich led her through her training.

Yergovich was a massive figure, taller than any man in camp except for the giant, Korolev. With his girth, he reminded one of a bear, especially with his thick brown beard and hairy neck and chest. He had a bear's power—and while he could not move as quickly as some of the younger men, he could anticipate their attacks almost before they had begun.

Years before, he had worked as a bricklayer. In a saloon he had gotten into a tussle with Tomorov. A few moments later, Tomorov and the others who had come to his aid were lying on the ground but not seriously hurt except for their pride. Yergovich had turned to the Ataman and said, "I can teach these young pups to fight properly." So he had joined them and proved himself worthy. Now none could defeat him except Korolev, who once nearly broke the old bear's head. But Korolev got a few bruises in the scuffle, along with a grudging respect for the big man. After that, they called him Great Yergovich, and he remained.

He was also obedient and trustworthy and didn't question things, which made him a good teacher for Paulina. He valued his position as instructor and enjoyed seeing the girl's progress. Great Yergovich had no family of his own, only a friendship with Shura, the only woman his age in camp. In a sense, it was Yergovich and Shura who had parented the growing girl.

Yergovich got on well enough with all the men but Korolev. He didn't like the way the giant looked at Paulina. Korolev knew enough to leave her alone, but Yergovich didn't trust the man, a tiger who played tame as it suited him while he waited, his tail twitching.

So the bear and tiger kept an uneasy truce.

Each day Yergovich led Paulina through a rigorous course of warrior games and exercises—running, swimming, climbing—and fighting skills some of the men had never seen. He had saved his secrets for her. The older man resolved to train Paulina so well that if the time ever came, and he wasn't there to protect her, she would at least have a fighting chance against the one-armed man.

KONSTANTIN, MEANWHILE, was hungry all the time. He grew out of his shirt and shoes. He had to go barefoot for a while until he found an old pair of boots in a pile of discarded clothing. He felt clumsy, and once in a while his voice cracked. He thought a lot about the older women and about what they did with the men and might do with him someday. Then he would think of Paulina and feel bad; after all, she was not quite a woman.

With all his changes, she remained his one constant—someone who cared about him no matter what. Konstantin now felt a jealous animosity toward Father Dmitri, whom Paulina still admired. She had seen only one side of the Ataman; to her he was a protective, demanding, involved father, interested in her progress. The Ataman had never given Paulina a reason to fear him. But she did not know the real Dmitri Zakolyev, and Konstantin could not bring himself to tell her.

At the same time, Konstantin did his best to hide his growing attachment to Paulina. Once he was like a brother to her, but his feelings had deepened and changed. He knew he should be thankful that the Ataman did not object to their friendship—as long as Konstantin didn't distract her from training.

He eventually accepted that his role in the band would remain as it had always been—a servant but never a warrior. His role had been defined years before, when the Ataman had first assigned him to help care for Paulina. So it was no surprise that none of the men encouraged him to learn fighting skills.

In fact, he was relieved to stay out of the raids and the killing; he had other interests and talents. From the growing pile of discarded belongings taken from murdered Jews, he found more books but also a precious set of brushes and colors. So while Paulina pursued her training, he practiced his own craft with charcoal and brush on paper or on any surface he could find. The hours would pass unnoticed as he drew and painted trees and houses and horses and sometimes images from his dreams.

But when Konstantin thought about his future, he couldn't imagine living this way for years—waiting in camp with the women and Yergovich for the "real men" to return from patrol. The other young men, some of whom now rode with the men, thought Konstantin strange.

Only Paulina understood him.

But now he wasn't so sure. When they found time alone, he felt awkward—no longer able to say what came so easily before. So he asked her about her training, and she told him with such enthusiasm that he would know they were still friends.

Konstantin loved the way Paulina's bobbed hair, the color of rich earth, bounced as she ran. And she was pretty, even in boys' clothing. He had tried to draw her face once, but they both laughed his first attempt. And he thought, I could draw her again and again from memory but never capture her beauty.

He knew that she would have been in danger from some of the men were it not for Father Dmitri's protection.

Father Dmitri. The thought of him brought a rush of righteous anger, burning like a fever at the great deception, the secrecy and lies. Paulina still saw only what she wanted to see—and what they let her know: the Ataman's disciplined life; going out on patrol in service of a faraway tsar. She never heard about the charred bodies left behind.

He knew that he should tell her, but every day he remained silent made it more difficult to speak. She wouldn't believe; she wouldn't trust him anymore. She might even hate him. And if she confronted Father Dmitri with what he told her, it could mean catastrophe for them both.

No, he would just have to wait until she woke up to the truth.

P OSSESSED OF A GOOD MIND AND HEART, Paulina assumed the same of those around her. She had seen Father Dmitri's moods and fits of anger, of course, but a child easily overlooks her father's foibles. Insulated from the world by his orders and preoccupied with the life he had arranged for her, Paulina had little time to consider life's larger questions. She had accepted that as the Ataman's child she received special training and responsibilities. She did not envy the other women's timid, submissive manners as they cleaned, cooked, carried water, and served the men.

But in the quiet moments before sleep, she thought about the world beyond the boundaries of the camp. And she wondered what it might feel like to live an ordinary life in the company of other women.

At least I have the old bear, she sighed. And I'll always have Kontin.

. 34 .

I T WAS SPRING OF 1905. Nine years had passed since Sergei had arrived on Valaam. Nine years of service, contemplation, and intense training in combat, and in life. Sergei was now thirty-two years old. His youthful temperament gave way to a more reflective state of mind, a sobering sense of maturity, humility, and perspective—the first stirrings of the transformation that Serafim had once predicted.

Since his wife's death, Sergei had spent more than a decade preparing for a single act of retribution. Sometimes it seemed a form of madness; other times it seemed a just and honorable cause. A man kills your family; you show him the gates of hell. It was as simple as that.

He was now a formidable warrior, having surpassed Alexei the Cossack and even Razin without realizing it. A growing energy and power flowed through him—intimations of mastery, of invincibility, tempered only by Serafim's regular thrashings.

With Sergei's metamorphosis came a growing sense of restless impatience as he confronted the question he had asked many times before: How long will I let Dmitri Zakolyev walk the earth? His mind stretched south, to the Pale of Settlement, where those men were likely shedding innocent blood.

Sergei decided that the time had come for him to leave. He could not wait any longer. Sergei both admired and envied Serafim for the peace he had found—a state of grace he might never know. But at least he had glimpsed the possibility that he might truly learn what the island father had to teach him and accomplish what he had first set out to do.

He announced his decision at their next meeting. "Serafim, it's time for me to be on my way."

Serafim only scratched his beard and said, "Well, that may be so . . . but I wonder, Socrates, how do you expect to destroy so many men when you can't yet defeat a tired old monk?"

"Are you saying that I have to defeat you before I can leave?"

"You can leave anytime you wish. This is a hermitage, not a prison."

"I mean leave with your blessings."

"You've had my blessings from the day we met. Even before—"

"I think you know what I mean, Serafim."

Serafim smiled. "Yes, Socrates. I believe we understand one another by now. I was merely suggesting that if you can defeat me in a sparring match, that would be a good sign of your readiness, that's all."

They had sparred many times in the past, of course, but this would be different. It would no longer be a child against a giant. Sergei had speed and youth and the edge of constant training. In his mind he practiced—while he ate, worked, sat, even while he slept. He was ready.

Sergei nodded, and so did Serafim. No other words were necessary.

They circled. Sergei took a deep breath and made a direct but deceptive attack, trying a feint. Unresponsive to bluffs, Serafim just stood there while Sergei danced around; then the old monk stepped forward and waved his arm. He almost threw Sergei off balance with this misdirection, but his student wasn't having any of it and maintained his focus and balance. Then Sergei managed to grab Serafim's robe and step in to throw, but the teacher seemed to disappear like a puff of air.

Sergei kicked and punched and swept and elbowed, but Serafim deflected so subtly that Sergei felt no resistance anywhere. Nothing connected. Serafim was never where Sergei expected him to be, so Sergei gave up expecting. In that moment he could see and feel everything: Serafim, the sky, the earth. Laughing with pleasure, Sergei threw him, and as Serafim fell, he threw Sergei, and they rolled to their feet in perfect unison. Their battle continued, but the conflict had disappeared. There was no Sergei, no Serafim, just energy moving.

Then, as Sergei stepped forward, before his foot touched the ground,

Serafim seemed to vanish from one spot and reappear in another, and his foot hooked the underside of Sergei's calf, and the next thing Sergei knew he was spread-eagled on his back. Serafim was above him, ready to deliver the final blow to Sergei's chest. The match was over.

It was the closest they'd ever come to a real contest. Serafim wasn't just toying with Sergei; he could no longer afford to. Sergei could now see the qualities his teacher possessed and where they were still lacking in him. Despite the outcome, this represented a major breakthrough: Sergei had learned months' worth of training in those few minutes. They both knew it. But Sergei was not going anywhere, anytime soon. His training would continue.

But it was about to change in a way he never could have anticipated.

As their next session began, Serafim announced, simply, "All your training was but a prelude and preparation for what I'm about to show you. I want you to respect and cherish all that your mind and body has absorbed, and let it filter into the cells of your body. Then set it aside. This is your rebirth, the one practice that is behind whatever modest skills I have attained. You could have learned it from the first day we met, but it would have taken twenty years. In preparing you, I've given you the shortcut you so devoutly wished. While I can't predict, with your present skill this final practice should take no more than a year to master. We shall see . . . "

It would be the most radical combat training Sergei had ever encountered.

"Prepare yourself," said Serafim. "I'm about to strike."

Sergei relaxed into an expansive state of awareness as he had been trained to do. He waited, ready. Then he waited some more. Serafim seemed to be just standing there. Sergei took a slow deep breath, and another. Finally, he said, "Well? When are you going to attack?"

"I am attacking," responded Serafim.

"I don't understand . . . "

"Shhhh. Silence please. Words only pull your attention into your lower mind, and you miss what's going on around you."

In the silence that followed, Sergei finally saw it: Serafim's arm and whole body were indeed moving toward him, but so slowly that the old monk appeared to be standing still.

A minute passed, then two. "Are you joking?" Sergei said. "What's the point of this?"

"Notice each passing moment," Serafim said slowly, in a soft voice. "Feel your entire body, from your toes to your head to the tips of your fingers. Match the pace of your response with the pace of my movement."

Sergei sighed and made the best of it, moving more slowly and deliberately than ever before. It felt both pointless and frustrating. Still, he followed the old master's movements during the minutes it took for Serafim to complete the hooking punch he had launched several minutes before.

Moving this slowly, Sergei noticed points of subtle tension and willed himself to relax his thighs, his stomach, his shoulders . . .

When the first movement was complete, Serafim began another, although it was difficult to tell. At this point Sergei broke the silence. "Serafim, I can appreciate the value of practicing in slow motion. But why this slow—hardly moving at all? I can easily block anything—I could run some errands and return before you hit me."

"Relax . . . breathe . . . observe," Serafim repeated. "Move as I do . . . "

So they continued, as slow and silent as the sun's path across the sky, into the dusk.

TIME STOOD STILL as the practice continued—his only practice—as weeks, then months, passed before the pace of Serafim's movement noticeably changed. At long last they still moved as if through thick molasses, but at least the motion was perceptible.

Soon the very practice that had seemed so irrelevant to combat was enabling Sergei to see and correct imbalances previously invisible and

unfelt and to relax profoundly as he moved. Whatever came, his body
responded naturally, without effort. Sergei's awareness now infused
every part of his body.

Sergei could feel the relationship of every body part, even his internal organs, and the bones and joints and the lines of energy flowing,
from the earth up through both their bodies, and their legs, torso, arms,
and legs became whiplike extensions of the body's core.

Once in a while Serafim would whisper something like, "Move like
seaweed . . . floating . . . rising . . . falling . . . turning." But mostly they
continued in silence, because no words were necessary. And the movement became a deep meditation, and at times, as energy welled up in
Sergei's heart, it became a form of prayer.

Subsequent months mirrored the first. Serafim would attack in a
slow, flowing manner with a punch . . . a kick . . . a knee . . . an elbow . . .
left hand . . . right . . . jab . . . hook . . . cross . . . kick . . . grab. From every
possible angle. The sun moved. The shadows changed. And the seasons
passed.

By midsummer, after thousands of attacks, each strike took only a
minute, and the sense of flow and rhythm grew. Sergei's thoughts had
abandoned him; now it was all a play of energy. Every response happened by itself, as if they were a being of one mind and mindless movement and response. Effortless. Sergei could have continued in his sleep,
yet this was the opposite of sleep: a total awareness, a transcendence of
the separate self. There was no "I" remaining; Sergei Ivanov was forgotten. So Serafim and Socrates moved mindlessly, like the wind, through
the seasons.

By autumn, each movement took only fifteen seconds . . . then ten
. . . then five . . . yet Sergei hardly noticed. The pace had become imma-
terial. Whatever force entered was absorbed, redirected; the principles
he'd learned had penetrated the marrow of his bones. His body was
manifesting every skill he had ever learned and more, but "he" was doing
none of it.

Then winter came, and the attacks whipped in rapidly, and every strike or movement was matched effortlessly. Sergei did nothing but remain aware.

In a moment of illumination, Sergei grasped how Serafim moved with an efficiency and grace he had not perceived before but now amazed him. More incredibly, he could feel it and had begun to do the same.

He had ceased all resistance in mind and in body, had become a hollow conduit of life force. He had long since learned to trust Serafim; finally he had learned to trust his body; only now did he begin to trust All That Is.

Then came the following spring—a cycle of the seasons. Serafim attacked like lightning—faster than the eye could see—but it made no difference at all. The movements were a blur of motion—so fast that a year ago he would not even have perceived them, much less had time to respond.

Then, without warning, Serafim stopped moving.

Sergei nearly fell over. His body was vibrating. He felt a huge mist of energy whirling around them.

"We created quite a stir," said Serafim.

Sergei nodded as spring sun disappeared over the hills to the west. "What now?" he asked.

"Nothing more," said Serafim. "Your combat training is done."

For a few moments Sergei heard only the wind in the treetops. Could it be? he asked himself, savoring Serafim's words. Not certain he had understood, he asked for a confirmation: "Are you saying that my training is over?"

"Training never ends," Serafim responded. "It only evolves, depending upon your purpose. You're ready—for what, I cannot say. But you now grasp the essence of movement, of relationship, of life. You've also learned something about combat—so you accomplished what you came for.

"Tomorrow we can go for a good walk and set aside this talk of killing. You may yet consider a higher calling.

"Serafim . . . you know—"

"Tomorrow," the old monk interrupted. "Let's speak of it tomorrow."

As soon as they met on the following day, Sergei began, "You know that I made a vow, on the grave of my family—"

"A vow you made to yourself, not to God. In truth, Socrates, you have no opponents but yourself. Find peace within you, and there will be no one who can overcome you. And no one you will wish to overcome."

"I once had a teacher who told me, 'Commitment means "no matter what"'—doing what you set out to do or dying in the attempt." Sergei turned to face Serafim and addressed him in his spiritual role. "I'm committed, Father Serafim. I have to face them."

The old monk looked weary. "Will you not stay here among us, as one of us, if only for a few more years?"

"More years? While those men run wild?"

"Men run wild all over the earth, Socrates. Nature runs wild—with hurricanes and earthquakes and plagues and locusts. Even now, innocents die by violence and by starvation, in the tens of thousands all over the earth. Who put you in charge? Who gave you the wisdom to know who is supposed to live and who should die, and by what means? Who are you to know God's mind?"

Sergei had no answer, so he asked a question: "To what God do you refer, Father Serafim? The God of mercy and justice who saw fit in his infinite wisdom to take my family? Is this God you pray to? Who is this God?"

Serafim raised his bushy white brows to convey a quizzical look. The monk seemed pleased by the questions. "Finally, Socrates, you ask what has been weighing on you for so long. I wish I had an answer—some sweet words to heal your heart and console you. But God remains a mystery even to me. There was once a wise man named Hillel," he continued, "one of the Hebrew fathers, who said, 'There are three mysteries in this world: air to the birds, water to the fish, and humanity to itself.'

"I have found God to be the greatest mystery of all, yet as intimate as our heartbeat, as close as our next breath . . . surrounding us, like air, like water . . . always present. But the mind cannot find God, only the heart . . . That is where you will find the faith—"

"I stopped believing years ago."

"Even nonbelievers are embraced by God. How could it be otherwise?" Serafim looked into his eyes and said, "Abide in the mystery, Socrates. Trust it. Let go of knowing what should and shouldn't be, and you will find your faith once again."

"Your words have always tasted of truth . . . but I can't quite grasp their meaning."

"Once you couldn't even grasp my robe. And look what has occurred with a little patience—"

"And a lot of practice."

"Yes. Perhaps it's time to practice another way." He paused then, waiting for the right words. "Socrates, your training has already taught you the limits of the mind. The intellect is a great ladder into the sky, but it stops short of the heavens. Sometimes only the heart's wisdom can show the way. Your namesake, Socrates, reminded the youth of Athens that 'Wisdom begins in wonder.'"

"So what am I to do?"

"What is anyone to do? Put one foot in front of the other! You are only a player in a drama greater than anyone but God can conceive— and sometimes I'm not so sure that even God can make sense of it!" he said, laughing. "You can only play the role you are given, my young friend. But I leave you with this: Those who appear in your life— whether to help or to harm—are all given by God. Meet all with a peaceful heart and a warrior's spirit. You will fail many times, but in failing you will learn, and in learning you'll find wisdom. In the meantime, surrender to God's will . . . to the life you were given."

"How can I know God's will, Serafim?"

"Faith does not rely on knowing anything with certainty," he said. "It requires only the courage to accept that whatever happens is for the highest good."

With those words, they reached the hermitage.

. 35 .

THE YEARS had not been kind to Dmitri Zakolyev, nor had the nights. Once lean and taut, he was now gaunt and drawn, his hollow cheeks giving the impression of a walking corpse. His eyes shone, not quite from madness, but from zeal over his single obsession. It was as if his vision, once grand and expansive, had shrunk toward a single point, and that point was Paulina's training.

Paulina, in the summer of 1906, was still lean and wiry, with new energy and awareness as she matured, and her progress had quickened, to the continuing amazement of those who watched her move. Yergovich had trained her well.

But Zakolyev no longer trusted the big man; he no longer trusted anyone except his daughter. Even Korolev was suspect; he had seen the way the giant sneered, how he turned away when his Ataman approached. Not only Korolev. He was losing their respect. Zakolyev heard them whispering behind his back.

His only hope lay with his daughter. She would win back his honor; she would give him peace. Nearly every day he watched her practice. But as he sat, his mind turned in upon itself; the daily world faded into fragmented sounds and images—words, grunts, screams, and blood.

Then he would come back with a jerk and remember where he was—weary to his very sinews, unable to fend off the living nightmare of the shrieks from the woman he had once called Mother as the monster cut her life to bloody ribbons of flesh. And her cries were joined by the Jews, the ghosts, coming for him, relentless.

He still led every frenzied raid. Every few weeks he demanded another onslaught, then another. Yet his mind wandered even then, preoccupied with Paulina.

Dmitri Zakolyev had placed his hopes, his very life, in the skillful hands of this girl turning to a woman, this woman becoming a warrior. Paulina was his dagger, his savior, his sword. Only her victory could stop the screams; only she offered a possibility for peace.

. 36 .

Over the next few days, Sergei spent hours in contemplation; he had much to ponder. He and Serafim went for walks together, sometimes speaking, other times in silence. They no longer discussed anything more to do with combat.

The questions inside Sergei were larger ones whose answers would come not from Serafim but only from within: Should he hold fast to his vow? Was he showing commitment or rigidity? Would he choose war or peace? Could there be a higher way? Maybe all these questions were a single question. Then he asked himself, Would Anya's heart be gladdened by the death of those men or by my own death in the attempt?

Sergei wasn't certain anymore, and he chastised himself for his lack of resolve. Maybe Zakolyev was right in calling him a weakling and a coward. If Sergei did not confront his enemy, what was the point of all his training these past years? He was like a loaded gun ready to be fired.

Yet a gun could be unloaded and a sword slipped back into its sheath. That was what Serafim would say.

A story came to him—one that Serafim had told some months before, perhaps intended for this moment. He had spoken of a proud and hot-tempered young samurai who routinely cut down any peasant who gave the least offense. In those days, samurai were a law unto themselves, and such behavior was accepted according to custom.

But one day, after another killing, as he cleaned the blood from his blade and returned it to his scabbard, the young samurai began to worry that the gods might disapprove of his actions and send him to a hellish realm. Desirous to know about eternity, he visited the humble abode of a Zen master named Kanzaki. With expected courtesy, the samurai removed his razor-sharp katana and set it alongside him, bowed deeply, and said, "Please tell me of heaven and hell!"

Master Kanzaki gazed at the young samurai and smiled. Then he began to laugh more and more uproariously, as if the warrior had said something hilarious. Pointing at the samurai's puzzled expression, Kanzaki wagged his finger and, still laughing loudly, said, "You ignorant bumpkin! You presume to ask me, a wise master, about heaven and hell? Do not waste my time, idiot! You are too stupid to possibly comprehend such things!"

The samurai's temper flared to the boiling point. He would have killed anyone else for even pointing at him in such a way! Now he fought to restrain himself despite these insults.

Master Kanzaki was not finished. He remarked casually, "It's quite clear that neither you nor your ancestors have half a mind between you. Your entire lineage of louts and fools could not understand a word—"

A murderous rage came over the young warrior. He grabbed his katana, leaped to his feet, and raised the sword to take the Zen master's head.

In that very moment, Master Kanzaki pointed to the samurai and said calmly, "There open the gates of hell."

The warrior froze. In that instant, a light illuminated his mind, and he understood the nature of hell. It was not a place he might go but a place within him. He dropped to his knees, laid his blade behind him, and bowed deeply to his teacher. "Master, my gratitude knows no bounds for this brave lesson you have taught. Thank you. Thank you!"

Zen master Kanzaki only smiled, pointed to him once again, and said, "There open the gates of heaven."

Maybe I'm that samurai, Sergei thought as he turned over the soil in the garden.

THE NEXT DAY, as they walked, Sergei told Serafim the story of his life, from his earliest memory to the time he came to Valaam. When

Sergei had finished, Serafim said, "Your story, Socrates, has only begun. And remember this: Your past does not have to determine your future. Yet you still carry your history like a bag of stones slung over your shoulders. The elderly stoop and bend not only from age, but from the weight of memories."

"Are you suggesting that I forget my past?"

"Memories themselves are faded pictures. Some we cherish; others we can't seem to get rid of. There is no reason to throw them away. Just tuck those you want to keep in a safe place, to review as you wish. The past is not meant to intrude on the present. What concerns me is not where you've been but where you're going."

"And where am I going?" Sergei asked. "Have you seen?"

Serafim looked at him intently. "I have seen something . . . but we will speak of that soon. To address your question in a broader way, I tell you there is nowhere to go. Now is all you have. Wherever you walk, you will always be 'here.'"

"But even now, the past is a part of me."

"Yes, in the form of memory. And the time has come for you to make peace with what was, just as you need to accept what is. What happened, happened. All a perfect part of the process of your life—"

"Perfect?" he said, suddenly angry. "The death of my wife and son?"

"Calm yourself, Sergei. You took in my words at a different level than they were spoken. I did not mean good or right; I spoke in the transcendent sense that it was perfect because it happened," he said. "It sent you to me, as God will send you onward, to whatever you need to experience next."

"How can you know this?"

"No one can know anything," he answered. "I don't know if the sun will rise or whether I'll wake up in the morning. I don't even know if God will grant me my next breath. So I choose to live on faith and accept whatever comes. Welcome or not, bitter or sweet—all of it, a gift from God."

"More words . . . Maybe they are true. But what am I supposed to do with them?"

Serafim began pacing. "You are right. Words are only words. So go beyond them to that place within you that already knows—"

"Knows what?"

"That each day is another life. Each moment you are born anew. This is one meaning of grace. What matters is paying attention, and doing the best you can in each moment."

"You make life sound so simple."

"It is simple; all the rest is complexities. But I did not say it was easy. One day you'll grasp its fullness, and it will all seem so clear that you will laugh with delight. All I can do is plant seeds. The rest is up to God."

SERGEI PONDERED Serafim's words, willing them to penetrate him. And another question arose. The next chance he had, Sergei asked, "Serafim, from the first time we met, how could you know so many things about me?"

The old monk considered the question and finally said, "Years ago, Socrates, before I became a monk, I was a soldier. I saw, and did, things that one does not forget. I fought in terrible battles and saw carnage that no man should have to see. Then there was another . . . difficulty . . .

"I traveled to the East, searching for meaning, for peace. I had little hope for either one. I visited many lands and learned of various paths to God. I learned that all paths are good if they lead to a higher life. I chose the Christian faith, but I haven't abandoned the gifts received when I studied other ways. They are all part of a great way, Socrates.

"I discovered that the gifts were always in me, but certain practices helped me to cultivate them. One is the gift of healing. Even as a boy, I had energy that pulsed through my hands. I believe it comes from a spiritual source. My other gift is insight—foresight, if you will. It's like a blossom that opens when the light enters. And I see things—in dreams and reveries. That is how I could know certain things, but never with certainty."

"I've wondered about this ability of yours . . . "

"To understand it, you have to experience it. When you open to God, you can know all because you are all. You discover that the past, present, and future are all occurring now. This is how I can sometimes see and know."

"Have you seen what my future holds?"

"I see what may be, not what must be. What you do now can change your future. Such is the power of free will."

"But can you tell me anything at all?"

Serafim paused to consider his words. "With every spiritual gift comes a responsibility. My visions are meant to help me advise, not predict. If I told you what I've seen, it might help or harm you—and I'm not wise enough to know which.

"In any case, it might interfere with your destiny. What if I had seen you vanquishing your enemies when you first arrived? Would you have bothered to train all these years? Would it have assured this course of action? What if I saw you lying dead? Would that have made you change your plans?"

Serafim again pierced Sergei with his gaze. "I don't always understand what I see, Socrates. I can't tell you with any certainty whether you will kill these men or forgive them."

"Forgive them? I'll send them to hell first!"

"They are already in hell."

"That's no excuse!"

"No, of course not," he answered. "There are no excuses for anything. Most of the time, I can't even find explanations. But one day you may come to see these men as part of your larger self. In that moment all else falls into place. You may be called upon to fight, but you'll know that you are only fighting yourself."

Serafim paced again as he continued. "What I'm going to tell you now, I've never revealed it to anyone, Socrates. But now it may serve a good purpose and help you to understand.

"I was once married, and we had three children. They rest under the same soil that holds you wife and son," he said. "When I was off to war, they were killed by brigands."

For a minute or more, the air was filled with silence. Then a bird sang nearby, and Serafim continued. "Like you, Socrates, I vowed to find those who committed this crime. And, like you, I prepared myself—"

"Did you?" Sergei asked, waiting for the answer, for a sign.

Another silence. Then Serafim answered. "Yes. I killed them, every one."

Sergei, struck by this tragic bond they shared, took a deep breath and said in a moment of profound empathy, "When you found out what happened to your family, was it also your darkest hour?"

Serafim shook his head. "I thought it was at first, but no, it was not. My darkest hour was the hour of my victory—after I had slaughtered those men. For in doing so, I became one of them—"

"But you weren't one of them! You aren't—"

"You fight the dragon, you become the dragon," Serafim repeated. "It still weighs heavily on my soul. I can't change what I've done. Ever. But do you now understand one of the reasons I decided to instruct you? Because I hope you won't make the same mistake."

In truth, Sergei was finally ready to seek another way of life, but a vow that deep—a vow he had worked nearly a third of his life to fulfill—left traces to which he still clung. "Even if I no longer seek revenge," he said, "someone has to stop them, Serafim. Why not me?"

Serafim looked into his eyes once more, searching, then he said, "Maybe you're right. Maybe you should go hunt them. Kill them all. Make them suffer the way you suffered. Do you think it will end there? You had better kill their children as well because they will come after you. So kill them too, and experience a hell deeper than you have yet seen. Or you may feel nothing at all. You may even find satisfaction in their suffering. If that happens, then you will know that you yourself have become the evil you seek to destroy."

After a time, Serafim added a final plea: "Your loved ones will find peace when *you* do, Socrates. So ask yourself: What is the way to peace? Must you make war to find it? Will it come only at the end of a quest? Or can you create it, here and now? Those at war with themselves are defeated at every turn. Only when you make peace with yourself can you become a true warrior.

"I understand the depth of your beliefs and your feelings—your memories and resolutions," he added. "But not every emotion needs to become an action. Whether you stay here, or whether you ride on, give your life over to a higher will. Master your emotions the way you weather a storm—by building a shelter of faith and patience until the storm passes. Liberate your life from the tyranny of impulse, desire, and compulsion. Become God's warrior, God's servant. God speaks through your heart, and your heart will show the way . . . to becoming a true man . . . and a peaceful warrior."

Serafim's words struck like arrows. Yet one question remained, a question Sergei could not dismiss: "What of those men?"

"Enough of those men!" Serafim said. "They seem to have possessed you! Have you not kept them alive in your mind long enough? Better to ask, 'What of faith? What of God? What of mercy?' Ask whether you have the courage to show them the very mercy and compassion they denied to you and your family. This question lies at the heart of Christ's teachings. But few listen. Are you listening, Socrates?"

Serafim paced again, as if words came more easily when he was in motion. "We both know that you are a formidable warrior. But can you wage peace? You know how to die, but have you learned how to live? Will you destroy or build? Will you behave with hatred or love? These are the questions you should ask yourself. This is the choice you have before you."

"And all my training?"

"Nothing is ever wasted," said Serafim. "You've learned the warrior's way—so fight! Make war on hatred, battle against ignorance, fight for justice! But I tell you this: You cannot kill darkness with more darkness. Only light can banish the shadows."

Sergei could hear Serafim's deep breathing as he gazed inside himself. Then Serafim said, "In any event, those men will die without your help."

"Have you seen this . . . in a vision?"

"Not a vision, no—only an understanding of how such men end up destroying themselves. They will all die, in any case, as all men must die.

"So the question remains, young Socrates: What will you choose?

Consider it carefully, and remember that this decision is not only about you. You were not the one killed. It is about Anya. What kind of a life would she wish you to live?"

When he was alone, Sergei walked the paths of Valaam. Serafim's words blended with his own thoughts. In all his years of training—facing his lust for the blood of evil men—he had come to know his own darkness. And Sergei finally understood why men and nations can rise up against each other and how each act of retribution, desperation, and ignorance fuels the tragic acts that follow.

His hatred, like any fire, had finally extinguished itself. And as he released the grip on his avowed mission, Sergei found in its place a troubled peace. For in letting go of the past, he seemed to be losing his future. Before, he knew what he was doing and why—and where he was headed. His mission to kill his enemies, his vow of vengeance, had ended. No clear goals or purpose remained.

Sergei floated between heaven and earth, connected to neither.

. 37 .

Having completed an intense training, every afternoon for all those years, Sergei now found a space opening in his days, and in his mind. A tremendous amount of energy once expended on his practice was now liberated, and pulsing within him. Sergei experienced a quickening and deepening of thought, insight, and understanding. He knew that this chapter of his life would soon pass into memory. New possibilities rose into his mind as he saw how his study of combat had finally revealed the path to peace.

He had come to a turning point, a crossroads: He forgave himself for his human failings and finally accepted that he did the best he could on that day in the meadow. Despite his efforts, he was not able to save his family. This truth helped him make peace with the shadows of his past. He had felt a weight resting on him. But for the first time in many years, since his family's death, he felt that the burden might be lifted from his shoulders. He might have a new life to live.

The time had finally come to write a letter to Valeria. He sat down immediately, in the common room where he had spent countless hours in training, and wrote the words that flowed from his heart to his mind:

Dear Valeria,

    I know that I have lost the right to call you Mother, but I continue to think of you that way, as Anya will always be my beloved wife. In the time that has passed, I hope your heart has healed enough that this letter will not reopen old wounds but instead may bring gentler memories of love and of family. I cherished what I found in your home. Overwhelmed by the loss of Anya, I was not able then to fully grieve losing you and Andreas as well.

I will not ask your forgiveness. I only send my love and gratitude for the kindness you showed to me during the happy times.

With abiding love, and prayers for your health,

Sergei

It was a long-overdue message, but he had needed the buffer of time before he could write it—and perhaps Valeria might finally be able to read it. He did not expect a reply. Sending it was enough.

. 38 .

THE NEXT TIME Sergei saw Serafim, the old monk took him completely by surprise. It was not a punch or kick this time, but it might as well have been. The first words Serafim spoke were, "You must leave the island, Sergei—and soon!"

Sergei stood there, stunned, his mind regrouping. "Leave?" he asked. "Leave to go where?"

"I'll explain as we walk. When I'm done, I hope you will gather your belongings and say your good-byes."

Mystified, Sergei decided to keep his mouth closed and listen. The father began. "Do you recall when, several days ago, you asked me where I thought you might be going, and I said that we would speak of it later?"

"Yes, I do."

"Well, I now know. The time has come. I only just received the letter. They are gathering at the roof of the world."

BY EARLY AFTERNOON Sergei had packed his few things and said his farewells to the brothers at St. Avraam Rostov skete. They nodded, smiled, then turned back to their duties.

Before meeting Serafim at the island farm, Sergei sat for a few minutes in a silence made more sacred by their imminent parting. In that silence, Sergei contemplated all that Serafim had told him . . . "Our purpose together is finished," the old monk had said. "But there are others who may be useful . . . a gathering of masters, all good and trusted friends. Each comes from a different religious tradition . . . They cherish their paths as I do mine. But they've transcended their reliance on the exoteric, or conventional, teachings and turned to the esoteric, hidden, truths and internal practices. They have found the common, intertwining roots underlying every religion.

"I can't be sure who will appear, but you may meet a master of the Sufi tradition . . . a Zen roshi . . . a Taoist sage . . . a yogi of the Hindu path . . . a rabbi of the Jewish faith . . . a woman Kahuna from Hawaii . . . a nun and Christian mystic from Italy . . . a Sikh master . . ." Then Serafim smiled, adding, "And you will likely meet a man named George, who fits into none of the traditions and all of them. It is he who has called them together.

"There is a proverb favored by those in this fellowship: 'One Light, many lamps; one journey, many paths.' Each of these masters serves as a such a lamp, bringing his or her own principles, perspectives, and practices to open doors to the world of spirit—the internal path of awakening—"

"Awakening to what?"

"To the transcendent," Serafim answered. "And in service of this purpose, they meet in friendly debate to compare and contrast, to test, and to share with one another in free and open inquiry. Their goal, I believe, is to find the most central, core practices for body, for mind, for spirit—to begin a universal path, free of cultural dogmas or trappings.

"I won't burden you with all their names, which you'll learn in good time. Just know that they will gather soon—in the next three months— which is why you cannot delay.

"The journey will be arduous," he added, "but you've made arduous journeys before."

"You haven't told me where I'm going," said Sergei.

"Yes—of course. Look here." Serafim reached into his robe and took out a map. "See, I've marked one possible route. You'll be riding to a point north of the Hindu Kush Mountains, in the region of the Pamir, which some call the rooftop of the world. That high place, at the crossroads of India and Tibet, China and Persia, is where I send you in my stead—to the Fergana Valley, and a city called Margelan."

Serafim handed him a letter. "It is a brief introduction. You go there to assist them . . . and to listen and learn. Consider it my parting gift.

"The timing seems too perfect for me to doubt the rightness of this opportunity," he continued. "This possibility fell into place only when you decided, of your own free will, to let go of your quest for retribution. That decision, that great step, makes this journey possible.

"Your decision to take a higher path justifies all that I've taught you over the years. In making that choice, Socrates—by not repeating my sad history, by avoiding that dark course—you've given me a gift whose full value I cannot fully express."

THE STURDY MARE, one of the few stabled at the little farm on Valaam, was a gift from Serafim. With the approval of the island fathers, Serafim had also provided supplies and a hundred rubles, in case of need. "The mare is yours to keep," he said, "as long as she will carry you."

Sergei named her Paestka, which means "journey."

Father Serafim stood watching as Sergei cinched up a saddle that one of the brothers found. The old monk's eyes shone, and his skin was translucent, as if he were made not of flesh but of light.

Before Sergei mounted, he turned to say good-bye, but Father Serafim raised his hand to silence him. "For us, Socrates, there are no good-byes."

Part Six

A

RISING

STORM

Talents are better nurtured in solitude,
but character is best formed
in the stormy billows of the world.

JOHANN WOLFGANG VON GOETHE

. 39 .

Two years later, in 1908, a man named Sergei Ivanov rode west, approaching St. Petersburg. Although his name remained the same, the man himself had changed in ways subtle and deep. This peaceful warrior breathed deeper, sat taller, and laughed easier. His eyes shone with an inner light and inner peace. Beyond these signs, an observer might think that little had happened to him in the town of Margelan.

He knew their names now, and their hearts: Kanzaki . . . Chen . . . Chia . . . Yeshovitz . . . ben Musawir . . . Pria Singh . . . Naraj . . . Maria . . . and George, who had called them all together.

After a difficult journey, Sergei had served as their assistant and a sort of apprentice. He listened as they spoke of different forms of meditation on images and inner sounds: chanting . . . breathing and concentration methods to amplify internal energy . . . inner work to open intuitive sight . . . hypnosis and working with the lower and higher mind . . . the three selves . . . from kirtan to kaballah, and the truth behind and within the holy books . . . and every kind of perspective about conventional and transcendental realms.

Those in the fellowship also practiced movements from various martial traditions, such as the slow-motion T'aiji, but such practice was aimed at efficient movement for vitality and health—for rebuilding, not destroying.

One day Yeshovitz and Naraj were debating a point, and Sergei found himself stepping into the fray. "I believe Yeshovitz has the more realistic view," Sergei said. Immediately, they asked him to leave for the day—for his audacity, he thought—but when he returned, they had decided to use him as an experimental subject: Sergei would practice each of the disciplines they agreed upon and report what he had experienced. So he came to understand in a deeper way—to actually experience the results of these practices.

After intensive months, he no longer recognized himself. His face had actually changed—healed. The scar on his arm had nearly disappeared. His body felt ten years younger, like that of a child. Only his white hair remained to remind him of the past. But the past, and time, had become nothing more than a useful convention, an illusory idea, as his attention rested in the present moment.

There was an initiation—a gauntlet of nine tests, which he would never reveal—that gained him welcome and entrance into the fellowship as one of their own.

Then it was time to part. Each of them carried new understandings and hope for humanity—that it was possible for anyone truly interested to awaken to an expanded sense of life and of reality. The ordinary could become extraordinary, and the so-called mystical states could be a normal part of human experience.

All this Sergei brought with him as he and Paestka entered St. Petersburg. He had thought about his most immediate plans: He would pay a visit to Father Serafim to relate the gifts and blessings he'd received and to convey his gratitude. After that, he would find work, save money, and make his long-overdue journey across the sea.

But first he would visit Anya's grave.

Standing there, in the meadow he had left so long ago, he surveyed all that looked the same, and what had changed. Flowers now grew upon the grave. A breeze caressed his face, and Sergei realized, as he stood in silent communion with the love of his life, that he was at peace.

In the next moment a new impulse arose: He would visit with Valeria and Andreas. Sixteen years had passed since he had last seen them. If he had made peace with the past, they might have done the same.

In the early evening Sergei found a stable for Paestka and a much-needed grooming and feeding and rest. As he had years before, he visited a barber, had a long bath, and again appeared at Valeria's door, completely open to whatever might follow.

Still, nothing happens exactly as you expect. And he had certainly not expected a crying Valeria to throw her arms around him, speaking so quickly he could barely understand.

"Sergei! Sergei! My prayers have been answered. We never thought we would see you again! After your letter came—it must have been two or three years ago—I sent Andreas to Valaam, to find you, but you had gone. Oh, Sergei, I grieved so for Anya, but then I grieved for you as well. You've no idea how much I wanted to take back the words I had spoken. Oh, but you've come back to us! Can you forgive me, Sergei? How you must have suffered!" Valeria began to cry again. Sergei reached around her aging shoulders and comforted her, and old wounds were healed.

Then, abruptly, Valeria's eyes opened wide. "Andreas—he doesn't know you're here. He will be so surprised! And Katya too—I didn't tell you—he is married, Sergei, and I have a grandchild, little Avrom, with another on the way."

Valeria was out of breath, but it didn't slow her down. "They will be home soon. I must make dinner, something special! Oh, Sergei, forgive me—I haven't let you say a word. You must tell me everything. Soon, when we are all together. And I have much to tell you too!" she called back as she rushed into the kitchen.

When Andreas arrived with his family, and he spied Sergei, he gave a joyous roar and a brotherly embrace. He too had changed over the years. Sergei guessed that Katya, a serene-looking, black-haired woman, now rounded with their second child, had much to do with this transformation. They made introductions, then Katya took Avrom away to change his diapers while Grandma made dinner and the men talked of many things.

Andreas began by telling Sergei of his own travels to Persia and his successful rug importing business. "And it wouldn't have been possible without—well, we can discuss that later."

DURING DINNER, after small talk, Andreas said, "The pogroms have continued under Tsar Nikolai—and on my travels I've seen terrible poverty and misery. It's been a golden age for those who have gold, Sergei, but the poor grow bitter, and there is talk of revolution. I fear for those who live comfortably here in St. Petersburg."

"All the more reason for you to consider emigrating with me to America."

Valeria took Sergei's hand and said, "In this I have not changed. I'm too set in my ways to leave the soil where I was born, and where my husband and daughter are buried."

A silence filled the room after that. It seemed the right time for Sergei to ask, "Tomorrow . . . may I take you to your daughter's grave?"

"Yes, I would like that," Valeria said with a sigh. "After all these years."

As soon as the dishes were cleared, Valeria said, "Now, Sergei, you must tell us about your life—all that has happened since our sad parting."

How does one convey the years, the life and depth and passion, into a few words told after a dinner meal? Sergei did his best to summarize his vow of retribution, and all the years of searching and preparation, ending on the island of Valaam, when Valeria interrupted—

"Oh! Sergei, I forgot—with all this excitement . . . seeing you again—there is a letter for you from Valaam. We received it six months ago, and I've saved it. Just a moment—"

Valeria rushed into her room then returned, handing him a brief note that said,

Dear Sergei,

I pray this letter finds you at the address you left with Father Serafim. He would have wanted you to know that he passed from this world last December. He was at peace with the world, and with God. If I may say, I believe that he remembered you with a certain fond regard.

Brother Yvgeny, skete St. Avraam Rostov

He would not be going to Valaam after all.

In the space of a deep breath, Sergei said a silent good-bye to his spiritual father, friend, and teacher. Blessings upon you, Serafim, he thought. I am one of the many souls you saved. Sergei would take more time later to reflect on his time with his old master, now residing with the other angels.

When he looked up he said only, "A good friend has passed away."

"AND WHAT are your plans?" asked Andreas.

"Please stay with us," Valeria interjected. "We can make room—"

Sergei smiled. "Perhaps for a little while, Mother—until I leave for America. I'll need to find employment, to earn my passage—"

"That won't be necessary," said Andreas with a broad smile. "Excuse me for just a moment."

When he returned, Andreas placed three jewels on the table in front of Sergei, saying, "These will cover your passage and more—not that we're in a hurry to see you leave . . . "

Sergei looked down at the sparkling gems. "Andreas—it's so generous, but I can't take your jewels."

Andreas laughed. Katya looked delighted. And Valeria was completely beside herself. Leaning forward, she said, "Sergei, these don't belong to Andreas; they belong to you."

"What? I don't understand."

"It was the clock," she said, as if those words revealed everything. Sergei's puzzled expression only made her smile more—but then it faded as she explained, "Years ago, on that terrible day . . . after I sent you away . . . the clock fell from the mantle and shattered. I was so distraught that I saw nothing. "

Andreas took over: "When I returned home and saw the smashed clock, I thought there might have been a robbery. I rushed through the apartment and found Mother in her room . . . and learned that what had happened . . . and we gave each other comfort.

"Only later did I return to the sitting room to clean up. That's when

I found them: Mixed with the clock fragments, an assortment of gemstones were scattered on the floor. I placed them in a cup and set them in the cupboard. In the back of my mind I knew that they were valuable, but neither of us could think about much of anything just then."

Sergei was starting to grasp it. "So my grandfather had hidden gems . . . inside the clock?"

Andreas nodded. "Twenty-four of them."

No one spoke as Sergei absorbed this revelation. His thoughts traveled back to the time he first found the clock and read his grandfather's note. It had said, *Always remember that the real treasure is within.* Sergei smiled as he imagined how Grandpa Heschel must have enjoyed writing those words, pleased by their double meaning.

He heard Andreas say, "The gems are your inheritance, Sergei. And you can't imagine our pleasure that you're here, and that we can pass them on to you."

Andreas looked at his mother, and at Katya, then said awkwardly, "I must tell you, Sergei, we kept them safe for five years, but when we heard nothing—we didn't even know if you were alive—we sold two of the smaller gems . . . to help me get started in my business, and to help with expenses. Now we have money enough, and I intend to repay—"

Sergei raised his hand to silence Andreas. "Please, say no more of it."

Andreas started to shake his head when Valeria interrupted. "Sergei, my son is too proud to ask. But if you could consider a gift of two more, for the growing family—"

"You shall have four more," Sergei said.

Valeria brought out a small velvet bag she had made, and she poured the gems onto the table between them. The afternoon sun glinted off their facets, causing some to sparkle a translucent green, others a deep rich red, and the clear gems diffracted rainbows.

Knowing that Andrei would take only the smaller gemstones, Sergei selected four different types of generous size and slid them across the table to Andreas. "For your family."

And it was done.

Valeria put the remaining eighteen jewels back into the velvet pouch and set them before Sergei. "Do you have any idea of their value?" he asked.

"Yes," said Andreas. "We sold the two stones to Yablanovich, a jeweler and trusted friend of your grandfather. He gave us sixteen hundred rubles for one gem and two thousand for the other—and those were the smallest in your collection. The rest he appraised. I remember it clearly.

"When I asked him the value of the stones, Yablanovich took an eyepiece out of his shirt pocket, examined the stones one by one—he turned them, weighed each—and then he said, 'I cannot tell you their value—that is for each person to decide—but I can tell you something of their worth in the marketplace. So let me put it this way. Today, you can purchase an excellent meal in a fine eating establishment for twenty-five kopeks. This stone,' he said, pointing to the smallest ruby, 'would buy you three such meals a day for many years. And this one,' he told me, touching an emerald, 'will purchase far more. As for the gems of alexandrite— they are more valuable than diamonds, and if you live modestly, they will meet your needs here or in America for the rest of your life.'

"That is what I remember," Andreas concluded. "You are a wealthy man, Sergei."

WHEN VALERIA and Katya had taken the dishes to the kitchen, Andreas drew Sergei aside and said in a more serious tone, "This may not be a good time, Sergei, but . . . could you tell me exactly what happened that day in the meadow? I've wanted to ask you all these years . . . if it's not too painful . . . "

"It will always be painful," Sergei replied. "But you should hear it all." So he told Andreas how his sister had died and what Zakolyev had done afterward. Seeing Andreas's face turn ashen, Sergei regretted saying so much.

"Thank you for telling me," Andreas said, staring down at the floor. "I would always have wondered . . ." He looked up and added, "Mother will also want to know. Now I can tell her the truth but . . . I'll spare her the details."

Sergei nodded.

Then Katya returned and the couple retired, leaving the rest of the evening to Valeria. She and Sergei spoke long into the night, bridging the years that had separated them.

. 40 .

THE NEXT AFTERNOON Sergei took Valeria and Andreas to visit the meadow and grave site. They sat quietly, together yet alone with their personal thoughts and prayers. Clouds, carried by the spring wind, passed slowly so that the temperature changed like their emotions, from the warmth of love to the barren cold of sorrow.

To Sergei, Anya felt so close that he could see her behind his closed eyelids. He saw her as she was then and would always be, forever young. He heard her voice and the sound of her laughter. He sensed her touch and knew that while he lived, she would always be with him, until they met at last in a place beyond this life.

The three of them spoke little on their return to the city, but Valeria reached out and took Sergei's hand—and she said something so softly he nearly missed hearing it. "Those poor babies . . . "

"*What?*" he said. "What did you say, Mother?"

She answered in a sad, wistful voice, "Oh, I was just thinking about the babies who died with their mother before they ever had a chance to be born . . . how they now rest in the meadow—"

"Babies?" Sergei interrupted. "I don't understand."

"I—I thought you knew, Sergei. Oh—I'm so sorry, you didn't—"

"Valeria, tell me."

"Anya had confided in me, but she didn't want to disappoint you if the midwife was wrong. But the woman seemed certain that Anya was carrying twin boys. I know that she was planning to tell you. I thought she already had."

Sergei stared blankly. *Babies.* Two lives inside Anya. Sergei's mind raced back in time, stitching together words and images: Valeria remarking about the size of Anya's swollen abdomen. Anya joking, "With so many kicks, I must have a dance troupe inside." Then the horrific image, the gaping wound, the bloody tangle of intestines and . . .

Sergei had seen the death of one child; then he had been knocked unconscious. He had found only one lifeless child. If there had been a second child, he would have seen it—

And so would have Dmitri Zakolyev.

In an instant Sergei knew the wonderful, terrible truth: Another child, most likely a twin boy, might still be alive. After all these years . . . in Zakolyev's sight, within his reach. There was no way of knowing for certain. But there was a chance—maybe a good chance—that they had a second child and that it still lived.

These revelations unfolded in a few heartbeats. Valeria would have had no way of knowing. She would have assumed that both infants died with their mother.

It was all he would ever let her know, unless he found his child and brought him home.

"Sergei? . . . Sergei?" Valeria's voice startled him back to this place.

"I'm sorry," he said. "I was just thinking . . . of Anya. And I was surprised to hear about the two babies. It . . . it's hard news, even now . . . to know what might have been. "

"Yes," she said with a sigh. "What might have been."

S OMETIMES we make choices, and sometimes they are made for us. And once or twice in a lifetime, we grasp how all that happened before has led us to this very moment. Sergei now felt a pressing new sense of purpose: If his son lived, he would find him. To do so, he had to find Zakolyev.

But what would he tell Valeria?

In truth, Sergei was no longer driven by hatred or a personal mission to use violence to stop the evils in the world. As Serafim had once said, he had neither the responsibility nor the authority to play God's assassin. But he would need a credible reason for his abrupt departure—one that did not generate in Valeria any hopes that might later be crushed. So he would tell her the truth—that he was leaving to search for Zakolyev and his men. His official motive—stopping evil men from doing more harm—was one that Valeria would support despite her concerns for his safety.

When Sergei told Valeria about his change of plans, she started to say something, to protest, but in the end she nodded sadly, resigned to his departure, and said only, "Please be careful, Sergei, my son."

In the morning Sergei made ready to go. "After that meal, Mother, I won't have to eat another for the next five days."

"I hope that you complete your mission before you're hungry again," she said. But she knew that Sergei might not return for months, or years—and while neither of them spoke of it, she also understood that they might never meet again.

As Paestka carried Sergei south across the rolling hills and plains, he took stock of the situation, drawing upon his past search for Zakolyev: It was not likely that one man on horseback could find a band of marauders that struck quickly, left no witnesses, then returned to hiding somewhere in the vast expanse of Ukraine. He could only trust that his senses, refined by life in the wild, years of contemplation, and his intuitive powers might show him the way. He would ride south to pick up a trail of rumors, smoke, and tears.

When he found them, he would use stealth and strategy, observing from a distance to discern their numbers and routines. He would seek out his son, if he was to be found, and wait for the right moment to speak with him alone. Such a plan wouldn't be easy, but it was far better than riding boldly into camp and starting a bloodbath that might endanger his child.

Beyond that, Sergei would just have to see what unfolded. Only a fool underestimated his adversaries. And as Serafim would have said, "All plans are tentative."

. 41 .

IN THE SPRING OF 1908, fifteen-year-old Paulina disobeyed her father's wishes for the first time: She told Konstantin her long-held secret. She knew that she could trust him to keep her secret safe. And by finally sharing her burden with him, she hoped that her clever Kontin might shed some light in the darkness that had recently descended upon her.

As she passed him on the way to morning practice, she slipped him a note she had printed in letters he had taught her: "Meet me in our special place. Before afternoon training."

Konstantin looked up from the note, enlivened by the prospect of a few minutes alone with her. He tried to imagine a future with Paulina, but it had never quite taken shape in his mind. How could it? He had nothing to offer her—no possessions except for the clothes on his back; even these were remnants discarded by others in the camp, plunder once worn by murdered men.

During the break between training sessions, as soon as Father Dmitri had left to talk with some men, Paulina ran into the forest and across the footbridge over the stream that tumbled down the falls. There in their small cave hollowed out of the thicket, where they used to hide as children, Konstantin was waiting for her.

In the few minutes before they would be missed, Paulina told Konstantin to lean close, and she placed her hand upon his shoulder. Then she whispered in his ear: "Years ago, my father told me a secret I was never to reveal: Elena is not my mother . . ."

She waited while he absorbed this revelation, unaware that her trusted Kontin already knew this, and more, then she added, "My real mother was killed by a monster with white hair, and . . . and ever since that day, I've had nightmares about a white-haired wizard who can paralyze with his voice, coming to kill me. I struggle to kill it before it can speak, but it always utters one word. I can never remember the word, but in the dream I die."

Her voice trembled as she whispered in Konstantin's ear. It was not likely that anyone would overhear them, but she leaned close and whispered because she enjoyed the closeness; she needed it. "It was so long ago that I thought it was only a dream, only a story, but Father Dmitri has told me that the monster is real. He is a man named Sergei Ivanov."

Then she stopped talking and moved back and watched Konstantin closely, searching for an expression, a reaction, a sign to justify the secret she had shared, the risk taken. Surprise, curiosity, even disbelief—anything.

He only furrowed his brow as he thought about that name.

"What is it, Kontin?"

Distracted by the memory forming, he said, "It's just that . . . I'm troubled to learn about your mother's death . . . and how it happened . . . "

He wasn't telling her something. Of this, Paulina was certain. She was about to speak, but then she jumped to her feet in alarm. "Oh! I have to go!"

Paulina scrambled out of the thicket. Yergovich would be waiting, and angry. He would not report her tardiness, but if her father had returned—

With that panicked thought, Paulina raced back across the footbridge over the stream and back to the camp.

KONSTANTIN WAS STILL thinking about the name, Sergei Ivanov. He had overheard it before, in a conversation long ago. He recalled the name for good reason: That man Sergei Ivanov . . . might be his father.

Konstantin had assumed he was one of the orphans whose parents had been killed—until he'd heard Shura muttering to one of the men about Sergei Ivanov. Konstantin had listened carefully and caught a few words: "one infant killed . . . a boy . . . the other taken." Konstantin had felt they were speaking about him, since he'd left Shura and Tomorov only moments before and then sneaked around to the back of the cabin to eavesdrop through a crack in the log wall.

He had to stop Paulina from hurting this Sergei Ivanov. But how could he tell her? If she spoke of it to Father Dmitri, the consequences were unpredictable and dangerous. Besides, he was not certain that Ivanov was his father. Everything could fall apart over a few words he might have misunderstood. Speaking out, even to Paulina, would mean his own death.

Yet how could he remain silent?

THAT NIGHT, as Paulina was about to fall asleep, Father Dmitri entered her room, sat on her bed, and gazed at her for a long time before he spoke. "Paulina, you have been a good and obedient daughter and have made me proud. I imagine that you sometimes wonder why you don't live like the ordinary girls. It is because you are not ordinary. You have special gifts and a rare destiny. Like your father."

He paused to let these words, as kind as any he had spoken, make their impression, then he reached behind his neck and removed something Paulina had never noticed before. He handed her a silver locket on a chain. She held it, not knowing what to do. "It is a gift," he said, "to celebrate the day you were born to me."

A single tear slipped down Paulina's cheek. Embarrassed by her tears, she turned away and wiped her eyes as Father Dmitri spoke again. "Open it," he said, pointing to a small clasp.

Inside the locket Paulina found a tiny, faded photograph of two faces—a man with a dark beard and a pale woman. As she gazed at the photograph, her father spoke again. "They are your grandparents," he said, "my mother and father."

Paulina felt her blood turn cold as Father Dmitri said, "Do you remember what I told you about the wizard who murdered your mother? The man Sergei Ivanov?"

She nodded.

"I must tell you now: He also killed your grandparents—these faces you see in the locket. It all happened on the same day." He took a long breath, and Paulina saw that even now he was grieving their loss. She reached out to touch her father's hand. "Oh, Father . . ."

He pulled his hand away and spoke rapidly. "We all lived happily in a small Cossack settlement. I had to go away on various duties, so I left you with your mother and grandparents in the safety of the camp. You were only an infant.

"I returned early from my business and found you with Shura, who told me that your mother and grandparents had left you and gone for a ride to a meadow by a lake. I decided to join them. Just as I rode into the meadow, I was surrounded by armed men who bound me . . ."

Trembling with rage, he continued, "While I was tied there, struggling so to free myself so I could save them, Sergei Ivanov raped and killed your mother, then turned on your grandparents. I looked on, helplessly, while he cut them down. I've waited all this time to tell you the whole story, but you had to know, because of . . . a duty I'm going to ask of you.

"Long ago, I vowed to find and kill this monster who took your mother, who took them all . . ."

Paulina had never seen Father Dmitri cry, and the effect was devastating. "I have men of my own," he managed to continue, "hard men like Korolev. But it's not for them to avenge the death of my wife and parents. That duty has fallen on me, as a matter of blood and honor."

He looked into her eyes and added, "I grow older . . . and I won't live forever . . . so I pass this torch to you." He watched her closely, studied her expression, before explaining, "Sergei Ivanov knows my face . . ."

Zakolyev paused to let Paulina grasp his meaning—that as a young woman and a stranger to this man, she would have a decided advantage. *And my child, my future,* he thought, *will take the life of the monster who has haunted me all these years.*

Then he added, "If I had a son, it would be his mission; instead I have a gifted daughter. Now you know why you've been training all these years; why I have such faith in you; why I gave you this locket . . . so you'll never forget who killed your mother and your grandparents."

"I won't forget," said Paulina, her eyes cold and hard—like those of her father, Dmitri Zakolyev.

THE NEXT MORNING Paulina rose early for practice. On the way to meet Old Yergovich at the barn, she saw Shura leaving her cabin to fetch water. Realizing that Shura must know the truth about her mother's and grandparents' death, she called out to the older woman.

Shura set down her buckets and approached, always glad to see Paulina. So when Shura's smile quickly faded, Paulina was confused—until she looked behind her and saw Father Dmitri standing by the cabin, watching both of them. He gestured to Paulina that she should get to training. When Paulina turned back to Shura, the woman had already picked up the buckets and hurried away without glancing back.

That day Paulina had one of her best practices. Father Dmitri saw her defeat multiple attackers. In years past the men had held back, treating her like a novelty. Now they sparred as roughly with her as they did with each other. She got some bruises and sprains, but they healed quickly enough.

The men outmatched her in reach and strength, but even Great Yergovich, who could squat under a small horse and lift the kicking animal off the ground, could not get his hands on her. Paulina was more supple and far quicker than any of them.

Old Yergovich had even told her that she seemed to be able to see into their bodies, sense their point of weakness, and throw them off balance. She guessed that was true. But what surprised them the most was her power. Paulina could kick like a horse. The force that came from her didn't seem possible in a woman; it was as if she were drawing her power from the earth itself.

Her hands, feet, and elbows could find the tender spots, the pressure points, that when struck would render the strongest man unable to move. If a fighter tried to grab her or throw a punch, she would punch a nerve in his arm. If a man kicked at her with his right leg, he would find the left one swept out from under him.

Paulina had no desire to kill anyone—not even the white-haired monster who had haunted her dreams. She wasn't certain she could bring herself to break his neck, crush his windpipe, or use a knife. Yet this mission meant everything to her father, so she did her best to prepare herself.

When she had asked why Father Dmitri didn't just use a rifle or pistol, he'd said, "A rifle can miss or misfire; so can a pistol. The hands or a knife are the surest of weapons at close range . . . and the most satisfying."

Satisfying. A strange word, she thought. But her father was, after all, the leader of a Cossack band, and an expert in such things. Yet elements of doubt began to seep into her mind—as if life now were a complex puzzle . . . and Pauline was just beginning to notice the missing pieces.

Within a few months Zakolyev knew that none of the men could defeat her—except perhaps for Korolev, who refused to "play games with a child." It was just as well because Korolev, like a provoked creature of the wild, might go for the kill; then one of them would die, and Zakolyev could not yet predict the outcome. It was enough of a challenge keeping the blue-eyed giant away from his daughter for purposes other than combat. So, despite this affront to his authority, Ataman Zakolyev let Korolev avoid sparring duty. He did it for Paulina. He did everything for Paulina.

Z<small>AKOLYEV AWOKE</small> in a sweat. Another night terror. The cries faded as his eyes snapped open. A wisp of memory appeared, then was gone. He rubbed his forehead, trying in vain to erase the ghostly afterimage, dreams of the dead . . . the voice of an old schoolmate . . . the face of a girl he deflowered . . . everyone whispering, walking away . . . a child receding . . . a day in the meadow . . . confusing flashes . . . all because of Sergei Ivanov, the monster who killed his wife.

He moaned aloud, then looked around to be sure no one had heard.

"Dreams, only dreams," he muttered, rising, pacing. Soon Sergei Ivanov would die at Paulina's hands. She would avenge her father, Dmitri Zakolyev. It had to be soon.

S TANDING ALONE under the stars, remembering her father's words, Paulina touched her locket. She sighed as she looked up into the night sky, wishing her father had never told her of her past or her mission. Her youthful innocence, believing in a world of love and kindness, had faded. And now Konstantin's growing distance, and this mission that darkened her future.

After that, no matter what she was doing, a cloud hovered over Paulina, and her rare smiles masked a growing melancholy and a terrible resolve—because she had accepted her father's mission and made it her own.

Aware of her father's suffering in the night as he muttered and moaned in his sleep, Paulina now suffered confusing dreams of her own—a mysterious, changing landscape of forest and meadow and the sad face of a woman who might have been herself, only older. This dream-woman's mouth moved, but Paulina didn't understand her words. And sometimes she saw the man, Sergei Ivanov, but his back was always toward her, so she never saw his face—only close-cropped hair as white as the clouds.

She awoke to a world no less confusing. Now that her body had started to fill out, the men looked at her differently—particularly Korolev, which made her skin crawl. She tolerated his presence by pretending he was only a ghost. While her father maintained his authority, she would be safe. And her fighting skills gave her less to fear from any man.

A few days later, as Paulina was about to enter the cabin, she heard Oxana speaking in hushed tones to Elena, just inside. Paulina stopped to hear her say, "Yes, the Ataman has grown 'concerned' and 'anxious' . . . and another of our men, Leontev, was killed in the last raid . . . Will these purgings never end?" Oxana quickly added, "I tell you this only out of love and concern for Ataman Zakolyev."

"Of course," said Elena.

When Paulina entered, the women changed the subject abruptly and Oxana hurriedly left with a concerned look back. Lately the camp had changed—people skulking about, speaking in whispers, wearing false faces. Elena was especially careful, Paulina had noticed. Then she wondered: Have they changed, or am I only just waking up?

Paulina continued to focus on her training and never asked for details about what the men did out on patrol. Maybe she didn't want to know. She had asked once when she was young and was told, "Patrols for the tsar."

She wanted to ask Konstantin about this—or Shura—but she rarely had the chance. Shura would nod respectfully when they passed each other, but they rarely spoke more than a few words.

So Paulina was surprised when, on the day after the men had returned to camp, Shura stopped and looked like she wanted to say something. "What is it?" Paulina asked.

Shura just stood there, looking at her.

"Shura?"

The older woman looked slowly right and left. Then she said, "I was there . . . soon after your birth. I nursed you."

A little embarrassed to think of such things, Paulina retorted, "Yes, you've told me—"

Shura glanced around then said, "Paulina . . . you do care about me, don't you?"

"Well . . . yes, but I don't understand—"

Again Shura interrupted her. "You wouldn't want to get me into trouble, would you? If I told you something, could you keep it secret?"

"Even from Father Dmitri?"

"Especially from . . . him," Shura answered, shuffling anxiously. Then she seemed to make a decision. "Things are not as they seem . . . the mark on your neck—"

Paulina touched her neck to feel the raised birthmark. "My birthmark? Like my father—?"

"Yes—no!" said Shura. "Not like his. It was a stick from the fire—oh, I can still hear the screams . . . "

"What are you saying?" Paulina cried, louder than she had intended. But when she saw the terrified look on Shura's face, which had turned pale, Paulina's voice softened. "Shura, I don't understand . . ."

But Shura only babbled, "So tiny . . . when they brought you. Such a precious child . . . you are not like him. He has killed so many . . ."

Then Shura saw one of the men approaching. She hurried off, leaving a shaken Paulina to sort out what the old woman had told her.

. 42 .

By SUMMER 1909, tired and discouraged after searching for more than a year without finding Zakolyev's whereabouts, Sergei had found the charred remains of isolated cabins and several burned farms that might have been Zakolyev's handiwork. He had marked each location on a map, but they revealed no pattern he could discern.

That night Sergei dreamed that Paestka and he were a tiny speck, eternally wandering across a huge map of Ukraine, looking for another dot that always moved away from them. He awoke in frustration. He was beginning to think that Zakolyev might have moved his camp to Siberia or to the north.

No, he reasoned, they had to be in Ukraine, where atrocities against the Jewish people continued. But Ukraine was a land so large it tested his heart and will. It stretched more than a thousand kilometers from the north to the south and from west to east. He might as well have searched for a single coin buried in a forest.

He zigzagged west then east and ever southward, toward Kiev, the center of Ukraine. He followed rumors like a scent but found only trails of smoke, dissipating in the wind.

Avoiding the larger city centers, Sergei sought out isolated cabins, farms, and small settlements, where Zakolyev's band was more likely to conduct a massacre. Near one such settlement he spoke with an elderly Jewish man who, lacking a horse or mule, was pulling his own cart. The old man offered to share a little bread from his meager stores.

"Thank you, but I need information more than food. Have you heard of any recent pogroms?"

"Who hasn't?" the elder replied. "In settlements outside Kiev, Minsk, Poltava, and elsewhere, horsemen appear from nowhere. Wolves dressed like men. No, worse than wolves because they kill their own kind—men, women, children, it's all the same to them. For what reason? What reason?"

When Sergei asked him where such marauders were last sighted, his eyes turned down and he would not or could not speak. He only shook his head slowly, back and forth.

As WINTER CAME, Sergei's patience grew thin. He rode across frozen soil, wrapped in his long burka, leaning into the wind. Grim and haggard, he pushed Paestka onward. But doubts plagued him.

For all his skill and discernment, Sergei could not track men by sniffing the air, nor could he see the faces of men in a bent twig. He needed tangible signs, omens, clues—a sense of direction. Until he found something tangible he could only follow rumors to gossip, and gossip to settlements, where he might find witnesses. In the meantime, his questions were answered by puzzled looks and fingers pointing in different directions.

He fasted and prayed for a clear path to his son, but no sign appeared. Then he thought, Maybe I'm asking the wrong question. His breathing changed, and he descended into a deep trance and lost all sense of his body. In that state he asked, *Where is Dmitri Zakolyev?*

The answer came in a form quite different from the one he expected. Out of the void, the face of Dmitri Zakolyev flickered before him—the same sallow skin, blond hair, and dead eyes. He had not imagined that face; he had actually seen it—and he felt the full force of Zakolyev's torment and madness. He felt it as his own.

. 4 3 .

NOT TOO FAR AWAY, and at that exact moment, as Dmitri Zakolyev lay sleeping, the face of Sergei Ivanov suddenly loomed before him. He awoke in a panic, seeing Sergei the Monster standing over him. He gasped for breath, his eyes wide, peering into the darkness. The face of his enemy showed no anger but something closer to . . . pity. Then the face vanished.

Zakolyev rose quickly and paced frantically, pounding his head with his fist. A momentary impulse arose, to tell his daughter the truth. But what was the truth? If only he could remember . . .

WHEN THEY WERE CHILDREN, Konstantin and Paulina were almost inseparable. Now Konstantin cherished each meeting—like the time he found Paulina sitting with her feet in the cold stream between training sessions. He sat down next to her, removed his shoes, and let his bare feet join hers in the brisk waters. In that moment, he nearly asked her to run away with him. But he had no idea where to begin. So he said nothing, out of cowardice, out of love.

Paulina now looked at her Konstantin in a way that made her blush at times. She had seen one of the men with Oxana, out behind the barn. It had seemed coarse and crude, with the noises they made. But now she wasn't so certain. It was as if her mind and body could not agree on this, the end of innocence. Paulina had no one with whom she could share her inner turmoil, not even Konstantin. Especially not Konstantin.

ONE MORNING after Elena had left the cabin, Paulina opened her locket and gazed at the faces of her grandparents—tiny faces she had examined under a magnifying lens and by now had memorized. Just then Father Dmitri passed by her room and said, "Get to practice. Yergovich will be waiting."

Paulina sighed. Yergovich was always there, waiting. One day she would rise earlier and get to the barn before him. But not today. She was too tired, and she felt off balance, cranky, and . . . something else she couldn't name.

She looked up as Father Dmitri was about to leave. Paulina pointed to the photograph and asked casually, "Father, I've been curious. Why you don't look at all like your father's photograph? Your hair is light and his is dark, and—"

"Do not trouble me with such nonsense!" he said. "Just remember who killed them, and increase your efforts in training!" He slammed the cabin door.

Hurt, then angry, at this unjust rebuff, Paulina trained so hard that morning that she pulled a muscle in her arm while throwing Great Yergovich. She flinched with a stab of pain.

"What's wrong, little one?" he asked.

"It's nothing, Bear, just a strain. I'll be all right. Don't tell my father." She tried to lift her arm, then bit her lip.

"No, it is not all right," he said. "Go put your arm in the stream until you cannot feel it. Then rest."

"No rest!" she cried. "I need to train harder!"

"First you soak your arm, then we'll see."

"First you soak your head!" she cried, running off too fast for the Bear to catch her.

Paulina sat alone in her room, as depressed as she could remember. She rubbed her arm, deciding that maybe she should put it into the cold stream. It would take her mind off her father's anger. She had no idea why she had displeased him with a simple question. He was the one who had given her the locket in the first place—and it was a natural question. But maybe not one he had wanted to hear . . .

She turned to find Father Dmitri standing in the doorway of their simple cabin. She had rarely seen him looking more distraught. She fought her emotions again, hating herself for losing control. She wanted to apologize, but something held her back. Why should she apologize? For what?

She just stood and stared at the floor until he spoke. "Paulina, I'm sorry I spoke with you harshly. I didn't want to talk about your grandparents because such talk. It brings too many terrible memories."

He came and sat on her bed. His voice was hoarse with emotion as he said, "I know that my father and I bear little resemblance, but not every child looks like his parent. It's lucky that you do not look like me. You were fortunate to resemble your mother. Still, we share a birthmark . . . "

He pulled back his straw-colored hair to reveal a red mark on his neck, like the one she had noticed on her own several years before.

"We are the same blood, you and I," he said, touching her hair. "That is why I've trusted you with my honor, with my life . . . why you need to train even harder. Sergei Ivanov is not merely a well-trained fighter; his voice also has the power to deceive and enchant. His web of lies can make you believe that earth is sky and black is white. When you meet him, you must not give him a chance to speak, or he will confuse and then kill you."

When Father Dmitri turned and left her, Paulina touched the raised mark on her neck. She hated the monster Sergei Ivanov for making her father suffer. One day she would find him. One day he would pay.

S EVERAL DAYS LATER, during an afternoon practice, Paulina was frightened to find blood on her pants and on her leg. Yergovich excused her without another word; he must have thought it was serious too. She ran from the barn back to her cabin and tried to find the wound. She wasn't hurting—just a little cramp deep in her belly. She wondered if it was some kind of illness.

Shura entered the cabin a few minutes later. "Yergovich told me," she said—and she was smiling, which only confused Paulina more. "It's normal, means you are a woman, now—no longer a girl. About time; you're later than most. The bleeding will happen every month. Now go change your pants. For a day you will probably need to train lighter." Shura gave her a few pieces of cloth and said, "When you bleed, put some of these up in between your legs." Then she turned and left before Paulina could ask her about anything else.

What other mysteries don't I know? she wondered. What else have they not told me?

Recalling what Shura had said about a burning stick, Paulina touched her neck.

THE NEXT DAY Paulina fell ill with chills and fever. She couldn't keep her food down. Her head spun, and she couldn't even stand. She had never been so sick. Elena avoided her, but Old Shura came and put cool cloths on Paulina's forehead, touched her cheek, and made warm drinks that tasted awful but that Shura insisted she sip.

Paulina's mind felt hazy, and images passed through her mind. She recalled, vaguely, something she was going to ask Shura, but she couldn't think of it just then . . .

This malaise, which forced Paulina to lie still, left her with questions that she had never thought to ask about herself and the world around her. What does my future hold? she wondered. She had not thought much about the future before. Would her entire youth be spent hunting a man who might not even be alive?

She needed to see her trusted Kontin, to talk with him. He had been her eyes and ears, her connection to the world around her—a world outside the barn.

Her reveries were interrupted by a harsh voice. "Get out of bed!" said Father Dmitri, standing stiffly in the doorway, staring at her. "You have to train, if only a little!"

Paulina tried hard to rise but fell back and slept.

When she next opened her eyes, a wet cloth lay across her feverish brow. She looked up to see her Konstantin sitting on her bed, stroking her hair. "Kontin!" she whispered. "What if my father finds you here?"

"Shhhh," he said. "He's away on . . . patrol." He sat with her, and his smile lifted her spirits, even though it was a sad smile. She closed her eyes to save his image as Konstantin spoke softly to her with a tenderness she had not heard before.

"Paulina," he began in a whispered breath, leaning close to her, his breath in her ear, his hand stroking her hair. "You once told me a secret. Now I'll tell you one so you will know that I trust you . . . and that I care." He took a deep breath and looked into the distance. "If you share what I'm about to tell you with anyone, it will mean my death . . . "

Paulina, half in and half out of delirium, murmured, "You'll never die . . . always here with me . . . "

"No, Paulina, listen—please! I need to tell you now, and you have to believe me! You've been kept in the dark about so many things—I don't know all of it. But you can't kill Sergei Ivanov—"

Konstantin turned back to Paulina. She was fast asleep.

As KONSTANTIN LEFT PAULINA to confused dreams about what she had heard, Zakolyev and his men were thundering down on a small, isolated farm. The farmer Yitschok had been urged by friends in a nearby town to move closer, where there might be help should trouble come, but Yitschok had disregarded their advice. "What is one to do?" he'd asked with a shrug. "The Pale is large. They have not come anywhere near. I am only one small farmer on land not even my own—just me and my wife and children. What would they want with me? And besides, would I be safer near a settlement?" His friends had shaken their heads, knowing that Yitschok was right. If these murderers came, he would find no more safety with them—no safety anywhere.

Zakolyev's band murdered Yitschok, and Korolev did more than his share before killing the woman. The others set the farmhouse aflame. Sullen, they moved mechanically, no longer under any illusions that they were serving the Mother Church or the Tsar—only the Ataman's will.

An argument broke out when some of the men wanted to take the children and others didn't. Zakolyev cut them off. "Kill them. Now. Do it quickly!"—his version of mercy—so they obeyed.

Before they torched the cabin, Zakolyev's band confiscated anything of value. Later, the Ataman would search through every trunk saved from the fire, rifling through photographs and other personal items. But today he found a special prize—one of the finest horses he had ever seen, deep chestnut, wild eyes, a warhorse if he had ever seen one. Raised from a colt by these . . . Jews.

As flames danced from the farmhouse behind them, lighting the evening sky, Ataman Zakolyev laughed. In a manic mood, he slipped a stolen halter over the frightened stallion and announced, "I name him Vozhd—Chieftain!"

All was well for another moment, until the fool Gumlinov blurted out, "He is indeed a great horse, Ataman Zakolyev—but of course you recall that my horse has also been called Vozhd these past three years. Surely we cannot both have a horse of the same name. After all, it was you who suggested—"

Gumlinov's words stuck in his throat when he saw Zakolyev's expression—abruptly calm, almost serene, a look that captured his undivided attention. Zakolyev approached Gumlinov's horse, joking to his trusted man, "Well, thank goodness you are named Gumlinov instead of Zakolyev, or people would have trouble telling us apart." This broke the tension, and the men, including Gumlinov, bellowed with nervous laughter.

Then the laughter died as Zakolyev drew his saber and with one stroke sliced through the knee of Gumlinov's horse and completely severed the leg. With a shriek, the shocked animal tried to rear up but instead fell, toppling, its severed leg spurting blood. Still calm, Zakolyev picked up the lower leg as the animal whinnied in agony. Gumlinov stumbled backward in horror, his eyes darting to his suffering horse and back to Zakolyev.

The men watched in silence, their mouths open. They had seen the Ataman do many strange things, but this—cruelty to a horse—was sacrilege, and some of the men's Cossack blood boiled.

So it was that the last of the mortar holding together Zakolyev's mind began to crumble. Waving the severed leg as if it were a piece of wood, Zakolyev said in a calm, lighthearted tone, "At least now we will be able to tell our two horses apart." Tossing the leg over his shoulder, he walked to his old horse and mounted, gripping the rope that held his new steed. He called down to Gumlinov, "Better find a new name for your horse— or better yet, find a new horse to name."

Zakolyev wheeled around, and the others followed, leaving Gumlinov to put the poor beast out of its misery. Soon the dead and bloodied horse lay at Gumlinov's feet. Twenty meters beyond lay the burning pyre, another family of Jews. Gumlinov turned, lifted his saddle over his shoulder, and started walking toward an old mare, let out of the corral, now grazing in the distance.

A loyal member of the band for fifteen years, Gumlinov did not hope to kill Zakolyev; he did not have the courage. But he would love the man who did.

He decided not to follow the others to their next raid farther north— not on a broken-down, swaybacked horse. Let them butcher the next village without his help. He'd see if this animal could get him back to the camp before he put it out of its misery. "I'm tired of killing horses," he said, "tired of killing Jews."

During her father's absence, Paulina grew strong enough to get out of bed and limber up. She had always liked stretching; it made her feel like a cat.

She missed Konstantin. She wanted to feel his hand stroke her hair again. Or had she just imagined it? Maybe it was only a dream, she thought. But he had said something to her; she could still remember his breath in her ear. Was it something about her father? She felt angry then, without knowing why.

The next day she asked Elena, "Have you ever seen Konstantin with any of the other girls?"

"I really don't know," Elena said curtly, "but I don't think so."

Paulina was relieved but wary. She placed little trust in Elena's words. The woman was little more than her father's servant, always formal and distant, ever so careful with the Ataman's daughter—as if Paulina were a duty like cleaning and cooking. In fact, Elena didn't like her; that was clear. Then why did she pretend? Why did everyone pretend?

Paulina felt like she lived in a cabin of secrets, in a camp of lies.

. 44 .

In April of 1910, as his search continued from village to village, Sergei rounded a hill and saw in the distance the still-smoldering ruins of a small farm. The stench called forth memories of the Abramovich cabin those many years ago. For a moment he felt physically sick with grief for those buried beneath the rubble.

Riding closer, Sergei spied a man standing near the ruins, stooped over by grief, his head bowed in prayer. Dismounting, Sergei walked the last thirty meters to avoid startling the older man, who might not welcome a mounted rider at the moment—especially one who looked like a Cossack. As Sergei approached, he continued scanning the ground for tracks.

When Sergei drew near to the grieving man, he stood respectfully and waited until he looked up, at last aware of Sergei's presence.

"I'm sorry," Sergei said. "Were they relations?"

"Are we not all related?"

"You speak like my grandfather. Are you a rabbi?"

"No, I am not. Was your grandfather a rabbi?"

"No, he only spoke like one."

The man nodded in silence, then said, "They were my friends. Now they are ashes."

Sergei waited in silence for a few moments, to show his respect, before asking, "Did you see what happened . . . the men who did this?"

"It was over by the time I arrived. I was riding to see Yitschok and his good wife . . . and his three children . . ." He sighed and after a long pause added, "and as my cart approached, I saw smoke in the distance. At first I hurried to help, thinking that the barn might be burning. But then—before the farm came into sight—I heard the shouts of men, then . . . then a woman's scream . . . and the children . . . oh, the children . . . "

"You heard men? How many?" Sergei asked, pulling him back to the present.

"How many? I don't know, maybe ten. I only saw them ride away from a distance. I was hiding . . . like a coward—"

"Like a wise man," Sergei said. "You saw them ride away?"

"Yes." The man shivered then shook his head sadly.

Impatient to follow, Sergei asked, "Which way were they riding? Please. It's important."

The man hesitated, then pointed to the southwest.

Sergei led Paestka twenty meters in that direction. His pulse quickened when he came upon the hoofprints of at least ten horses—the freshest trail he had found since his search began. If Zakolyev's band had done this, they might have only an hour's lead—two at the most.

Before riding off, he returned to the old man. "Can you describe any of them?"

"No, I was hiding. But there was one, who seemed taller than the rest—a giant. That's all I know."

"Thank you, Father," he said out of respect. "I'm so sorry about your friends. Do you need anything before I go?"

"Nothing you can give me, I'm afraid. I will go and tell the others. They will come. We live in a settlement twenty kilometers to the south. If you ever come there, ask for Heitzik."

He nodded in farewell and was about to leave when Sergei saw him falter, clutch at his chest, and fall.

Sergei ran to him. "It . . . it's all right," he said, trying to rise, clearly in great discomfort. "It's happened before. Just the shock of seeing this."

"What can I do?" Sergei asked.

"If you could help me to my cart." He rose slowly, painfully. He tried to walk but couldn't, so Sergei carried him. "Thank you. It's all right now. My horse is as old as I. She knows the way."

Clouds were building; it might rain soon. Now Sergei had a trail he could follow, and perhaps he could overtake them before they reached the forest. Sergei's son had never felt so close.

Heitzik grimaced in another wave of pain. "I'll be all right," he said. "You go . . ." He could barely hold the reins.

Sergei sighed. "Give me just a moment—I'll ride with you to your settlement." Heitzik nodded, and Sergei saw the relief on his face.

He quickly mounted Paestka and did another quick ride around the ruins. The tracks led south. He also found the body of a horse, its throat cut and one leg severed at the knee. A swarm of flies buzzed around the carcass.

He ached to follow these men while the trail was warm. He looked back at old Heitzik, hunched over on the cart seat. He tied Paestka to the back of the cart, climbed up, and took the reins. "All right, horse," he said. "Take us home!"

"The horse's name is Tsaddik," whispered the old man. He added, "I only reveal his name to friends." Then he was quiet.

By the time they reached Heitzik's settlement, it was nearly dusk. Rain clouds had settled heavily over them. A woman ran out to meet them and pointed to Heitzik's home. By the time Sergei got him to the door, it was dark. The rain had begun to fall in a drizzle, then a downpour.

Few tracks, if any, would remain.

While Heitzik's wife, Devorah, was helping her husband to bed, she spoke to Sergei as if he were family: "It's dark. It's raining. Please—put your horse in the barn across the street and stay the night. In the morning, you'll have a good breakfast with us. With food in your stomach, you can be on your way. Or stay with us as long as you wish." Then she hurried to attend to her husband.

Sergei had also heard her unspoken words: Thank you. May God bless you. You are not a stranger to this house.

Serafim had once said, "A man's character reveals itself most clearly when he makes a choice under pressure." Sergei had made a choice; he hoped it was the right one. He believed it was what Serafim would have done. But in making that choice, he knew he might have lost the way to his child. He wasn't going to be able to find tracks at night in the rain, so he would accept the hospitality of these Jewish people—Grandfather Heschel's people.

. 45 .

.

On an otherwise pleasant day in early spring, the dogs began barking wildly. A stranger had entered the camp. Nearly naked, his clothing torn and shredded, he cursed loudly and waved a saber in the air. His hair and beard were long and tangled, as if he had lived in the wild—no longer a man but more like a forest creature. One of the dogs growled ferociously, just out of the man's reach. Another attacked and was cut down.

Zakolyev and his men were away on a raid, and nearly all the boys including Konstantin were in the forest gathering wood, leaving only Great Yergovich on guard. On seeing the savage, a child cried out in alarm and ran screaming. Paulina emerged from her cabin just as Great Yergovich rushed to investigate.

Yergovich and Paulina saw the stranger at the same time, but they were both too late to save Shura, who was just rounding the corner carrying water from the stream. Startled, the nameless man spun and slashed Shura with the sword, nearly severing her head. Yergovich dashed in to take both the sword and life of this stranger, but he made the fatal mistake of underestimating his adversary, thinking him a *bezoomnii*—mindless, crazy. Yergovich approached boldly to frighten off the poor witless fool.

As Yergovich drew near to him, the man threw his sword in a spinning arc. It pierced the chest and heart of Paulina's Old Bear, who stumbled backward and fell with a look of surprise on his face as the light faded from his eyes.

Paulina stood stunned, at first thinking that the wild-eyed stranger might be the monster Sergei Ivanov. She trembled with dread and resolve. But she quickly realized that this crazed and babbling bearded man was not a monster but another intruder possessed by demons and bent on destruction. He would surely attack the other women and children.

An instant later, Paulina confronted him. She had no memory of what happened next—but Oxana, peering out the door of her hut, saw it all.

SOON AFTER THIS INCIDENT, the boys returned, their arms filled with firewood. When they saw the bodies of Shura and old Yergovich and a stranger lying facedown, they dropped the wood and ran to investigate. Konstantin was the first to reach Paulina, slumped against a wall nearby and weeping. He sat down next to her, put his arm around her, and held her close.

Just before dusk, Dmitri Zakolyev, Korolev, and most of the others returned. As soon as the Ataman saw the bodies of Yergovich and Shura—and the corpse of a stranger lying farther away—he cried, "What happened? Where is Paulina?"

"I saw it, Ataman," said Oxana. "A crazy man came into the camp!"

Zakolyev leaped off his horse and shook her. "Where is Paulina?" he repeated, but Oxana babbled even faster, as if to save her life.

"After he killed Shura he threw a saber and killed old Yergovich—but Paulina saved us! She walked up to the wild man and held up her hand as if to say 'Stop!' He pulled the saber out of old Yergovich, and he let out a horrible shriek and attacked Paulina. She moved so quickly! She was in front of him, and then she was beside him, so his saber missed her. Then she hit him many times, and he fell and died."

Zakolyev was breathing hard, trying to control himself—there was no reason to hurt the woman. So he said softly, "Oxana, I'm going to ask you only one more time. Where is Paulina?"

She pointed toward the Ataman's cabin. "I . . . I think Konstantin— he walked her back to your cabin—"

Zakolyev released Oxana and ran toward the cabin.

Paulina had begged Konstantin to leave the instant they heard the men riding in. When Father Dmitri found her she was sitting alone, in a kind of trance, staring into space. She had avenged the death of Shura, who had mothered her, and the death of the man who had taught her better than he knew. She was sickened by how easy it had been to take a man's life—sickened because she had wanted to kill him but also because of something he had said . . .

At first he had only raved in words she didn't understand, but then he'd muttered a few words in Russian. That's when Paulina realized that he had not just stumbled onto them, he had searched for and found the camp. He had cried out, "Murderers! . . . killed my wife . . . my children . . . for what reason? Because we are Jews!" There were tears in his wild eyes. She didn't understand the rest of his mutterings. He was crazed, yet his voice had the sincerity of one who spoke the truth.

The wild man's words made Paulina face what she had long ignored: where the men had found the horses, sheep, trunks, tools, books, and many other things as well.

Just then her father burst into the room in a panic. "Are you all right?"

Her answer came slowly, her voice a monotone. "I'm not injured, if that's what you mean." She looked up and saw what she had never seen with the eyes of childhood: Her father had aged; he was drawn and weary.

Zakolyev let out a sigh of relief. "All right then. You did well—Oxana told me—and soon you'll be ready." He started to reach out to touch her hair, but she moved away.

He pretended not to notice. "You rest," he said. "Tomorrow I will find you another instructor."

Staring at the floor, Paulina responded, "I don't think I'll be needing another instructor, do you?" When she looked up, the doorway was empty.

Dmitri Zakolyev had left to wash himself in the river, to scrub his body raw, to cleanse his mind. Then he would try to sleep. He did not

like losing Great Yergovich and the woman Shura. They were both useful—and he was furious about this breach of security. Yet this strange
twist of fate had tested his daughter in mortal combat. So it had turned
out well in the end.

She was ready.

SOON, SHE THOUGHT. He had said it would be soon. She hoped
so; she wanted to get it done, get it over with, find out if she had any life
on the other side of this mission. As the reality, the inevitability, of it
dawned on her, Paulina shivered. She knew she could fight—and now
she knew she could kill—but was she truly ready to kill Sergei Ivanov?
Paulina touched the locket, held it gently in her fist, as if it contained
the souls of her grandparents. She tried to imagine what her mother
must have thought before the demon killed her.

Yes, she could kill him, and she would. Everything depended it. Not
only her life, for if she failed she would surely die. But in the event she
survived and he escaped, she could not live with the shame.

She wondered what had happened to her, a girl once so full of
dreams now replaced by a single dark purpose. Paulina sighed. She
wished her father had never given her this weight to carry. But he had.
So she would not fail him. Now seventeen years old, Paulina wondered
how much time, how much life, she might live beyond that.

THE NEXT DAY the Ataman began muttering about leaving the
camp. Pacing like a caged tiger, he spoke without direction, as if he were
talking to the air or to himself. "We have grown soft and comfortable,
like a quaint village of Jews!" he ranted. "Remember what I told you long
ago: We must be moving targets—so we move!"

He slipped in and out of a dark inner world that no one could reach.
Then, without apparent cause, he would wake from his trance and issue
orders with complete clarity. Some hoped he would forget about leaving
the camp. Others whispered about leaving themselves.

Zakolyev could no longer clearly distinguish between the waking world and the nightmares that raged in his sleep, shifting and changing like patterns of smoke rising into the night sky.

But he took consolation in one certain knowledge: Someday soon, Paulina would be the last sight that Sergei Ivanov ever saw.

If he saw her coming at all. And justice would be done.

Meanwhile, Korolev watched Zakolyev's descent into madness with growing disdain. And whenever the ripe little Paulina would pass, Korolev's cold blue eyes would follow.

. 46 .

S ERGEI LEFT Heitzik's village with little hope but with the blessings of his family and new provisions. The cold rain had ended, leaving the air crisp and fresh—a good day for tracking, if any tracks remained.

He returned to the ruins, now cold, and to the spot where he had seen the tracks. Now there was only mud, without a trace of horses' hooves. Still, he had a direction. Or did I? Think! he told himself. Would these men, led by Zakolyev, whose existence depended on secrecy, leave the scene of a massacre in the exact direction of their camp? Not likely. Their initial trail led southwest, toward the Podolia region, and Bessarabia beyond—not the best region to hide.

But suppose they changed course and circled—where? To the north, his instincts said. Toward the forested region near Kiev where he had once found tracks before they disappeared in a streambed. He knew the region well by now, and if he were Zakolyev, that's where he would go.

His knees told Paestka to go forward at a walk, along the line of old tracks. Up ahead the ground might be harder and show some sign. He found nothing for fifty meters . . . a hundred . . . two hundred. But at about three hundred meters, he saw the traces of hoofprints—many riders. He followed whatever tracks he could find until they disappeared.

He backtracked until he found the hoof markings again. Then he rode in a circling course almost ninety degrees to the right until he was heading northwest. He found nothing, so he backtracked again, then rode in ever-widening circles all afternoon. As the sun dropped low in the short days of early spring, he was about to give up for the day when something caught his eye. It was a hoofprint. He walked in a circle and found more—many more—leading north and east. He had found their trail. He was certain of it.

There were times he lost the tracks again, but he could see other signs where they had ridden through tall grasses or underbrush. He looked for broken branches at the height of a rider's head or shoulder or slung rifle, places where horses pulled up plants to eat while walking, or shrubs pushed out and down due to the circular motion of their hooves. He silently thanked Alexei for those few lessons in tracking.

He had hoped that they would head directly back to their camp, but the trail led to the outskirts of the town of Nizhyn, where the tracks were lost in a morass of hoofprints and the ruts left by of many travelers on horseback and buggy. There was no trail left to follow.

It was not likely that they had remained long in the town. But on the faint hope that he might learn something, he entered and decided to spend the night in a room and eat a prepared meal.

He found a barn for Paestka and a small boardinghouse for himself, run by a heavy, middle-aged woman with a bun of gray hair pinned to her head. She showed him to his room and announced that the dinner meal would be ready in twenty minutes.

Sergei decided to go down to the saloon across the street and question a few locals about riders who might have passed through. But first he would have a little vodka to warm his bones. Ordering a bottle, he sat down, poured himself a glass, and drank its contents. Then he found himself pouring another, and downed that one. He was just raising the third glass to his lips when he heard a man at the table behind him muttering to himself: ". . . sick of it . . . slaughtering pigs . . . no honor . . . Zakolyev's crazy . . . last time I'm going . . . "

Suddenly alert, focused, and sober, Sergei quietly put the glass down. He sat still and listened, but he heard nothing more than the man's breathing, pouring, swallowing. He picked up the bottle and casually walked to another table and sat at an angle to him, where he could watch the man closely. He was alone, dressed in the clothing of a Cossack. It had been many years, but he still had a familiar look about him. One does not forget such men.

Soon the man rose unsteadily and, still muttering, staggered up the street to another boardinghouse. Sergei followed from a distance, never taking his eyes off him. Then he stood outside and waited and watched through the long night, his dinner and bed forgotten.

In the morning, he thought, this man may return to his camp.

. 47 .

Even before the incident with Gumlinov's horse, the men had unspoken doubts. Now they had no doubts left. Everything was falling apart, and the Ataman was acting like a crazed jackal.

Later, in another raid, two more men died—one killed by a Jew who charged with a pitchfork as his wife hugged their children in the doorway. He managed to stab Chertosky before one of the men cut him down. Another of their men was stabbed in the back by a boy who had leaped out of hiding. That boy had courage—but it was his last act.

The men had had their fill of it by the time they rode back to camp. Those well out of the Ataman's earshot muttered about riding off, sickened by what their lives had become. One of the men said softly to a nearby rider, "Perhaps I'll become a monk."

The man answered, "Too late for that. Our souls are already lost."

Just before her afternoon practice session, which she did out of habit and in solitude—and before her father's expected return from patrol—Paulina searched the camp for Konstantin. She found him sitting on a rock outcropping overlooking the falls, staring down at the water pounding on the rocks far below. Sitting down next to him, Paulina told her Kontin that she would soon be leaving to complete the task her father had given her. "Few young women have ever undertaken such a mission," she said, as if trying to convince herself. "For this purpose he freed me from the duties of other women . . . gave me special privileges and protection . . . "

Paulina looked intently at Konstantin, desperate for his approval, but his expression revealed nothing. "He told me I was born to do this," she continued, her eyes pleading, her hand grasping his arm. "Oh, Kontin, I hope I'm ready! My father needs this victory so badly for his . . . peace of mind."

Then she reached down the front of her blouse—a gesture that made Konstantin gasp—and pulled out her locket. She showed him the faded picture of her connection to a past of which she had no memories. "I do this for them as well," she said. "Father insists on sending Tomorov with me. I wish it were you instead . . . "

He nearly spoke then—almost told her everything he knew—but what did he know for certain? And if he told her, would she believe him? It could mean his death; it might even be dangerous for Paulina . . .

Paulina had hoped that Konstantin might share her sense of destiny, that he might be glad for her. But the growing look of dismay on his face, despite his efforts to hide it, filled her with a sadness she didn't understand.

THAT VERY AFTERNOON, after Paulina left him for her training, Konstantin decided he must leave this camp—that he must risk everything and convince Paulina to leave with him. He had gone over it again and again, but any path his mind traveled, it reached the same destination: They had to go together; it was their only chance for happiness. They would run for their lives and for their future. This very night they would take flight.

Konstantin was no fool—he knew that choosing between familiar lies or bitter truth would not be easy for Paulina—and he held only the barest hope that she loved him enough to abandon all she had known.

If she could not bring herself to join him, then he would go alone, carried by the hope that he might one day make his fortune and return for her. And at least he would be able to say good-bye to the one person who reminded him that love was still possible in this dark world.

KONSTANTIN RAN to the barn, where Paulina practiced, looked around to make sure no one else was inside, and said quickly, "Paulina, this afternoon, meet me at the falls. Tell no one you're coming!" And he thought, If we leave in the night, no one will miss us until morning.

All might have gone well if Elena had not just returned from the latrine. Overhearing Konstantin's words to the girl, she stopped, just out of sight until the boy ran off, then she continued back to the cabin.

As KONSTANTIN SAT QUIETLY in the thicket of brambles near the top of the falls, he had time to think of many things. He wondered why Father Dmitri had never discovered this spot, then worried that perhaps he had.

Konstantin also thought about prayer. Some of the men had spoken of God and heaven and hell, but that was the extent of his religious education. He had never prayed before, although he had seen others do it. He prayed now, not quite sure whom he was addressing—but if there was some all-powerful being who might be listening, he asked for Paulina's safety. He could not pray for her love, for that was only hers to give.

Dark clouds had blown in, turning a bright afternoon to dusk. Konstantin had an hour to wait, maybe more. "Please," he whispered fervently, "if you're listening, God, let her go with me!"

A steady rain had begun to fall, which might cover any tracks in the forest. He would be a rabbit that would evade Zakolyev the fox.

Two rabbits, he reminded himself. Two.

. 48 .

By the late afternoon, Sergei had to drop far behind or risk being seen by the rider ahead. This meant that he could no longer see his quarry, either, but the trail was fresh and easy to follow, despite the rain showers. Eventually, the tracks led to the edge of a forest. Sergei quickened his pace; he could draw closer without being seen.

An hour passed. Sometimes the hoofprints were mixed with others, until Sergei came to a rushing stream, where the tracks disappeared altogether. Tracks don't just disappear, and horses don't fly, thought Sergei; the man's horse had walked upstream. So Sergei followed, checking the banks on either side as the water rushed past Paestka's knees and then her strong thighs. It would be deeper ahead, and faster. Soon he heard white water surging over rocks. It was not a river for travel by boat—a good place for an isolated camp.

Sergei listened for any telltale sounds but heard only the steady pounding of a waterfall just ahead.

Part Seven

———

THE
SEARCH
FOR PEACE

Everything that begins also ends.
Make peace with that
and all will be well.

THE BUDDHA

. 49 .

W HEN THE MEN RETURNED in the late afternoon, a few smiling women and children ran to greet them. Their smiles quickly faded when they saw the grim expressions on the dirty, tired, and sullen faces of the men. Covered with blood and soot, they had brought back two more riderless horses. No bodies were draped across the horses because the dead were thrown into the flames.

"The Jews killed Chertosky and Larentev," muttered one of the men to Oxana before he headed for his cabin. Oxana had lived with Oleg Chertosky. She cried over his loss, but she could feel no hatred for people who were only defending themselves.

The Ataman was in a bad state. He had killed a woman before Korolev was finished with her, and they'd had angry words. As soon as they arrived, Zakolyev turned his back on Korolev as if the man didn't exist. Then he led his new horse into the corral, quickly removed the saddle, and carried it to the barn, where he planned to check on Paulina's practice.

She was finishing her routine when she saw her father standing in the doorway, staring at her but not really seeing her. He nodded absentmindedly before departing. When he arrived at his cabin, tired and distracted, he hardly took notice of Elena, sitting by the fire, until she looked up at him and forced her usual smile.

T HE ATAMAN had lost control of his mind and his men. Korolev was convinced of this after they had almost come to blows during the raid. It was time to leave; he, Korolev, would never again take orders from any man.

But before he rode away, he would have the girl, Paulina—as a parting gesture for the lunatic leader. He had waited far too long to pluck the ripe young woman. He would only have to wait a few moments more, just out of sight, until Zakolyev left the barn and headed to his cabin.

Paulina had just finished her stretches, and her body still wet with perspiration. She was about to rush off and tidy up before meeting her Kontin, eagerly anticipating what he might say or do, when Korolev entered the barn, his knife drawn.

"Get on your knees!" he commanded, shutting the door.

Paulina knew that the time had come. Korolev was going to force himself on her . . . and her father was not going to be able to protect her this time.

Just then Korolev threw a kick to her belly. The kick missed, but Korolev had known it would and had followed up with a backhand strike to where he anticipated she would move. It stunned her, but Paulina rolled and recovered.

They both knew it would be over in a matter of seconds, one way or the other. Korolev had tremendous power, devoid of mercy or conscience. Paulina had speed and determination—and a primal hatred of this brute.

When he came at her again, she leaped aside and spun and kicked him in the groin. The air escaped his lungs, and he went down. As she came in to finish him, Korolev swept her support leg and kicked the side of her knee.

Paulina gave way to minimize the force, but the kick had done its damage. When she took a quick step, her leg gave way and she fell. Then he was on her, straddling her hips, pinning one of her arms with his knee, sweating, excited, victorious—

Out of the corner of her eye, she saw the blade flashing down. In that fraction of a second, she realized he was going to kill her and *then* rape her—it made no difference to him—and a fury coursed through her body. Since his one arm held the knife, he was momentarily open. As the blade descended to pierce her chest, she moved, deflecting the blade and in the same motion thrusting her knuckles deep into Korolev's windpipe. She heard a crunch, and then he was raising the knife again . . .

But it never came down because he had released the blade and instinctively clutched at his throat, trying to get air as she shot her good leg up and kicked straight into his groin, lifting the giant off the ground with a terrible sound. He lay there making sucking, gasping, choking noises, vomiting, but it stuck in his throat, and with a shudder, Korolev died as violently as he had lived.

A RAIN BEGAN TO FALL as Paulina hobbled in pain back to the cabin. Finding no one there, she collapsed upon the cold hearth and cried in convulsing sobs. She dreaded what her father might say or do when he learned that she had killed his second in command. Then she realized that she didn't care. If any man ever deserved death . . .

Still, she was badly shaken; she needed to talk to Konstantin—

All at once she remembered: She had just been leaving to meet him when the brute had attacked. She hoped he was still waiting! Paulina leaped to her feet and started to run but cried out in pain and fell. She pounded the stone hearth. Furious at her father, at her leg, at the world, she rose again and forced herself into a limping run toward the stream, to the falls, to her Kontin.

. 50 .

THE RAIN, and a forest full of chirping, made Konstantin want to scream for silence. Another hour had passed as he sat here, listening intently for her footsteps. He did not really believe she would come, but he could hope. If she came, all would be well because they would be together. And if she did not come . . . He tried to imagine what he would do.

I can read and write and draw, he thought, and I know my numbers. I will find work in a city far away, perhaps even in America. I will learn a new language, and I will make my fortune. Then I will return one day and ride into the camp on a great horse with a sword and rifle and with a band of fighting men I've hired. And I will tell Dmitri Zakolyev, "I come from America. I have come for Paulina!" I will say the words in English, and if he does not understand, that will be too bad!

Just then, as a rain began to fall, Konstantin thought he heard something over the sound of crickets and the water's thunder at the base of the falls below. He heard approaching footsteps.

Ecstatic that Paulina had come, Konstantin emerged from the foliage, his face radiant—but instead of Paulina, he found Ataman Dmitri Zakolyev standing before him, not three meters away.

A MOMENT of cold panic washed through him, followed by an impulse to run. Such a gesture would have been futile, desperate, and hopeless. So he froze in place and waited as the raindrops fell.

Dmitri made no attempt to approach. Instead, the Ataman seemed relaxed, even friendly. Konstantin glanced around—the Ataman seemed to be alone, and he softly spoke words that Konstantin never imagined he would hear. Ignoring the rain that would soon soak them, the Ataman said, "I have known for some time that you care deeply for Paulina. I've also noticed that she cares for you. And why not? You have a bright mind and good character.

"It may seem strange, my coming to you now, here, but there are pressures building for everyone, and I have given it considerable thought. You know I have always liked you, Konstantin." Sitting on a large stone, Zakolyev gestured for Konstantin to join him. "I expect that Paulina will want to marry before long. And I will not have her marry any of the other men, nor will I have her passed around from man to man. So marrying you may be the best solution. But you and I must have an understanding."

Konstantin could not believe his ears. He was suspicious, of course; yet what the Ataman said made sense, and he truly sounded sincere. In any case, Konstantin knew two things for certain: Either the Ataman was telling the truth, in which case he was safe for the moment and his life might work out far better than he had ever imagined, or the Ataman was lying, and he was in grave danger. But if he rejected this offer, sincere or not—if he turned and ran—he would not live out the next hour.

He approached warily, as Father Dmitri patted the wet stone next to him. This was Konstantin's moment of truth. As he sat down, Father Dmitri smiled and placed a hand lightly on Konstantin's shoulder and said with what seemed genuine affection, "You have grown, Konstantin. Yet you still look Paulina's age."

Konstantin risked a smile in return. He wanted so much to believe Father Dmitri that his wary mind did not consider three critical questions: First, if Father Dmitri truly wanted his daughter's happiness, why had he trained her as an assassin—to kill or be killed? Second, and more pressing, how had the Ataman known he was waiting here? And third, where was Paulina?

SERGEI HAD LOST THE RIDER'S TRACKS, but he continued upward, following the turbulent river on faith, until he reached the base of a high waterfall, where he found a winding path upward—a path made by men. He tethered Paestka to munch on the wet grass. Wiping his rain-soaked hair back from his eyes, Sergei climbed the steep and slippery trail.

As he reached the top of the falls, he thought he heard, over the sound of the roiling water far below, someone speaking.

PAULINA LIMPED along as fast as she could, but her painful leg had given way and caused her to fall again. She could see Konstantin's face in her mind's eye, with his sad smile. He was waiting for her, and once she reached him all would be well. She struggled on through the slick mud, blinking in the downpour, peering ahead into the cloud-shrouded light. Now twenty meters from the stream, she could make out two figures sitting together on the far shore of the rushing stream, near the top of the falls.

She stopped and stared. It was Konstantin . . . and her father. Then they stood and turned as a third man stepped out of the forest.

WHEN SERGEI EMERGED from the forest, he thought he had stepped into a dream. By Zakolyev's expression, he didn't quite believe it either; he stared as if he were seeing a ghost. Then his face quickly returned to the familiar mask as he wiped back his wet hair.

Seeing that man for the first time since Anya's death, Sergei felt his body tense for an instant; then he took a breath and let himself relax, his senses on full alert, scanning the immediate area above the falls.

They were alone, just the three of them: Sergei, Zakolyev, and a young man about the age his son would be.

Sergei turned his attention back to Zakolyev and wasted no words: "I've come for my son."

Zakolyev sighed, as if resigned to some unpleasantness. He knew that the moment of reckoning had arrived. "Sergei Ivanov," he said, forcing a mirthless smile, "we meet again. And you say you've come by to pick up your son . . . without even a word of greeting? Well, I'm willing to overlook your lack of courtesy. As it happens, you're in luck. As you see, he stands here before you. His name is Konstantin, and I give him to you."

Konstantin, elated by this wondrous turn of fortune, started to speak as Dmitri Zakolyev reached around his shoulder.

Sergei saw the knife flash just as Zakolyev grabbed the boy's head, put the knife to Konstantin's throat, and cut—

In the next instant Sergei had transported himself three meters forward, as if by magic, and slapped the knife hand down to the boy's chest, pinning it. He broke Zakolyev's arm and disarmed him and with his other hand grabbed Zakolyev's hair and jerked his head back so far it nearly broke the man's neck; then Sergei pushed Konstantin out of harm's way as he stunned Zakolyev with an elbow strike, knocking him to the ground, semiconscious.

Just then Paulina arrived, in a state of total confusion. She had just seen—or thought she had seen—Father Dmitri try to cut the throat of her Kontin, but the white-haired man had saved him.

Zakolyev came to quickly, but seeing Paulina, he did not rise to fight. His right arm and wrist broken, he lay back in pain and screamed at Paulina, commanding her with all his authority, "Kill him! Kill the monster!"

"No!" yelled Konstantin. "Paulina, no! You can't! He's my father!"

The words made no sense. Nothing made any sense. But Paulina's body responded to years of training and followed the will of the man who had raised her. Her painful leg forgotten, Paulina closed the distance and flew at the white-haired monster who had killed her mother and haunted her dreams, leaping in with a devastating kick—

She landed with a splash in the stream above the falls and whipped her head around. The white-haired man was no longer there. She rolled, twisted, spun, saw him behind her, and attempted a leg sweep, but somehow it missed. Without hesitation, she leaped up and launched a barrage of lightning blows, but Sergei Ivanov evaded her every strike.

Something felt wrong. Nothing in her years of combat training had prepared her for this. It made no sense; the monster had not struck a single offensive blow. Was he truly a wizard or merely playing with her?

Again she lashed out at him—and again the man deflected but did not return a single blow. Panting, she stopped for a moment to gather her wits.

Just then the rain stopped, and clouds parted, opening to the last rays of the setting sun. And in the soft light of early evening, Sergei got his first clear look at the face of this amazing assailant: It was the face of a girl—not any girl, but the face of a young Anya. In that moment of recognition, a ray of sunlight glinted off the locket around her neck. And he knew beyond any doubt.

His search was finally over.

Again Zakolyev screamed, "Kill him! Now is your chance!" But the authority was fading from his voice.

Konstantin cried out again, "Stop, Paulina, please! He's my father!"

"No," Sergei said to the boy without taking his eyes off the girl called Paulina. "I wish I were your father—but I don't have a son. I have a daughter, and she is standing before me now."

Paulina stood frozen, not knowing what to do.

Zakolyev lay still, his eyes waiting, watching, then he commanded her one last time: "Kill him, Paulina!" he yelled, his voice shrill and desperate. "Complete your mission! He killed your mother!"

She crouched, circling the white-haired man. He stood relaxed; his face was serene, and he was crying.

Confused, not knowing what to think, how to feel, she pointed to Father Dmitri, then said to the white-haired man, "But . . . he's my father—"

"No!" This time it was Konstantin's voice, as he walked toward her, his wet shirt bloody from a cut on his chest. "No, Paulina. I'm so sorry—

but I've known for a long time, always known. He has never been your father. I was a little boy, but I remember when they brought you—"

Then Zakolyev was on his feet with another knife in his left hand, his mind gone, madness driving his legs forward in a frenzy, leaping—

Sergei looked over Paulina's shoulder to see Zakolyev flying toward them both—and he couldn't tell who Zakolyev was aiming to kill. Moving faster than Paulina could see, Sergei drove her back and through the air to land three meters away.

As she fell and rolled, for an instant she thought it was an attack. But when she came up she saw Father Dmitri Zakolyev, his knife raised, flying at Sergei Ivanov.

Sergei watched Zakolyev careening toward him in slow motion. The world was silent. Not a sound intruded, as he waited, relaxed, breathing, his hands resting at his sides. This was the moment he had trained for.

As Zakolyev rushed in and the knife stabbed downward, Sergei moved like a ghost, and at the last instant—as the point of the blade was about to pierce coat and flesh and penetrate his heart—Sergei was no longer there. He had somehow moved off the line of attack, turned his body slightly, and with a subtle wave of his arms had thrown Zakolyev headlong into the river toward the edge of the falls.

And as the mystified assailant flew past his enemy, he reflexively reached out and clutched Sergei's coat—

Zakolyev's momentum, combined with the treacherous footing and powerful current, jerked Sergei off his feet.

Horrified, Paulina and Konstantin watched Dmitri Zakolyev, flailing and struggling, and Sergei Ivanov, turning toward the precipice. Then both men slid over the edge and disappeared.

.51.

Twilight. A clearing sky. The last rays of the dying sun shone upon Paulina's confused and anguished face as she limped along the shore to the top of the falls and peered down to the rocks far below to view the twisted, broken, lifeless body of Dmitri Zakolyev.

Sergei Ivanov had vanished.

She couldn't yet grasp the truth or take in all that had happened. But she felt as if a spell had lifted. Her shattered past had opened the way to a new future. She could not articulate or understand this truth, yet Paulina sensed that she now lived in a different world.

In a sort of trance, she looked to Konstantin's bleeding chest before they slowly made their way down the winding path to the foot of the falls.

Amazed by his survival, in a state of grace, Sergei crawled up the bank of the river about twenty meters below the falls to see Paestka peacefully grazing nearby, unconcerned with the dramas of the human world.

Sergei was bruised and cold but bore no serious injury. He made his way back to the foot of the falls, found Zakolyev, and pulled him out of the pounding water and into the underbrush. For a moment Sergei saw images of their boyhood together, as fellow cadets, and their survival training, and their struggles. Then the images faded as Sergei took the small shovel from the saddlebag and dug a final resting place for Dmitri Zakolyev, covering him with the wet earth.

He had no stone to mark the grave nor any words to say, but as he gazed down at the mound, Sergei faced the fact that his worst enemy had midwifed his daughter into the world, had protected her and trained her, and in his troubled way had fathered her. And he gave thanks.

He was aware that Paulina and Konstantin had joined him there, each with their own memories and farewells.

As the people of Zakolyev's camp went about their business, ignorant of what had transpired, the three of them hiked back up the winding path—Sergei leading Paestka, and Paulina and Konstantin clinging to each other's hands.

While they ascended, Sergei told Paulina the story of the locket— where it came from and how it came into her hands. Not the details, but just enough so she might begin to understand.

By the time they returned to the top of the falls, Sergei had finished his story. A soft light still infused the purple sky when they heard shouts of alarm from the camp, carried through the still evening air.

"Korolev is dead!" someone shouted.

"The Ataman is missing!" yelled another. "We are under attack!"

A few moments later Tomorov and five other men carrying saber, knife, and pistol caught sight of the three of them standing there and raced toward them to kill the white-haired intruder.

Sergei stood relaxed. Expecting nothing, ready for whatever came—

As the fierce-looking men drew near and started to spread out, Paulina stepped in front of Sergei and faced the men. "Stop! All of you!" she said, her small voice ringing with authority. As she raised her arm, the men stopped and waited. "It's over!" she said. "Ataman Dmitri Zakolyev is dead—gone over the falls. And believe me when I say this: You do not want to fight this man! If you do, you will face me as well!"

The leaderless men grumbled and stared and shuffled their feet. They didn't take orders from a woman—not even Paulina. But there was something familiar about that man . . .

Tomorov the scout had a long memory. He recognized the white-haired man—the one who had followed after they had beaten him and killed the woman and child. Tomorov remembered enough. "Come on!" he said to the men. "We have no more business here."

They backed off and away, and like a horse without a head, they stumbled as lost men to gather their belongings and saddle their horses. The camp suddenly stank of death, and they wanted no more of it.

Sergei looked at the wound on Konstantin's chest. "It isn't deep and will heal well enough," he said.

"Better my chest than . . . thank you for saving my life," Konstantin said. "I . . . wish that you were my father too."

Sergei looked at his daughter, and, seeing how closely Paulina held this young man, he smiled and said, "We may yet find a way to grant that wish."

The events of that day—the death of Korolev, Kontin nearly taken from her, and the end of the man she knew as her father—rushed in upon Paulina. She started to pant, and her chest heaved. Konstantin held her as she found release.

Some time later, when she was able to speak again, Paulina looked up at the man who claimed to be her father. "I had learned to hate you . . . all my life . . . How can you be my father? How can I know that it's true?"

Sergei had no proof to offer. So he said, "You've had a difficult day, Paulina. We all have. Let's ride away from here, make a camp in the woods. And in the morning things may be more clear."

His words made good sense.

S ERGEI, PAULINA, AND KONSTANTIN rode out of the camp together. No one interfered or seemed to care. Someone had set the barn ablaze. Looking back, Paulina said to Konstantin in a weary voice, "Today, before I came to the falls, Korolev tried to . . . attack me. We fought . . . and I killed him."

Sergei turned to her. "Did you say you killed the one-armed giant, the man Korolev?"

She nodded, biting her lip. "Do you know him?"

He hesitated, then decided that she should know: "Korolev was the man who killed your mother."

Paulina turned her head away so he would not see her private tears, as she realized that she had completed her mission after all, killing the monster who had murdered her mother. Her years of training had not been wasted after all.

That night Sergei lay awake for a time, wondering how he might earn her trust.

The next morning he was already up and tending the fire when Konstantin woke, then Paulina. They didn't speak at first, but Sergei knew what was on her mind—the proof she sought. When he had first awakened, an idea had come to him. He would have to take a risk.

As Sergei handed the two of them some berries he had found near-by, he said to Paulina, "Do you notice the resemblance between me and your grandfather . . . in the locket?"

She didn't need to look; she had memorized their faces. "Yes," she said. "But many people may bear a resemblance."

"There's something else," he said, "if it's still there. You see, when your mother and I were married, I took five strands of her hair and wound them into a tiny circle—a lock of hair the same color as yours—and I placed that lock behind the photograph of my parents—your grandparents."

Paulina's eyes opened wide. She had never thought to look behind the photograph. She quickly opened the locket and carefully pried up the round piece of photographic paper and looked as Sergei held his breath—

There was no lock of hair to be seen—nothing. When Paulina looked up, her eyes were again guarded.

"Wait!" said Konstantin. "There's something stuck to the back of the photograph." Paulina turned the photograph around to see the white backing. And there, pressed into the faded paper, was a tight little cir-cle—five strands of her mother's hair.

Sergei smiled. "Her name was Anya, and she was as lovely as our daughter."

Soon after, they broke camp and mounted their horses.

Paulina had brought only the locket and a few personal items. Konstantin had left everything behind save for a few of his drawings, folded and placed into the cover of a book.

"Your book," Sergei asked as they rode north. "What is it about?"

"About a journey to America, by a writer named Abram Chudominsky," he replied.

Sergei nodded, committing the book and author to memory. "America is where I intend to go," he said. "And I hope you will both join me . . ."

Paulina said only, "Where are we going now?"

"To meet your family. You have a grandmother and an uncle who would like very much to make your acquaintance."

T HEY RODE IN SILENCE a while after that—not because they had little to say, but because they had so much to it was difficult to know where to begin. Sergei thought it best to wait until Paulina was ready.

About midday she began, with one question following another. Sergei answered them all, telling the story of his life and her lineage, until she seemed satisfied.

It wasn't until the second day of their ride north that Paulina spoke of her life—slowly at first, then faster, as if to reassure herself of her memory and hear it aloud in the safety of Konstantin's company. She told Sergei Ivanov all that she remembered of her life. Konstantin embellished where he could and told his perspectives as well.

Sergei took it in and silently grieved her strange childhood and all the years they had lost.

. 5 2 .

On their sixth night at Valeria's table, Paulina and Konstantin shared their first Shabbat meal with Sergei, Valeria, Andreas, Katya, and their children, Avrom and Leya. Grandmother Valeria Panova took special joy in this sacred occasion.

To Sergei the scene had a dreamlike quality, as if all the paths of his life had led to this family gathering. He slowly looked around the table at these faces he would remember all the days of his life. Realizing that this moment would not last, he cherished it all the more.

Sergei stole yet another glance at his daughter. He marveled at her resemblance to Anya—the eyes, the hair, the shape of her cheeks, the line of her mouth—so alike yet so different. Paulina was only now learning about the larger world.

In the past few days, Valeria and Andreas had taken Sergei, Paulina, and Konstantin on a tour of St. Petersburg. Konstantin, curious about everything, had a hundred questions about customs and social manners, banks and commerce and travel. Paulina spoke less but looked and listened.

That Shabbat night, during a lull in the conversation, Sergei quietly announced that he had three small gifts for Paulina. He reached out to take her hand, but she pulled it away. So instead he placed the three gemstones on the table in front of her. "These jewels," he said, "come from your great-grandfather Heschel Rabinowitz, and from his father before him. I now pass them to you. They are quite valuable and will provide funds for you to begin your new life together."

Paulina looked down at the gems, glittering in the candlelight, her eyes wide. She turned to look at Konstantin, unbelieving, then back to Sergei. "I . . . I thank you . . . Father."

Paulina was quiet the rest of that evening—preoccupied. Her mind had accepted that all the people around the table were relations: father, grandmother, uncle, aunt, and young cousins. Yet they were all strangers to her. Even this brave and generous man Sergei Ivanov, whom she had known for only a short time.

After the meal, Sergei spoke again of America, where he and Paulina and Konstantin would go. He made a last plea for Valeria, Andreas, and Katya to join them, but without success. He glanced again at Paulina and caught her watching him intently. The instant their eyes met, she looked away.

As Sergei had contemplated their future, Paulina had reached a resolution about her past: She would put it behind her and never speak of it again.

On the previous night, Paulina and Konstantin had made another resolution as well.

THE FOLLOWING WEEK Sergei returned with all necessary certificates and papers for Paulina and Konstantin. "A little money in the right hands can work wonders," Sergei explained with a smile. He had also booked their second-class passage out of Hamburg on the great steamship S.S. König Friedrich.

Five days later—after a bittersweet farewell and promises to write—Sergei, Paulina, and Konstantin set out toward Finland, to find passage on the Baltic Sea to the port city of Hamburg.

DURING THEIR TRAVELS to Hamburg, conversations seemed strained and awkward, sometimes dying out almost as soon as they had begun. Sergei realized that while Paulina had accepted him as her father and Anya as her mother, they were strangers. Still, Sergei made an effort, and so did Paulina—if not out of familiar affection, at least out of courtesy.

During the first week of their voyage to America, Paulina and Konstantin kept mostly to themselves. Sergei missed seeing her, but he understood. They still took most of their meals together, and he was glad for that, but their voices were drowned out by many others at the table.

Then, almost two weeks into the voyage, as the great ship neared the coast of America, Paulina made an extra effort to include Sergei in the conversation over dinner.

It seemed she was about to say more, but she fell silent, as if unsure how to proceed. She glanced at Konstantin. He gave her a look and a nod, then he said, "There will be no better time than now."

Paulina turned to Sergei. "Father . . . Sergei, could we go up on the deck—somewhere to talk?"

On the aft deck, out of the wind, Paulina drew Sergei aside. At first, her carefully rehearsed words failed her. So she took a deep breath, drew upon the courage she had cultivated over years, and said slowly, "I—first I want to thank you for saving Konstantin's life. You have done so much for us . . . and what you went through to find me . . . all your kindness . . ."

Sergei started to speak, but she silenced him and her words tumbled out: "I am glad that you—a good man—are my father. Maybe there is also some goodness in me . . ."

She hesitated again and closed her eyes before adding, "And now you have completed what you set out to do, and . . . and Konstantin and I must go our own way . . . just the two of us."

Paulina looked up into Sergei's face. When she saw his expression, her eyes brimmed with tears, but then her face grew more resolute and she quickly wiped her eyes. "I am not a little girl anymore—that is past. For my whole life I have been instructed, guided, told what to do. Now Konstantin and I must explore the world together. I am a grown woman, and I can take care of myself. We will go to find our life as you must find yours. I wish for you a good life, wherever you may go . . ."

Konstantin appeared, slipping one arm around Paulina. With the other he reached out to clasp Sergei's hand and said, "When we find our

place and have news to tell, we will write to Paulina's grandmother."
With a nod, he excused himself. Paulina started to follow but turned and
added, "I believe that my mother would be proud of you for what you
have done."

Then, for the first and last time, Paulina drew close, reached up, and
kissed Sergei on the cheek—a daughter's kiss so tenuous and tender that
Sergei's heart nearly broke open. He could not even protest when she
took the locket from her neck, took Sergei's hand, placed it in his palm,
and closed his fingers around it.

When they had left him, Sergei stood and stared out to sea.

Serafim had taught him, many years before, to expect nothing but be
prepared for anything. A wiser part of him had known this parting would
occur, just not so soon.

So many emotions washed through him that it was impossible to distinguish one from another. Despite his hopes or plans, Sergei had to face
reality: When they reached America's shores, Paulina and Konstantin
would vanish from his life as abruptly as they had appeared.

All in all, it had turned out well. Sergei had found his daughter and
enabled her to build a new life. And she had just done the same for him.
Now she had spoken her truth. And it set him free.

As THE SHORES OF AMERICA came into sight, Sergei stood
alone on deck as the bow of the great ship cut the ocean waves. His eyes
took in every detail—the sparkle of sun, the textures of earth and sky,
the life abounding in his new land. Someday, he thought, men may voyage to the stars. But that adventure will be no greater than this.

Stepping into a sheltered place, out of the wind, he reached inside
his shirt pocket and took out the locket. Carefully opening the clasp,
Sergei gazed at the photograph of his mother and father then peered
behind it, expecting to find the lock of Anya's hair.

For a few moments, Sergei forgot the world around him, and the taste
of his tears mingled with the scent of sea. For he had found not one, but
two separate locks that he would treasure for the rest of his days.

He said a silent prayer for his daughter as a wind gusted in from the north, and it seemed that Sergei could hear Anya's voice, as it had once spoken to him in his darkest hours. She had said, "Have faith, my darling. Our child is safe in God's hands."

So she is, he thought. So are we all.

When I was young, I had hoped that one day my life
might unfold in an orderly way, according to my hopes.
But now I understand that the Way winds like a river,
always changing, ever onward,
following God's gravity toward the Great Sea and Source.
My journeys revealed that the Way itself creates the warrior;
that every path leads to peace,
and every choice to wisdom.
And that life has always been,
and will always be,
arising in Mystery.

FROM SOCRATES' JOURNAL

REVELATIONS FROM THE YEARS THAT FOLLOWED

FAMILY SECRETS

In writing this story, I expected that I might learn more about my own family's heritage. All four of my grandparents came from Ukraine, but I was especially close to my maternal grandparents. When I was a boy, Grandpa Abe used to tell me stories while we cracked opened walnuts from the tree in their backyard. Like many people from the old country, he didn't say much about Ukraine or Russia but spoke of smaller, more personal incidents that could have taken place anywhere—a horse he had longed to ride, a favorite river where he learned to swim by jumping from a rowboat into the cold, clear waters. He awakened my imagination with folktales, like the one about a rainbow bird that no one could catch except a clever and patient little boy like me . . .

Grandpa Abe died when I was still young.

My grandma, whom we called Babu, didn't tell stories. But she made the best peanut butter and jelly sandwiches and was an expert at cleaning behind my five-year-old ears. I remember Babu fondly, as an old white-haired woman who wore shapeless flowered dresses and looked just the way grandmas were supposed to look. When I stayed overnight, she took good care of me.

When I grew up, I went away to college. I didn't see Babu except for brief visits.

In the 1970s I moved back to southern California for a time and was able to visit Babu. She was about eighty years old then, mostly bedridden, and her eyesight was failing. I had begun writing, so when I visited her I read aloud from one of my various works in progress.

One Sunday I decided to read her an early draft of this book. Since the story took place in Russia, in the old country, I thought that Babu might enjoy it. As I began, I wasn't at all sure that she was paying much attention—that is, until I first said the name Sergei Ivanov. Hearing that name, Babu leaned forward, and her clouded eyes opened wide.

"Are you okay, Babu?" I asked.

"Yes, yes—go on," she said, staring into space.

The name Sergei Ivanov is not uncommon in Russia, so I thought she might have known someone by that name.

It wasn't until I spoke of the boy, Konstantin, that Babu held up her hand and interrupted me. "Stop right there!" she said.

I had never heard her speak so emphatically before. But it wasn't just her voice that got my attention. It was the tears filling her old eyes. Wiping them gently with a tissue, Babu began telling me about her early years, and the story of her life . . .

WHILE ON BOARD their steamship to America, Konstantin met a well-dressed French-Canadian émigré. The man, a Monsieur Goguet, owned a fashion design company. After studying several of Konstantin's sketches, Goguet offered him a job on the spot, making illustrations in the company catalog.

So directly after they arrived in New York, they emigrated to Toronto. There Konstantin and Paulina rented a small flat.

Paulina eventually gave birth to two daughters. In 1916 they journeyed across Canada to Vancouver, British Columbia, and from there they finally moved to the west coast of the United States.

As for Sergei, he traveled on foot, by horse, and by train for a time, and his occasional letters to Valeria and Andreas bore postmarks from places across America. Later he again made contact with one of the masters he had met in the Pamir and was called back across the sea on an urgent mission. Their correspondence ceased for a time.

In 1918, after Valeria passed away, Andreas managed to get his family out of Communist Russia just before the iron curtain closed. And as happened in so many immigrant families, everyone lost touch.

Sergei finally returned to America and settled in Oakland, California, a mere five hundred miles from his daughter, although neither of them knew the other's whereabouts.

Sometimes he thought he saw Paulina in a crowded marketplace and almost called out her name. He often wondered where she was and how she and Konstantin were faring.

Paulina and her husband were doing well, devoted to their family and future. But their daughters never learned more than the most sketchy details of the past.

However, the story doesn't end there.

Years earlier, when Paulina and Konstantin had first emigrated, Konstantin was asked to state his name. Since he didn't have a last name, he decided to take a new name for a new country. The only one that came to mind was Abram Chudominsky, the author of his first and favorite book. When they entered the new country, the clerk at immigration wrote it down as Abraham Chudom. So it was done, and Paulina took his new last name and changed her first name to Pauline.

Pauline and Abraham named their two daughters Vivian and Edith. Both girls grew to adulthood in southern California, where their parents lived. One of those daughters, Vivian, married a good man named Herman Millman, with whom she had two children—a daughter named Diane and a son named Daniel.

Not until my grandmother Babu, whose legal name was Pauline Chudom, told me her story—from the time she grew up in the camp of Dmitri Zakolyev to her motherhood in a new land—did I grasp the hardships, heartbreak, and eventual triumph that was my grandmother's life.

So it was that my great-grandfather, Sergei Ivanov, whom my mother had never known, became my mentor, when we eventually met in 1967 in Berkeley, California.

Now I understand why he smiled that night that I impulsively chose to call him Socrates, after the Greek sage so admired by my great-great-grandfather Heschel Rabinowitz and his beautiful daughter, Natalia.

M Y GREAT-GRANDFATHER was a resourceful man—more than I ever could have realized. Those of you who have read Way of the Peaceful Warrior may recall that in 1968 Socrates told me, "I've been watching you for years." A few years after that, when I first opened his journal, I noticed that his first entry was dated February 22, 1946—the exact date of my birth, twenty-two years before we ever met.

During our time together, Socrates never revealed our family relationship—maybe for the same reason he chose not to intrude in (my grandmother) Paulina's life or that of her family. Nor did his journal notes make that final connection. I had to learn the truth from Babu herself. She also told me that she had written once to Valeria many years before, to inform her about their new names, their whereabouts, and their children.

Babu told me that she briefly met and exchanged a few words with Sergei only one other time—at my grandfather Abraham's (Konstantin's) funeral. Later I searched my earliest memories, and an image came to me: I was only three or four years old then, standing next to my mother and fidgeting in my dark suit a size too big. As they lowered a shiny box bearing Grandpa Abe's body, my mother started to cry, so I tried to be still.

I looked up and around at the faces of the people gathered there and noticed an old, white-haired man looking right at me. He looked different from the other people—maybe because he smiled right at me and nodded before he faded back into the other faces and was gone.

I now realize that he knew of my birth and chose to begin writing his journal on that day so that he might someday share it with me. That same journal, along with the story of Babu's life, enabled me to share his story, their story, with you.

I believe that my great-grandfather Sergei Ivanov had watched over me all those years like a guardian angel. I believe that he was waiting for the right time. Socrates was good at waiting. He had learned patience many years before, on his many odysseys, on his long journeys to the light.

> *Late one night, in the predawn hours,*
> *an ageless man sits quietly outside an old Texaco station*
> *leaning his chair back against the wall.*
> *He owns the station and works the night shift.*
> *His name is Sergei Ivanov.*
> *Dan Millman, a young college athlete,*
> *is walking home from a late-night date when he stops*
> *and, on impulse, approaches the station office.*
> *He's not sure why he does this—*
> *maybe to get a soft drink or late-night snack . . .*
> *Socrates smiles to himself through half-closed eyelids.*
> *He is here. It begins. The final chapter.*

Acknowledgments

No one is smarter than all of us. Many people past and present helped bring this book to life. Many writers, philosophers, and mentors served as way stations on my odyssey. And of course there's Socrates.

A varied cast of characters played essential supporting roles.

Candice Fuhrman, my literary agent, first told me to write the book about Socrates and guided the project from the beginning.

In the early stages of development, Sierra Prasada Millman, Joy Millman, and Nancy Grimley Carleton all provided invaluable editorial feedback from first to final draft. Sierra's brilliant editorial analysis of the first draft enabled me to see the story with fresh eyes, to reshape the narrative, and to make that literary leap to the next level.

Publisher Stephen Hanselman acquired the book in an act of faith, generosity, daring, and uncanny good taste. Gideon Weil, my capable editor, provided skill and support at every level of the publishing process. With the rest of the outstanding HarperSanFrancisco team of Jeff Hobbs, Sam Barry, Linda Wollenberger, Claudia Boutote, Margery Buchanan, Terri Leonard, Priscilla Stuckey, Mickey Maudlin, Mark Tauber, Jim Warner, Anne Connolly, and JulieRae Mitchell, Gideon took the book from manuscript to finished form and out into the world.

John Giduck, founder of the Russian Martial Arts Training Center in Golden, Colorado, gave generously of his time and expertise, providing detailed research notes and invaluable suggestions about both Russian culture and martial arts.

The Russian System Guidebook, written by Vladimir Vasiliev, one of the world's foremost teachers of the Russian Martial Art, served as a rich resource. And special thanks to Valerie Vasiliev, who, while caring for her family and performing innumerable other tasks, answered many questions that helped establish authenticity related to Russian traditions.

Other experts in their respective fields who helped me keep my facts straight include: Rowan Beach, Elissa Bemporad, PhD; David E. Fishman, professor of Jewish history at the Jewish Theological Seminary of America; Lawrence H. Officer, professor of economics at the University of Illinois at Chicago; Professor Harlan Stelmach and Mary K. Lespier, Humanities Department, Dominican University of California; Four Arrows (Don Trent Jacobs), professor at Northern Arizona University and Fielding Graduate Institute; William Harris, MD; David Galland, MD; Father Vladimir of the Holy Trinity Russian Orthodox Church, Toronto, Canada; and Joe Cochrane of the North Bay Cooperative Library System.

Any errors in the text are mine, not theirs.

Thanks also to manuscript readers Linda and Hal Kramer and Sharon and Charles Root for their insight, candor, and encouragement.

Each of my daughters (in birth order)—Holly, Sierra, and China—has contributed, in ways both practical and mysterious, to my creative endeavors and reminded me about the important things.

My wife and guardian angel, Joy, for three decades has renewed and enriched my life through her loving support and practical wisdom. Always my first and final reader, she offers sage advice that helps me improve both my writing and my life.

Finally, I want to acknowledge the loving sacrifices and generosity of spirit provided by my late parents, Herman and Vivian Millman, which made possible all that has followed, and my grandparents, Pauline and Abraham Chudom, and Rose and Harry Millman, all émigrés from Ukraine, on whose courage we relied, on whose labors we depended, and on whose shoulders we now stand.